HARLEQUIN SMALL TOWN
CHRISTMAS COLLECTION

It's a wonderful time of year! A time when friends and family gather to celebrate the joy of the season with good food and beautiful gifts.

And where better to meet than in a small town? The warmth of community adds extra delight to Christmas. Even the hardest of hearts is warmed by the sight of Main Street wearing its festive finery. Seeing the town square decked out in bows, lights and holly brings a smile to every face.

There is even the possibility of romance for the unsuspecting beneath those sprigs of mistletoe!

So join us in this special 2-in-1 collection as we bring romance and good cheer to this special holiday.

If you enjoy these two classic stories, be sure to look for more books set in small towns in Harlequin Superromance.

JANICE KAY JOHNSON

An author of more than eighty books for children and adults, *USA TODAY* bestselling author Janice Kay Johnson is especially well-known for her Harlequin Superromance novels about love and family—about the way generations connect and the power our earliest experiences have on us throughout life. Her 2007 novel *Snowbound* won a RITA® Award from Romance Writers of America for Best Contemporary Series Romance. A former librarian, Janice raised two daughters in a small rural town north of Seattle, Washington. She loves to read and is an active volunteer and board member for Purrfect Pals, a no-kill cat shelter. Visit her online at janicekayjohnson.com.

Be sure to look for other books by Janice Kay Johnson in Harlequin Superromance—the ultimate destination for more story, more romance! There are new Harlequin Superromance titles available every month. Check one out today!

USA TODAY Bestselling Author

Janice Kay Johnson
and
Holly Jacobs

THE BABY GIFT

⬦ **HARLEQUIN**® SMALL TOWN CHRISTMAS

Recycling programs
for this product may
not exist in your area.

ISBN-13: 978-0-373-60675-7

The Baby Gift

Copyright © 2014 by Harlequin Books S.A.

The publisher acknowledges the copyright holders of the individual works as follows:

The Baby Agenda
Copyright © 2010 by Janice Kay Johnson

Unexpected Gifts
Copyright © 2009 by Holly Fuhrmann

Printed in U.S.A.

CONTENTS

THE BABY AGENDA
Janice Kay Johnson

CHAPTER ONE

EVEN THOUGH THE GALA was part of a professional conference, it looked as though almost everyone had arrived two-by-two. Moira Cullen had known they would, and decided to come anyway. So what if this, like most social occasions, had too much in common with Noah's ark? *She* was supposed to have been half of a couple tonight, too, until she'd gotten the email this afternoon from Bruce.

I'm sorry, Moira, but I won't be able to escort you tonight after all. Something has come up. I know you hadn't planned to attend until I asked you, so I hope it won't be too big a disappointment.

He'd signed off with "Bruce." Plain and simple. No "Love, Bruce," or "I'll think of you tonight and wish we were dancing together," or even "I'll call tomorrow and explain."

She still had no idea what could have happened since this morning, when they'd parted after a conference session. She and Bruce Girard both had been attending the conference held in Redmond, across Lake Washington from Seattle, for members of the building trade. He was a real estate attorney, she was an architect. They'd been dating for nearly six weeks, and she'd decided that tonight was a fitting time to invite him into her bedroom for the first time.

And she'd bought the most beautiful dress!

In a spirit of defiance, she'd decided to come to the gala anyway. Lots of attendees were from out of town and had come without significant others. A single woman would surely be asked to dance. It could be fun, she had decided, surprising herself with her determination. Bruce was probably disappointed, too, and would undoubtedly be in touch. They'd have other nights. She had no reason to feel hurt.

She hesitated only momentarily in the lobby, then walked toward the ballroom, telling herself she looked voluptuous in her new dress, not fat.

Repeat after me: I am not fat.

She *knew* she wasn't. Believing, though, that could be another story.

Right by the open doors, she saw a man she knew. She'd worked with Stan Wells on a job a couple of years ago. He appeared to be by himself.

He turned, looked her up and down, and said, "Well, *hello,*" then did a double take. "Moira?" He sounded stunned.

Stan had never once looked at her as if he'd noticed she was a woman when they had worked together.

She smiled pleasantly and said, "Hello, Stan," then strolled past him, enjoying the knowledge that he'd swiveled on his heel to watch her walk away. The dress must be as flattering as she'd imagined it to be.

It was also formfitting, which meant that she scanned the buffet table with a wistful eye but didn't dare partake. So what. She wasn't here to eat.

Moira made her way around the outskirts of the ballroom, pausing to chat a couple of times and to promise a dance once the musicians started to play. She'd been right to think she'd have fun—it was nice to come to a party where she actually knew many of the people.

Then her roving gaze stopped on a tall, handsome man with sandy hair and a lopsided grin. Bruce Girard, wearing a well-cut suit, had his head bent as he talked to a beautiful, slender woman in a fire-engine red dress cut short to bare long legs. Moira stared in shock. She wouldn't have dared wear a dress that short, because she didn't have legs like that. On her, the razor-sharp, chin-length bob wouldn't have emphasized sculpted cheekbones, because she didn't have those, either. And—oh, God—if she'd worn a red dress, never mind the slash of scarlet lipstick, her hair and freckles would have looked orange.

They *were* orange.

She had to quit staring. Moira knew that, in some distant part of her mind. It would be humiliating if Bruce were to happen to glance her way and catch her gaping.

Maybe, at the last minute, his plans had changed and he'd come on the chance that she would be here. If he'd tried calling her at home, and thought that because she didn't answer…

He laid his hand on the brunette's lower back. Really, almost, on her butt. The way his hand was splayed there was unmistakably proprietary and…sexual. Recognizing it, the woman smiled and tilted her head so that it, very briefly, rested against his upper arm.

Pain squeezed Moira's chest. Surely he hadn't been seeing someone else all this time. Or was even married? They had several mutual acquaintances who knew they were dating each other. Wouldn't someone have said something?

And—face it—why would he have dated her at all if he had a wife or a lover who looked like that?

The backs of her eyes burned, and she suddenly felt homely and *fat*. Probably Stan Wells had turned in incredulity at the amount of flesh she'd squeezed into this damn dress.

Breathe, she told herself, and couldn't.

She couldn't seem to make herself move, either. She was frozen between one step and the next, excruciatingly self-conscious. What she'd convinced herself were curves were really bulges. And no one thought a woman whose skin was spotted was sexy. With self-loathing, she wondered who she had been kidding.

Then, to complete her misery, Bruce's head turned and their eyes met. His face went still. Knowing a riptide of red was sweeping up her neck to her cheeks, Moira forced herself into motion. With her redhead's skin, she didn't blush, she flamed. Even from a distance, he would see.

Her eye fastened desperately on a bar ahead. She could pretend she'd been looking for a drink. That gave her a goal. Made her feel as if she was less pathetically, obviously alone.

Except, of course, that she was.

There was a short line. The couple ahead of her were strangers and paid no attention to her. She wished someone else would join the queue, someone she could hide behind. Unfortunately, in her peripheral vision she could still see Bruce and the woman. He spoke to her, then left her watching him speculatively and approached Moira.

If only she could cool her cheeks, she might be able to handle him with savoir faire. A surprised glance, an, "Oh, you made it after all?" If only she had any actual confidence.

"Moira." He was here, at her side.

She tilted her chin up and, somehow, smiled. "Bruce. I didn't expect to see you."

"I didn't think I'd see you, either."

Anger was her salvation, or maybe it would embarrass her, she didn't know which. She went with it anyway.

With raised eyebrows, she glanced toward his date. "Yes, that's obvious."

"Ah…I'm sorry about this. I should have told you."

"That we weren't dating each other exclusively?" She was proud of her level tone.

"It's not like that." He frowned at her. "We were. I was. It's just that I ran into Graziella and…" Bruce spread his hands and shrugged. "We'd broken it off, but as soon as we saw each other again we both knew we'd made a mistake."

In other words, Moira realized, he'd been in love with another woman the entire time he'd dated her. No wonder he'd been so patient. He'd been filling time with her. Licking his wounds. She couldn't even flatter herself that he'd been on the rebound. He hadn't been interested enough in her for their relationship to qualify.

It hurt. Her heart or her pride, she wasn't sure which, but either way, it did hurt.

The couple in front of her stepped up to the bar. She moved forward.

"Honesty would have been nice."

"I didn't lie—"

"Yes, you did. If only by omission." Anger was still carrying her along, thank goodness. "I didn't understand that I wasn't supposed to come tonight. You've embarrassed me. That wasn't necessary, Bruce." Drinks in hand, the couple stepped away. To Bruce, Moira said, "Please excuse me," and turned to the bartender. "A martini, please."

By the time she'd paid, Bruce was gone, striding across the ballroom toward his Graziella, whose name was as exotic as her looks.

Moira took a huge gulp of the martini and wished she could go home. But if she did that, the jerk would know that she wasn't just embarrassed, she was humiliated and wounded. And she refused to give him that satisfaction.

She'd dance, and maybe even get a little bit drunk. She would clutch at her pride, because that's all she had. And she wouldn't let herself think until she got home about the fact that Bruce Girard hadn't wanted her, not really.

Men never did.

WILL BECKER LEANED AGAINST the railing, his back to the view of dark woods that somehow still existed within a stone's throw of the Redmond Town Center mall and the surrounding upscale hotels and restaurants. Instead, nursing a drink he didn't really want, he looked through the floor-to-ceiling glass at the ballroom where other people seemed to be having a fine time.

Him, he hated affairs like this. He was content lurking outside, glass separating him from the gaiety within.

Circumstances being different, he wouldn't be here at all. As it was, he and Clay had attended a few conference sessions together, but the real point of the weekend had been for Will to introduce his brother to everyone he knew. This had been a four day long changing of the guard, so to speak.

"Yes," he'd said dozens of times, "Clay will be taking over Becker Construction. He knows the business. Hell, better than I did when I stepped in for my father." *Got stuck,* was what he really meant. "I have confidence in Clay."

That was the important part: to convey to everyone that he believed Clay could replace him without one of the county's biggest construction companies suffering even a minor hiccup.

"I have plans," he'd said vaguely when asked what he'd be doing. Only to a select few had he admitted that a week from tomorrow he was flying to Zimbabwe to begin a two-year commitment to build medical clinics. He only knew how to do one thing—build—but at least he'd be having an adventure. That, and doing good, instead of adding another minimall where it wasn't needed.

Now, he was lying low. He'd done his duty this evening and would have left if Clay didn't still seem to be having a good time.

Music spilled from the crowded ballroom, and he idly watched the dancers. Not for the first time, Will found his gaze following a redheaded woman whose lush body was poured into a high-necked forest-green dress that might have been demure on someone else— someone who didn't have a small waist, a glorious ass and breasts that would overflow a man's hands, even hands as large as his.

The guy she was dancing with kept trying to pull her closer, and she was refusing to relax into him. She sure as hell had no intention of melting against the guy, which seemed to be frustrating him no end.

When the music ended, he said something to her, his hand still resting against her waist. She shook her head and walked away, straight to the bar.

Will had noticed that, too. The beautiful redhead was putting away the drinks. Not enough yet to have her tanked, but more than was wise if she intended to drive home. And he guessed she'd need to, because he hadn't seen any sign she was here with anybody, friend or date. In fact, for all the dancing she was doing, she didn't look like she was having a very good time. Maybe a mistaken impression, but…he didn't think so.

She took her fresh drink and this time headed for the doors that stood open to the terrace where he currently lurked. Just like he had, the redhead went straight for the dark perimeter where light from the ballroom didn't reach. She didn't realize she wasn't alone until she was almost on top of him.

When she started, Will said, "Hey," making his voice soothing. Even if he hadn't been standing in the dark, his size tended to alarm lone women. "Want to hide out here with me?"

She blinked owlishly. "I didn't see you."

"I know. That's okay, I wouldn't mind some company." Hers, anyway. To himself, he could admit that he'd been humming with a low level of arousal since he'd first set eyes on her. He didn't like bony women, and this one had the most luscious body he'd seen in longer than he could remember.

He wished he could make out what color her eyes were. He knew she had a pretty face and a mouth made for smiling. But her eyes, he hadn't been sure of from a distance. Brown? Didn't most redheads have brown eyes?

"I don't want to intrude," she said after a minute.

Will shook his head. "You're not. I was watching you dance."

Her head tilted his way. "You were?"

Some undertone in her voice puzzled him. She sounded surprised. Or even disbelieving.

"You're beautiful," he said simply.

His mystery redhead snorted. "Yeah, right. That's me."

Oh, yeah. Definitely disbelieving.

He grinned at her. "You think I'm full of hot air."

The pretty mouth was mulish and *not* smiling. "I know what I look like."

He was tempted to end the argument by kissing her, but he didn't make a habit of grabbing women he hardly knew. And anyway…she wasn't being coy. The words had been pained, as if pushed through a throat that was raw.

"Did somebody insult you?" Will asked gently.

She took a long swallow of her drink, swayed and clunked it down on the railing beside his. Liquid splashed. "You could say that," she said in a small, tight voice.

He was hardly aware of his hands tightening into fists. Partly to keep them off her, and partly because he wanted to slug the bastard who'd hurt her feelings.

"Who?"

She blinked at him again.

"Who?" he repeated.

"Oh, it was my own stupid fault," she said finally. "I guess I was supposed to get the message when he let me know he wouldn't be bringing me tonight." She heaved a sigh. "The part I missed was that he was bringing someone else."

"He thought you wouldn't come."

"Bingo."

Will's eyes narrowed. "So he's here."

"Yes. With Graziella." She grimaced. "Of course she couldn't have a name like Ethel."

Not many women in their twenties or thirties were named Ethel, Will thought with a trace of amusement. But he liked the way she said it, and the way she spit out *Graziella*.

"I'll bet you're nothing as plain as Ethel, either."

"No," she mumbled, "I'm Moira."

"As Irish as your hair."

She reached up and touched the skillfully tumbled mass of red curls atop her head as if to remind herself what was up there. "I suppose."

"I'm Will," he said, and held out his hand. "Will Becker."

She laid hers in it and they shook with an odd sort of solemnity. "Good to meet you, Will Becker."

She sounded as if the booze was starting to go to her head, as if she was having to form words carefully. He hoped she'd forget she still had most of a drink.

"Having a good time anyway?" he asked.

Moira sighed. "Not especially. You?"

"No. I'm not a real social guy."

She stirred. "You probably wish I'd leave you alone."

"No." He clasped her wrist loosely. "No. Don't go."

After a moment she said, "Okay." She didn't seem to notice he was holding on to her. "I kind of wish I could go home, 'cept…*except* I don't want *him* to catch me slinking out. You know?"

"Is he really worth the heartburn?"

"I thought so," she said sadly.

"Have you been seeing him long?" Will didn't actually want to know; he didn't want to talk about the scumbag at all. But he also didn't want her to go back in, and he couldn't think of anything else to talk about. Sure as hell not the local building trade, since as of Monday morning he was no longer president of Becker Construction.

"I don't know," she said in answer to his question. "A month or six weeks."

Will slid his hand down and laced his fingers with hers. It was almost more intimate than a kiss, he thought, looking at their clasped hands. There was something about being palm to palm.

She didn't seem to notice that they were holding hands now.

"I just want to forget about him," she declared. "And *Graziella*."

There it was again, the name as abomination.

Will laughed. "Definitely forget them. Talk to me. Did you grow up around here?"

She turned to look at him instead of the ballroom. "Uh-uh. Montana. Missoula. You?"

"I'm a local boy."

"So your family is here?" She seemed bemused by the idea.

"Yeah. Not my parents, they're gone. My mother when I was a kid, and then my dad and stepmom in a plane crash when I was twenty. One of those freak things, a sightseeing flight—" He stopped. Sharing long past tragedy wasn't the way to get the girl.

Not that he was trying to *get* her. Not when he'd be winging to Africa a week from now. He just wanted to enjoy her for a little longer.

"But I have two brothers and a sister," he continued. "From Dad's second marriage."

She nodded her understanding.

"The youngest just graduated from college. My sister, Sophie. She'll be going to grad school come fall." He smiled. "And that's more than you wanted to know, I bet. Do you have sisters or brothers?"

Moira shook her head. "There was only me and my mom. I didn't really even know my dad. My parents split up when I was two."

And her father was a jackass who hadn't bothered to make time for his daughter, Will diagnosed. He really, really wished he could see her face better. Once again, she sounded a little sad, but he might be imagining things. He was surprised to realize that, for the second time tonight, he was feeling protective and angry on her behalf. He thought he'd worn out all those instincts getting his siblings safely raised.

"Have you ever been river rafting?" he asked, at random, determined to lighten the conversation.

She made a little gurgle of amusement. "I can't swim. So no."

"You can't swim?" Will repeated. "How is that possible? Doesn't every kid take lessons?"

"Not this one." She opened her mouth as if to say

something, then closed it. "And I'm not about to start now," she finished with a hint of defiance.

"So, is taking the ferry across the Sound your worst nightmare?"

"No, the ferry is okay. I keep a close eye on the lifeboats. Now, those I wouldn't like, but it's a comfort that they're there. My worst nightmare…hmm. Sailing cross the Atlantic."

"*The Perfect Storm* wasn't your favorite movie?"

"I never have liked horror movies."

He found himself smiling at the description. Standing here this way felt good. Somehow they'd come to be closer together than they had started. His much larger hand enveloped hers. Their voices were low, as if they were lovers murmuring secrets to each other.

"What's your worst nightmare?" she asked.

Will had to think about that. He didn't have any phobias, per se. He guessed he might be a little claustrophobic; he'd had a construction site injury once and when the doctor sent him for an MRI he'd found the experience hellish. Given the breadth of his shoulders, he'd been crammed in that damn tunnel as if it were the skin of a sausage and he was the innards. And he'd had to lie there for an aeon. Yeah, being buried alive wouldn't be high on his list. But it wasn't the worst thing, although it was oddly akin.

"Being trapped," he finally said quietly. "Any freedom of choice taken away from me. Spending my entire life doing what I have to do, no matter how desperately I chafe at it."

Now where had *that* come from? It was true, every word of it, but he didn't think he'd ever spoken the words aloud. God help him, that's what his life had been like since the day he'd taken the phone call in his college dorm telling him his parents were dead. He hadn't known what he wanted to do with his life yet, but it wasn't going to be construction. He'd worked summers for his dad for the past five years, and that was enough.

Until all choice had been yanked from him when he realized his brothers and sister had no one else.

He couldn't regret the decisions he'd made then. He loved Clay, Jack and Sophie. But these past couple weeks, knowing the end was in sight, he'd felt like a kid who'd suffered through his school years looking toward high school graduation.

Free at last.

He felt Moira's scrutiny. Finally she nodded, but said softly, "Life's made up of obligations, though, isn't it?"

"But we ought to be able to choose the ones we take on, don't you think?"

Her head tilted, reminding him of a curious bird. Perhaps the owl he'd likened her to earlier, with downy, unruly feathers around the enormous, unblinking eyes.

With that tilt of the head, enough light touched her face that he thought, *green.* Her eyes were green.

"Yes," she said. "I'm a big fan of free choice." Her fingers wriggled in his, and she glanced down in apparent puzzlement.

So she'd finally noticed that they had been holding hands for the past ten minutes. Although reluctant, he released hers.

"If you'll excuse me, my feet are killing me and I think I had too much to drink. I'm about to conk out."

"You're not planning to drive, are you?"

She shook her head. "I think I'll get a room."

Will smiled at her. "I'll walk you down."

"You don't have to—"

"It would be my pleasure," he said with a formality unusual to him.

After a moment, she murmured, "Then, thank you." She started toward the open doors, and he strolled at her side.

When they reached the ballroom, he could hardly tear his eyes from her face. She was indeed pretty, but in a way that contrasted with her curvaceous, seductive body. Her cheeks were round, her forehead high, giving her an unexpected look of vulnerability, and her milk-pale skin was dusted with pale gold freckles. Her eyes were green, but flecked with gold, too. And her eyebrows, like the hair on her head, were the pure color of copper.

She looked...innocent, which made him feel guilty for wondering if the rest of her body was freckled, too, if the nipples crowning her generous breasts were pink or dusky brown, whether her pubic hair was copper bright, too.

He almost groaned. Yes, of course it was. And, damn it, he had no business thinking this way when he couldn't start anything with her. He was tying up the last strands of this part of his life, not opening any new packages. However enticing this one was.

Moira greeted a couple of people, and he did the same. They even had a few mutual acquaintances, none of whom seemed to think anything of the fact that they knew each other. He wondered what she did for a living, but decided he didn't want to know. He'd prefer to remember her as his mysterious redhead.

Then she stiffened. Raising his eyebrows, Will saw

the couple directly in front of them. Good-looking guy, beautiful woman if you liked hip bones sharp enough to draw blood and thought counting ribs was an excellent postcoital activity.

The scumbag, clearly, and *Graziella*. Feeling Moira's tension, Will wasn't nearly as amused as he'd been when she last said the name.

"Bruce," she said coolly.

Some instinct made Will lay his hand on Moira's back in a way any other man would recognize. *Mine*. He nodded, making plain his disinterest, and steered her around the other couple.

"Aren't you Will Becker?" the other guy said.

Will nodded. "Yes." And kept going.

Moira gave another of those little gurgles of laughter that sounded like a small brook tumbling over rocks. "Well, that was rude."

"Yeah, and I enjoyed it," he said truthfully.

She turned that laughing face up to him, her eyes sparkling, and said, "Thank you."

"You're very welcome." He kept his hand on her until they reached the front desk, at which point he stood back and let her take a credit card from the small, sparkly bag she'd carried over her shoulder. When eventually she turned around, he asked, "All set?"

"Yes. You don't have to walk me up, Will."

"Yes, I do."

She bit her lip and studied him for a moment, her eyes curiously vulnerable in a way that gave him a pang. Twice now he'd thought of her as such, which had to mean something.

He knew what that something was. His gut was telling him to say good-night to her outside her hotel room door and leave. Don't kiss her. Don't step over the threshold. She wasn't a one-night stand kind of woman, and he wasn't interested in anything but.

Moira nodded and let him walk beside her to the elevators. One opened as soon as she pushed the button, and they rode upward in silence, side by side. He heard the soft sigh of a breath from her, caught an elusive scent that seemed old-fashioned. He had a flash of standing on the deep front porch of his family home, the sky purple with twilight, and that scent filling his nostrils.

Lilac.

The elevator opened and he said, "What's your room number?"

She stumbled, stepping out, and he wrapped a hand around her arm to catch her. "Um…" She looked at the small folder she held. "Two-eighteen."

Will nodded and directed her to the right. The hall was broad, the plush charcoal-gray carpet inset with maroon. He stopped in front of 218 and watched as she fumbled with the card, finally getting it into the slot correctly and turning the knob when the green light flashed.

"I should say good-night now," he said hoarsely.

Holding the door open, she met his eyes. "Did you mean it, when you said…" She seemed to lose courage.

"Said…?" His heart was hammering.

She whispered, "That you think I'm beautiful."

"I meant it." He lifted a hand, hesitated, then only grazed her round, plush cheek with his knuckles. "You are."

Her tongue touched her lips; she took a deep breath. "Then will you stay?"

CHAPTER TWO

Stunned pleasure blossomed inside him like the warmth from good whiskey.

"You're sure?" Will asked.

Had she really invited him in? Could he get this lucky?

But already Moira's eyes had widened, as if she'd shocked herself, and her face flushed. Even so, she mumbled, "I think so."

Despite the rising tide of hunger, he found himself smiling. "That wasn't the strongest yes I've ever heard."

Now her gaze was shy. "I haven't done this in an awfully long time."

His every instinct was to kiss her and keep kissing her until she was past any second thoughts. Damn, he hadn't had sex in…it had to be a year, since he'd parted ways with Julia. But as desperate as he felt, Will wasn't willing to risk making love with a woman who might hate herself or him immediately afterward.

"It's been a good long while for me, too," he admitted.

"Probably not as long as it's been for me." This mumble was so low he doubted it had been for his ears. It was a good reminder that his redhead had maybe had too much to drink. She was clutching onto the door frame pretty hard.

"Why me?" he asked.

She raised her chin. "You can just say no."

"I don't want to say no."

"Oh." Her lashes fluttered. "I'm attracted to you. I suppose…I needed someone to tell me I'm beautiful. You sounded like you really did mean it." Her shoulders moved in an oddly unhappy jerk. "This is only for tonight…"

"It can only be for tonight." His voice came out harsh.

Now alarm flashed in her green eyes. "You're not married?"

"No." He laid a palm against her cheek and felt the heat of her blush. "No," he said, softer. "Nothing like that."

"Okay." Her breath tickled his wrist. "Then…?"

"Are you on birth control? I don't have anything with me."

Now her cheeks blazed. "I do. I was planning…"

He got it. The jackass downstairs was supposed to be standing here, not him. He was a substitute.

This was one time, Will thought with amusement and a leap of desire, that he didn't mind filling in.

"In that case," he said huskily, "I'd love to stay."

He had a fleeting moment of being bothered that she looked surprised—had she really thought he'd say *no?*—but it was forgotten when he stepped forward until their bodies touched, chest to thighs. He took the hotel key from her hand and urged her backward, until the door swung shut behind them.

The room was dark; he fumbled for a switch and

batted at it. The lamp beside the king-size bed came on, casting a golden circle of light. Perfect.

Damn, she was pretty. Will tossed the hotel key onto a dresser top and divested her of the small evening bag, sending it after the key. Then he cupped her face in his broad palms and bent his head.

He didn't feel gentle, but he made sure his mouth was. Simply a little friction on her lips, a nibble, a stroke of his tongue. He could taste the martini, and something more. Something, he thought, that was distinctly *her*. He lifted his head and looked down at her face where color still blossomed. This close he could see that her lashes were darkened with mascara. Their natural color was undoubtedly that same bright copper. He'd like to see her without the mascara, with no defenses.

Although she had precious few now. She might have started with lipstick, but it had worn off, and the roses in her cheeks were surely her own. It would take a lot of powder to cover her freckles, and why would she bother trying? He liked those freckles.

"Can I take your hair down?" he whispered.

Her eyes were dazed. "I… Yes. Of course."

When he delved his fingers in, he found an intriguing texture. As he removed pins, curls sprang free. One leaped around his index finger as if to entrap it. Her hair was thick and strong, strands sleek but not downy soft. Despite the sexual tension that gripped Will, he found himself foolishly smiling, imagining her trying to tame this mass every day.

"It's awful hair."

"It's glorious." Pins showered to the carpet; he was too busy playing to care. The curls tumbled below her shoulders. He guessed if her hair had been straight it might have fallen to the middle of her back. He could see that calling it *copper* wasn't right: a hundred colors seemed to be mixed, from hairs as pale as flax to ones a deep auburn, and every shade in between. It was beautiful in this light. With sun shining on her head, she must glow.

"Man," he whispered, and buried his face in her hair. The lilac fragrance was coming from it, and he let himself wallow happily for a minute. Then he pulled back enough to nip her earlobe and finally string kisses across her cheek to her nose and mouth.

This time he kissed her deeply, hungrily, sliding his tongue past her teeth to stroke hers. She made a muffled sound and wrapped her arms around his neck. Her body molded itself to his as if they were custom shaped. Sensation piled atop sensation: her tongue, slippery and sinuous against his, the plump, firm pillow of her breasts pressed against his chest, the vitality of the curls tangled around the hand he had cupping the back of her head.

He wanted her *now,* and fought to hold himself in check. That bastard downstairs had made her feel undesirable, and Will needed to fix that. Come morning, he was determined that she had no doubt in her mind how much he'd wanted her and how rich her own response was.

As he slid her zipper down and trailed his mouth over her throat, he murmured disconnected words meant to tell her what he felt. Her skin was unbelievably soft, and the leap of pulse under his lips aroused him like he couldn't remember being. He nipped at her neck, wanting to leave a mark but careful not to.

He couldn't claim the right, not when he wouldn't be around tomorrow.

She let out little gasps as he eased her dress down and peeled it off her arms then over her hips. His blood surged at the sight of her deep purple satin bra and a skimpy pair of matching panties.

"Beautiful. So beautiful," he managed to say, although the words came out sounding raw. Her dress fell to her feet and he scooped her in his arms and moved her a few feet closer to the bed.

She wore no stockings, only strappy high heels and the bra and panties that were… His hands explored. Not a thong, but there wasn't much there except the generous curve of butt that had him so hard he hurt.

Damn. He kissed her again, both his hands gripping her ass to hold her tight to his hips. They rocked where they stood, as if they couldn't help themselves, and a groan tore its way from his throat.

He eased back and started yanking at his own clothes, flinging his suit coat to the floor, his tie after it the moment he got the damn knot undone. Moira was wrestling with the buttons of his shirt at the same time, and it fell to the floor, too.

Somehow he got the covers pulled down and laid her across the wide bed, her sprawl so wanton he couldn't do anything but follow her even though he wanted to finish stripping. He had to cradle his erection between her thighs or he thought he might die right now.

They kissed and rolled, his hands everywhere on her body, hers on his. Not until she rose above him, sitting atop him, did he manage to undo the catch on her bra and free the most beautiful breasts he'd ever seen. Her chest was freckled, and a scattering of paler freckles danced down over the creamy skin traced with faint blue lines, as though her skin was more transparent than normal. Her nipples were pink, the aureoles larger and just a little deeper in color.

Will heard himself making sounds that weren't even words as he tugged her near so that he could lave her nipples with his tongue, first one then the other. Kiss them softly, blow on the damp skin until she shivered, then suckle her, pulling the hard nubbin deep into his mouth as his cheeks flexed.

She clutched his shoulders and whimpered. Her hips rose and fell on his as if she couldn't help herself, but he was afraid he'd come right now, in his pants, if she kept riding him that way. He rolled her onto her back so that he was on top, able to savor her breasts for another few minutes before he rose to his knees and tugged her panties off. There were the curls as bright as the ones on her head, nestled between a smooth, freckled stomach and perfect legs that were freckled, too. He wanted to kiss every single freckle, but he knew he wouldn't last that long.

Her stomach. He'd start there. He loved the give of it; she had a tiny waist, but not the washboard abs of a woman who worked out every day. She felt intensely feminine, the ripples of reaction under his mouth amazingly erotic.

He finally had the strength of will to retreat enough to remove her shoes and, with clumsy hands, unbuckle his belt and shed his pants and socks. Then he kissed and licked his way up her legs, from the quivering arch of her feet to the sensitive back of her knees and the velvet softness of her inner thighs. He nuzzled her curls and inhaled her scent, his head swimming. A few strokes of his finger told him she was hot and wet and ready. Her cries had become something closer to mewls, and her head was flung back, her hair a halo against the white sheet.

He moved up between her thighs and got as far as pressing against her opening when his brain finally kicked in.

A condom! What in the hell had he been *thinking?*

He all but sprang from her. "Your purse?" he asked.

For a moment he could tell she didn't comprehend, but then her eyes widened in shock that matched his. They'd come so close. Too damn close.

"Yes." She swallowed. "Yes. I don't know where…"

"I put it…" He turned his head and spotted the glittery bag. He leaped out of bed. When he got his hands on the bag, he dumped the contents on the dresser top, not caring that some fell to the floor. Between folded bills was one small packet, and that was it.

He wished she'd brought more than one.

Will ripped it open and put on the condom. Two long steps and he was at the bed, where her legs were still splayed wide. He ran his hands up them, caressing, squeezing, until his fingers reached her damp center and he stroked as he knelt there. Not until her hips rocked again did he lower himself, taking her mouth in a deep, hungry kiss even as he pushed inside her.

She was tight. So tight he had a brief, horrified moment of wondering whether she might be a virgin. But he met no barrier, although he had to quit kissing her to grit his teeth at the exquisite pressure her body put on him. He was a big man, but he'd never felt anything like this.

"Am I hurting you?" he asked roughly.

She was panting for breath and her eyes were dilated. "No," she whispered. "Oh, no."

Will moved. Out, in, slowly this time. He was near to exploding, but he had to give her pleasure first. Had to.

"Never felt…anything…this good," he groaned against her throat.

"Please." She wrapped her legs around his hips and rose to meet his next thrust. "Oh, please."

He knew what she needed. He just wasn't sure he could hold out long enough. He tried to blank his mind as he plunged, again and again, clasped so tight by her. He'd been holding his weight from her on his elbows, but now he reached down with one hand and gripped her hips, lifting her higher, changing the angle at which their bodies met.

"Will?" She sounded…almost frightened. Stunned, certainly. And then she cried out, and her body spasmed. He drove himself in her as deep as he could go and let the climax roll through him, the pleasure so powerful he couldn't have formed a coherent thought if his life had depended on it.

He collapsed on top of her and couldn't move.

Through a haze, it occurred to him that he'd never felt this amazing in his life. That sex had never *approached* being this powerful. He didn't know how or why it had been this time. Maybe something about the night, about having watched her for so long through the glass. And they didn't know each other.

That was it: anticipation, and mystery.

Eventually he made himself roll to one side and tuck her against him, her head on his shoulder, her hair tickling his chin. Eyes closed, he smiled, imagin-

ing those tendrils reaching for some kind of toehold,
like ivy scaling a brick wall.

"You're amazing," he murmured, his voice thick.

She snuggled closer and said nothing.

Will let himself drift, aware of the change in her breathing as she fell asleep. And, in drifting, he slept himself.

It was probably the unfamiliar weight of her head
on his shoulder that awakened him. Will was disoriented only for a moment. He reached up with his free
hand and brushed curls from his mouth, then tilted his
head enough to be able to see her face. Her lips were
parted, and a faint snore came to his ears.

His body stirred, and Will wished again that they
had more than one condom. He supposed he could call
down to the front desk… But she was sound asleep.
She didn't surface when he gently disentangled himself. Wishing for another condom had reminded him
that he hadn't removed the last one, or cleaned up.

What he should do was get dressed and go. Staying
longer wouldn't bring anything but frustration and, come
morning, an awkward conversation he'd as soon not
have. She'd asked for one night; he'd told her it couldn't
be any more than that. What else was there to say?

Will eased away, used the bathroom, then quietly got
dressed. He found a pen on the desk and wrote quickly
on the back of one of his business cards:

You are beautiful. I wish more than one night
had been possible.
Will.

He underlined the *are* with a dark slash.

He picked up her clothes and laid them over a chair,

then tucked the covers under her chin. She sighed and shifted before sinking back into deep slumber.

Will took one last look at her face and the vivid hair spread across the pillow, turned off the lamp and quietly let himself out of the room.

MOIRA WOKE WITH A START. Her mouth felt disgusting and she tried to work up some saliva. When she moved, a headache blossomed. Ugh. Was she coming down with something…?

She opened her eyes and remembered. *Oh, Lord,* she thought in shock. Had she really…? She squeezed her eyes shut. Yes. Yes, she had.

Behind closed eyelids, she pictured him, broad and tall in the darkness, the way she saw him first, then his rough-hewn face above her here in this bed, his short dark hair and the deep brown eyes looking so intensely into hers. She saw him so vividly, she expected to see him in reality when she opened her eyes, even though she knew better.

When she rolled enough to check out the other side of the bed and the room, it was to find herself alone. He was gone. They'd had sex, and he'd left her sleeping.

After, Moira noticed, picking up her clothes so they weren't left wadded on the floor.

With a groan, she got out of bed, snatched up her clothes and rushed into the bathroom. Her stomach felt queasy but not too bad. She couldn't exactly say she was hungover, although she wished she hadn't had the last drink or two. Maybe, with a clearer head, she'd have had more sense than to take a hotel room and invite a perfect stranger into bed with her.

Shame crawled over her skin like goose bumps.

What on earth had made her do something like that? She'd had only one lover in her whole life, and that was a college boyfriend. All these years since, she'd never even been *tempted* to have a one-night stand.

Until last night. When she'd not only been tempted, she'd done it.

The shower was blessedly hot, and she stayed in it for a long time. Getting dressed afterward wasn't fun, given that she didn't have clean underwear and had to put on an evening gown and high heels. She'd have killed for coffee and breakfast to settle her stomach, but no way was she going in a restaurant dressed like this, advertising that she'd had a hard night. She could order from room service… But that seemed silly. She'd be home in forty-five minutes.

With no brush, either, all she could do was loosely braid her wet hair. Her evening bag…she spotted it lying atop the dresser, next to a TV schedule and some local promotional brochures. Her keys had fallen to the floor for some reason, and as she bent to pick them up she saw her lipstick, too. She grabbed the purse and straightened, stuffing the lipstick inside as she turned for the door. Moira had no idea where the room key was and didn't care. At last, gingerly, she picked up the business card with the short note written on the back. A painful lump seemed to form in her chest.

Why can't *we have more than one night?* But she wouldn't call him. He'd made clear his limitations. If he wanted to, he could find her.

Moira dropped the business card in her purse and let herself out of the room. All she wanted was to get to her car, preferably unseen, and go home.

Then she would try to understand why she'd so foolishly gotten naked with a stranger, however kind and sexy he was.

But she knew, of course: her feelings had been hurt and she'd needed consolation. *Foolish* was the word for it, Moira thought, blushing as she crossed the hotel foyer under the gaze of a woman behind the front desk.

And *risky*. That was another word for having sex with a stranger.

Except, he hadn't hurt her, and she knew he'd used the condom. Because *he'd* remembered, not because she had. She'd been lucky. Done something dumb, and escaped any of the myriad possible consequences. She should be old enough not to have to learn a lesson this way, but apparently she wasn't.

Moira got into her car and momentarily laid her forehead against the steering wheel.

I learned. I did.

Time to go home and... No, she wouldn't wish Will Becker would call. Instead, she'd do her best to forget last night ever happened.

THE SECURITY LINE at the airport lay just ahead. This early in the morning, it was short. He'd have plenty of time for breakfast and coffee once he got through it.

Will had intended to take an airporter to Sea Tac, but Sophie insisted on driving him. During the past week, he'd signed over the title to his pickup to Jack and piled a few plastic tubs filled with his possessions in the basement of the family home. This morning, he had taken one last look at his bedroom, stripped of personality, and felt something unexpected: grief. He was saying goodbye to his entire life to this point. He had grown up in this house, played with plastic dinosaurs on the floor of this same bedroom, fought later with his stepmother over how clean he had to keep it. Sneaked a high school girlfriend in here and had sex with her after his parents were in bed and asleep. Returned the one summer after his freshman year in college, swearing that it would be the last time he'd work for his father, the last time he'd swing a hammer.

Then he'd come home to stay after his parents died. He'd never considered moving into the master bedroom, which was still empty. It was stupid, really, with Jack, Sophie, Clay and him all here, all in small bedrooms designed for children. He hoped, if and when Clay got married, that he'd have the sense to overcome the past and make the house his. Really his.

Something Will hadn't done, in part because he hadn't wanted the house, or the company, and he sure hadn't wanted to be a twenty-year-old stand-in father of three, responsible for the financial and emotional well-being of his young sister and brothers.

And now, he thought, standing in Sea Tac airport at the crack of dawn, he was done with all of it.

He turned to face his sister. "Thanks for bringing me."

Sophie was the shrimp of the family, and still stood five foot ten. "*Somebody* had to see you off," she insisted.

"Yeah." He grinned at her. "Don't do anything I wouldn't approve of, okay?"

Her brown eyes filled with tears. "Oh, Will!" she wailed. "I'm going to miss you!"

His arms closed fiercely around her. "Damn it, Soph. I thought we had this goodbye crap out of the way."

She shook her head hard. "I know it doesn't make sense, when I've been away at college the last four years, but...you were always here. And now you won't be."

"I'm sorry," he heard himself say. "Do I still need to be?"

She shook her head again, then pulled back to give him a watery smile. "Of course you don't. I'm being silly. It's just...I'll miss you, Will. I'm *glad* you're going. I know how much you need this. How much you gave up for us."

He scowled. "Don't start with that. I did what I had to do. I have no regrets."

Her smile became more genuine. "Yeah, sure you don't. Just, um, have a fabulous time, okay? And email."

"Yeah, yeah." He kissed her wet cheek. "I love you, Soph. I won't disappear, I promise."

"Okay." She sniffed and swiped at damp eyes. "I'm going. You don't need this. Just...take care." She gave him one more fervent hug, then hurried away.

He watched her go, not looking back, and remembered taking each of his siblings to college to start their freshman years. Helping them haul their stuff into dorm rooms, wishing he was the one there to stay, then driving away with the feeling that a big hole had opened in his chest. Except for the envy he hadn't been able to help, he'd been all parent, a little shocked to find out how much he was going to miss first Clay, then Jack, then Sophie.

By the time Sophie started her freshman year, Clay was home again and working with Will. Unlike Will, he had loved the summers he'd worked construction.

It seemed to be in his blood. He'd learned the business eagerly and had a natural air of authority.

Will shook himself now, surprised again at how alone he felt. Glad he was, but a little sorry all the same. Maybe he should have expected these mixed emotions, but hadn't. He'd expected to be celebrating this morning.

He went through security, taking out his laptop, putting his shoes on the conveyor belt, having to go back and empty the change out of the pockets of his pants. Then he put himself back together and headed for the closest place to have breakfast.

Although he'd brought the morning *Times* to read while he was eating, Will found himself thinking instead about his redhead. He kept thinking he should have tracked her down and called her. Maybe she felt fine about making love with him, but maybe she didn't. He hated to think she was embarrassed.

He wished…oh, damn, he wished he'd met her at another time and place. That he'd been able to call her the next day and ask her out to dinner. Let her know that she could be special to him, not merely a chance to get his rocks off.

Face it, he thought harshly; that's all she'd been. And she deserved more.

He'd feel worse if he was sure saying "Thanks, but no thanks," would have been the right thing to do. Will was still afraid that would have hurt her, that she'd been emotionally fragile enough to *need* a man to want her.

And maybe he was trying to excuse himself for taking what she offered because he wanted to, whether it was a crappy thing for him to have done or not.

He hoped she didn't give the jackass another chance if he came begging.

Forget it, he told himself, frowning as he rose to walk to the gate. There was nothing he could do now. This was his new beginning. He should be rejoicing.

Too bad he wasn't already in Harare, instead of facing thirty-six hours on airplanes and airport layovers in Frankfurt and Addis Ababa, Ethiopia. He hoped like hell the promised aisle seats materialized; he was way too big a man to spend that many hours cramped between other passengers or at the window.

Half an hour later, his flight was called. Thinking, *Here goes nothing,* he took out his boarding pass and joined the line. But he was still picturing an apple-cheeked, freckled face with pretty lips and green eyes when he wedged himself into his airline seat and buckled the belt.

CHAPTER THREE

STANDING ATOP THE ROUGH concrete foundation, Moira studied the completed framing of the building that would house doctors' offices and an outpatient surgical center.

"Looking good," she told Jeb Morris, a contractor with whom she'd worked before. These visits were almost a formality with Jeb; he knew enough to spot problems before they tripped him up. And he maintained high standards.

A short, stocky man with a close-cropped beard, he pushed his hard hat back, his gaze resting on her. "Everything okay, Moira?"

She looked at him in surprise. "Sure. Why do you ask?"

He shook his head. "You seem distracted today."

Moira forced a smile. "I guess I am. Just things on my mind. Sorry, Jeb."

"Hey, no problem. I'll walk you to your car."

Because she was visiting several sites today, she'd worn her clunky work boots, jeans and a green flannel shirt over a T-shirt, in case the day got warmer. It was May, tulips were in bloom, but the morning had been chilly.

She was trying very, very hard to think about the job site and the wiring and electrical and plumbing that would soon go in, about spring flowers and how she was meeting Gray and Charlotte for lunch later. Gray Van Dusen was her partner in Van Dusen & Cullen, Architects, and her best friend in the world. Charlotte had quickly become almost as good a friend.

Moira was doing her best to think about anything and everything except the fact that she was almost positive her period was late. At least a week late. Maybe ten days. She didn't keep exact track, so she wasn't sure. But…it should have come and gone.

Sickening fear rose from her belly to swell in her chest, as it did every time she let this worry creep through her defenses. She felt Jeb's scrutiny and made a point of smiling again and asking about his oldest son, who was a senior in high school waiting to hear which colleges had accepted him.

Jeb's face brightened. "Didn't I tell you? He received early acceptance to Stanford. Can you believe it?" He wore a goofy grin. "My kid, going to Stanford."

She laughed. "Your kid, your tuition bills."

That didn't wipe the smile away. "Worth every penny." He slapped the top of her car. "Take care, Moira."

"Yeah, thanks, Jeb." She put the key in the ignition and closed the door as he walked away. Not wanting him to turn back and see her sitting here, she reversed then drove across bumpy ground toward the street. Meantime, her stomach churned.

Was it too early for a pregnancy test?

Once out of sight of the construction, she pulled to the curb and set the car in Park. Still holding on to the steering wheel for all she was worth, Moira let the fear wash over her. It sensitized her skin, set her to rocking, made her pant.

How could this *be?* He'd used the condom. She knew he had, saw him put it on.

Yes, but condoms had a failure rate a whole lot higher than birth-control pills. Which she wasn't on. Hadn't wanted to start until she was sure her relationship with Bruce was moving to that point.

She'd had sex once. Once! *And* they'd used a condom. Even if it had failed—had a hole, or leaked, or whatever went wrong—a woman shouldn't get pregnant the one and only time she'd had sex in over ten years. Wasn't there some justice, somewhere, that would keep her from being punished so severely for her foolish need to prove she was desirable?

And to make matters worse, she wasn't even convinced she'd proved that much. Yes, he'd made passionate love to her. He'd said the right things. He'd touched her with such care, such longing, and his eyes had darkened to near black when he thrust into her. But…he had also left the minute she fell asleep, simply stole away.

And even though he'd said it would be only the one night… A part of her couldn't help wondering why. Why, in the three weeks that had passed since then, he hadn't made the effort to find out who she was, hadn't called. She would have been easy to find, Moira knew, with her flaming red hair and freckled face. They'd known people in common; all he would have had to do was make a phone call or two.

But he hadn't done that.

Please don't let him be married, she prayed. *Don't let him have lied. I'd hate to have to live with that. Especially now, especially if…*

If she was pregnant. Moira bit her lip so hard she tasted blood.

What would she do if she was pregnant? Would she track him down and tell him?

Still rocking herself, she thought, *No*. If this was anyone's fault, it was hers. She'd asked him to make love to her. The condom was hers, so she couldn't even blame him for using a defective one. He'd warned her that the one night was all he could offer, and she'd agreed. How could she now contact him and say, "Hate to tell you, but you're going to be a father, so how do you feel about paying child support for, oh, say, the next eighteen years?"

That wasn't the deal they'd made.

My fault, my risk.

And—oh, Lord—she didn't know if she could face him anyway. Maybe the standards she'd grown up with in Montana were dated, but the closest she'd come to shaking them was sleeping with her college boyfriend. Having too much to drink followed by a one-night stand… She shivered. She'd all but *begged* him to have sex with her.

Moira was whimpering now, the fear swamping her. She felt like a drowning victim, going down for the last time, desperate for a hand to reach for her. But there wasn't one. Wouldn't be one. If she made Will Becker take responsibility, all she'd be doing was dragging him under with her.

It was a long time before she felt able to drive again. She'd made one decision: she would wait another week before she bought a home pregnancy test. Heck, maybe her anxiety was holding off her period. A watched pot never boils, after all. And…really, was there any advantage to knowing for sure this early? Abortion wasn't an option for her, she knew that. She *wanted* to have children. She'd always assumed she would be married by the time she had a baby, that there would be a father in the picture, too, but hard reality was that she was thirty-four years old. Maybe she should be grabbing at any chance to have a family, even if it wouldn't be the ideal one.

Moira wished she wasn't supposed to meet Gray and Charlotte. Hiding her distress would be hard. And the truth was, if she really was pregnant, carried the baby to term and kept him or her to raise, Gray would pay some of the price, too, however unfair that was.

When he got the idea of running for mayor of West Fork, they'd had a long talk. He wasn't married then, hadn't even met Charlotte, so it was only the two of them making the decision. The mayoral job wasn't full-time, or he wouldn't have considered it. But he'd have to cut back substantially on how many architectural commissions he took. Unless they wanted their revenue to decline substantially, Moira would be carrying more than her share of the work.

She'd liked what he wanted to accomplish for this town that was now home for both of them, and understood why it mattered to him. Understood more, probably, than he'd be comfortable realizing. Gray was usually closemouthed about his deepest motivations, but they had been best friends in college. There'd been a couple of times when he'd had too much to drink and had told her things he had probably regretted—assuming he'd remembered the next day.

She knew he had had a twin brother who died in an accident when the two boys were ten years old. They had been riding bikes together, racing down a hill. Garret had pulled ahead, just a little. He slammed into the side of a car passing on the street that intersected the foot of the hill. Gray shot past the rear bumper. A split second one way or the other and it would have been different. Garret might have been fine and Gray dead. Or both fine. Garret went into a coma and never came out before dying two days later. In their grief, Gray's parents pulled away from each other and ultimately divorced, his mother moving to Portland, his dad to Boise. They'd left behind the small-town life that in later years came to seem idyllic to Gray, who had also had to cope with the realization that he was a constant, aching reminder to both of his parents of the son they'd lost.

In coming to West Fork, Gray was trying to recapture everything *he* had lost. She knew that, and feared it was impossible, but had agreed to open their architectural firm here anyway. To her surprise, he seemed to have found what he was looking for. The satisfaction of shaping the town to suit himself, a woman to love, the start of a family.

But Moira wasn't going to be able to keep her end of the agreement. Would she even be able to work full-time when she got near the end of her pregnancy? Didn't most new mothers have to take some time off? And then, how many hours a day could she bear to leave her baby in day care? There was no way Gray would be able to continue serving as mayor, not if Van Dusen & Cullen, Architects, was to survive.

And that made her feel horribly guilty.

Fortunately, if she was quiet during lunch, neither Gray nor Charlotte seemed to notice. They talked some about their current projects, some about Charlotte's pregnancy, which was starting to show, and some about Charlotte's twin sister, Faith, who had recently married West Fork Police Chief Ben Wheeler and who was also thinking of starting a family.

Call her pathetic, but it made Moira feel even lonelier to imagine Charlotte and Faith both pregnant at the same time as she was, but the two of them having men who loved them and worried about them and hovered over them. While all Moira was doing by getting pregnant was screwing up her life.

Worry about it when you're sure, she told herself.

A WEEK LATER, MOIRA BOUGHT a pregnancy test at a pharmacy in Everett where nobody knew her, and decided to wait until after dinner to use it. She should be hungry, but wasn't. A part of her knew it wasn't only anxiety, that the lack of appetite and faint queasiness of the past few days shouldn't come as any surprise.

She peed on the stick, then sat on the edge of the bathtub waiting, staring at it. Maybe the watched pot *wouldn't* boil. If she didn't take her eyes off it, didn't blink....

But she couldn't help blinking, and the blue color first tinted the slot, then brightened.

Oh, God. Oh, God.

All of her fear poured back. She dropped the stick in the wastebasket and bent forward, holding herself as tight as she could as a hundred different emotions eddied and tumbled like flood waters, almost more than her body could contain.

In the end, all she could think was, *I'm pregnant.*

And now she had to live with it.

"LUNCH?" MOIRA SAID. "Um…sure. Now?"

Oh, heavens. She'd done her best in the two months since she realized she was pregnant to…not avoid Gray, how could she when they were partners and friends? She saw him every day, and she had dinner with him and Charlotte at least once a week. But she had tried not to spend time alone with him, not to let conversation become really personal. It hadn't been as hard as she'd have thought. Mostly in the office they talked business, exchanged ideas, looked over each other's preliminary sketches and made suggestions, offered solutions to jobsite problems. Lunch for Gray was usually fast food or a deli sandwich, snatched between city hall and their architectural office or a job site.

But today, he'd appeared earlier than she had expected him, and now stood in the doorway waiting.

"If not now, when?" he asked with his usual good humor.

She saved her CADD drawing and closed out the program, then took her purse from the bottom drawer of her desk. Gray stood back to let her out the door, then flipped the sign to Closed.

"The Pea Patch?"

"Fine." Perfect, in fact. The small vegetarian restaurant used only organic, healthful ingredients, exactly what a pregnant woman should be eating. Gray had probably taken to eating there with Charlotte.

He didn't say much during the short drive and found parking right in front. The main street of West Fork probably hadn't changed much since the 1950s, with false-fronted buildings and small, locally owned businesses. The Pea Patch was relatively new, of course, as was the antiques store beside it, but the barbershop and hardware store could have starred in a Norman Rockwell painting. One of Gray's goals had been to maintain the old-fashioned atmosphere of downtown and keep people shopping here.

Moira ordered the day's special, a bowl of split-pea soup and a half sandwich, Gray a burrito. He glanced at her sidelong when she asked for a juice instead of the latte that had been her habit.

Once the waitress took the menus and left them alone, he contemplated Moira over the table. Gray was a handsome man with calm gray eyes and sun-streaked light brown hair. They had dated a time or two when they first met, then fell into friendship instead of romance. Gray wasn't the first or the last guy to see her as buddy material instead of potential girlfriend. In his case, she didn't regret it. He'd become family to her, a lot more important than the college boyfriend with whom she'd lost touch shortly after graduation.

"Something's off with you," he said bluntly. "Or maybe with us. Have I been unavailable when you needed to talk?"

Swallowing the lump in her throat, she shook her head.

"Then what, Moira?" His eyes were kind.

Her chest hurt. "Oh, Gray."

"What?" He leaned forward and reached for her hand.

"I've been dreading telling you."

"Telling me what?" His fingers tightened. "You're not leaving me, are you?"

Even in her misery, Moira giggled. "Do you know what that sounds like?"

A grin tugged at his mouth. "Yeah, someone who

knows I'm married might wonder." The smile faded and he repeated, "What, Moira?"

She had to tell him eventually. Now was as good a time as ever.

"I'm pregnant."

He jerked. "Pregnant?"

"Jeez, tell the whole town, why don't you," she said indignantly.

He looked around. "There's nobody close enough to hear." He paused. "Is it a secret?"

"No." Damn it, she felt watery again. "I guess it'll be obvious anytime."

"How far along?"

"Um...three months."

He frowned. "You've lost weight instead of gaining, haven't you?"

"Didn't Charlotte?"

"You're sick, too?"

Moira nodded. "Well, not sick. Just...icky feeling. I don't dare do more than nibble at any one time."

He was staring at her. "Pregnant," he repeated. His expression hardened. "Who's the father?"

She gazed steadily back. "No one who is in the picture."

"It was that son of a bitch Girard wasn't it?"

Moira gave a choked laugh. "He is a son of a bitch, but no. It's not him, Gray."

"Then who?" This man, her best friend, sounded implacable, as if he intended to beat the crap out of the man who'd impregnated and abandoned her.

She swallowed, the backs of her eyelids burning again. "It really doesn't matter. He...used a condom. It's just one of those things. Not his fault. And we didn't have the kind of relationship that means I'm going to stick him with this."

The waitress appeared with their lunches, and Moira sat silent, head bowed, while Gray said the right things. The minute the waitress was gone, he said, "You're having the baby." It wasn't really a question.

"I'd have done something about it long ago if I wasn't."

He gave a one-sided shrug, as if to say, *Oh, yeah.* "Why did you dread telling me? You're not planning to move home?"

"Home?" She wished she could laugh. "Missoula? Are you kidding? I love my mother, but…no. I'm not going anywhere. It's just that…"

Neither of them had reached for a spoon or fork.

"You're trying to tell me I'm going to have to start carrying my fair share of the work, aren't you?"

"Probably more than your fair share," she said in a rush. "Gray, I'm sorry. We had a deal, and now I've blown it."

Suddenly he was smiling, so tenderly the tears she'd kept at bay filled her eyes. "Moira, falling in love and having babies are way more important than who does what share of work. You gave me my chance, I had fun. But I won't run for reelection. I can't even say I mind that much. It's been a lot tougher than I envisioned, trying to hold down both jobs. I didn't mind so much before Charlotte, but things are different now." He picked up a napkin and dabbed at her cheeks. "It's past time I take up the slack at work. It's you I'm worried about."

On the verge of major blubbering, she gulped and leaped to her feet. "I'm sorry, I—" She hurried to the bathroom, a small, unisex one where she could lock the door and sob without embarrassment.

It didn't take her long; heaven knows, she'd cried enough lately, and should have had it all out of her system. Even though she splashed cold water on her face, she was blotchy when she returned to the table.

Gray gave her a comprehensive look, but all he said was, "Eat. Your soup's getting cold."

She sniffed and picked up her spoon.

"Do you mind if I tell Charlotte?"

"Of course not. I'll be showing before I know it anyway."

He nodded, and they ate in silence for a few minutes. Moira was hungrier than usual, she was surprised to discover. Maybe something had loosened inside her, now that she'd told Gray.

As though his mind was following a similar path, he asked, "Does your mother know?"

Moira groaned. "No."

His mouth quirked. "Unless she's planning a visit, you have six months to work yourself up to it."

"She'll be supportive."

"Then…?"

"This isn't the way I ever imagined starting a family," she heard herself telling him. "I hated not having a father. It seemed like everyone else did. I always swore—" Her throat closed up.

Once again, his hand enveloped hers. "You know I'll be there for you as much as I can."

"Yeah." She felt her smile wobble. "I do know. Thank you, Gray. But we'll be fine." Unconsciously, she laid a hand on her belly. "Mom and I were fine. It's not as if I grew up unloved."

He was quiet for a moment, his gaze perceptive. "Your baby does have a father."

"I haven't told him."

"I'd have been pissed if a woman I was involved with kept that kind of secret from me."

Admitting something like this was hard, but... "It was a one-time thing, Gray. We weren't involved. He doesn't even know my last name."

His eyes narrowed. "But you know his."

After a moment she nodded.

"Damn, Moira."

Heat swept over her face. "I've never done anything like that. Doesn't it figure I'd get caught, big-time, when I did."

"You know I love you."

She nodded again. "I've cried enough, okay?"

Gray gave a low chuckle. "Okay. But let me say this again. Unless you know the guy's a creep, I think you should tell him. If I had a kid out there, I'd want to be part of his life. Give the man a chance."

She sighed. "I think...I've been trying to pretend it didn't happen."

His eyebrows rose. "An immaculate conception?"

Once again he'd managed to make her laugh despite everything. "Something like that." She folded her napkin, then folded it again. And again. "I'm embarrassed to talk to him," she mumbled. "And...it really doesn't seem fair to me to ask anything of him."

"He was there." Gray's voice was hard.

Yes. Will Becker definitely had been there.

"Give him a chance," Gray repeated.

After a moment, she nodded. "Okay. You're right. I know you are."

He smiled then, satisfied, and reached for her hand. One quick squeeze conveyed plenty. "Let me know what I can do, all right?"

There wasn't any point in saying more, not yet. She hated to think he wouldn't be able to finish his term in office, that he'd have to resign early, but they'd have a better idea later when she found out how she was affected by the pregnancy. His term ended the first of the year, and her due date was the middle of January, so they'd be okay as long as she could work until the end.

She should feel better, having gotten this out of the way. And in a way she did. He'd reacted exactly the way she had expected he would: with understanding and affection.

But she still felt guilty, and panic still whispered at the edges of her awareness, prepared to engulf her if she let it.

No matter what, her life would never be the same again.

And now she'd committed herself to calling Will and saying the unthinkable: "I'm pregnant with your baby."

CHAPTER FOUR

BY THE TIME HE REACHED the outskirts of Harare, Will was weary and grateful to be back. He'd spent the past two weeks in rural east Zimbabwe, negotiating with workers, suppliers, local officials, town leaders, hell, even the community *n'anga,* or healer, who seemed to be particularly influential in that district.

The job had turned out to be nothing like he'd envisioned. When he'd first arrived, it hadn't taken him two weeks to discover that the architectural renderings drawn by a firm in Providence, Rhode Island, were useless; that nothing near as elaborate as the original plans was required; that, if these community hospitals and medical clinics were to be useful, they needed to spring from local needs and with local approval. He'd made the mistake, too, of believing he could conduct most business in English, the official language. Zimbabwe had been, after all, a British colony when it was Southern Rhodesia. But, while road signs and the like were in English, it was mostly spoken in the cities. In the countryside where he was working it was another matter. He was now learning Shona, the language of the majority tribe. He still needed a translator, but was gaining confidence in his ability to understand discussions before they were sanitized and translated for his benefit. He was already adept enough to conduct the ritual conversations that preceded any real business.

"How is your mother? Your father? Your son? Good, good," he would say with grave nods. Then, in answer to the requisite polite questions for him, "I don't often speak to them, but my brothers and sister are well."

Nothing happened rapidly, and getting frustrated did no good.

He pulled his ancient Datsun pickup truck into a curbside parking spot in the block adjacent to the foundation offices. As he got out, his mouth quirked as he imagined what Clay would say about the irony of Will, the strong, silent member of the Becker clan, having to spend his days and weeks and months in seemingly never ending conversation. Or—most delicious irony of all—being good at it. But these first months, Will had realized, would build the bridge of friendships strong enough to see a dozen medical clinics and two community hospitals built in the next two years. Or it wouldn't happen.

Harare was Zimbabwe's largest city. It had a surprisingly European look, to his eye, and a population of over a million people. Every time he reached the outskirts of the city after days' or weeks' absence, tension melted away. He was American enough to feel most at home here. There were Western-style grocery stores. He could dine out on Italian food, Greek, Chinese. Hold conversations with American businessmen and women.

He felt rueful amusement when he thought of the last cocktail party he'd attended. He wasn't any better at that kind of socializing. Lurking in a dark corner, he'd wished for his mysterious redhead.

In the first week Will had rented a small house

less than half a mile from the office. Even though he seemed to be away more than he was here, he needed a base. And he'd somehow acquired a full-time house-keeper-cook.

At home in the U.S., the closest thing to a servant he'd ever had was a woman who came in to the Becker home weekly to clean. He'd seen her once in a blue moon; mostly they communicated by notes. *Please clean the refrigerator this week,* he'd write. *I'll be coming on Tuesday instead of Thursday next week, if that's okay,* her sticky note would inform him. But having someone *wait* on him...well, that was different. He'd intended to take care of himself. But he'd barely moved in when women began knocking on his back door asking for work. He was met with blank astonishment when he said he didn't need anyone, thank you. And it wasn't totally true, he discovered; buying food in the unfamiliar markets where English often wasn't spoken was a hassle, and he'd come to Africa with the intention of immersing himself in the culture, not living in a bubble like a tourist admiring the scenery. Yeah, sometimes he appreciated seeing familiar brands on grocery-store shelves, but he didn't want to shop only in the Western-style supermarkets. God knows, he wasn't much of a cook. He had no microwave here. And unemployment was sky-high. He could afford to give someone a job.

So now, when he was in town, he came home to *sadza* ready when he sat at the table. *Sadza* was the word commonly used for any meal, but also for the sta-ple of the diet: a sort of stew served on cooked grain. Jendaya, his housekeeper, most often used chicken in the stew, although she was scandalized that he preferred it to goat, which his relative wealth would have permitted. He liked the stew without meat at all, and she obliged with scandalized shakes of the head. Only the poor didn't put meat in their *sadza,* she made sure he knew. When he was in Harare, he usually ate lunch out, so Will was content with the traditional evening meal even though it varied little.

Jendaya had expected him back today, so he assumed dinner at home would be ready at the usual seven o'clock. That gave him time to stop at the office and check email. He hadn't even seen an internet café the past two weeks—to find one, he'd have had to drive into Mutare, the city closest to the Mozambique border, and it hadn't seemed worth the bother. One of the pleasures of getting home was anticipating email: responses to questions he'd asked of the foundation headquarters, and especially to hearing from Clay, Sophie and Jack. Will missed them more than he'd expected.

The early evening was cool enough to remind him of home as he walked the half a block to the two-story stucco-fronted office building. He'd become accustomed to the rich scent of the air: diesel fuel, wood smoke, ripe fruit and the heady scent of flowers in bloom. September was spring here, south of the equator, still dry, the reverse of seasons in the Pacific Northwest. The hard rains, he was told, fell during the summer in Zimbabwe, therefore at the same time as they would be falling in Washington State.

The front door to the foundation headquarters was still unlocked, although he was greeted with silence inside. He'd started up the stairs when a light went out in an office at the top and Perry Marshall rushed out. Another American, he'd arrived only a few weeks before, and would be acquiring the equipment, furniture and supplies for the clinics as they were built.

"Will!" He paused on the stairs. "Good trip?"

"Yeah, I think so."

"Can we talk in the morning? We're having a dinner party, and Rachel's going to kill me if I'm late. You'd be welcome to join us," he added.

Will smiled. "Thanks, but I suspect Jendaya will have dinner ready. And I've got to tell you, I'm beat."

The other American's bushy gray eyebrows rose. "Then what are you doing here?"

"Just wanted to check email."

"Internet's slow today," Perry warned him, and kept going.

It was, but Will got on eventually and relaxed in his chair, glad the building seemed otherwise empty, as he watched a dozen messages load. Good, a couple from each of his siblings. He liked hearing from them so often. There was one from an unfamiliar address and he clicked on it first, figuring it would be a quick delete. But it wasn't the junk he expected. It was short, only a paragraph, and ended with *Moira*. His pulse quickened.

His mysterious redhead. What the hell? His thoughts had turned to her with disturbing frequency, but if she hadn't tried to get in touch in four months, why now?

Will, I've hesitated over contacting you at all, but I think you deserve to know that I'm pregnant. I don't know what happened; I suppose the condom tore or something. You need to know that I don't hold you responsible. I invited you to stay, I knew you weren't offering anything but the one night. Heck, I was the

one who provided the condom. But…I am pregnant.
I intend to have the baby, and am well able to afford
to raise him or her. I have friends and family. I'm not
asking for help from you, or any involvement. I'll be
honest. I'm not even sure I would welcome either.
Since you don't know me, you may not even believe
the baby is yours. That's okay, too. I thought I should
tell you, and now I've done that.
Moira

Stunned, he stared at the computer monitor, reread-
ing the email a second time, a third time.

She was pregnant.

The first wave of anger took him aback, because it
was a stupid thing that pissed him off. Did she really
think he wouldn't believe her when she said the baby
was his? He'd have had to be an idiot not to recognize her essential innocence. His redhead didn't sleep
around.

"I haven't done this in an awfully long time," she'd
said. He'd wondered then how long that actually was.
A year? Five years? She'd been incredibly sexy but
also…awkward. Unpracticed. No, if she was pregnant,
it was his baby she was carrying.

Not *if*. After four months, she might even be showing.

He shook his head in…not disbelief, not shock, but
something related. He was going to be a father.

A sound escaped his throat. A father was the last
thing in the world he'd wanted to become, at least for
the next few years. He'd already raised a family. The
idea of starting over appalled him. And yet…that was
his baby she was carrying.

He shoved his fingers into his hair. As things stood, his son or daughter would grow up without him, and it sounded as though that was what she'd prefer.

He should be grateful. *Glad* she wasn't demanding he be an every-other-weekend father, or that he send child-support checks. She was right; they didn't know each other.

Numbly, Will sat back in his chair. It would be worse if he hadn't liked her, if it really had been a typical one-night stand. A chance-met stranger encountered in a bar, say.

Wasn't that what it was?

He found himself scowling. No. No, he'd been drawn to her from the minute he set eyes on her. He'd ached the next morning to call her. The temptation to see her in the few days left to him had been acute. Now…hell. Now he wished he had. At least then they *would* know each other better.

He felt another surge of anger. She wouldn't welcome his involvement? Did that mean she hadn't liked him nearly as much as he had her? That he really was nothing but an available sub for the jackass?

Had it occurred to her that, if she'd had sex with *him,* using that same condom, she might still be pregnant? Would she prefer that, even given the way the creep had treated her?

I have friends and family, she said. Will gritted his teeth. A mother. She had a mother. Had she forgotten that she'd told him it was just her and her mom? Okay, she probably did have friends, but friends had their own families. With the best will in the world, how much good was a friend going to be to her, caring for a baby by herself?

He swore aloud, his voice hoarse. He didn't know what to tell her. How to respond. Damn. He looked again and saw that her email was dated almost two weeks ago, in fact the day after he'd left Harare. She had probably already concluded that he wasn't going to reply at all.

Maybe she was relieved. That idea pissed him off yet again.

One more day wouldn't matter. He had to think about this.

At last he made himself read the emails from his brothers and Sophie. None had any real news. Clay had met a woman shortly after Will left and sounded as if he might be serious about her. Jack had had a minor accident in a company pickup, and Clay was ragging him. Sophie was renting a room in a house with other grad students in L.A., where she'd be attending UCLA, classes to start next week. She'd met with her faculty advisor, and told a few amusing stories about her roommates, two guys and two girls.

Will responded to their emails with a general one telling them about this latest trip. He tried to draw word pictures, so they could see the general meeting held under a baobab tree, with him in a metal folding chair facing the sixteen men who'd sat comfortably on the dusty ground despite Western business attire that made him suspect they'd dressed up for his benefit. He described the tea plantations, with leaves as big as elephant ears, and the kraals of round mud huts with thatch roofs, women wearing Western garb cooking on open fires outside. He made fun of his more ludicrous language mistakes.

He didn't say, "Hey, the real news is that I'm going

to be a father." Although he'd have to tell them eventually, wouldn't he? After years of lecturing them on safe sex.

Yes, but he'd used the damn condom. He'd come close to forgetting it; closer than he'd ever come in his life. But he'd remembered in time, so he couldn't blame himself now for carelessness. He hadn't seen any obvious tear when he disposed of it, although now he wasn't sure he'd even really looked. He'd been wishing he had another condom, wishing he wasn't leaving his redhead to awaken alone in the hotel room.

Will sent the email, figuring he'd write shorter, more personal ones to each of them individually tomorrow. Then he read Moira's one more time, as incredulous and confused as he was the first time. Finally he closed the internet and turned off the computer.

What was he going to say to her?

IT WAS FIFTEEN DAYS AFTER she'd made herself write that hideous email and send it before she saw a reply in her in-box from Will Becker. The first week, Moira had compulsively checked her personal account at least twice a day while she was at work, something she rarely did, then a couple more times at home. When there was nothing from him, she'd...not given up, *relaxed*. A better choice of words. Since then, she'd gone back to reading personal email in the evening at home. Tonight, she'd sat at the computer while leftover casserole was heating in the microwave. At the sight of his address, her heart took an unpleasant bump and her hand was actually shaking when she reached for the mouse.

She distantly heard the microwave beep and ignored it.

Moira,

I'm sorrier than I can say that you've had to deal with this on your own. I should have told you that night why the one night was all I could offer. I suspect that, despite my denial, you still worried I might be married, engaged, whatever. It wasn't anything like that. I had just accepted a job from a nonprofit committed to build schools and medical clinics in sub-Saharan Africa. I've been in Zimbabwe for nearly four months now, and have made a two-year commitment. I often have no access to email for weeks at a time. I just read yours last night.

It would never have crossed my mind to think you'd tell me the baby was mine if it wasn't. Maybe you believe I don't know you, but I thought I did. Well enough to be sure you're honest, and that your invitation to me was out of the ordinary for you. I hope you know me well enough to guess what I'm going to say now. No child of mine is going to grow up not knowing his father. I can't do much to help you right now, although I am more than willing to offer financial support if you find you can't continue to work all the way through your pregnancy. I ask that you stay in touch and let me know how you're doing. I'll be back in the States every few months, and we can talk the first time I am. Come up with a plan. But fair warning: I will be involved.

He gave her the website address of the foundation he worked for in case she was interested, and repeated that he wanted to hear from her. He closed by asking what she did for a living. *Tell me about yourself,* he said. *Please.*

Moira cried for the first time in months, and she

didn't even know why. She *didn't* need him. She kept
remembering the intense note in his voice when he told
her about his worst nightmare. "Being trapped. Spending my life doing what I have to do." There was more,
but she'd known what he meant.

This was what he'd been trying to say. Getting stuck
with an obligation he hadn't willingly, wholeheartedly
made. Having to accept responsibility for helping raise
a child he couldn't possibly want.

Her email, she thought wretchedly, was his worst
nightmare.

TWO DAYS LATER, moira replied.

Will,
Now I think I'm sorry I told you. I remember that you
said your worst nightmare was to get stuck, to spend
your life fulfilling obligations. I don't want to be your
nightmare. And please, please don't feel you have to
be involved if you'll resent it. That would have to be
awful for a kid, don't you think? I barely remember
my father—did I tell you that?—but even though I
often wished that he was around when I was growing up, I know it might have hurt worse if he'd been
there because he felt he had to be. I really will be
fine, you know. We won't starve without you.

If you want to look me up when you get home,
that's fine, though. I live in West Fork, and work here,
too. I'm an architect, in partnership with a friend. Van
Dusen & Cullen. I'm Cullen. I guess you can tell that
from my email address, huh? It's not a real physical
job, which is good right now. And I'm hoping I can

bring the baby to work some of the time. I know
Gray, my partner, won't mind.

She went on to say that she'd looked at the foundation website and was impressed with what they were
trying to accomplish. She'd taken the time to read some
about Zimbabwe, too, and knew how high the rate of
AIDS and HIV was and how desperately more acces-
sible medical care was needed.

Will brooded some before he hit Reply, trying to get
over being mad before he said something that would
stiffen her resolve to keep him at a distance. And yeah,
that made no sense when he didn't *want* to be a family
guy, but, man, had she turned him into a mass of war-
ring emotions. She could enrage him quicker than the
most venal local bureaucrat, and he'd done his share
of teeth grinding these past months dealing with them.
She also had a way of zinging him with powerful protective impulses.

Did she really think so little of him, she believed
he'd let any kid of his feel *resented*?

Damn it, damn it, damn it, he wished he couldn't
so easily picture her as a freckle-faced kid herself who
couldn't understand why she didn't have a daddy like
everyone else did. He wished he hadn't seen that fleeting, wistful look in her eyes as she remembered.

Finally he sighed and started typing.

Moira, I can promise you I won't feel resentment.
Someday I'll tell you why I said that, about my worst
nightmare. It doesn't really matter now. You reminded
me, as I recall, that life's made up of obligations. Not
all kids are planned. They should all be loved. I never

doubted that my parents loved me, and I was lucky enough to have a stepmother who did, too. Another promise: I'll love any child of mine.

Will hoped that was true. He wanted to believe it was. The idea of holding that baby was pretty abstract right now.

But he thought of himself as a decent man, and even though there'd been times he *had* felt resentment for getting stuck raising his siblings, he thought what they'd most been aware of was security and love. Yeah, they'd probably known on some level how he felt. No twenty-year-old kid was capable of completely hiding his shock and desperation. But he'd tried, they'd understood, and he was damn proud of how they had all turned out.

He went back to his email.

You don't say whether you're feeling okay. Aren't pregnant women supposed to be sick to their stomachs and tired? Or is that the exception?

You're right about the toll AIDS is costing here. It's painful to see. Unlike in South Africa, the majority of AIDS orphans are being raised by relatives, which is a testament to the power of family here. This is a country of astonishing contrasts. The literacy rate is quite high and schools good. Meantime, out in the countryside, medical care is close to nonexistent, and what itinerant medical clinics are held are often outside, with patients lined up waiting to see a nurse who sits at a folding table beneath a shade tree. Not much that nurse can do for the desperately ill. I'm often struck by the patience people here seem to have. I imagine

Americans throwing a temper tantrum because the line for the drive-through window at McDonald's is four cars long.

My part in this project is less important than the care that will be provided—the nurses and doctors, the AIDS cocktails, the surgical supplies. I provide only the walls and roofs, and simple ones at that. We've finally broken ground on the first clinic, and it will have brick walls and a metal roof, like the store in the village. The homes are crude, with thatched roofs.

He told her about the architectural drawings he'd scrapped and why, about his need to build structures that belonged, that people would be comfortable going to. In fact, when he reread his email a few minutes later, it was to find he'd waxed eloquent, revealing more of the passion quietly building in him than he'd intended. He frowned, finally, and left what he'd written. She was an architect herself; she might be interested. And anyway…he wanted to know her. To be fair, he had to reveal something of himself in return.

By the next day, he had an email back from her. *She* waxed eloquent on her belief that structures should meld with their surroundings. Her partner, apparently, teased her about emphasizing function over form, although Gray, too, she said, preferred to design buildings that didn't immediately command attention. She told him about her partner's house, which appeared to be part of the riverbank so that a fisherman casting his line below might not even notice it was there atop the bluff. She thought many of the more admired homes featured in magazines were hideous. Original, yes, interesting, but jarring.

I'm content to design staid but dignified office buildings that have grace and pleasing proportions but do
not startle. If I were to plan a medical clinic for a small
town in the African savannah, I'd go with mud brick
and a metal roof, too. Good for you.

Will found himself smiling.

I was sick to my stomach for a couple of months, although not as miserable as some women are—Gray's
wife, Charlotte, could hardly keep any food down—
but it's passed, thank heavens. Now I'm starved all
the time, making up for the weight I lost. I dread my
next monthly weigh-in and the lecture I'm bound to
get from the doctor. I'm trying very hard not to gain
too much. I am a little more tired than usual, but all
it means is that I go to bed earlier than I used to. No
big deal. So you see, I really am fine.

Without you, was what she meant. Will suppressed
his irritation.

He wrote an email in response longer than the ones
he'd sent Clay and the others. He felt a strange tension,
sitting here digging into himself for what was most important to tell her about his life and values. It was as if
they were connected by a thread so delicate, he could
snap it with the wrong word, but perhaps with the right
ones he could lend it strength. He was hungry to hear
back from her. Half an hour ago, when his messages
had been loading, it was *hers* he'd hoped for with eagerness that embarrassed him.

He felt, Will realized after he'd sent his response,
like a boy with his first crush. Ridiculous, maybe,

when they'd already made love and now he longed for so little: the equivalent of a shy glance.

This time she didn't write back right away. Stuck in Harare meeting with government officials, Will was therefore able to obsessively check his email in any stray minutes, which made the three days before he did get a reply from her seem endless. But her response was long and satisfying. She'd read more about Zimbabwe and wondered whether he was in any danger, a white man in a country where white-owned land was still being violently snatched by black mobs.

She was worried about him. He felt a warm glow to realize it.

She told him about a movie that had recently been released about South Africa and talking to a woman whose daughter was currently in Ghana with the Peace Corps.

Several people I know who've been to Africa tell me they'd give anything to go back. They always have this look in their eyes, as though there's some kind of magnetic pull. Although that's silly, isn't it? Africa is an enormous continent. I'm sure Zimbabwe is nothing like... I don't know, the Ivory Coast or Kenya. See, I've revealed typical American ignorance about a huge swath of the world.

He assured her that, as a foreigner, he felt safe and that people were warm and friendly. He told her more about what he'd seen, about the astonishing sight of elephants ambling across the road in front of his Datsun, about seeing so many hippos in a river he could have walked across, stepping on their backs. About

Victoria Falls where water plummeted into a canyon and raised a cloud of spray so vast, it created a rain forest for miles about. He told her that he hoped soon to go see the Great Zimbabwe, the granite ruins of the greatest city in ancient Africa. About the rock art, more faint traces of people long gone, that could be found everywhere.

For all my wonder, I feel an astonishing pang of home-sickness every so often. I didn't expect that. To miss my brothers and sister, yes, but not the mundane reali-ties of everyday life at home. For all the beauty here, I sometimes feel a strange sense of not-belonging. As if I never could, even if I lived here for the rest of my life. It works both ways, though. I met a white couple a few weeks ago who fled the country some years back, when it was obvious what was happening, but after staying for two years in England—where their daugh-ter and her family live—they came home even though there was no way they could recover their farm. That was how they put it: they came home. It was too late for them to really belong anywhere else.

Four days later, without having heard from her again, he left Harare, this time for the eastern lowveld near the Sanyati River. He sent Moira a quick email before he left, telling her he'd be out of touch for two to three weeks.

Then he worried. Had he said something wrong in his last, long email? Or did she not want to con-tinue exchanging long, chatty communications with the man who'd fathered her baby but whose involvement in their child's life she didn't *welcome?* Was she not feeling good?

God. Had she lost the baby? Will thought most miscarriages were earlier in the pregnancy, but he didn't know. He was astonished at how sick he felt at the idea. Did women die when they miscarried? Surely not anymore, not at home, anyway, with modern medical care readily available.

If anything was wrong, would she let him know? Would anyone else?

Had she told anyone he was the father of her baby? He bounced irrationally from the cold sweat of fear at the idea of her sick or hurt or grieving to sharp anger because she might not want her mother or her friends to know who he was.

Checking email wasn't an option; he hadn't even driven on this trip, but had been flown along with Chionesu, his translator, into a dusty bush airstrip in a thinly populated region where the roads, he'd been told, were abysmal.

He evaluated, he met with local leaders, he chose a site. He slept in thatch-roofed huts and dined with host families, sitting cross-legged to eat *sadza* out of a communal pot. Will had become adept at molding the thick millet or corn cereal into a shape he could use to dip stew.

And the whole damn time, all he could think about was Moira. By the time he was on a small bush plane taking off from the same dirt airstrip, he'd made up his mind he would take a trip home to the States. He had to see her.

CHAPTER FIVE

"I'M GOING TO GRAB some lunch on my way to city hall," Gray said. "You want me to get you something and drop it off here?"

Moira straightened on the tall stool in front of her drafting table and rolled her shoulders with a groan she hoped Gray didn't hear.

"Thanks, but I brought a sandwich." She smiled at him. "Come on, when have you ever known me to let myself go hungry?"

He grinned. "Well…you were looking a little peaked there for a while."

"I'm making up for it," she said ruefully. "I swear, I'm ravenous all the time. It's awful."

He laughed, a warm rumble. She expected him to head for the door, but instead he leaned a hip against his desk and kept looking at her. Finally he said, "I haven't wanted to push, but curiosity is getting to me. Have you contacted your baby's father yet?"

Heat rose in her cheeks. "Yes. I sent him an email…"

His eyebrows rose.

"I tried calling first!" Moira snapped. "It's not my fault I had to email instead. Turns out he's moved to Africa for two years."

"Good God."

"He's, um, actually been really nice. We've exchanged half a dozen emails. I told him he was off the hook, but he insists he doesn't want to be, that no kid of his is growing up without a father."

"Told you so."

She rolled her eyes. "It was a one-night stand. I might have picked a scumbag to sleep with."

"Nah. Not you." He straightened, came to her and kissed her cheek. "I know you better than that, Moira."

They hugged, and for a moment she closed her eyes at the pleasure of his solid embrace. Then he stepped back. "What's the guy doing in Africa?"

She told him, and Gray nodded. "Would I know him?"

Moira hesitated.

Gray looked sardonic. "Aren't you planning to put his name on the birth certificate?"

She grimaced. "Yes, of course I am. Uh…his name's Will Becker."

Her partner's eyes narrowed. "Of Becker Construction?"

"Yes, but his brother Clay has taken it over now, with Will gone."

"Huh."

"Do you know him?" she felt compelled to ask. Oh, Lord—was she wrong about Will?

But Gray shook his head. "I hear they do good work. Mostly stuff that wouldn't interest me. Shopping centers, grocery stores, that kind of thing."

"I don't think it interested Will, either. There's some reason he threw it over to build mud-brick medical clinics in Africa."

Gray laughed. "Yeah, I guess so. Okay. Is he planning to help financially? See the baby?"

"He says he'll be back in the States every so often, and the next time he is we'll talk." Moira bit her lip. "He did say he'd be glad to help financially if I can't work all the way through the pregnancy, so I guess he probably will offer child support at least."

"Good. Not as good as his being here, but better than nothing." Gray jiggled his keys in his pocket as if to make sure they were still there. "I've got to run. See you tomorrow?"

She nodded. "Except I'll be out at the Fletcher house first thing in the morning."

They exchanged a few words about the project that had turned into a huge trial for her, with the clients changing their minds about what they wanted at least weekly.

"Don't worry about the cost," Jennifer Fletcher would say blithely. "It's important to get it right. Tearing it out at this point is better than living with a layout that isn't perfect."

Jennifer would undoubtedly want something else torn out this week. The contractor, Dave Hendricks, was getting even more aggravated than Moira was. During most of their meetings, she played peacemaker.

Waiting until the door had shut behind Gray, she strolled to her desk and took out her sandwich. She might as well have lunch now, too. She'd intended to make herself wait another hour, but…damn it, she was hungry. And anyway… She peeked out the window at the parking lot to be sure Gray wasn't coming back for something he'd forgotten, then, when she saw his car gone, sat in front of her computer and went on the internet. There hadn't been one word from Will in three full weeks. He'd said it might be that long, but she couldn't help worrying. He'd dismissed her concerns, but from what she'd read, Zimbabwe under Mugabe *wasn't* a safe place. Not many nonprofits were working there right now, and she suspected the potential danger was why.

There was no email from him today, either, she was disappointed to see. She'd send him another one tonight, Moira decided, something chatty and casual. She could tell him about the Fletchers. He'd undoubtedly had difficult clients and would sympathize.

She ate quickly, drinking cranberry juice with her ham sandwich and longing for her usual iced tea. She missed caffeine. She *craved* caffeine. Especially these days, when she tended to get drowsy right after lunch. Her body really, really wanted her to take a nap. Even the nine hours she'd slept last night apparently didn't cut it.

Ruefully she laid her splayed hands on her belly and gently rubbed. For Pete's sake, she was only halfway through this pregnancy, and she was so blasted *big.* Didn't it figure? Of course, Will was an exceptionally large man, which meant his child probably wouldn't be petite. She thought he was at least six foot three and maybe taller, with shoulders so broad he'd alarmed her at first sight. His enormous hands had dwarfed hers. She imagined what his hand would look like on her rounded stomach, and felt a disturbingly sexual twinge at the image. No one had ever touched her the way he had, so gently even though she could feel the power he kept curbed. She wondered if, as big as he was, he often felt like the classic bull in a china shop.

With a sigh, Moira managed to get herself back to work.

Jennifer Fletcher *did* want something else torn out when they met the next morning.

Bright eyed, her dark hair artfully disheveled, she swept in and said, "I keep worrying that there won't be enough storage here in the kitchen. And last night it came to me. What if we bump out the dining area here with a bay window instead—" she waved one hand toward the large, small-paned window she'd been measuring for blinds last week "—and then we could squeeze in a sort of butler's pantry on the other side of the doorway?" She gave first Moira, then Dave, a limpid look and waited expectantly.

Moira heard a rumble rising from the middle-aged contractor and interceded hastily. "Let me do some measuring and we'll see, Jennifer. Did you consult with Stella?" The kitchen designer, Moira suspected, had long since thrown up her hands, or maybe thrown in the towel was more accurate, but she might be a voice of reason.

"Oh, I know Stella will agree with me. Absolutely she will." Jennifer's smile was radiant. "With Ron and I entertaining so often, we can't live without enough storage for serving pieces. And I have four different sets of china, you know."

Moira knew. Normally this would be Dave's problem and Stella's problem, not hers, but if they were to knock out this wall…

She made no promises, but soothed Jennifer, who made a whirlwind tour of the unfinished house, pronounced herself delighted and left. Another fifteen minutes, and Moira had Dave settled down, too.

As she walked to her car, the faint flutters she'd been

feeling in her stomach intensified, as if the baby had decided to take up swimming the butterfly.

"Just wait'll you're in the last month and the kid weighs thirteen pounds. And *then* discovers the trampoline," Charlotte had warned darkly. She was eight months along now and could hardly get out of a chair. Moira had heard Gray clearing his throat to suppress his laugh at the idea of a thirteen-pound fetus, but he'd had the wisdom to have noticed that Charlotte's sense of humor seemed to have waned recently. Moira was beginning to see why.

She settled with relief behind the wheel of her car and carefully arranged the seat belt around herself. Everything took longer these days, and it was going to get worse, not better.

She treated herself to the guilty pleasure of a burger and fries on her way back to the office, even though it was awfully early for lunch. She'd probably put on a pound with the one meal.

"I'll have a salad for dinner," she said aloud, and knew she lied. Maybe a salad and a grilled cheese sandwich. And frozen yogurt after. She'd developed a sweet tooth lately.

At the office she told Gray about the latest hitch at the Fletcher house, he commiserated then grumbled in turn about the city council. He swore they'd gotten less cooperative now that they knew he was on his way out. Moira felt even guiltier about that than she did about the sinful lunch. She was glad when he left for city hall.

She determined that yes, they probably could install a bay window and find room for Jennifer Fletcher's new pantry, called Dave who ranted for a few minutes, then went back to the drawing she'd begun yesterday

of a building that would house a new real estate office.
She used her computer at a certain point, but liked to
rough out ideas with pen and paper, and found that clients liked a drawing, too.

A client popped in at one point and looked at preliminary sketches, after which Moira checked email for
the second time today. Still nothing from Will.

It wasn't like they were best friends, she reminded
herself. She hadn't even wanted to tell him about the
baby, for heaven's sake. But she was honest enough
with herself to admit that, somehow, in the past six
weeks he'd become important to her. Only because
knowing she had some support from him made her feel
a little less scared about the future, she tried to convince herself. She knew it was more than that, though.

When she read his emails, she could almost hear
his voice, as if he were talking to her instead. He had
a good voice, deep and relaxed, laced with amusement that she sensed was often directed at himself
instead of at other people. The emails reminded her
why she'd trusted him enough to make love with him.
She'd freaked the next morning, but the truth was
she couldn't remember ever liking anyone as much
so quickly. She guessed in some ways he'd reminded
her of Gray. There was something rock solid about
him. She'd be surprised if he had one-night stands with
women he barely knew very often.

Her mind wandered; her hand stilled.

Had he really thought she was beautiful? she wondered wistfully. He said he'd been watching her for
quite a while through the glass. That might have been
a line, one of those things he'd have said to any woman
who joined him out there. But she thought maybe he'd

meant it. He didn't seem…slick. The way, she had belatedly realized, Bruce was.

When the door opened, Moira turned in surprise, her hand pressing her lower back as she summoned a polite smile. They didn't get that much drop-in traffic. Who…?

She gaped. Will Becker, who was supposed to be in Africa, had just walked into Van Dusen & Cullen, Architects.

"WILL?" SHE WHISPERED.

He'd been dreaming of Moira for months, and still she looked better than he remembered. Although… different. He took in the sight of her freckled face and astonished green eyes, the copper bright curls escaping the knot she'd fashioned at the back of her head, then lowered his gaze to the unmistakable swell of her belly. The knowledge that she was pregnant suddenly became a whole hell of a lot more visceral.

"Can you feel the baby moving?" he heard himself ask.

She nodded and stared at him from her perch on a tall stool in front of a slanted drawing table that stood before one of the large windows.

He wound his way past desks until he was only a couple of feet from her. Made a little uneasy by her obvious shock, he cleared his throat. "I should have told you I was coming."

She blinked a couple of times in quick succession. "I thought…you were still out, um, wherever you went."

"I got back to Harare a few days ago, and caught a flight as soon as I could. I, uh, needed to clear some decisions with people back here." That was a flat-out lie; sure, he wouldn't waste his time here, but he'd endured the twenty-five-hour flight to see her.

Will still wasn't sure why that had been so important. There'd been a couple of emails from her waiting for him when he got back to Harare. He'd known she was fine, the baby was fine. But once he'd let himself formulate the desire to see her, he couldn't seem to let go of it. He *had* to see her.

And there she was, right in front of him, lush, curvaceous and pregnant with *his* baby.

"How are you, Moira?" he asked quietly.

"You didn't believe me when I said I was fine?"

"You have a backache."

She hastily withdrew her hand from the small of her back and clasped her fingers together in front of her. "I've been bending over all afternoon."

"What are you working on?"

She seemed to hesitate, then swiveled toward the drafting table. "You can take a look, if you want."

It was a typical architect's rendering, but skillfully done. He liked the look of the bungalow-style building with a deep front porch.

"A real estate office," she told him.

"I like it," he said simply.

"I can't believe you're here."

"I kept thinking about you," he admitted. She was even prettier close up, with the sunlight slanting in the window turning her freckles to pale cinnamon. This was the first time he'd seen her in daylight. He wished he could tell better what she was thinking. She was surprised, certainly, maybe even stunned, but beyond that... Was she glad to see him, or unhappy?

His mysterious redhead, he thought, was still mysterious.

"I was a little worried," she admitted. "When I didn't hear from you, I mean."

Chagrined, he said, "I should have emailed. Once I realized I had a chance to come home, I wanted to surprise you. I don't know why."

And that was no lie. He didn't understand a damn thing he'd felt since he'd gotten that first email from her.

I think you deserve to know that I'm pregnant.

She'd thrown him for a loop from that moment on.

No, he thought, she'd done that from the moment she walked onto the terrace and straight to his dark corner.

"Well." She took a deep breath. "You can see what I mean about the weight gain."

"Actually..." Will frowned. "Your cheeks look thinner. Are you sure you're eating enough?"

Moira laughed, a flash of genuine humor that relaxed him. "You're kidding, right? Nobody has ever accused me of being skinny."

"You have a perfect body." And, damn, he was getting aroused.

She laughed again, but less happily, and looked down at her stomach. "Right."

"I love the way you look."

Her cheeks flushed, and he saw the shyness in her eyes. She mumbled. "Um...thank you."

Why was she so determined to believe herself to be unattractive? Will wondered, puzzled. It couldn't be only the scumbag. Her doubts had to be more ingrained than that. Someday he'd find out, he promised himself. But that kind of question wasn't exactly the ideal opening salvo today.

"Will you have dinner with me?" he asked.

She looked around as if she'd find an excuse floating in the air like a dust mote, but finally took a deep breath. "Yes. Sure. I suppose we should talk."

Gee, thanks. He'd only flown halfway around the damn world to see her.

Hiding his frustration, Will asked calmly, "What time do you close?"

"Five. I don't have any more appointments today."

"All right. I'll be back at five."

More color flowed into her cheeks, but she nodded. "Okay."

"If you don't mind eating that early."

"I could eat six times a day," she told him ruefully.

He smiled at her, said, "You decide what sounds good," and left.

He didn't go far, only to the parking lot. He'd brought a book, but thought he might close his eyes. He could set his cell phone to wake him up. At this point, Will's sense of time was so screwed up, he had no idea whether his body thought it should be the middle of the night or what. Mostly, he was disoriented. He'd gotten into Sea Tac early this morning and surprised Clay and Jack, too, at the breakfast table. Scared the daylights out of them, actually, when he'd strolled in the door as if he'd been out getting the newspaper. Will grinned at the memory.

He got in his truck—not really his anymore, but Jack had let him drive it today—and pushed the seat back. He could tell the minute he closed his eyes that he wouldn't actually be able to sleep.

He was buzzing, in that irritating state where tiredness kept him awake. And simply being here felt strange, to put it mildly. Everything looked wrong, from the trees to the cars to the people driving them, all white. The smells were wrong. Even this morning, when he'd walked into the house where he had lived for most of his life, he'd almost felt as if he existed in two different dimensions. In one, he was where he belonged; he'd reached for his mug in the kitchen cupboard without thinking about it, poured coffee, known which shelf in the refrigerator the milk would be on. All the while, on another plane he had thought, *I'm not really here. I don't belong.*

The weirdness of international travel, of being hurtled by an airplane that chased the setting sun from one continent to another, so that you had breakfast one morning in Africa and the next morning in Lynnwood, Washington, was partly to blame. But Will knew that it was more, that he *didn't* belong. He would never move back into that house, no matter what. Right now, not much would have drawn him home to Washington at all.

Only his redhead.

Even with his eyes shut, he saw her. Actually seeing her was as weird as being here. He knew her and yet he didn't. He'd had the best damn sex of his life with her, he'd sucked on her bare breasts, touched her everywhere, been *inside* her, and now he wondered nervously how she'd react if he kissed her.

Will gave a grunt that wasn't quite a laugh. With outrage, is how she'd react. They'd never even been out on a date. What they had done was meant by both of them to be something not quite real, remembered later as if it might have been a dream.

The most erotic dream in the world didn't result in pregnancy, however. Fate had apparently grinned wickedly and said, "Gotcha!"

He returned to her office at five on the nose to find Moira plucking a purse from a drawer and holding keys in her hand.

"Your partner's not around?" he asked.

She glanced his way. "No, Gray's at city hall. Or on city business, anyway. Did I tell you he's mayor?"

"No." He frowned, not liking the implications. "You mean, you're the whole firm right now?"

"No, the mayoral gig, as he calls it, is part-time. He's putting in really long hours keeping up at least half his usual workload here, sometimes more, *and* being mayor."

He stood aside as she locked the door. "Leaving you, almost five months pregnant, to keep your firm alive."

"It's not Gray's fault I'm pregnant," she said sharply.

Will winced.

They walked together outside, where the chill of evening was making itself felt as the sun dropped low on the horizon. A row of small hybrid maple trees marched along the sidewalk, their leaves—a vivid orange—beginning to fall. One crunched under his foot.

"He isn't running for reelection." Moira's head was bowed and her voice had become more subdued. "Because of me." She touched her stomach. "He'll be out of office in January, about the time I'm due."

I have family and friends, she'd told him, and this was partly what she'd meant, Will realized. How good friends were she and this Gray?

"Why don't I drive?" he suggested. "I'll bring you back to your car later."

"Fine."

She hoisted herself into the cab of the pickup without too much trouble. Will reached to help her but she didn't see his hand and he let it fall as she settled into the seat. She was doing fine without him. She'd said that enough times.

When he got in, she suggested a restaurant right there in West Fork, and directed him. "It's mostly a steak house," she said a little apologetically. "But I seem to be more of a carnivore these days than I used to be."

He glanced at her belly and smiled. "Do you suppose every baby has his own tastes?"

"You mean, the next one might be a vegetarian?" Quickly she added, "Assuming I have another one."

He ignored that. "Yeah, or be especially fond of... fish. Italian food. Nothing but Italian food."

Moira sounded more relaxed. "Pregnant women are famous for their cravings."

"Pickles."

"Right. Charlotte—Gray's wife, who is eight months pregnant right now—has a thing for lemon-meringue pie. And lemon bars. Lemon pudding." A dimple appeared in her cheek. "The pudding, she says, is for emergency fixes. Otherwise, she keeps baking."

Will laughed. "You?"

She sighed. "I don't dare. I put on weight if I take too deep a breath around fresh-baked goodies. Charlotte can afford the calories."

"What's with the obsession about weight?" he asked.

Moira leveled a look at him. "I see the obstetrician every month. I get weighed. Then I get lectured."

"Oh."

"See, there's this ideal. You have to gain enough, but not too much. And I don't want to gain too much, because then it would be hard to lose it. As if," she added gloomily, "it's not going to be hard enough to lose the weight anyway."

"How much are you likely to gain?"

Her face was cute scrunched up in a grimace. "Like, twenty-five to thirty-five pounds."

"And babies are, what, seven or eight pounds?"

"Right. You do the math."

He did, silently. The baby wasn't all that came out when a woman gave birth, though, he knew that much. There was the umbilical cord, and afterbirth, and whatever fluid the baby had been swimming in. Still...

"Do you plan to nurse?" he asked.

Moira gave him another look, this one startled and rather shy. "Yes." Then, unnecessarily, she said, "This is it."

"I see." He pulled into the nearly empty parking lot of the River Fork Steakhouse. They were definitely beating the dinner crowd.

The place was nice in a casual way, the booths deeply padded, the lighting designed to give a sense of intimacy even when the restaurant was busier. Moira studied the menu with more care than she probably needed, given that Will assumed she'd eaten here often. They both ordered steaks, baked potatoes and salads. She asked for a glass of milk. He'd have liked a beer, but didn't dare. With his luck and lack of sleep, even a little alcohol would probably knock him out, and he did have a forty-five-minute drive home after he dropped Moira off.

He felt a strange ache. He'd wanted her to run into his arms today when he walked in. He wanted to be going home with her, to see her new curves, unclothed, to sleep wrapped around her.

Yeah, and he'd have been scared to death if she'd flung herself at him. He was offering the minimum a decent man would offer, and no more. Better if they maintained a relationship that was cordial, not sexually charged. If they both forgot—or at least pretended to forget—how she'd gotten pregnant with his baby.

The silence between them was beginning to seem stifling, alone as they were in this part of the dining room.

Will reached out and touched the back of her hand. "I'm sorry. I did wear the condom."

Beyond the faint quiver he'd felt beneath his fingertips, she didn't react. "I know. I saw." She hesitated. "Thank you, for believing me."

He nodded. After a minute, he said, "I'll expect to pay child support."

Her eyes searched his. "I meant it when I said you didn't have to."

"Yeah. I could tell. But I want to."

She dipped her head once, in acknowledgment.

"I really am committed in Africa for two years. Actually, for just over a year and a half, now. But after that, I'll want visitation."

Her lips compressed, but she nodded.

"You'd rather I ditched you?"

She couldn't hide her turmoil. "No. In some ways, it would be easier, but…" Her fingers drummed on the table. "I keep thinking about how much I wished my father cared at all." She focused briefly on him. "I remember telling you that I didn't know him."

"Yes."

In a near whisper, Moira said, "This isn't the way I wanted to start a family. But…I wouldn't undo it, either. I just turned thirty-five, Will. If I was going to have a baby at all, it was going to have to be soon. I'm sorry I stuck you with responsibility, but otherwise… I'm glad, now that I'm over the first shock."

"You knew for a long time before you emailed me," he said slowly.

She nodded. "I thought about not telling you at all. You'd made pretty clear that you didn't want any future involvement."

He closed his eyes. "If things had been different, I would have. I'd have called you the next day, Moira."

Her half laugh was disbelieving. "It doesn't matter," she said, although he suspected it did. "Gray chewed me out and said I had to tell you, that he'd be angry to find out he had a child he'd never been told about."

"Then I owe him one."

She didn't say anything; didn't believe he was grateful any more than she'd believed he actually liked her. Will wanted to shake her father and everyone else who'd ever made this woman feel unlovable.

The knowledge that he'd contributed curdled in his stomach. He'd screwed her then slipped away in the night. He couldn't quite convince himself that child-support checks and occasional weekend visitation made him in any way noble or good.

Anger came to his rescue, roaring through him like the blustering winds of winter. What the hell else was he supposed to do? Throw over his life again? He'd done it once. Wasn't that enough?

He stared at her averted face, and had no idea what to say to make any of this better.

CHAPTER SIX

AFTER THAT INCREDIBLY AWKWARD dinner, Moira couldn't believe she'd invited Will to go with her to her monthly checkup with the obstetrician. And poor Will—he was likely horrified, but what could he say?

What he *had* said was, "I'd like that."

Now she snorted. Probably he couldn't think of an excuse quick enough.

With a sigh, Moira got out of her car in front of the clinic, a block from the hospital. Thank goodness West Fork had a hospital. Otherwise she'd have had a half-hour drive to Everett when she was in labor. Even so, she was already worrying about getting to the delivery room when the time came. There had probably been pregnant women who'd had to drive themselves to the hospital. Hey, she could pull over to the shoulder every time a contraction hit.

Of course that was silly. She'd have a list of friends prepped to go. One of them was bound to be home.

Except, what if the baby decided to make an untimely appearance, when no one did expect to hear from her? Or—her new nightmare—what if a winter storm knocked out phone service and she *couldn't* call anyone?

She'd keep her cell phone charged.

But *their* phones might all be out.

Jeez, she thought, disgusted with herself. Then I stagger over to a neighbor's house and hammer on the door. Do I *need* to find things to worry about?

Will had arrived at the clinic ahead of her. The minute she walked into the waiting room, he rose from one of the chairs. "Moira," he said, in that quiet, deep voice of his.

"You're here." Oh, brilliant.

Pretending she hadn't said anything so inane, she checked in at the front desk and then they sat next to each other. They weren't alone. A very pregnant woman was in the corner, flipping through a magazine, and a couple holding hands had come in behind Moira. Their warmth and intimacy were so obvious, she had to tear her gaze from them.

When she looked at Will, it was to find him watching her, his brown eyes unreadable but his expression gentle. "I'll really be able to hear the heartbeat?" he asked.

"I'm sure the doctor will let you."

His gaze lowered to her stomach. A couple of lines between his dark eyebrows had deepened, not quite in a frown, but as if... Moira wasn't sure. As if he was unsettled, maybe.

"Moira Cullen?"

Moira stood automatically and turned toward the smiling nurse who held her chart. She was aware that Will had risen also and was following her.

The nurse said, "Oh, good. You brought the father today."

"Uh...yes."

She produced a small cup and handed it to Moira.

"Why don't you give us your sample first, and then we'll weigh you."

Will looked so horrified, Moira had to swallow a giggle even though she was probably blushing, too. She'd had *sex* with the man, for Pete's sake. Why should she be embarrassed to talk about peeing in front of him?

She was relieved when she came out of the bathroom to find the nurse, a comfortable woman in her fifties, had shown him to the exam room so that he didn't see her step on the scale. She had gained four pounds this month, which horrified her even though she knew it was normal. After spending a lifetime battling her weight, though, it was killing her to watch it climb.

The nurse led her to an exam room, which had never looked so small. Will really was a very large man, Moira realized afresh. He backed out of the way and wedged himself into the V between the table and the cabinet so that she could sit in the one visitor's chair to have her blood pressure and pulse taken. He seemed unwillingly fascinated, she thought, by the whole process.

The nurse finished up then. She told them the doctor would be a few minutes and left, closing the door behind her.

"I'll hop up on the exam table," Moira said. "Then you can sit."

"You don't have to get undressed?"

She shook her head and muttered, "Thank goodness."

"You have to pee in a cup every month?"

"They're looking for protein in the urine and things

like that. That's how they know if something's going wrong."

"Huh."

Having him sit didn't reduce the way he dominated the room. The effect was partly physical, partly just presence. It was funny, she thought, because Will didn't give the impression of arrogance, but she also couldn't imagine anyone not assuming that he was in charge on sight. He was simply that kind of man. She doubted he ever had to raise his voice.

The door opened then, and Dr. Engel darted in. A tiny woman, she'd reminded Moira from the beginning of a hummingbird constantly hovering rather than settling in place. She listened, though, when Moira had questions, and answered without any impatience, her head tilted in a way that was birdlike, too.

"Marcia Engel," she said, thrusting out her hand at Will.

"Will Becker. I'm the father."

"Ah. I'm glad to see you here." She took him in with one sweep of her bright blue eyes. "How much did you weigh at birth?"

He looked startled. "Almost ten pounds. My two brothers, too. My sister was eight and a half pounds."

"Then chances are we can expect the same for this one, Moira. Well." She set the open chart on the small counter and skimmed the newest information. "Things are looking good. I'm glad to see you putting on weight now."

Moira made a face.

"She wasn't?" Will asked.

"Nausea," the doctor said. "Not unusual, but always

a concern." She gave him a sharp look. "You didn't know?"

"I've been away."

"Will and I don't live together," Moira said. "He's being good enough to share responsibility for the baby, that's all."

His mouth tightened, but he said nothing.

After one more appraising look, Dr. Engel ignored him and smiled at Moira. "Lie back now, please." When Moira did, she raised her shirt and pushed down the waistband of her maternity pants, exposing the freckled mound of her belly. Moira knew she was blushing, which seemed to be a redhead's curse. It was dumb. He'd seen her stomach before, and a whole lot more, but she couldn't make herself look at him.

Even so, from her peripheral vision she knew he was staring.

The doctor manipulated gently, then blew on the bell of her stethoscope to warm it before placing it on Moira. Listening intently, she moved it several times, and smiled. After a minute, she glanced at Will. "Would you like to listen?"

"Please." He stepped forward, bent and slipped the earpieces of the stethoscope in place. He frowned. "I don't hear anything."

Dr. Engel moved the bell half an inch, then, after a pause, another half inch. The expression on Will's face transformed. Now Moira couldn't help watching him, seeing what wonder did to the hard lines of his face.

"It's so fast," he whispered.

"Normal for a baby."

"I guess I knew that, but..." He kept listening, and when at last he removed the earpieces and handed the stethoscope back to the doctor, Moira could see his reluctance. "Amazing." His eyes met hers. "You've heard it?"

She nodded.

"Have you felt the baby move?" Dr. Engel asked him.

He shook his head and looked again at Moira's belly.

"Let's see." The doctor gently pressed, sliding her fingertips around. Finally she reached for his hand and laid it where hers had been. Will's was so very large, it covered much of Moira's stomach. A movement came inside, the flutter and swirl. Will stood very still, concentrating, then cleared his throat. "Thank you," he said, sounding hoarse. "Wow."

Dr. Engel pulled up the waistband of Moira's pants, drew down her shirt, said briskly, "One month," and breezed out.

Moira shifted her weight to an elbow to lever herself up. Without a word, Will wrapped an arm around her and helped her to a sitting position.

"That's only going to get harder, isn't it?" He sounded amused.

"I've perfected the art of rolling out of bed."

The amusement left his face. He was silent as they walked out and she scheduled her next appointment. Still quiet until they were in the parking lot.

"If you have an emergency, do you have someone to call?"

"Of course I do," she said. "But I don't expect an emergency."

"No." He had that look on his face, the not-quite-a-frown one. "Four more months."

Moira nodded, unlocked her car door and opened it.

He gripped the top of the door and watched as she got in and put on the seat belt. "I'd like to see you again," he said quietly. "Before I go."

Her throat felt clogged, as if she wanted to cry.

When she didn't say anything immediately, his hand tightened until his knuckles turned white. But his voice stayed calm. "You're not comfortable with me, are you?"

Breathe in, breathe out. A chance to practice her Lamaze techniques, Moira thought a little hysterically.

"I don't know why you're here," she said. "You can't possibly want this baby."

"You don't know what I want." The timbre of his voice had roughened.

She stared at him fiercely. "Be honest. You were horrified when you got my email."

"Shocked," Will admitted after a moment. "Yeah, I was. I'll bet you were, too, when you first suspected."

"Yes." She had to be honest. Not just shocked: terrified. She wasn't going to tell him that. "But I do want the baby now. What I don't want is to…oh, count on you in any way then have you back out. Do you understand? It's not money, it's…everything." She hardly knew what she meant herself. It was dumb to feel so distraught when she didn't even know why she did. "I don't want her to count on you if you're not going to stick it out."

His gaze flicked to her belly. "Her? Do you know it's a girl?"

"No." Oh, damn, damn. Her voice was thick, and she *would not* cry. "I was just…"

"Talking about yourself," he said softly.

They stared at each other.

"Maybe," she whispered.

Will circled the car door and squatted close to her. "Have you told your mother yet?"

Moira bowed her head and saw a tear splash onto her maternity top and soak in. She took an angry swipe at her face. "No. I don't know why. I...keep putting it off."

"Like you put off telling me."

"I'm used to doing things for myself. I'm *good* at taking care of myself." It seemed important that she convince him. She didn't want him feeling guilty in some way. "I'm not telling you that I need you," she said, looking fully at him despite a nose that had probably resembled Rudolph's. "I just want to know. If you're going to send support checks, that's great, but then... then don't come and see me, and be nice, and..." Crap. Her vision was blurring again and she hated herself. She was doing the absolute last thing in the world she wanted to do, which was laying a guilt trip on him. "No," she said suddenly. "No, I don't want to see you again. All right? My hormones are going crazy, and I'm up and down, and I'm confused about you, and I don't want to see you tomorrow or the next day when you won't be around again for another six months."

Something happened to his face, although she couldn't see clearly and didn't want to. She thought it contorted briefly. Then he stood so she couldn't see it at all.

"All right." His voice was low and scratchy. "Thank you for this. For today. Please keep letting me know how you are. Will you?"

She swallowed and nodded.

After a moment, he said, "Goodbye," closed her door and walked away.

Moira sat with tears running down her face until she saw his pickup drive out of the parking lot and knew he was gone. And she didn't even know why she felt like her heart was breaking.

FOUR DAYS LATER, Will got on the goddamn airplane and felt like scum. Worse than scum. All he could see was her face, all he heard was the way her voice broke when she said, "Then don't come and see me, and be nice, and…"

Every time he thought about her, he felt as if his guts were spilling out, and it *hurt*.

He shouldn't have come at all. She was right. They *didn't* mean anything to each other, and he'd let himself start thinking they did, as if there must be a connection between them if they were having a baby together. He'd never imagined having a child with a woman who wasn't his wife, a woman he didn't love. Somehow he'd turned things around in his head and gotten to believing he felt things he didn't. That was all this was.

He closed his eyes and ignored his seatmates, who seemed to be ignoring each other, too. Three strangers, compelled by circumstances to sit shoulder to shoulder, thigh to thigh, for hours.

It was all Will could do not to jump up, grab his carry-on and bulldoze his way off the airplane before the door was shut. But he sat where he was, muscles locked with the effort not to move, and thought, *What the hell's wrong with me?*

Torturing himself this way was stupid. Moira had a mother, she had friends. Single women had babies all the time. He could tell she meant it when she said she really wanted this child. There wasn't a reason in the world she wouldn't do fine without him.

So why was it killing him to know that he wouldn't be in the States for another five or six months? That she'd already have had the baby by then? That at best he'd have a brief visit before he was off again?

The expressions on his brothers' faces when he told them hadn't helped. He'd done it last night at the dinner table.

"This woman," Clay had said slowly, as though to be sure he understood, "is having your baby while you're off in Africa."

"I didn't know her well. We had sex. I used a condom, but it apparently failed."

Jack had offered a profanity. Clay never took his eyes from Will's face.

"You came back to make sure she's all right."

He unclenched his jaw. "Yes."

"Is she?" Clay might be young, but he had the implacable expression Dad had done so well. Funny, until that moment Will hadn't realized how much his brother had come to look like their father. More so than Will did.

"Yes," he said. "I, uh, went to the doctor with her. Heard the baby's heartbeat."

They were all quiet for a moment. "Well, damn," Clay said at last.

"I don't like it," Will had told them finally. "I don't like anything about this. The only thing that would have been worse is if she'd aborted my baby. Okay?"

"The timing is piss-poor," Jack said thoughtfully.

Will turned on him almost savagely. "You don't have

to tell me. I should have kept it zipped. Do you think I don't know that?"

Goddamn it, right now Jack looked like Dad, too. Dad had believed there was right, and there was wrong, and not one hell of a lot in between. He'd taught his children his unbending rules. Will couldn't remember even hesitating about whether he'd come home and take Dad's place after he died. That was the right thing to do.

The plane was accelerating down the runway, then lifting off, tilting upward to climb. It was too late now to sprint down the aisle and beg to be let off. Sitting here, his body still rigid, Will thought, *This is wrong*.

But, for one of the first times in his life, he had no idea what the right thing to do was. He'd believed he was doing the right thing. Maybe this was one of those hellish situations where there was no right.

What stayed with him all the way to New York then across the Atlantic was the knowledge it wasn't the baby he was worrying about. He didn't doubt that Moira would be a good mother. The best. No, what was tearing him up inside was Moira herself, the woman whose vulnerability he'd seen from the beginning. No matter how beautiful he'd thought she was, he wouldn't have stayed talking to her so long that night if he hadn't seen that someone had hurt her. Yes, he'd wanted her, but even more, he had wanted to be the one man who would make her feel good about herself.

And look what he'd done instead.

He'd known grief twice in his life, once when he was a boy and his mother died, then again when his father and stepmother were killed. This shouldn't have been as bad. Nobody had died. Nothing was unfixable. But by the time he got off the plane in Harare, his heart felt like a rock in his chest, and not one that had been tumbled smooth. This stone was so rough, it scraped his sternum and ribs every time he took a breath.

THE HOSPITAL HELD REGULAR cycles of childbirth classes. The sessions were eight weeks long, and it was recommended that expectant mothers not wait until the very end. After all, the online description pointed out, not all pregnancies went full-term.

Charlotte would have been her first choice for a partner, but Gray had woken Moira at 4:00 a.m. five days ago to let her know their baby had been born. A little girl, Emily Faith Van Dusen. Moira didn't think she'd ever heard him sound so exhausted and so happy. And all at the same time.

He hadn't looked or sounded any more rested since, and Charlotte, who was breastfeeding, was probably even more tired. Obviously, she was out as a labor partner for Moira.

And even if Gray had been willing to leave Charlotte and Emily for the weekly class, Moira didn't want him. The fact that he was a man and she was a woman didn't usually seem to matter. For heaven's sake, he'd even had her stand up for him at his wedding. She'd always thought, if she got married, she would ask him to do the same for her. But she wasn't asking him to coach her in childbirth the same way he had his wife, the woman he loved.

Sheila Daniels would be her next choice, but Sheila lived in Mukilteo. Only a forty-minute drive from West Fork, but Moira suspected she'd want someone *now* once labor started. Bonnie Pappas was another possibility, or Jill Shore… Moira's brow wrinkled. No, with two young kids of her own, Jill might have a hard time getting away for the weekly classes, never mind at whatever hour of the night or day Moira went into labor. Bonnie, then. But Moira didn't call her. She had time. She didn't have to start childbirth classes quite yet.

What she did have to do was call her mother. Admitting to Will that she hadn't told her had made Moira shrivel inside, knowing how Mom was going to feel about her having kept this secret. Will hadn't looked too happy himself when he did a mental count and realized how long she'd known she was pregnant before she'd told him. And Moira had even less excuse where her mother was concerned. Worse yet, she and Mom talked every couple of weeks, so she'd been lying by omission for months now.

Filled with resolve, she called that evening.

"Sweetie," her mom said with pleasure. "How nice to hear from you."

Moira gulped. "I have something to tell you. I've been putting it off for ages."

During the ensuing pause, she could all but see her mother's eyebrows arch. "Oh?"

Deep breath. Bald words. "I'm pregnant."

This silence was even longer. "Pregnant?" Mom whispered.

"It was, um, an accident. The guy isn't anyone I was seriously dating… He wore a condom, but…" She stumbled to a stop.

"Oh, honey."

Moira squeezed her eyes shut. "I'm sorry, Mom."

"Please tell me you're not apologizing to me," her

mother said tartly. "Are you sorry in the sense you wish you weren't pregnant?"

"No." She took a deep breath. "No, actually I've become reconciled to that. I want to be a mother. I'd even given thought these past couple years to... I don't know, adopting, or looking into a sperm donor bank. No. I'm excited about having a baby. I just wish I'd fallen in love and gotten married first. I know raising a child alone wasn't easy for you."

"It was also the greatest joy of my life," her mother said.

Moira sniffed. "Oh, Mom."

Her mother's laugh was warm and familiar, almost as good as an embrace. "When are you due, honey?"

"Oh, uh, January. My official due date is January 14."

This silence fairly crackled. "You're six months pregnant."

"Yes." She closed her eyes and said again, "I'm sorry. I guess I've been ashamed to tell you. Which I know is dumb. It's not like I'm sixteen. Or that you wouldn't have guessed I'm not a virgin."

"No, although I've wondered... Well." Mom cleared her throat. "I'd like to be there when the baby comes, or whenever you need me most." She hesitated. "Is the baby's father going to be involved at all?"

Moira found herself telling her mother about Will, including his visit and her own bewilderment. It felt like it had when she was a confused teenager who'd been able to cuddle up to her mommy on the sofa and confide all her troubles. She'd been the envy of her friends because she *could* talk to her mom. Of course Mom wouldn't be ashamed of her or ever have anything but faith in her. She didn't know why she'd ever feared otherwise.

She was the one who didn't have faith in herself. Who'd been ashamed of herself.

Moira swallowed a few lumps in her throat, told her mother she loved her, and finally hung up the phone feeling both better and terribly, inexplicably sad.

Until she'd felt the first movements inside her, she hadn't realized how lonely she was. She had friends; Gray, especially, would do almost anything for her, she thought. But Mom was the only person in the world for whom she, Moira, came first. And…it wasn't supposed to be that way. By her age, she should have found someone else to love her completely, so much that she never had to doubt it. Instead, she would turn the fierceness of her love on her child. She could see herself replicating her mother's experience, her own experience, and it scared her to wonder if she hadn't somehow made this happen because it was the only kind of family she knew. Maybe she wasn't capable of loving a man and being loved by him, of forming a true family circle.

She sat in the quiet of her house and thought, with a kind of chill but also the knowledge of her own strength, *If that's the way it is, so be it.*

There were worse fates. She was lucky enough to have the chance to be a mother. Mom had talked about joy, and she'd have that. The man-woman thing…so, it hadn't happened. She'd have a rich, satisfying life anyway.

To heck with Will Becker. Who needed him?

CHAPTER SEVEN

"YOU UNDERSTAND," THE SMALL, balding man told Will, "that I will need to get permission from higher up for these plans."

The government office looked like those the world over, although the desktop computer was an antique by American standards. Will had had to wait for over an hour for admittance to see this official, who had then, of course, been extremely cordial. Now, twenty minutes later, they were getting down to the nitty-gritty.

Which, as expected, was that this particular man couldn't make that decision. Nobody, Will had long since discovered, ever admitted to being able to make a final decision about anything. The buck was always passed upward. No one ever wanted to look him in the eye and say, "Sorry, no can do." Or even, "Sure, no problem."

He'd been a model of patience until these past few weeks. Become damn good, if he did say so, at these protracted negotiations, all seemingly friendly.

Today, he seethed, even as he said with hard-won civility, "Indeed, these matters are complex. It's my hope that a man in your high position can get the needed permissions. It would be unfortunate if we couldn't proceed before the heavy rains. Building might not be possible until fall, if we don't start soon."

Yes, yes, summer was not the season to build, indeed it was not. Ten minutes of amiable, time-killing conversation later, Will escaped.

Just for the day, he was in Mutare, Zimbabwe's fourth largest city and very close to the Mozambique border. Also European in looks, Mutare was beautiful, surrounded on all sides by mountains, green on the slopes and crowned by tumbles of granite. He was working toward building two clinics in the area, one to the south in the rich, agricultural valley below the Vumba Mountains, one not far north in the Nyanga region. Yesterday he'd taken the time to wander the ancient remains of Nyangwe Fort, a stone enclosure built of granite blocks and slabs that wouldn't have looked out of place in the Peruvian Andes. He'd driven through the Nyanga Mountain National Park and seen tumbling rivers and wildlife.

And all he could think about was Moira. He'd been back in Zimbabwe for four weeks, during which time she'd sent exactly three emails letting him know that she was fine and commenting pleasantly on the humorous stories he'd shared of his adventures. The tone of her missives enraged Will, even though he knew damn well he didn't have a right to expect anything different.

She was now seven months along. He'd close his eyes and picture her pressing a hand to her lower back, or climbing awkwardly onto that exam table. He saw her sitting in her car, not looking at him, tears thick in her voice as she told him to get lost.

Will had emailed Clay last week and asked him to check on her. She'd probably be ticked, but he didn't care. He'd noticed an internet café earlier, and now decided he could walk to it rather than move his truck. A row of red blooming poinciana trees arched overhead, and he passed pedestrians: men in business suits, some teenage boys with a scrawny dog, a pair of women in bright colored western sundresses. Both women had babies slung in equally bright slings on their backs, while one balanced a full duffel bag on her head, the other a tote bag topped with a bulging white plastic grocery sack. Their arms were free, their gaits graceful despite the burdens. Their burst of chatter didn't register as words with him; although his Shona became more fluent by the day, he still had to concentrate and hope the speaker talked slowly.

He bought a tea in the café and waited for a computer to become available, then waited longer to get online and finally for his email to load. He immediately sought Moira's email address; nothing. But Clay had replied.

I met your Moira. Damn it, Will! She wasn't in the office, but a man was. Gray Van Dusen, the partner. I had the feeling he was real glad to be able to send me to a new development out by Lake Stevens, built on a hill. Said he'd offered to go in her place and she wouldn't let me.

Will's gut knotted. He wasn't going to like any of this.

I've gotta tell you, it's done nothing but rain buckets all week. I've had to idle a couple of crews, if that gives you an idea. The house I found her at was down a lo-ong steep driveway. The ground is ankle deep in mud. I mean, sucking-your-feet deep. The walls were up, the inside rough. She's in there, pissed about the grade of plywood, the foreman is yelling at her, she backs up and damn near falls over an exposed pipe. I flung myself forward to catch her. I don't know much about pregnancy, but man, her belly is sticking out there. As imbalanced as she is, I don't know how the hell she got down the driveway. I know how she got up, because I waited around to walk with her. Slowly, me hovering to grab her although I didn't have to. She's sturdy, I'll give her that, but I had to boost her into the SUV she was driving, with it tilted off the road the way it was. She went on to a second house in the development, and I let her go when I saw that the driveway wasn't as long or as steep, but, crap, she has no business being there in her shape.

She was friendly enough, but looked surprised when I told her you were worried about her. I half expected her to say, "Will who?"

So okay. I checked. She's alive, maybe not big as a house but holy shit she's getting there, and apparently not willing to cut herself any slack because of it.

Damn, I wish you hadn't sent me.

Clay

Will felt sick. What was she thinking? But he knew—what she was thinking was that she had to be independent. She couldn't start letting herself lean on her partner because she might keep leaning. She wouldn't take any more help than absolutely necessary, because she didn't feel entitled to it.

Didn't she believe that any of them cared?

He closed the program without reading any of the other messages. He stood and walked out, started down the street toward his Datsun, otherwise oblivious to his surroundings and passersby. He churned inside: stomach, mind, heart. With ruthless honesty, Will admitted to himself that he'd wanted Clay to say, "Yeah, we met. Nice lady, she seems to be doing great." His anxiety would be quieted, if temporarily. He'd be able to keep justifying having left her.

Left? Abandoned. That's what he'd done. Will reached his pickup and laid both hands flat on the rusting roof, bowing his head and surprised to discover he was panting. No, they hadn't had a relationship, not really; he hadn't promised her anything, she didn't expect anything of him. But no matter how it happened, she was carrying his baby, and he had goddamn abandoned her to do it alone. He'd heard the heartbeat, felt his child move beneath the hand he'd spread over the firm swell of Moira's belly. He'd seen fear on her face and taken it as a ticket to go. Nope, she didn't need or want him.

But she did, whether she knew it or not. And while the commitment he'd made here could be fulfilled by someone else, the one he owed her couldn't be.

Will was scared as he hadn't been since Sophie fell off the monkey bars during recess at school and remained unconscious for three terrifying hours. He had the sudden, unreasoning conviction that Moira *would* fall, that she'd lose the baby if she kept plodding on alone. Maybe just as bad, he couldn't imagine that she'd ever believe in any man again. The scumbag hadn't dealt the deathblow; Will had. And yeah, he knew that was irrational, too, but he still believed it.

There might be a blurry gray area between right and wrong, something like the eternal drizzle of a November back home, but he wasn't standing in it. Will knew what was right, and he knew he'd been wrong.

No, he didn't love Moira Cullen. He didn't know her well enough to feel anything like that for her. But the possibility had been there from the moment he first saw her in that ballroom, dancing with another man. There was a reason he hadn't been able to forget her, even before he learned she was pregnant.

Will straightened at last, clearheaded for the first time in months. His choice made, he wished he could head straight to Harare this minute, but it was too late in the day for the drive over mountainous country. He'd find a room here instead of going back to Nyanga as he'd intended. Tomorrow morning, Harare. He could be home in the U.S. within the week.

Whether his redhead liked it or not, she'd have him beside her as long as she needed him.

Because he couldn't live with himself if he wasn't there.

"NO, I'M GREAT, CLAY." Moira managed a chuckle into the phone. "I'm pregnant, not disabled." She was trying, damn, she was trying, not to sound sharp, but she was getting awfully tired of everyone fussing. For Will to have sicced his brother on her was the last straw.

"I just don't like the idea of you taking a tumble," he said. For the second time. "That driveway was steep and slick."

Yes, it was. And, unfortunately, he'd seen her struggle up it. By now he'd probably reported back to his big brother, who would likely then send his *other* brother to check on her, too, and maybe his sister and an aunt and who knew who else. And it wasn't as if she didn't already have Gray on her case.

"You can reassure Will," she said, "that I'll be careful. I have every intention of cutting back on anything physical these last couple of months. Okay?"

Eventually she had him soothed. She was just banging the phone down when the office door opened and Gray walked in. Her glower honed in on him and had him pausing.

"Problem?"

"I'm mad at you all over again. I didn't need another nursemaid."

He grinned. She'd torn a layer of skin off him last week because he'd had the nerve to tell Becker's brother where to find her. "That was Clay Becker on the phone?"

"Yes!"

"Good. Seemed like a nice guy."

"*Seemed* is the word for it. Neither of us knows him. I don't want to know him. I resent Will making him come here. I've told Will repeatedly that I'm fine, and he refuses to believe me." She was shouting, Moira realized in surprise. She never shouted. But frustration and, yes, fear had swelled in her chest until she felt like she could burst with it.

She didn't want to admit that Gray might be right, that Will's brother might be right, and that she shouldn't have gone out to Lake View Heights last week. It was her job. What good was she if she couldn't do the follow-up work on her own plans?

But she'd been scared when she parked and walked to the top of that damn driveway, when she'd teetered there on the edge of the drop-off and wondered how she could get down. She'd felt a sharp kick in her belly, as though her anxiety had awakened the baby, and she'd gulped as she took the first couple of steps, figuring out how her ungainly weight should be balanced over feet that were trying to skid out from under her despite the deep tread of her work boots.

Maybe next time she'd accept Gray's offer to go in her stead. But how could he do that very often and keep up with his own schedule? They were both hoping he could hang on until his term of office expired in January. It was bad enough that he hadn't been able to run for reelection, but if he had to quit early because of her, she didn't know how she could live with it.

Gray dropped his briefcase on his desk and strolled over to hers, where he half sat on a corner she kept clear for him. Smiling, he said, "You're a stubborn woman, Moira Cullen. Must go with the red hair." He reached out and fingered an escaped curl.

She slapped his hand. "That's a stereotype."

His smile widened. "Maybe."

"Once upon a time, a woman would work in the fields until the baby dropped out, then sling it on her back and keep working."

"Now, why do I suspect that's apocryphal? Probably no more true than claiming all redheads have tempers and a tendency to dig in their heels."

She felt like tearing at her hair. "I have two more months to go. What do you suggest I do, take a lot of bubble baths and watch soap operas?" Moira let out an annoyed puff of air. "No, forget the bubble baths. I'm not allowed to take a hot one, and who wants a tepid bath?"

Gray listened to her indignation with clear amusement, but his gray eyes held a glint she recognized as serious. "Will is right to worry about you," he said bluntly. "Nobody has suggested you sit around and watch *Days of Our Lives.* All I'm asking is that you use some common sense."

Interestingly, his voice had begun to rise there toward the end. What temper Gray had most often came out in quiet, steely orders.

"Men," she muttered.

"If women worked the fields until they gave birth in the good old days, it was because they did it every day. They had the muscles for it. They didn't sit in front of a computer four days a week, then spend the fifth scrambling over concrete foundations with exposed rebars and pipes just waiting to trip them up." Now he was definitely yelling, too. "Especially not when they reach the point where they can't see their feet!"

Moira blinked. "You're really worried about me."

He sucked in a huge breath and closed his eyes when he exhaled. "Damn it, Moira, yes."

"Oh." She looked down to see her stomach take a bounce. When she laid a calming hand on it, a knob bumped into her palm. An elbow, a knee, the heel of a foot, she didn't know, but felt awe every time she came that close to touching her unborn baby. Her shouting had upset him.

She almost snorted. *Him.* If it was a him, he was probably anticipating the chance to do his own yelling. Yee-haw.

"How on earth," she wondered aloud, "did I ever become best friends with a *guy?*"

"The same way I became best friends with a redhead."

She grinned at him. Then her smile vanished and her eyes narrowed as what he'd said sank in. "So, you're telling me women in the good old days had muscle, but me, I'm in such lousy shape I'm not safe to let out of the house."

"Oh, for God's sake," he snarled. "You're making me crazy."

"You've already made me crazy."

They glared at each other.

He sighed. His shoulders relaxed. "I've got to tell you, until recently I thought Charlotte was the most difficult woman in the world."

"I'm telling her you said that."

Gray only laughed. "She knows." He hesitated. "Why won't you let me do anything for you?"

"I will. When I need you," she said, knowing perfectly well that she *was* being stubborn, but not why.

He stood, shaking his head and muttering something under his breath that she suspected was an obscenity.

"I got a call yesterday," he told her. "From Reynolds."

Sam Reynolds was the contractor building both houses in Lake View Heights that she'd drawn the plans for. Moira stiffened.

"He doesn't want you out there again. Says the homeowner won't accept the liability."

Her eyes widened. "It was Curtis Tate. That creep," she stormed. "I caught him using lower grade materials than I called for, and he's getting back at me. I'm going to call Sam right this minute—"

"You ever think maybe you scared Curtis?"

"No."

They were back to glaring at each other. Moira was

too mad and too upset, too tangled up altogether, to talk about this as if it was an everyday problem. And she was afraid that if she let Gray have a glimpse of her confusion, all she'd be doing was confirming to him that she was too weak to do her job.

"I'm going home," she snapped, shooting to her feet. Too fast—her belly bumped the desk and the chair scooted backward several feet. She ignored it, didn't care that her computer was still on or that she had a couple more calls she should make. She grabbed her purse, said goodbye and stomped out.

She thought she was doing well, out of respect for the attorneys across the hall, not to slam the door behind her.

WILL WALKED INTO Van Dusen & Cullen, braced to see Moira, but her corner of the big space was unoccupied. There was a guy sitting at the second drafting table, although he wasn't working; he was frowning into space until he heard the sound of the door opening. This must be the partner.

He was good-looking, gray-eyed, with shaggy hair that was almost light enough to be called blond. The minute he saw Will, those eyes narrowed.

"Will Becker," Gray said slowly.

"Have we met?"

"I found a picture of you on the Becker Construction website."

Will winced. It was a crappy photo, almost ten years old, and should have been replaced with Clay's by now.

"Met your brother last week, too." Van Dusen seemed to be musing aloud. "There's a resemblance, although I might not have recognized you just from that."

"He's better looking."

"Yeah, he is."

The other man was bristling, Will could feel it. Could even understand it. Van Dusen and Moira were close. Best buddies, and maybe more. Sister-brother, on a level that had nothing to do with genetics? Will wouldn't have felt real cordial, either, toward a man who'd screwed Sophie then walked away, leaving her pregnant.

But reassuring Gray Van Dusen wasn't Will's priority right now. "Where is she?" he asked.

"She went home."

Worry speared him. "Is something wrong?"

Gray clasped his hands comfortably behind his head and leaned back in his leather desk chair. Surveying Will, he began to relax.

"She's mad at me," Gray said. "I was coming down hard on her, probably for the same reason you're here."

Will's mouth tightened. "Clay emailed me."

"She's been banned from the Lake View Heights development by the contractor, who claims the home-owner doesn't want the liability for a pregnant woman scrambling around a half-built house on a steep hillside."

"She could scream sex discrimination."

"Oh, I'm sure Moira will think about that," Gray said drily. "Once she cools down a little."

Will felt the first stir of humor in days, although it didn't last long. "She scared the crap out of Clay."

"So I gathered. He just called. That's what set her off in the first place."

Eyebrows rising, Will said, "Clay called?" Apparently his little brother shared Will's overdeveloped sense of responsibility more than he'd realized.

"Had the gall to ask how she was, apparently. Moira's not about to tell anyone that, about midafternoon, it's all she can do to keep from falling asleep across her keyboard." Gray's expression hardened. "Or that her back aches whether she's been sitting too long or on her feet too long."

Will sat abruptly in one of the upholstered chairs in their small conference area. He hadn't had any choice; his knees had given out on him. "She swears she's fine. Doesn't need me. Doesn't want me."

"And you? What do you think?" Gray still lounged in his own chair, but the posture, Will guessed, was all show. Probably he wanted to ram his fist into Will's face. He had to have been seething for long months because Moira was pregnant and alone, and now the guy to blame was right there, in front of him.

It was understanding that allowed Will to meet Gray's eyes steadily. "I think she's wrong," he said quietly. "I'm back to stay."

Moira's partner began to smile. He straightened in the chair, then stood and walked over to Will, who rose at his approach.

Gray held out his hand. "Glad to meet you, Will. I'm Gray Van Dusen."

Will didn't smile, but shook his hand with a strong clasp. "You going to give me her home address?"

MOIRA HAD JUST LAY DOWN on her sofa, cozily warm beneath a throw, when her cell phone rang. She'd set it on the coffee table within reach, in case someone needed to contact her. She'd been hoping nobody would—a nap sounded really, really good, even though she'd be sorry come bedtime if she took one. When she saw the number, she almost didn't answer. But on the fourth ring, she sighed and did.

"Gray."

"What made you think I'd let you get the last word?"

How was she supposed to stay mad at him? But she pretended she was. "Now what?"

"Your doorbell's going to be ringing in about five minutes. Thought you deserved a warning."

Her eyes widened and she sat up. "What? Who?"

"Will himself. We met, we talked, he persuaded me to tell him how to find you."

"Will?" she repeated numbly. "He's *here?*"

"Yep."

"But...why?" she all but wailed.

"Seems he's been worrying about you."

The undercurrent of amusement in Gray's voice made her grit her teeth. "He wasn't satisfied by his brother's report? He had to come and see for himself? I told him—" She bit off the rest and closed her eyes. *Breathe. Deep and slow.* Hyperventilating wouldn't help. "Why did you tell him where I live?"

"You're in the phone book, Moira," he said patiently.

"Without my first name."

"Hmm. M. Cullen, with a West Fork address. You think he couldn't have figured that out?"

A car pulled into her driveway. No. She stood and peeked. A pickup truck that she recognized. "Oh, God. He's here. Damn it, Gray."

"Do you want me to come over, Moira? I can be there in a minute."

"No." She was being silly. She could handle Will. "No, of course not. He's a nice guy. Just…"

"Stubborn?" Gray suggested, and she knew—*knew*—he was smiling.

With a growl, she disconnected then thought, *Oh, my God, my hair!* Bathroom… No, there wasn't time. Her purse. Where had she put her purse? There, on the kitchen table. She hurried around the sofa to it and groped frantically in the depths until her hand closed on the bristles of her brush. Even as the doorbell rang, she ran the brush through the hair she'd released from a bun the minute she got home.

Then, steeling herself, she opened the front door.

Neither of them said anything for a long moment. He made no attempt to hide his thorough appraisal. She couldn't help feeling a moment of weakness, of—heaven help her—longing, to be wrapped in his arms for a minute. He was so big and solid, and from the moment she'd met him she'd heard something in his deep, slow voice, seen something in his brown eyes, that made her feel as if she'd be safe with him.

Get real. All she had to do was look down at her belly to see how deceptive appearances were. *Safe* was the last thing she'd been with him.

"Will," she said, finally.

His gaze met hers. "You're not surprised I'm here."

"Gray called."

"Ah. May I come in?"

"I suppose," she said, embarrassed at how ungracious she sounded. Okay, she *felt* ungracious, but still had this compulsion to be polite. She stood aside and let him past.

He stepped into her living room and glanced around

in an appraisal as blatant as the one he'd given her all-too-ripe figure. "Nice," he said after a minute.

The interior of her house owed as much as she could afford to the Arts and Crafts movement of the late 1800s and early 1900s. She loved the combination of strong, clean lines and sophisticated sensuality. Mostly her furniture was reproduction, but she'd started collecting pottery from the period. Will went immediately to the glass-fronted case where she displayed her pieces.

"Genuine?" he asked.

"Yes." Reluctantly, Moira joined him. "That's a Grueby." She pointed at a particular favorite, a small vase with the classic stylized designs in a matte green glaze, then gestured to a second pot, this one cylindrical with hand-incised, extraordinarily delicate geometric designs drawn in brown, rust and pale orange glazes. "Do you know anything about pottery of the time? That one's from Marblehead Pottery. I like that it was started to teach ceramics as therapy to sanitarium patients."

"That's interesting," he said. "I know enough that I'd have snapped one of those up if I saw it at a garage sale, but not enough to identify the pottery." He turned to face her.

Her interest was caught despite herself. "Do you go to garage sales?"

"Weirdly enough," he admitted, "I can't resist a garage or yard sale sign. I've found some good stuff at 'em. Mostly tools, but a couple pieces of furniture, too."

What an odd thing to have learned about him.

"Do they have them in Zimbabwe?" she asked.

His mouth quirked. "Not that I've seen. They have

street markets instead. They're as irresistible, in their own way."

So much for the niceties. She took a deep breath. "Will...why aren't you *in* Zimbabwe?"

"I didn't like how we left it between us," he said bluntly.

Moira's heart began to hammer. "That's it? You flew home so we could...what? Have a heart-to-heart chat?"

She couldn't be sure, but she thought his expression had become wary.

"No," he said. "I came home to ask you to marry me."

CHAPTER EIGHT

MOIRA COULD ONLY GAPE at him. "You have got to be kidding."

Marry him? Was he nuts?

Dark color streaked Will's cheekbones. "No. I'm serious, Moira. We're having a baby together."

She backed up to the sofa and sank onto it. "Will... this is the twenty-first century. The word *illegitimate* has pretty much disappeared from our vocabulary."

He shoved his hands into the pockets of his trousers. In dark pants and a rather wrinkled, button-down gray shirt, he was dressed more formally than she'd seen him since the night of the gala. If he'd worn a tie, he'd shed it at some point and rolled up the cuffs of his shirt to expose wrists that had to be twice the size of hers. He looked as if he might have come from a day-long meeting. Or, it occurred to her, straight from the airport. If so, he must be exhausted.

"I'd rather my child have my name," he admitted, "but I'm more concerned that he knows his parents were both committed."

Stunned beyond belief, Moira said, "We're not."

He considered her for a minute, expression unreadable, then said quietly, "I am."

"I don't understand," she whispered.

Will came to sit on the coffee table facing her, his

knees touching hers. He reached out and took her hands, engulfing them in a warm, steadying clasp. "I don't want you to be in this alone. I'm not asking you to promise me forever, although I'd like us both to go into this with the idea that we'll try to make our marriage work. But even if it turns out to be temporary, I'd like to stay here with you. I intend to take you to the doctor, do any work that needs doing around the house, cook dinners, drive you to job sites. I want to be there when the baby is born. Take my turn at diaper duty. I want him to know my voice as well as yours. When he's a few months old, then we can talk."

All she could think to say was, "You're supposed to be in Zimbabwe."

The deep color of black coffee, Will's eyes held hers. "You're more important."

"You loved what you were doing."

"I did." His pause was awkward. They both knew he couldn't with any honesty say, *I love you more.* Of course he didn't. She'd become a responsibility to a man who took them seriously. "We're having a baby together," he repeated instead of claiming any feelings for her whatsoever.

"Oh, God." Moira wrenched her hands away and covered her face with them. "I should never have told you I was pregnant. I knew better. I knew you'd feel stuck."

"Moira." He gripped her upper arms, squeezing gently. "I don't feel stuck any more than you claim you do. I like the idea of being a father. It didn't hit me as soon as it did you, but…I can hardly wait."

Slowly she let her hands fall, her eyes searching his. "You're just saying that."

He let out a rough laugh. "No. I admit I've surprised myself. I'd have probably preferred to wait to start a family, but..." His gaze flicked to her belly. "I keep thinking about the baby moving inside of you. I want to put my hands on you and feel him move again."

"What if he's a she?"

His smile was curiously tender. "That's more than okay. I hope she has bright red hair and freckles."

"God forbid," Moira muttered.

Will lifted his eyebrows.

"I've always hated my freckles. And when I was a teenager I would have killed to have plain brown hair so I could blend in. I would have dyed it, except with the freckles that would have looked dumb."

He laughed again, more naturally this time. "Moira, honey, you have gorgeous hair and lovely skin. That night, I wished I'd had time to kiss every single freckle on your body."

Like an idiot, she blurted, "That would have taken—" She stopped before the last word could emerge. *Forever.* That's how long it would have taken.

"Weeks," he said softly. "Months, maybe."

Get a grip, Moira Cullen. "You're crazy," she told him.

"No. What I am is determined."

"You're already committed, and not to me."

Now his tone was completely inflexible. "I'm going to quit my job with the foundation. They can replace me."

"Midway through the job?"

"I've given them a good start. Someone else can take over."

He was serious, she realized. She couldn't tell at all

from his face how he really felt about walking out on something that had meant so much to him. No, that was stupid; of course she knew how he felt. But Will Becker was made up of bedrock that was…traditional, maybe, but solid enough to be earthquake proof. The fact that the condom had failed was no one's fault, but he'd still feel responsible.

No. Her forehead crinkled as she kept studying him. That wasn't it. The thing was, this baby was his. It carried his genes. That was what he took so seriously.

"How old were you when your father and stepmother died?" she asked.

A ghost of some emotion passed through his eyes. "Twenty."

Her suspicion solidified. "Clay's a lot younger than you, I could tell. And he's the next oldest, right?"

"Yeah. Dad didn't remarry right away. Clay is seven years younger than I am."

"And you said Sophie just graduated from college. So she's…twenty-two?"

"Twenty-one, actually. She got a year of college credits while she was still in high school." He realized he'd never told her how old he was. "I'm thirty-five, in case you wondered."

She nodded acknowledgment, but stuck to the point. "Who raised them?"

Other than the flex of muscles in his jaws, Will was expressionless. "I did. I was an adult. There wasn't anyone else."

"Did you go to college?"

"I dropped out."

She pictured him, a shocked, grieving kid as immature as she and Gray had been their sophomore year in college, only Will had left behind dorm life and gone home to console three children who'd lost their parents. In the years to come, instead of studying and going to keggers, arguing all night with friends about American policy abroad, dating coeds and soaking up knowledge, he'd been making school lunches, attending parent-teacher conferences, taking his young brothers and sister shopping for new shoes. His sister for her first bra.

Moira ached for that boy.

"And the construction company. You took it over for your dad."

"Yes."

"You gave up everything for them." She sat looking at this big, kind, sexy man and said, despite the pain in every word, "That's what you meant, isn't it? When you said your worst nightmare was being trapped. Spending your whole life doing what you have to do."

He didn't respond.

"I can't do this to you, Will. No. No, I won't marry you."

"This isn't the same."

"It is."

"No. No, Moira. Leaving you and flying back to Africa was torture. Right now, all I want is to be with you. I want to hold our baby as soon as he's born. I *want*." His gaze bored into hers. He leaned forward, took her hands again, his grip tighter this time. "Listen to me. Don't think I'm making a sacrifice I'll regret. Life is full of choices, and I've made mine. I'm not going away, no matter what you say today."

She couldn't seem to speak. Emotions were rising in her like floodwaters, dark and tumultuous. She didn't know what she felt, only that it was too much. All she could do was shake her head hard.

"Don't say no, Moira." Like that day outside the obstetrician's clinic, Will's face spasmed with some emotion she couldn't read any more than she could understand her own. His voice was hoarse. "Please. Don't say no."

When she still failed to say anything at all, he let her hands go and leaned forward until he could draw her into his arms. Gently but inexorably, he tugged her forward until her brow rested against his broad chest and he could settle his chin on top of her head.

"Marry me, Moira," he said, so low she barely heard him. "Let me do this for both of us."

She could hear his heartbeat, as strong and steady as he was. Maybe the powerful rhythm was what allowed the floodwaters of her confusion to subside, the emotions to resettle into their places. She didn't ache anymore when she finally sat back, separating herself from Will.

"Are you sure?" she asked. "If this makes you miserable, I'll know eventually. That would be worse for both of us than being honest now."

"I've never been more honest in my life."

"Then…" Well, shoot, *now* she was going to cry. Didn't that figure. "Then yes," she managed to get out. "Yes, I'll marry you."

"Oh, sweetheart." He framed her face with his hands and caught the tears with his thumbs. "I'll try to make sure you're never sorry."

For some reason that struck her as funny, so that she laughed even as she wept. He kissed her forehead, then pulled her to him again, so that she got the front of his crumpled cotton shirt soggy.

"That's it. Let yourself cry," he told her, sounding so blasted *comforting* that she did, even though she couldn't help thinking of how often he must have cuddled his brothers and sister when they cried. When he was trapped, being a daddy whether he wanted to be one or not.

IT WAS ASTONISHINGLY EASY to get married, Will found. Easier than it ought to be, in his opinion. But then, divorce was easy these days, too.

He didn't want to think about that.

They got married in the church the Becker family had always attended. Will couldn't claim to be much of a believer—nothing had happened in his life to make him one—but his parents had insisted on Sunday attendance, and for their sake he'd done the same with Clay, Jack and Sophie. Moira resisted initially the idea of a church wedding, which annoyed Will. Was she trying to make sure she felt less guilt when she walked out on him a few months from now? But she eventually gave way, as most people did when Will dug in his heels. They were getting married, and they were going to do it right.

They did it on a Saturday so her mother could fly over from Missoula for the ceremony without missing any work. She was trying to save her vacation to be available when the baby was born if they needed her. Sophie came from L.A., too. There was no maid of honor. Instead, there were two best men—Gray for Moira, Clay for Will. There were only a handful of other attendees: a couple of friends of Moira's, Dennis

Mattson, a good friend of Will's, Gray's wife, Charlotte, and her twin sister, Faith, who'd also brought her husband, Ben, the police chief of West Fork. Jack and Sophie, of course.

Moira had refused to make a big deal out of walking up the aisle, which was fairly short anyway in a church that was in temporary quarters while the congregation was remodeling and expanding the original building. Instead of preceding her, Gray walked her the short distance, her hand resting on his arm.

Will was stunned by how much he felt at the sight of her. She hadn't worn white, which annoyed him in one way, but he suspected the rich shade of cream was a better color on her anyway, setting off her fiery hair and redhead's skin. She was so gorgeously rounded with pregnancy, full with his baby, he found himself both choked up and aroused as he held out a hand to her. Then she looked at him, her green eyes scared and worried and vulnerable, and damned if it wasn't like being shot by a nail gun in the chest.

Somehow, from somewhere, he found a smile for her as she searched his face anxiously for that brief moment when it seemed as though they were the only two people there. He didn't know if the smile reassured her, but she did take a deep breath, square her shoulders and turn to face the pastor. Will did the same.

The church might be modern, but the promises they made were the same ones their grandparents and great-grandparents would have made. That's the way Will wanted it.

When Pastor James said, "You may kiss the bride," and Will drew Moira gently to him, her stomach lurched and bumped against him. Startled, he looked down, and Moira laughed. He liked kissing her when her lips were curved with pleasure. His lingered, and she didn't object. She was breathless and startled by the time he eased back.

My wife, he thought, undecided whether this felt unreal or more astonishingly real than anything else he'd ever done.

Clay hugged Will, giving his back a good, firm whack, then kissed Moira's cheek. Jack followed suit, and Sophie, tears in her eyes, rose on tiptoe to kiss Will then turned to embrace Moira. Moira's mother—good God, his mother-in-law—kissed them both, too. Moira all but disappeared in the bevy of women, leaving Will at Gray's side.

"I'm still stunned you were able to talk her into this," Gray said softly.

Will grinned. "I'm a persuasive man."

The other man's eyes met his. "Don't hurt her."

I won't, snagged in his throat. He had even less idea what was to come than most grooms did. The best he could do was a quiet "I'll try not to."

"Good," Gray said. "Moira is…" He seemed to be searching for the right word.

Thinking of everything he'd seen in her eyes when she was distressed, Will said, "I didn't marry her just because she's pregnant. I'm not stupid enough to do that. It's…Moira," he finally finished, unable to find the right thing to say himself but hoping Gray understood.

A smile warmed the face of Moira's best man. "Good."

Will knew the minute she turned, looking for him. He went right to her side. Taking her hand, he said to the small crowd, "Everyone knows where we're going?"

Everyone did. Mom was riding with Moira; Will would be following in his pickup truck. The others were taking their own cars to the restaurant where they'd reserved a private room for lunch.

He had barely met her mother before the ceremony. Will had half expected her to be a redhead, too, but she wasn't. She had short, brown hair frosted with gray she hadn't bothered to color. She was a pretty, slender woman whose blue eyes had filled with tears when she embraced Moira after the ceremony. Sitting side by side at the restaurant, their heads bent together as they talked quietly, there was a palpable warmth and closeness between them that didn't surprise Will. They'd had only each other. He couldn't help wondering why a woman as attractive as Sylvia Cullen had never remarried. He supposed she'd kept her ex-husband's name because of her daughter.

"Aren't you curious whether you're having a girl or a boy?" Sophie asked at one point during lunch. She was seated halfway down the table, but didn't mind talking around several other people. Sophie wasn't shy.

Moira smiled. "Of course I'm curious, but I like the suspense."

"Do you have a preference?" Clay asked, from Will's other side. Apparently nosiness ran in Will's family.

She glanced down at her stomach. Will thought he caught something on her face, but he couldn't pin it down. "No," she said, after a moment. "No."

Was that true? She might feel more comfortable if she had a little girl. She would know better how to raise one, especially if she were on her own. Will clenched his jaw at the idea, then deliberately relaxed it. At this speed, his dentist would notice he was grinding his molars down. And he had no right to feel irritated because Moira felt emotions that were surely natural. She had no reason to trust he was in this for the long haul, no matter what he said.

He'd count his blessings. She'd said, "I do." He was going home with her tonight.

Actually, he and her mom both were going home with Moira tonight. He'd overheard her mother at the church earlier saying, "Moira, honey, I really wouldn't mind at all getting a hotel room. For heaven's sake, it's your wedding night." Clearly, they'd already had this argument.

"Don't be silly," Moira said. "You know our marriage isn't like that." He'd ground his teeth at that point, too. She had continued, "Besides, I want to see you while you're here. I wish you were staying longer."

Conversation became general again. Will was a little surprised at how well this mixed group of people seemed to get along. His gaze moved down the table. Dennis, an electrical contractor, was having an animated discussion with one of Moira's friends, while Sophie was listening, seemingly rapt, to some story Charlotte's sister, Faith, was telling. Jack was quizzing Ben Wheeler, the police chief; no surprise there, Jack had briefly considered a career in law enforcement.

The wedding cake the waiter brought in was a surprise to Will and Moira both. A couple of people pulled out cameras and took pictures while the newly married couple cut the cake together. Moira's cheeks flamed.

Will and Clay wrangled briefly over the bill for the meal, Clay winning. Little brother was coming into his own, which apparently included the familial stubbornness.

"You didn't give us time to think of decent gifts," he said. "I'd like to give you at least this much."

In lieu of a gift, Jack had given Will back his pickup truck. With a grin, he'd said, "Clay's paying me slave wages, but, you know, I can afford to buy my own."

More hugs and kisses were exchanged in the restaurant then in the parking lot as the crowd broke up. Will walked Sylvia and Moira to her car. His pickup was loaded with his suitcases and a few of the boxes he'd stored seven months ago at the house. He had spent his last night in his old bedroom, but this time, closing the door behind him, he'd felt none of the pang he had the night before he left for Africa. This house where he'd grown up didn't feel like home anymore, not the way it had. He hoped like hell Moira let him feel at home with her and didn't treat him like an inconveniently lingering guest.

As she drove out of the parking lot, he turned to his own vehicle to find Clay leaning against the bumper. His brother rose to meet him. Clay looked good. Unfamiliar, but good in a dark suit and red tie.

"So, you're a married man," he remarked.

"Yeah." Will looked down at his hand. For the first time in his life, he wore a ring, a simple gold band. The sight of it induced something between panic and satisfaction in him. "Guess so."

"You quit officially with the foundation?"

"Yeah," he said again.

They'd professed to understand, but had to be disappointed in him. During the interview process, they'd heavily stressed that he was making a minimum two-year commitment. "No problem," he'd said. Uh-huh.

"Your old job is waiting for you," Clay said. "I figured you might want a week or two to settle in with Moira before you pick up the reins, but…"

Will shook his head. He should have foreseen this conversation and headed it off. "No. I'm not coming back, Clay. I told you before I left that I wasn't. I meant it."

His brother frowned. "Then what the hell do you plan to do?"

"For now, take care of my pregnant wife."

"You really think she's going to let you trail behind her all day, every day?"

"I'm assuming there are days she doesn't leave the office and I won't have to hang around. If she goes out on a construction site, I'll be with her."

"Then what?" Clay asked.

This was the part Will didn't like to think about. Funny, when he'd spent years craving his freedom like a sober alcoholic did the drink he wouldn't allow himself. But now that he was free in a way he'd never intended, Will felt like as if he'd stepped out of an airplane without knowing whether he'd be able to reach the ripcord. It was unsettling.

"I don't know," he admitted. "I've got time to think, and I intend to use it."

"Have you considered going back to college?" Clay asked, his tone tentative.

"I'm too old." Will moved his shoulders uncomfortably. "No, that's not true. I'd do it if I was sure where I was going. Say, I hankered to be a lawyer. But right now, if I went back to school I'd be taking classes like any eighteen-year-old with no idea what I wanted to be doing with my life."

"Would that be so bad?"

"I like building," Will said slowly. "More than I realized all those years. I want to build something that matters. And...I discovered over there that I was better at persuading people to do what I wanted them to do than I expected to be."

Clay grinned. "I could have told you that. You're the original immovable object. People *always* do what you want them to. You didn't notice?"

"Being bullheaded is one thing. Patient and diplomatic is another."

"Hell, maybe you *should* think about law school."

"Maybe so." Will shrugged. "Like I said...I've got time."

Ignoring the uneasiness that rose at the idea of so much unstructured time and an uncertain future, he reached for his brother and gave him a hard hug.

"Thanks."

Clay hugged him back, just as hard. "We've missed you."

Stepping back finally, Will said, "I missed all of you, too. Those first weeks were a little like going off to college. Caught me by surprise, but I was homesick as hell."

"See? You could be eighteen again."

A reluctant laugh escaped Will. "Got to tell you, I don't feel that young. Thank God. No eighteen-year-old should be a father."

"Man, I'm going to be an uncle." Clay shook his head. "That day I went out to meet Moira, I kept feeling weirded out when I thought about how it was your kid in there."

They said their goodbyes and Will started, at last, for West Fork. He'd expected to be right behind Moira, although he doubted that she was watching her rear-view mirror. She didn't need him when she had her mother with her.

Clay, he thought as he merged onto the freeway, wasn't the only one occasionally weirded out by the stunning realization that Moira was carrying his baby. It amused Will to realize that he also felt a whole lot of satisfaction and some primitive, male triumph.

Maybe that was even okay now. After all, Moira was his wife. She and the baby both were his.

Temporarily.

His hands were rhythmically squeezing the steering wheel. He heard it creak.

What a time to discover that he hated a state of uncertainty. He'd married a woman who'd agreed only because she'd grudgingly conceded she could use some help. For now. And, oh yeah, he was unemployed.

It didn't make him happy to realize that he was a hell of a lot more nervous now than he'd been the day he got on the airplane to start a new life in Africa.

CHAPTER NINE

WILL HADN'T ARGUED AT ALL when Moira had informed him, the day he asked her to marry him, that she wasn't ready to share a bed with him.

"I don't know you well enough," she'd whispered, knowing how dumb that sounded under the circumstances. "And with me so pregnant…"

Watching her, seeing the distress on her face, he'd only nodded calmly and said, "We'll have time."

She hadn't been able to tell if he minded her ultimatum. Probably not. Just because he'd had sex with her once—at her invitation—didn't mean he really lusted for her.

And things were different now anyway. She'd wondered ruefully whether men ever genuinely lusted for a woman who was starting to waddle from pregnancy. She hadn't quite worked up the nerve to ask any of her friends whether their husbands had found them sexy this far along.

Now it was not only Moira's wedding day, Will was moving in with her.

He had arrived twenty minutes after she and her mother got home. He rang the doorbell, probably for the last time. She had a small burst of panic. She'd have to give him a key. From now on, he would simply walk in. It would be *home* for him. Wow.

Leading him down the hall, she explained, "I'm going to pull out the couch in the living room tonight for Mom. She slept in the bedroom last night, but I've already changed the sheets."

"You didn't have to displace her," Will said mildly. He was close behind her, a big plastic tub in his arms. "I'd have been okay on the couch."

"You have all your stuff." Which he'd refused to allow her to help carry. "It makes sense for you to go ahead and settle in now."

Her mother came out of the bathroom as they passed. "Oh, I thought I heard voices. Will, can I help?"

"No, I can get it all."

Gee, of course he didn't want a woman carrying anything when he—a man—was around to do it. Moira was beginning to wonder—oh, shoot, why kid herself? she'd wondered all along—what she'd gotten herself into. Will Becker, she suspected, was sexist and overbearing, even if he mostly disguised those tendencies behind a relentlessly pleasant manner.

Mom laughed and said, "I can certainly pull a suitcase," and went out to his truck.

His eyebrows drew together as he watched her. After a minute, evidently resigned, he passed Moira and walked across the guest room to set the tub on top of the dresser.

"The drawers are empty and the closet is mostly," she told him hastily. "I have some extra bedding in there up on the shelf…"

"I don't need that much space." He glanced around, his gaze finally settling on the open doorway beside her. "Is that your room across the hall?"

"Yes. I have a second bathroom in there. You can put your stuff in the one out here."

His expression told her she sounded like a bellhop unnecessarily pointing out features of a hotel room. She couldn't seem to help herself. This was so bizarre. A man she hardly knew was moving in with all his worldly possessions.

She was wearing a wedding ring that he'd put on her finger.

Gulp.

"Uh…let me check that there are clean towels in the bathroom."

With a nod, he left. Moira still hadn't moved when her mother pulled a giant suitcase in, said, "I'll go back for another load," and disappeared again. Moira hurried to the bathroom before Will could catch her still standing there like a dolt. She already knew there were clean towels in here because she'd hung them on the rack not ten minutes ago, but this was a good place to hide briefly. And heck, while she was here she had to pee anyway. That was pretty much a given these days. She was awfully glad the master bedroom had a separate bath, or else he'd hear her getting up all night long.

She made a face. Not that he could live with her for long without noticing she needed the bathroom constantly. Gray hadn't commented, but that was probably only because he was used to his pregnant wife doing the same.

Thank heavens Mom was here tonight. Her presence made Will's feel less strange. More as if Moira simply had houseguests, two of them instead of one. Of course, one of them was going to be staying a whole lot longer than the other.

Marriage might have been an even bigger mistake than sleeping with him had been in the first place. Moira stared at herself in the mirror and saw how dilated her eyes were, how shell-shocked she looked. And how not married. The first thing she'd done when she got home was change out of her wedding dress into a denim jumper over a forest-green turtleneck. Nicer than she probably would have put on if she'd been by herself, but comfortable. And a contrast to Will in his well-cut dark suit.

Seeing him today at the church, she'd wondered whether it was the same suit he had worn that night at the gala. When she'd approached him at the altar and he held out his hand to her, the moment had felt eerily familiar. As if the two scenes had layered one over the other, she'd seen him stepping into the hotel room, his eyes devouring her face. His expression had been similar—intense, maybe hungry, and yet also tender.

It was the tenderness, she admitted to herself, that got to her.

She slipped out of the bathroom after hearing his footsteps going down the hall. She lurked in the kitchen pretending to be thinking about what she'd make for dinner even though she already knew. What was she going to *do* all afternoon?

Will appeared in the kitchen. "What are you up to?"

"Um…making sure I took the chicken out of the freezer."

"You look tired." His voice was gentle. "Why don't you lie down for a bit?"

The minute he suggested it, Moira wanted that nap with all the desperation of a chocoholic grubbing for a hidden stash of Hershey's Kisses. She needed sleep. More, she needed oblivion. A chance to recharge.

"You know, I think I will. If you don't mind."

"No." He smiled at her. "You'll feel better."

"Where's Mom?"

"She's as determined as her daughter. She's out getting another load."

"Oh. Will you tell her…?"

"Yeah."

He didn't touch her as she went by, but she felt his gaze following her all the way to her room.

As overwhelmingly sleepy as she suddenly felt, Moira expected when she lay down to spend some time thinking about Will and the fact that they were married now and what that meant, but it didn't work that way. She kicked off her shoes, slipped under the covers and conked out.

THIS OUGHT TO FEEL SIMILAR to living at home, Will thought a week later. Somehow it didn't, even though he was used to sharing his home with a woman.

But Moira wasn't Sophie. He didn't feel about her the same way he did about his sister.

The two women had things in common, though. Neither of them took direction well. They were both smart, too, and curious. And they both had smiles that warmed his heart.

In some ways, of course, Moira was the more confident of the two. She was in her thirties, not twenty-one. She had a successful career. She'd won recognition as an architect, had homes and commercial buildings she'd designed featured in Sunday supplements of the *Seattle Times* and *The Herald*. She was more of an artist than most architects were, Will had seen; her sketches weren't only clear, they had grace and deserved to hang framed on the wall.

What he couldn't figure out was why she also had a quality of vulnerability that Sophie, who'd lost her parents early, didn't. Why that trace of sadness clung to Moira, why he'd been able to tell that she wasn't surprised at all when Bruce Girard treated her the way he did. Moira maybe wasn't beautiful by the standards set by fashion magazines, but Will was a hell of a lot more attracted to her generous curves than he would have been to any skeletal runway model. She was vibrant and sweet and yet had a quality of innocence that made him think of Botticelli's Venus, or maybe a Renaissance Madonna. Pregnant, she embodied fertility, but he never saw even a hint that she was aware of herself as a sensual woman.

He found he wanted to know badly whether she'd had her heart broken. Who had hurt her and why. Why she'd never married and had reached the point of being grateful to have become pregnant during a one-night stand.

Since their wedding day, she'd been as skittish with him as the dainty impala he had startled once at the edge of a Zimbabwe woodland. A patient man, Will was smart enough to bide his time. It was easy to talk about work, about clients and friends, to draw her out. He waited several days even to ask how she and Gray had gotten to be so close.

They were eating a dinner he'd cooked—grilled salmon and baby potatoes sautéed in butter and dill. Moira wrinkled her nose at the broccoli, but took a decent helping. He'd noticed that she wasn't fond of most green veggies, but Will was trying to make sure she ate right.

"How'd you and Gray get to be friends?" he asked, helping himself to another serving of potatoes, his tone deliberately casual.

"Our freshman year we were in the same dorm, same hall." Moira's smile was soft as she remembered. "We flirted a little, went out a couple of times and had a really great time. He kept coming by my room to hang out. We talked and talked, and somehow never got around to seriously making out or anything like that. Even then, Gray was always totally up front. One day he said, 'You're, like, the best friend I've made here, but I sort of get the feeling neither of us has the hots for each other,' and I realized he was right."

Had she really felt the same? Will couldn't help wondering. Or had she fallen in love and, given her lack of experience, was waiting for Gray to make a move?

Sounding breezy, she went on, "He told me about the girls he was seeing, I talked about guys. I ended up getting pretty serious about this one guy my junior year, and even so there's stuff I'd have never in a million years have told him that I'd already told Gray. When we graduated, we promised each other that someday we'd open a firm together."

"Promises like that are easy to make," he observed.

"And unlikely to be kept? That's what I thought. I went home to Missoula. I'd worked summers there for this firm and they offered me a job. Gray took one in Portland. I figured we'd drift apart."

"So what happened?" Will asked.

"It was Gray more than me. More than anyone I've ever met, when he says something he means it.

He had a goal, and he never let himself forget it. We talked often, emailed all the time and we both saved money. When we thought we had enough, Gray told me he'd found the perfect town. Aside from nixing a few places—with my skin, I don't do well at all in hot climates—I didn't care so much where we opened our firm. Gray, though, had this ideal town in mind, and as far as he was concerned West Fork was it. Small town, but close enough to Everett and even Seattle that we're not dependent on a strictly local clientele. And he was right. It's worked great."

"Was he already married when you moved here?"

She shook her head. "No, Charlotte had grown up on a farm here, but she came back to town again only last year when her dad needed her. She got pregnant pretty soon after the wedding. I don't think she and Gray planned it. Which I think is funny, because Gray plans *everything*."

Will nodded. There was no reason for him to be jealous of her relationship with Gray Van Dusen, but he felt a jab now and then anyway. There was a sense of intimacy between the two of them that made him wonder whether Moira would have liked her *friend* to feel more for her. Will knew she wouldn't admit it even if he asked, though, so he didn't.

"What happened with the college boyfriend?"

One shoulder lifted in a dismissive, who-knows shrug. "It wasn't the romance of the century. He met someone the summer between our junior and senior years and I didn't actually care."

Yet another guy who'd ditched her. Or was he reading entirely too much into normal stories of youthful romance? He'd had a girlfriend himself his freshman year, and he couldn't remember her last name or quite picture her face.

"Anybody serious since?"

She didn't quite meet his eyes. "Not really."

He wasn't buying that; she was thirty-five, not twenty-five. Most people their age had had a few near misses, at least.

Suddenly stunned, he thought, good God, what if it was true? What if she hadn't had the high of knowing a man she liked was falling for her? What if that college boyfriend had been the last? Was it possible?

After a moment, she said, "You?"

Surprised and pleased, since up to this point she'd avoided asking him anything very personal, Will said, "I've had a couple of relationships that lasted a year or more, but…" He frowned, mulling it over. "Truth is, I was pretty tied up, between the business and my sister and brothers. I was doing well to sneak away for a date once a week." His mouth tilted in a rueful smile. "Plus, I made a house rule that none of us could have overnight guests of the opposite sex. I was the one who suffered the most from it in the early years, but I didn't want home to degenerate into a frat-house atmosphere. Especially with my sister being the youngest. The rule broke down eventually, when each of them had college friends stay, but the friend always had a bed made up in the family room. If anybody sneaked down the hall…" He laughed. "I pretended not to notice."

She was smiling, too. "Even when it was Sophie's boyfriend doing the sneaking?"

"I might have been a little stricter with her. I guess you've noticed that I'm an old-fashioned kind of guy."

Quietly, Moira said, "We wouldn't be married if you weren't."

He couldn't read much with her eyes downcast. "No," he said after a moment. "I guess we wouldn't be."

"Dinner was good." She gave him a bright, artificial smile. "Thank you."

Right now, he was the original house-husband. What else did he have to do but grocery shop and cook on days when she didn't need him? A week into it, he'd have thought he would be bored to death, but strangely he wasn't yet. He'd been reading voraciously, a pleasure he hadn't been able to make much time for even once Sophie was off to college. Will had found he enjoyed accompanying Moira to job sites, too, seeing her in her element demonstrating a quickness of mind and creativity he admired. The contractors, electricians and plumbers she dealt with were almost universally men, but aside from a certain nervousness when their gazes strayed to her protuberant belly, they treated her straightforwardly and with respect. Will knew some of them, and he'd been careful to deflect any attempt on their parts to include him in discussions.

"This isn't my job," he'd say briefly. He wouldn't blame Moira for getting her back up if anyone tried to defer to him instead of her. Will did stay close to her from the minute they got out of her car or his pickup. If she so much as stumbled, he'd grab her or wrap his arm around her waist.

He thought she was starting to get used to having him touch her, progress of a kind. The first few times he'd laid a hand on her lower back as they walked, or reached for her to help her out of a vehicle, she'd been obviously startled. Today, she had walked in the front door looking exhausted, and when he pulled her to him she'd simply leaned, as if she had waited all day to do just that.

"No," he said now when she stood and started clearing plates. "I'll clean the kitchen. You sit."

"If you cook, I should clean."

"You worked today. I didn't." He took the empty serving bowl and plate out of her hands. "Want me to put hot water on for tea?"

She followed him to the kitchen but settled on a stool at the breakfast bar. At his question, she sighed. "No, it'll only make me have to, um…"

It amused him that she should be shy about something like that.

"Get up at night?" He raised an eyebrow at her. "According to the book about pregnancy I've been reading, that's pretty normal."

"You've been reading a book about pregnancy?" Moira looked aghast. "Why?"

"I want to know what to expect," he said simply.

"Speaking of which…" Color tinted her cheeks. "I need to start a childbirth class. Actually, I should have started a couple of weeks ago. And, well, I need a labor coach." She was talking faster and faster. "I wondered if you wanted to go with me. Except it would mean you being there. I mean, when I have the baby."

He'd opened the dishwasher, but now he straightened. What the hell? Had she been thinking of asking someone else? "I told you I intended to be there. Of course I want to be your labor coach."

"Oh. Well." Moira rubbed her fingertips on the tile counter. "Okay. Then I'll sign us up. It's only once a week."

He nodded, willing himself not to get pissed off. He felt more married than she did, but he couldn't blame her. He'd pushed her into this.

He was getting damn tired of repeating that to himself, but he'd keep doing it as long as he had to.

"We can practice the breathing at home," he said.

Moira nodded, then said a little tentatively, "I was thinking we might get a Christmas tree pretty soon. Unless you want to go to your brother's, or..."

"You mean, do *we* want to go to my brother's?"

He must have sounded ticked, because she looked wary. "I did assume you wouldn't take off Christmas Day and leave me behind. Although I spent last year with Charlotte and Gray and Faith and...oh, everyone. I'm sure we'd be welcome if we'd like to do that."

Damn it, this wasn't a minefield. She shouldn't have to watch her every word.

"What do you want to do?" he asked. "Can your mother come for the holidays? Or would she rather wait until you have the baby?"

"I think that's what she has in mind." She hesitated. "We should have Christmas with your family. Maybe have them here."

He reached across the counter and took her hand. "Yeah, I'd like to do that. Maybe just us Christmas Eve, unless you want to do something with Gray and Charlotte."

"They're having a party the Saturday before." Her smile was a little tremulous. "I'd like to get a tree. And maybe put up lights. If you don't mind climbing the ladder."

"I'd rather you keep both feet on the ground." He grinned at her. "I like Christmas. Bring it on."

Her smile brightened and he saw a glow of excitement in her eyes. "Have you shopped yet? I mean, for Sophie and everybody?"

"For a change, yeah." He laughed at her expression. "What did you think? I'm a guy. But in this case I brought presents from Africa." For her, too, but he didn't mention that. "I even have a few extra things. A basket your mom might like, for example." He'd packed a whole suitcase full of things that had caught his eye.

Moira gave a happy wriggle. "Let's get a tree next weekend."

Will felt a glow of his own, centered right under his breastbone. "Works for me."

Their first Christmas.

She might assume it would also be their last, but Will was finding that he liked being married to Moira. Failure wasn't an option. Starting a few traditions together spiced by Christmas spirit might be just the thing to convince her that they could be happy together.

"Oh, my," the childbirth instructor said when she saw Moira. "When are you due, dear?"

She must be enormous. Everyone who set eyes on her thought she should be ready to go into labor. "Not as soon as I look," Moira said. "My doctor wondered earlier on about twins, but my husband was a big baby and she thinks this one is going to be good-sized too."

The instructor's assessment was practiced. "You may not make it full-term. Well." She smiled at Moira then at Will, who stood behind her. "Welcome. Why don't you take a seat on one of the mats?"

Moira glanced around. There were six other couples and one very pregnant woman whose labor coach was likely her mother, given the resemblance between the two women. Will stood over Moira while she clumsily got to her hands and knees then sat with a groan.

"I feel like a...a hippopotamus," she mumbled to Will.

She loved his smile.

"They're actually graceful in water, you know," he told her. "It's when they lumber *out* of the water that they, uh..."

"Resemble me?"

His laugh was a low, husky rumble. "Something like that."

He sat behind her, spread his legs to each side of her and said, "Lean back against me."

With a sigh, she did. In theory, she still had a month to go, which made her wonder if she'd be able to get out of a chair by the last week. She was more grateful than she wanted to admit for Will's frequent helping hand. In fact, she was beginning to wonder how she'd have managed at all without him. And that made her uneasy. When was the last time she'd actually *needed* someone?

The class started off with breathing exercises. Moira felt silly lying on the mat panting and blowing, but the other women were doing it and Will had listened to the explanation with a seriousness that Moira found touching. Not that she would have expected anything different. He wouldn't be here with her if he didn't take *all* his responsibilities seriously.

And clearly, she was number one these days.

Kneeling beside her, he counted for her until the instructor had the women roll onto their sides.

"Coaches, now we're going to practice massage

techniques. Touch is important at keeping your partner relaxed. Some women feel their contractions in their lower backs. Others gather tension in their necks or between their shoulder blades. They might suffer from cramps in their calves. You'll learn to feel when the muscles knot and take advantage of the breaks between contractions."

She walked around the room, pausing to give suggestions. Moira had been embarrassed at the idea of Will giving her a back massage, but, honestly, it felt so good from the minute he laid his big hands on her shoulders that she only closed her eyes and sank into bliss.

He seemed to know how much pressure to bring to bear, working his way from her shoulders down her spine to her incessantly aching lower back.

"We'll do this at home, too," he murmured, kneading more firmly down there.

Moira couldn't help letting a groan escape her.

His hands momentarily went still. "Did I hurt you?"

"No. It felt really good," she admitted.

"Ah." After a noticeable pause, he resumed the massage.

The instructor stopped, watched for a moment and said, "Excellent."

She had already set up a projector, and she gave them the option of sitting on folding chairs or staying on their mats to watch a short film on the progression of labor. Will looked at Moira, and when she said, "I'm so relaxed now I don't think I *can* get up," he smiled, helped her sit up and drew her back to lean against him again.

At first she had trouble concentrating on the film.

With the lights dimmed, she was even more conscious of being wrapped in his embrace. He held her so securely, one hand splayed on her belly. The baby must like the feeling of his hand there, because he got active. After feeling the movement, Will chuckled quietly and began to rub her stomach. The gentle motion of his hand was astonishingly seductive.

But the film got more and more explicit. Moira found herself tensing up and gaping. When the credits rolled, she whispered, "Oh, my God."

"*That* was supposed to reassure us?" he said.

"I guess we're supposed to go into this knowing what to expect."

"I'd rather not, thanks."

His obvious shock lessened hers to the point where she could laugh. "Too late."

Will gave her a dark look, then hoisted her to her feet. Moira staggered on legs that felt as if they'd gone to sleep, and tipped against him. Once again, he enfolded her in his arms as if that's where she belonged.

Increasingly, she wished that was true. Wished they hadn't gotten married only because they'd accidentally made a baby together.

But it could be more. Couldn't it? Will had thrown himself wholeheartedly into the marriage as well as into impending fatherhood. If she did the same, they might make something of this. Maybe their marriage would never be the love match Charlotte and Gray had, but they could be happy. Moira wanted to believe it was possible.

They were both quiet walking out to the car. They were halfway home when Will said thoughtfully, "Do you suppose the baby will come early?"

"Dr. Engel didn't say anything."

"No." He'd accompanied her to her appointment today. "I just can't imagine you, a month from now…"

She couldn't, either. "If I'm a hippopotamus now, what will I be then?"

He chuckled and reached out to take her hand. "To tell you the truth, I've been thinking pygmy goat."

Moira faked indignation. "Wow, that's flattering!"

Will laughed again. "I happen to think they're cute."

When he said things like that, she got this warm flutter inside. She hoped, so much, that he meant it. If he really did like her, if he really *was* attracted to her, then maybe there was hope.

He was going to work with her tomorrow, as she had a couple of construction sites to visit. Both were on flat ground and were nearby, but he had insisted anyway, and Moira wasn't going to argue. His presence was reassuring in a way she didn't want to examine too closely. On the way into the house, they talked about her schedule. Then she said, "I think I'm going straight to bed."

Will nodded. "I'll probably read for a while."

The most awkward part of this whole marriage business was saying good-night. Tonight was no different. She wondered if he ever thought about kissing her. She knew that he always had the same expression on his face when he watched her turn to go down the hall, or when they parted outside their bedroom doors. It was… pensive. He was thinking really hard about something. He always stood where he was until she went into her room. A couple of times this week, she'd glanced back, to find his eyes on her.

Tonight she couldn't resist. One hand on the doorknob, she looked back. He was standing by the kitchen, one shoulder propped against the wall, his hands in his pockets. When their gazes met, Will didn't move, not a muscle, but although he gave the impression of being relaxed she somehow knew he wasn't at all. She'd have sworn his eyes had darkened. The air between them all but shimmered with tension. Moira found she was breathing hard when she slipped inside her room and closed the door behind her.

Maybe a man *could* lust after a very pregnant woman.

Or maybe she only wished Will could. Was.

It took her longer than usual to fall asleep. She kept listening for his footsteps or the bathroom door opening or closing and not hearing either. The baby decided this was an excellent time for some gymnastics.

She hadn't looked at the clock and didn't know how long it was before she had to go to the bathroom again. A half hour at least. She was getting back into bed when she finally heard Will's footsteps in the hall.

Sleep kept eluding her. Fifteen minutes later, sighing, she got up again. She hadn't had anything to drink all evening. She couldn't possibly have to pee again! But once she started thinking maybe she did, she couldn't get the idea out of her mind until she gave up and went to the bathroom.

As she was pulling up her nightgown, she thought she felt a damp spot in back. Alarm quickened in her. That was bizarre. She couldn't have wet herself in bed without realizing it, could she?

But she felt dampness between her legs, too. Really scared now, she sank down on the toilet and looked down at herself. Blood streaked her thighs.

CHAPTER TEN

WILL HAD JUST TURNED OUT his bedside lamp when he heard the soft snick of Moira's bedroom door opening. He didn't like it that she closed it at all; he had been leaving his open at night in case she ever called out for him. He lay rigid, waiting. She might be going to the kitchen, she might not need him at all....

"Will?"

He sat up and reached for the lamp. "Moira? What's wrong?"

The light came on, and he saw that she had taken only a couple of steps into his room. A long flannel nightgown enveloped her from neck to ankle. But it was her face he focused on, and the fear he saw.

"Will, I'm bleeding." Her voice was tremulous. "I think...I think I'd better go to the emergency room."

"God." He surged from bed and crossed the room to her. "Should I call 911?"

She bit her lip. "No, it's not that heavy. It's just... well, not quite spotting, a little more than that, but..." She drew a shuddery breath. "I don't think I should be bleeding at all."

Will gripped her upper arms and squeezed. "Even if they have to do a C-section right now, the baby should be mature enough to survive." He sounded one hell of a lot calmer than he felt. "Let's get to the hospital, okay?"

"Okay. Um…let me get dressed."

"I'll help. No. Hell. Let me throw on some clothes first." He'd worn only pajama bottoms to bed. "Go lie down."

Moira nodded and disappeared, ghostlike, from his room.

He'd never gotten dressed so fast. Will didn't bother with socks, simply shoved his feet into his running shoes. Then he went to her room. She'd actually curled up on the bed rather than ignore him and dress herself.

"All right. Tell me what you need."

"I already put on panties. A top and bottoms. There are some in the closet."

He grabbed the first ones his hands touched. Gently he helped her struggle out of her gown. Trying not to focus on her naked breasts, larger than they'd been, he tugged a knit shirt over her head then helped her slide on loose pants.

Moira insisted on walking, and he let her, although he kept an arm around her the whole way. Outside *was* cold, frost sparkling on the grass beneath the streetlight. Despite her parka, Moira shivered as he backed the pickup out of the driveway.

Will broke speed limits all the way to the hospital. She sat silent and tense beside him. Not until he braked in front of the brightly lit emergency entrance to the hospital did she say very softly, "I'm scared, Will."

"Oh, sweetheart." He hugged her, quick. "Let's not worry too much until we know there's reason to. Okay?"

She pressed her lips together and nodded, but her eyes were huge, her gaze clinging to his.

A couple of people in scrubs had come out, and

within moments had her in a wheelchair. He had to park the pickup before he could sprint in.

The next two hours were hellish, even though the emergency-room doctor found the baby's heartbeat immediately. The doc seemed okay, although he was younger than Will liked. He had a million questions. How much bleeding? When did it start? What color was the blood? Was she cramping? Had she had sexual intercourse this evening?

Moira flushed at that question and cast Will an agonized look before shaking her head.

Had she fallen? When had she last seen her doctor?

It seemed to Will that the level of tension in the room dropped noticeably after Moira told them that she'd seen her doctor today and that yes, she'd had a pelvic exam.

Nonetheless, they took her away for an ultrasound, and when they brought her back he still wasn't allowed into the curtained exam cubicle because now the doctor was doing yet another pelvic exam and cervical culture. Will hated like hell that he was out here and she was alone with her fear, staring at the ceiling while some strange doctor had his hand inside her.

Sitting in a plastic chair in the hall, Will prayed as he hadn't in years. Amazing how much more faith a man *wanted* to have at a moment like this. He'd read about some of the things that could go wrong in late-term pregnancy, including placental abruption, when the placenta separated from the uterine wall. If she started to hemorrhage, it could kill her as well as the baby.

Will groaned. He rubbed the back of his neck, wishing he hadn't educated himself, that he didn't know how serious the trouble Moira might be in.

"Mr. Becker?"

He looked up to see the green-garbed nurse, who said, "You can come in."

Will followed her through the gap in the curtains, his broad shoulders causing them to rattle on their rings. Lying on the narrow bed, Moira was covered now by a white blanket. The nurse had been bringing her warmed ones because Moira kept shivering as if she were cold. Cold, or in shock.

The moment he stepped into the cubicle, her eyes fastened desperately onto his face. A lump in his throat, he went to her side and took her hand in his, then looked at the doctor.

"At this point," the doctor said straight-out, "I'm not very concerned. The bleeding was minor, and it seems to have stopped. The fetus shows no signs of distress. I think this was likely triggered by the exam Mrs. Becker had earlier today. Minor instances of bleeding are most often associated with a pelvic exam or sexual intercourse. I have some question about the possibility of placenta previa—which means that the placenta is implanted over or near the opening to the birth canal. If it's the case at all, however, my guess is that it's resolving itself, as most often happens. Your doctor will want to keep an eye on it, however. And I'm sure it goes without saying that you need to let her know about any further bleeding."

Moira nodded. She looked drained, almost numb.

"I would certainly speak to Dr. Engel before you consider resuming sexual intercourse—"

"Fine," Will interrupted. "Should Moira be on her feet at all?"

"Assuming there are no further episodes of spotting, I see no reason she can't resume normal activity. No dancing." He chuckled, uttered a few pleasantries and went away.

Will breathed an almost-silent profanity and sank onto the chair beside the bed. "Damn. Does that mean we can go home?"

"I think so." Moira sounded uncertain. "I guess you were right that I panicked unnecessarily."

"You weren't the only one panicking," Will admitted. "I just tried to hide it."

Her smile trembled, but it was a smile. "I'd never have known. You're always so…steady."

"Practice," he told her. "Clay mostly avoided hurting himself, but I had to rush Jack and Sophie to Emergency way too often. You get inured." Which was a lie. Yes, he'd gotten so he barely rolled his eyes at a broken finger or even a broken arm—Sophie in particular had been an adventurer. But tonight, he'd been more scared than he could remember being in years. At least.

The nurse came in with discharge papers, and Will went to get the truck. They wheeled Moira out, helped her in, and not many minutes later he pulled into the driveway at home once again.

"Wow." Moira fumbled to unbuckle the seat belt. "I think I'll reschedule the stuff I was supposed to do tomorrow." She focused on the dashboard clock. "Not tomorrow. Today."

"How about you sleep in? Maybe even take the day off."

She must be shaken, because she nodded. "I think maybe I will. I'll set the alarm and call Gray—"

"I'll do it." When she opened her door, he said, "Wait until I get around there."

Wonder of wonders, she was docile again, waiting for his hand to take hers. She climbed the few steps to the front porch slowly, leaning a little as she went. When he helped her out of her coat right inside the front door, Will couldn't help thinking about how fragile she was. Generous curves or no, her bones were almost delicate. With the bulk of her pregnancy, it was easy to forget that.

"Let's see if I need to change any of your bedding," he said.

She went to the bathroom while he checked and found that her nightgown had apparently soaked up any blood and the sheet was fine. He pulled open drawers in her dresser until he found a clean nightgown. When she came back, she didn't argue when he reached for the hem of her top and drew it over her head. Moira did cover her breasts protectively, though. Again he tried not to look, but couldn't help himself. God help him. She had the most beautiful breasts he'd ever seen, ripe and full, creamy skin dusted with freckles paler than the ones on her face and shoulders. He regretted letting the gown drop to cover her body.

When he eased her back on the pillows, Moira said, "I'm not helpless."

"Tonight, let's pretend you are. For my sake."

She looked up at him, her eyes very green, and finally gave one small nod.

Bracing himself for argument, he said, "I'm going to sleep with you. I want to be right here, and know you're okay."

Her lips parted, then, after a perceptible pause, closed. She swallowed. "All right."

"Give me a minute to get undressed."

Will went back to his room and shed his clothes as quickly as he'd put them on. He thought about leaving on the T-shirt but decided not to. He'd always worn pajama bottoms because he'd had to get up often enough during the night with one of his brothers or his sister. That was as far as he was willing to go.

Moira watched warily when he returned to her room. He was grateful she had a queen-size bed, at least. They'd want a king-size eventually, he thought, but this would do for now. He slipped in on the far side from her, then rolled toward her.

"Do you sleep on your back?"

She shot him a glance that made him think of a spooked horse. "No. I was, um, waiting to turn out the light."

"Okay," he said agreeably.

Moira reached for the lamp and plunged them into darkness. After a moment, he felt her moving, settling. He reached out a hand and found she'd turned on her side facing away from him. Probably on the very edge of the mattress. No surprise. He gently rubbed her back. "Sleep tight, sweetheart."

After a moment of silence, she whispered, "Good night, Will." Yet another pause. "Thank you. For… being here tonight. For…I guess for being here at all."

He smiled. "You're welcome."

Then he waited. Waited until she relaxed, until he heard her breathing deepen and slow. Only when he was sure she was asleep did he move the last foot closer to her, slide his arm under her head, and spoon their bodies together. He went still when her breathing hitched, but she sighed and, it seemed to him, snuggled against him.

He lay there in the dark, her springy hair tickling his chin and throat as it hadn't since that first night, and smiled again. Very carefully, so as not to awaken her, he splayed his hand on the large mound of her belly. Then, his wife and child held safe and close, Will let himself welcome sleep.

WILL HOVERED THE NEXT DAY. There was no other word for it.

At first it was kind of nice. But nice wore off, and after a while, his edginess made hers worse. She'd stand up to go to the bathroom, and he'd automatically rise with her, as if she was bound to collapse going ten feet. She'd look up and discover he wasn't reading at all, he was watching her.

In case she didn't notice gallons of blood gushing forth.

By midafternoon, she was snapping at him. When all he did was raise an eyebrow, she huffed out a breath. "Maybe I should go into the office."

"No, you shouldn't."

Moira's eyes narrowed. "You know, I'm usually pretty competent at taking care of myself."

Will was sprawled in her easy chair, leaving the couch to her. He smiled. "I imagine you are."

"Last night excepted."

"Uh-huh."

"I freaked. I admit it. Today, I'm fine."

"Good."

"You're looking at me like you expect the worst."

"Maybe you should go take a nap," he said gently.

"Are you going to come in and stare at me while I sleep?"

He fiddled with the book he so obviously wasn't reading. "Can I check on you a time or two?"

"No." Moira rose from the couch and marched out of the living room. He was smart enough not to follow her.

She closed her bedroom door behind her with a satisfying click. Not quite a slam because that wasn't justified. But firm enough to make a statement.

She didn't even know why she was mad. Maybe it wasn't at Will at all. Maybe she was upset about her own predicament, for which God knows she bore almost all the responsibility, whatever Will said to the contrary. Yes, it took two to make a baby, but she'd practically shanghaied him. And now he was being so damn *kind,* and she was all mixed up because it felt so good to have someone to lean on, but it was also scary and unsettling because she'd gotten so used to not having anyone. All these emotions seemed to tangle inside her, like a knot that got tighter and more complicated the more she picked at it trying to separate one strand from another.

She would never in her life forget how it had felt this morning to surface and find her head pillowed on his biceps, his warm, strong body touching hers from neck to calves. His breath had tickled her hair and raised goose bumps on her nape. His other arm en-

closed her firmly and his hand lay open on her belly.
One of *her* hands had clutched his arm as if to make
sure he didn't get away. And she had loved waking up
that way. She couldn't help thinking about the night
she met him, the night they made this baby, and how
much she had wished he'd still been there the next
morning. How maybe everything would be different
if he'd hung around. This awful, almost painful longing swelled in her chest.

And, damn it, she had to pee! So instead of lying
there quietly savoring the experience of being snuggled by this man, or at least trying to deal with all
these complicated feelings he brought to life in her,
what she did was wriggle out from under his arm and
rush to the bathroom. And by the time she came out
he was awake, and his eyes on her embarrassed her, so
she collected clothes and went back in the bathroom to
shower—aka to hide out.

The rest of the day so far, nothing had felt quite
right. She both wanted and didn't want him to fuss.
All this emotional tumult annoyed her, it was so unlike her prepregnancy self.

Hormones. And the aftereffects of last night's scare.

I'm fine. Lying in bed so that she faced the side Will
had slept on last night, she stroked her stomach and
turned inward. *You're fine. Oh, baby, I was so afraid.*

If Will hadn't been here...

She'd have managed. As it turned out, she could
have driven herself. Or called Gray, or 911. Or even
Joan Phillips next door. She didn't *need* Will.

Eyes wide, she stared unseeing at the wall. Tonight
he'd return to her guest room across the hall, and she

wished that wasn't so. If they were really married…
But she didn't know whether they were or not.

He said he was committed, he said she was more important than his project in Africa, but…he'd also said that when the baby was a few months old, they'd talk.

And *that's* why panic swirled among all her other emotions, because it would be much, much worse to let herself believe he was really hers if he was only here on loan, so to speak.

She didn't know if she could bear it if that's all this was, all he was offering.

Oh, God, Moira thought, *I'm falling in love with Will.*

She was all but hyperventilating.

I'm already in *love with him.*

And he was so totally not in love with her, or he wouldn't have screwed her then slipped away into the night the way he did, not bothering to get in touch until he found out she was pregnant with his baby.

He was a good man doing the right thing, and how could she let him know she was starting to feel things that would tie him to her even more tightly? Her love would probably feel like ropes of guilt on top of his sense of responsibility. He probably thought they were becoming friends; wasn't that what always happened to her? And friends didn't want to wake up every morning for the rest of their lives with each other.

Instead of agonizing in silence she could ask if he saw himself going back to Africa in a couple of months. She lay staring at the ceiling knowing she didn't dare. What if he said yes? Think how miserable she'd be having to depend on him then, once he'd confirmed her fear that her need was all that held him here!

But if he didn't—if he said of course not…would she believe him?

Moira closed her eyes. No. No, she wouldn't.

WILL COULDN'T FIGURE OUT what was going on with Moira, but he was damned if he was going to give her the space she clearly wanted. What had she thought? He'd go snowboarding up at Stevens Pass and leave her alone for the day after she'd spent two hours in the emergency room the night before?

He kept getting this cold feeling. He had been wildly attracted to her from the minute he set eyes on her, but maybe for Moira he really had been nothing but a substitute. A bird in the hand, and she was tipsy enough not to be too particular, but now to her horror she was stuck with him.

God. What would he do if that's how she felt?

His throat almost closed up. Let her go. What else?

In a fit of frustration and something that might have been anger but was probably wounded feelings, he threw the paperback book across the living room, then winced when it thudded against the wall. Way to go. Throw a tantrum. What if she came out to see what the noise was?

Will made himself pick up the damn book and toss it on the coffee table. Then he went out on the front porch, needing the bite of fresh air. The neighborhood was quiet at this time of day, with most people at work and kids in school.

Half the houses or more already had Christmas lights up. Maybe he'd finally put up Moira's tomorrow, if he could get her to agree to stay put at Van

Dusen & Cullen. She'd like to see the lights up. That might make her smile.

Shit. What did it mean that he was still thinking of them as *Moira's* lights?

A sound escaped his throat, one he couldn't even identify. Despair, disgruntlement, who knew? For only a moment, Will had a longing vision of the highveld in Zimbabwe, vivid green fields of tea leaves, a kraal of round, thatch-roofed huts housing the workers, tumbled slabs of granite topping a ridge. Some uniquely African baobab trees that would look so alien if they were transported here. His nostrils flared, trying to catch smells nothing like the sharp, cold air of winter here in the Northwest, air that carried a whiff of wood smoke. And that probably illegal, with the frequent burn bans aimed at reducing smog.

Then he remembered the way Moira had looked at him last night as if he was her everything, as if she did need him, and the angry tension left him. Just like that.

What an idiot he was. He was expecting too much, too soon. He had his own mixed feelings, of course she did, too. There must be times he felt like an intruder to a woman who had indeed taken care of herself just fine for…years. Had she ever lived with anyone else after she'd left home at eighteen?

Yeah, she was probably wrestling with the adjustment, the same as he was. He'd been careful not to let her see any of his regrets, and he needed to keep it that way.

Will shivered. It hadn't gotten above freezing today. Ice still glittered on the lawn. And he was standing out here in his stocking feet and shirtsleeves.

Feeling like an idiot, he went inside.

Yeah, Christmas lights along the eaves tomorrow. That would be good. Right now, he'd think about dinner. One thing Moira hadn't objected to was his cooking. Evidently, she wasn't real fond of cooking. So that was something he could do for her.

But give her space? No, Will decided. With her so wary, it was up to him, if he really wanted this marriage to amount to anything. And maybe he was still a little stunned over the right turn his life had taken, maybe he still wrestled with some doubts and some regrets, but he also knew he'd never walk away from Moira and his baby, not of his own volition.

A big empty pit opened in his stomach when he thought of having to walk away because she sent him, because she didn't want him.

She was a complicated woman with secrets he hadn't yet plumbed, but he had to believe she could come to trust him and maybe even love him.

They were married. Last night, they'd shared a bed. And as far as he was concerned, continuing to share a bed was a step in the right direction. Actions were what counted, not words.

HE WAS A BULLDOZER. A steamroller. Moira already knew that, but wasn't thinking it when, at nine o'clock, she said good-night.

Will stood. "I think I'll go to bed, too."

Feeling him practically breathing down her neck as they went down the hall, she was glad to turn into her room.

"Leave your door open," he said.

She hesitated. Was that an order? A request? But truth was, the closed door was more symbolic than anything, and maybe she would feel better knowing he'd hear her if she called out. So she nodded. "All right."

She plucked her nightgown from under the pillow and went to her bathroom. She'd corralled her hair in a loose braid that morning, and now she decided to leave it. Who cared what it looked like? She dutifully flossed and brushed her teeth, dropped her dirty clothes in the hamper, and, after taking one alarmed look at her naked self in the tall mirror on the back of the door, hurriedly put on the gown.

I'm pregnant. Not fat.

She had to tell herself that ten times a day. She'd once been fat, and she wasn't going to be again. She tried really hard not to think about the way her weight had climbed. Even more with Will cooking. According to the doctor, she was doing fine, so she shouldn't recoil every time she caught a glimpse of herself.

But…wow. She *looked* fat.

Feeling more hippopotamuslike than ever, she got herself settled in bed and was reaching for the lamp switch when Will strolled into her bedroom as if she was supposed to be expecting him. Last night, she'd been too shaken up to notice how sexy he was wearing nothing but a pair of flannel pajama pants hanging low on his hips. Those shoulders were so broad and powerful. Dark hair dusted a wonderfully muscular chest and narrowed into a line that disappeared beneath the waistband of the pajama bottoms. Despite herself, her gaze lowered, taking in the whole length of him. It didn't help that she *knew* what was below that waistband.

"What are you doing here?" Her voice squeaked.

He stopped at the foot of the bed. "I'll sleep better here with you."

She felt silly, sitting up and clutching the covers to her like some Victorian maiden afraid of being defiled. Even so, she heard herself say, "Well, maybe I won't."

"Moira, we're married."

"You agreed we wouldn't—"

"I'm not trying to seduce you. I only want to sleep with you. You scared me last night. I like being here where I can touch you. Hear you breathing." He paused. "Didn't you find it a little bit comforting to have my arms around you last night?"

Oh, God. Yes. *Yes.*

Moira opened her mouth and nothing came out. She closed it, opened it again. Every instinct screamed, *Don't let him this close or you won't be able to save yourself,* but the truth was, she wanted him here. The idea of his hand spread protectively over her belly made her feel warm and weak enough in the knees it was lucky she wasn't standing up.

"Okay," she finally said, in a small gruff voice, and lay down.

Will didn't smile or say anything. He simply climbed into bed. He didn't reach for her the way she half expected.

Hoped.

Moira turned out the light. She lay completely still, excruciatingly conscious of Will beside her.

After a minute, she whispered, "I'm sorry."

The pause was so long, she wasn't sure he was going to respond. "For what?" he asked.

"I've been awful today. I know I have. I just, uh…"

She just what? Was scared to death, not of losing the baby but of losing Will?

As if he had known right where her hand was, his closed over it. "It's okay," he said, his voice low, rough. "Believe it or not, I understood. Sometimes I should back off, but…"

A bubble of laughter rose, warming her chest and catching her by surprise. "You're a bulldozer. I've noticed."

"Sometimes ground needs clearing." Now there was a smile in his voice.

"Sometimes it does," she admitted, and realized she was smiling even though he wouldn't be able to see.

"I like being here with you."

"I, uh, kind of like it with you here, too," Moira said shyly. "I'm…not used to it."

"I'm not, either." He squeezed her hand. "We can get used to it together."

"Okay," she whispered.

"Would you mind if I cuddle you?"

She shook her head, realized he couldn't see her. "No-o. Except I do get up several times a night, you know."

"I know." She heard his amusement. "Even with the door shut, I can hear water running in the pipes after you flush the toilet."

"Great," she muttered.

He laughed, let her hand go, then gathered her firmly into his arms. She found her head right where it had been when she woke up this morning, and had the fleeting wish that she wasn't wearing a nightgown. She would have liked to feel his skin against hers. But despite the strangeness of being held like this, it felt so good that a soft, whispery sound of pleasure escaped her lips.

Will's chest vibrated with a silent chuckle. His hand on her distended belly moved in a soothing, circular pattern.

Moira was smiling as her eyes drifted closed.

CHAPTER ELEVEN

FOUR DAYS BEFORE CHRISTMAS, Moira had scheduled a site inspection. The client was mad because he'd carried a tape measure on a walk-through of his framed-in house and found that the downstairs powder room was six inches narrower than the plans showed. If he was right, she wasn't going to be happy, either. What she specified was what got built. Now, by God, she and the contractor were going to measure every room, wall and door opening.

Well, probably Will would find a place to tenderly deposit her while *he* and the contractor measured. He was a bully that way.

He'd left her alone for the morning, but came into the office at noon, several white bags dangling from one hand, a plastic grocery sack from the other. In jeans, heavy sweater and down vest, he looked even bigger and more imposing than usual. He brought in a rush of cold and the scent of winter. White flakes dusted his dark hair.

"It's snowing?" she said in surprise, turning to look out the window.

"Yep. Just a skiff, nothing to worry about." He smiled and set the bags on her desk. "Lunch, as promised."

"I suppose it's wholesome," Moira said gloomily.

She liked salads, mostly. Or the veggie wraps from The Pea Patch. Just, once in a while... Her nostrils flared and she snatched at the first sack. "Do I smell...?"

"I thought you deserved a treat." He sat on the same corner of her desk Gray had made his own. "Burgers and fries."

Moira moaned and took out a small carton of French fries.

Will laughed, but something flared in his eyes as she popped the first deliciously salty fry into her mouth.

"Damn, woman," he muttered.

She swallowed and reached for more. "Better eat, or there won't be any left."

He shook his head, still laughing. "Want a drink?"

"Please, please tell me it has caffeine in it," she begged.

"Apple juice or milk."

"Well, damn." She waffled briefly. "I guess I'll forgive you. Given how very, very grateful I am for the cheeseburger. It does have cheese on it?"

"Would I leave it off? You've got to get your calcium."

This was absolutely the best lunch she'd had in weeks. The worst for her, but he was right: she did deserve a treat, and she wouldn't feel guilty.

"Milk," she decided. "Unless you'd prefer...?"

"Juice is fine by me." He unscrewed the lid from the bottle and took a long swallow. "I got something else you'll like, too."

Moira paused with a burger halfway to her mouth. "A present?"

"Not exactly, but it's Christmassy." He shook his

head before she could say a word. "Patience, patience. You have to wait to see."

He entertained her while they ate by telling her about all the children he'd seen that morning, from what he swore was a brawl being conducted on an elementary-school bus he'd followed for blocks—the driver oblivious in front—to a baby that screamed non-stop the entire time Will was in the grocery store.

"Man, it was like a fire engine," he reminisced. "Undulating. When that kid hit the high notes, the glass on the freezer cases shivered."

"It did not."

"Cross my heart." He did just that. "The glass wasn't all that shivered. I did, too. What are we in for, Moira?"

"Sleepless nights?" She wadded up her lunch wrappings and dropped them in the trash can, then heaved herself out of her desk chair. "I suppose we'd better go."

Gray arrived and stood there smirking as Will bundled Moira into her parka and checked to be sure she had gloves and a knit hat.

"My mommy used to do that for me." He paused. "When I was four."

Moira made a rude face. "Will's being a gentleman."

Her partner's chuckle followed her and Will out.

A very few flakes of snow still floated lazily down from a sky that was pearly gray. Maybe they'd have a white Christmas. The moment she saw Will's pickup, she smiled with delight. He'd affixed a big evergreen wreath decorated with holly leaves and berries as well as a fat red bow onto the hood so that it hung above the license plate. It was an unexpectedly frivolous note on his utilitarian, slush- and mud-splattered, black vehicle.

"It is Christmassy. Thank you."

"I deserve a kiss, don't you think?" her husband suggested.

Wow. As always when she thought of him that way, Moira felt a punch of surprise. *Her husband.*

When he bent down, she brushed her lips over his. His tongue took a lazy swipe inside her lips before he lifted his head. "Milk," he murmured.

Tingling from the pleasure of a too brief kiss, she ran her own tongue where his had sampled. "Apple juice."

Will opened the passenger door for her and boosted her in. "We live wild."

"Right." Moira groaned.

On the verge of shutting the door, he yanked it back open. "What? *What?*"

"I just remembered we have the childbirth class tonight."

"God." Will pressed a gloved hand to his chest. "Don't scare me that way."

"Wimp."

He snorted and slammed her door. Once he'd gotten in behind the wheel, he said, "So, where are we going?"

The development was on the west side of the freeway, just north of Lake Ki. She told him, saw him nod and make mental calculations, then put on the turn signal. She'd been impressed by how quickly he'd learned how to get around the north county, as if he'd drawn a mental map in his head. Moira got lost easily. She had to go someplace two or three times before she could reliably find it again without her GPS.

"Expect problems?" he asked.

She told him about the call from the homeowner and he grunted.

"Well, that sounds like fun."

"Yes, and it will get us all into the holiday spirit."

Their holiday spirits did lift when they arrived at the house-in-progress to find that Christmas lights were strung along the eaves and were plugged in. The lights, twinkling against unfinished wood, seemed to represent hope.

"Oh." Moira smiled, feeling suddenly more forgiving even if Ralph Jakes, the contractor, wasn't responsible.

Will parked behind three pickups, then came around to help her out. The raw, uneven ground was frozen solid and she had to pick her way. Moira had never been more grateful for Will's strong supporting arm.

She could hear the whine of a circular saw, the rhythmic punch of a nail gun at work, male laughter. The front door, still lacking knob and dead bolt, stood open.

"Hello," she called as soon as they were inside, and the saw paused.

Ralph appeared at the top of the roughed-in staircase. "Moira." He nodded resignedly. "I hear we screwed up."

"So Chuck says."

"Hell, we're already tearing it out."

She relaxed. She'd worked with Ralph before, and had believed him to be solid. "You checked other dimensions?"

"Yeah, but I'll bet you're going to do it again."

She grinned at him. "Yep. Will and I will. Have you met my husband, Will Becker?"

She *had* gotten almost used to introducing him that

way. In fact, instead of uneasiness she'd begun to feel a small surge of proprietary pleasure in claiming him.

Unease tiptoed down her spine. What if by spring he was gone, and she had to tell all these same people that she was getting divorced?

She wouldn't think about that. Not now.

A flicker of interest showed in Ralph's eyes at the introduction. "Becker Construction?"

"My brother Clay is currently heading it."

"You're the one went off to…was it China? Something like that?"

"Africa." Will's voice was neutral. "That was me. I'm back." His hand moved in a seemingly unconscious yet reassuring way on the small of Moira's back, under the parka.

The contractor's attention switched to her. "Hell, Moira, you look like you're going to pop any minute. You sure you should be out here?"

She sighed. "My design, my job, Ralph. Though Gray will be stepping in for a few weeks."

He left them alone. She heard him yelling at someone upstairs.

Moira unrolled plans on a sheet of plywood atop two sawhorses that was being used as an impromptu table. Then she held one length of the metal measuring tape and let Will do most of the work. He referred frequently to the plans. It took them an hour to be confident the powder room was the only foul-up. She was pleased with how the house was going up otherwise. On a cold, clear day like this she could appreciate the way the sweep of windows took advantage of a view of the lake, the privacy gained by her having angled the house slightly to tuck it behind a mature stand of fir and cedar. She still thought the kitchen would have worked better without quite so much floor space, but the client had insisted.

Ralph walked them out so that he could discuss a couple of minor problems, one of which was going to necessitate her tweaking plans. With electrical in, he reminded her, an inspector would be out after the new year.

"We're winding up tomorrow," Ralph told her, "then taking the week between Christmas and New Year's off."

"Makes sense," she agreed. "You can't get wallboard up until we clear the inspection."

As she and Will started the drive back, he said, "Something I've been wondering."

Still thinking about the tweak she'd be making, she made an absentminded, questioning noise.

"Your house. Looks like it's, what, 1940s?"

She started paying attention. "Uh-huh. Postwar."

"You're an architect. Why buy an older place? Why haven't you designed your own?"

She asked herself that once in a while. The stock answer was easy enough, though. "When I first came to West Fork, I was focused on the building that houses our office."

Will glanced at her with interest. "You designed that?"

"Yes. We own it. Gray and I."

"So you're landlords."

Moira smiled. "We have trouble-free tenants. No one has trashed our office yet." She shrugged. "As for my house...I thought about renting for a while, then building like Gray was doing, but I didn't like the idea of having to move twice in a short time. So I went ahead and bought. I guess…" The snow had quit falling and barely dusted the pasture beside the road. A promise, like the Christmas lights on an unfinished house. She concluded, "I wasn't ready."

"Because you didn't have a family to share it with?"

"Maybe," she admitted.

"But Gray did build his own place right away, and he wasn't married, either."

Will and she had been to Gray and Charlotte's for dinner a couple of times already, and she'd been able to tell how much he admired the house.

"He's different. I've told you what Gray's like. He had a plan."

"A plan?"

"Choose town. Check. Establish firm. Check. Build house. Check. Get married. Took him a *lo-ong* time to put a check there. I think he was a little disconcerted that his perfect woman didn't appear on schedule. Everything was supposed to fall into place." She found herself smiling as she remembered. "And when she did appear, Charlotte wasn't so sure she *wanted* to cooperate. Gray isn't used to being thwarted."

"But he got his way in the end." Will sounded reflective. It occurred to Moira, not for the first time, that the two men had quite a bit in common. In their own, equally agreeable ways, they were both bulldozers. Steamrollers.

"Gray usually does," she said simply.

Will drove with effortless competence. She suspected he was being particularly careful for her sake not to take corners sharply or stop too abruptly. She noticed that he never got in that first thing he didn't glance at how she'd positioned the two straps of the seat belt around the increasingly gigantic swell of her belly. It was probably a surprise that he didn't minutely adjust the belt before he was willing to start out.

From her peripheral vision she caught Will's quick glance. His tone, though, betrayed nothing but mild curiosity. "So he had a plan, and you didn't."

"Didn't I say Gray always has a plan?"

Will's hands flexed lightly on the wheel. "Because he's an optimist."

She frowned a little. "I suppose that's it."

"And you? You're a pessimist?"

Disconcerted, she took a moment before she answered. "Not in some ways."

"But your personal life. Hard not to tell that you have trouble expecting the best for yourself."

Maybe that's because she'd never gotten it.

The whisper came from deep inside. It wasn't so much bitter as sad. And it shocked her.

She hadn't had a terrible life. She'd had a happy childhood. She loved her mother. They'd stayed close, even when other kids her age were all rebelling against their mothers. And Gray. She'd been so lucky to find him. His friendship had changed her life.

Still stunned, staring blindly ahead, Moira thought, *Yes, but...*

There had always, in her mind, been a *but*. Maybe rooted in the fact that her father hadn't wanted her, maybe not. Deepened by those painful years when she'd been overweight and therefore self-conscious, when she hadn't been so much teased as friendless. Then later, even after she'd lost the weight, she hadn't really known how to flirt, and the boys she'd grown up with had gotten used to seeing her in a certain way so she didn't date. She didn't get invited to her senior prom.

She had felt such hope when she went off to college. It would be her new start. And it had been, in some ways. There was Gray, and she did date, and eventually she'd had a serious boyfriend for most of a school year.

But—yet another *but*—even that romance had fizzled, and though she'd dated off and on in the years since, the relationships never passed casual. Men didn't fall in love with her. They didn't want her passionately. And knowing that hurt.

For the very first time, Moira wondered if it was possible that *she* hadn't seen herself as lovable, as desirable. Whether other people might have if she had. Was she inadequate, or did she just think she was?

The very idea shook her. She didn't know which was worse: to *be* undesirable, or to have wasted years of her life because she was so screwed up.

God. I'm pathetic.

Self-pity was not an attractive quality.

She suddenly became aware that Will had parked in front of Van Dusen & Cullen, Architects, and had even turned off the engine. He'd half turned in his seat, his forearm laid across the top of the steering wheel, and was watching her sit frozen with her unwelcome self-revelation.

"Wow," she said, trying for a laugh that was such a failure it was—oh, God—pathetic. "You set me off. And not in a good way. You're right. I'm doom and gloom, and I didn't even realize it."

"Not doom and gloom." He had a way, even with that deep, sometimes rumbly voice, of sounding so gentle her defenses crumbled. "That's not you at all, Moira. But I feel a sadness in you sometimes that I don't understand."

"I don't understand it, either," she whispered. "I didn't know."

He reached out and squeezed the back of her neck with a big, warm hand. His fingers had become practiced at easing muscle tension even in a brief caress. This one wasn't brief; he worked her neck until she bowed her head, closed her eyes and let go of her bout of bewilderment and unhappiness.

Eventually she managed to clear her throat and lift her head. She met his steady, dark gaze with the flicker of a genuine smile. "Man, you should change professions. A Will Becker massage fixes all problems."

He laughed for her sake. She knew it was for her, because his eyes remained dark and worried.

"I'm just trying to understand you," he told her.

I'm trying to understand me, too.

And why, she had to ask herself, *is this suddenly all about me?*

Wasn't *Will* the one who'd given up everything for his sister and brothers, then had to do so again for her? Did she understand *him?*

Had she tried?

"I know," she said, a little shakily. "I do know. I'm… really lucky to have you." She managed a smile. "And now I'd better get back to work."

"Okay." His knuckles brushed her cheek, then he released her seat belt and his. He issued his standard order, "Wait for me," and got out to help her down.

She was so lucky.

And hated the whisper, the pathetic whisper, that

said, *Yeah, you're lucky right now, but how long will all this last, given that he only married you because he thought he had to?*

CHRISTMAS WAS...NICE. Will and Moira didn't do anything that special on Christmas Eve, their gifts to each other weren't extravagant, but they were right. He could tell she really did love the soapstone bowl and the wooden carving he'd brought her from Africa, and she'd bought him an unbelievably soft alpaca scarf the exact color of his eyes—she said—as well as a couple of books that he had trouble tearing himself away from once he flipped open the covers. Her choices told him she listened to him and paid attention to what he said and maybe even to some of his silences.

One of those books was about a project not so different from the one he'd taken on in Zimbabwe, this one in South Africa. He could hardly wait to read it, but even a glance inside at the photos gave him a pang. He tried to hide that, though, when he looked up to find Moira watching him.

"Looks interesting," he said, more casually than he felt, and set it aside.

He'd built a fire in the fireplace, and he and Moira snuggled on the sofa sipping hot chocolate and gazing dreamily at the lights on the Christmas tree they had put up two weeks before. The sharp scent of fir needles reminded him of Christmases past, of times before he'd lost his parents, of trembling in bed waiting for the first light of dawn before he could wake Mom and Dad to open presents. Of his first bike, of the year he'd itched like crazy from chicken pox and was mad as blazes because he'd gotten it over the holiday and wouldn't even have the benefit of missing school. His first car, a used clunker, had been a Christmas gift, too, the year he was sixteen. He thought about the effort he'd put into making sure Sophie, Jack and Clay had memories as good as his of the holidays.

He found himself talking about them, about how glad he'd been the first year that Sophie, then seven, had become disillusioned about Santa Claus.

"It was sort of sad," he said, "as if that one year all her illusions got shattered, but, man, it would have been hard to keep that one propped up if she'd been young enough to beg Santa to bring her mommy back." He fell silent, remembering that particular Christmas when they had all ached with loss and any celebration was more pretence than reality. Even then, though, it had never occurred to him to say, "Let's skip it this year."

Moira, tucked under his arm, was for once utterly relaxed. "I forget sometimes that you're an experienced dad."

He gave a short laugh. "Not with babies or diapers. When Clay was born, I was still pissed that my father remarried and had another kid to threaten my place. By the time Jack came along, I was too tough a guy to be talked into helping with any baby. And I was a teenager when Soph was born. I sure as hell didn't want anything to do with her bare bottom."

"And then you ended up daddy to all of them."

He grunted an agreement. "Fate does throw you a curve ball sometimes, doesn't it?"

"You must still get nightmares about that first year or so," she said quietly.

"You're back to me admitting I felt trapped," he realized. "I can't lie. I did at first, and I guess I never

threw that belief away. I tucked it in my wallet like…
damn, a Dear John letter. I could pull it out now and
again even as the folds on it frayed and the ink became
unreadable. And yeah, I still know what it said, but…"
He shrugged, knowing she'd feel the motion. "Truth
is, when I think back most of my memories are good
ones. I didn't know how good until I went away and
found out how much I missed them. It shouldn't have
been such a surprise, because when each of them left
for college I had this big hole inside." He touched his
chest with his free hand. "But I'm stubborn. I guess
you've noticed that."

She gave him a quick, amused grin.

He laughed. "The thing is, I'm stubborn enough not
to always admit I was wrong even when I should. Or
even to realize that I was. I saw myself as having to
give up everything I'd ever wanted to fill in for my dad.
I was mad at him for dying. But now I think…sure, I
lost a lot of choices I might have made, but somehow
the four of us cobbled together quite a family. And my
life has been pretty damn rich to this point. I still don't
know what I wanted to grow up and be. Who's to say it
would have been any better than what I had?"

Moira was silent for a long time. "Do you mean
that?"

Will could admit to himself that he'd started with
the intention of reassuring her that taking on an unexpected family wasn't so bad the first time around,
which meant he really didn't mind having his life de-
railed a second time by yet *another* unexpected family. The funny thing was, as he'd talked he had known
he meant it. He was as proud of Sophie and his brothers as any father would have been. He *liked* all three

of his siblings. When he looked back, he remembered doing a lot of laughing along with the quiet swearing when he was by himself.

Keeping the business in the black those first years had been the most hair-raising. He'd known the construction side, but not the business itself. He'd made a lot of mistakes, lost good employees, hired some lousy ones. But after a couple of shaky years, he had found his footing and made a success of Becker Construction, too. He'd built it into a bigger company than his father had left him, one with a solid gold reputation. He was proud of that, too. Proud he'd saved a legacy from Dad for Clay and Jack.

"I do mean it," he told Moira. "I'm a different man than I would have been if my dad and stepmom hadn't died when they did, but it's possible I'm a better one."

In a strange, gruff little voice, she said, "I think you're a very good man, Will Becker. I just wish I didn't think you're such a good man, you'd lie to me to keep me from believing I've taken advantage of you."

He had a fleeting and uncomfortable instance of wondering if he might be lying even to himself. He didn't think so, even though it was a little unsettling to realize he had been looking at his own life upside down all along. No matter what, it didn't seem like words were going to convince her that she could count on him. She wouldn't believe him if he said, "I love you." Time, he thought, might be his only hope.

What he did was lay a hand on her stomach and rub. "This is *our* baby, Moira. This time, I really will be Daddy. I wouldn't want to be anywhere but here."

And that *was* the truth, whether she wanted to believe it or not.

She took a sip of her now cooling cocoa and didn't say anything else. But her belly surged under Will's hand and a knob poked his palm.

"Amazing," he murmured.

"It is, isn't it?" Moira whispered.

He turned his face to nibble her earlobe. "Merry Christmas, Mama of my baby."

He felt more than saw her smile. "Merry Christmas, Daddy," she said softly.

THEY MADE TWO MORE CHILDBIRTH classes, one the week before New Year's, one the week after. Two more visits to her obstetrician, too. Her due date was the fifteenth, but at the last visit, Dr. Engel said, "You're *sure* about when you conceived this baby?"

Will and Moira exchanged a glance. Newly self-conscious, Moira nodded. "Very sure."

"I doubt you'll last another week." She smiled at them. "Daytime labor would be nice."

Apparently that was a joke. They both laughed dutifully.

Once the doctor had whisked out the door, Will helped Moira sit up. It wasn't easy. Chuckling, Will said, "Now you're a pregnant pygmy goat."

All she muttered was, "God."

On the way home, she made a few observations about how unlikely it was that this gigantic, linebacker kid of theirs would be able to exit her body in any approved manner. Under her breath, she said, "It's the *Invasion of the Body Snatchers*. No one else in the Lamaze class looks anything like me."

"Most of them aren't as close to due."

"Mindy is. Did you *see* her?" The tiny blonde was

the hateful kind of woman who'd have her prepregnancy figure back two weeks after she delivered.

"Her baby'll probably be five pounds and have to spend two weeks in an incubator."

"While ours will come out crawling. At *least* rolling over. He sure does plenty of that now. Especially when I'm trying to sleep."

Will thought that was funny. He wasn't the one who was barely sleeping in brief snatches.

Moira sighed. "I am so ready." She brooded on that for a moment. "What if he's *late?* If I have *weeks* left?"

"You won't." Will patted her hand. "I promise."

Like he had any more idea than she did.

He parked in the driveway at home and turned to look at her. Abruptly, he said, "I don't want you going back to work."

She'd managed half days this week because four hours was as long as she could bear either to sit in her desk chair or perch on the stool at her drafting table. Gray and Will had, together, nixed any more site inspections for her, and she hadn't argued.

"Gray's got another—" she had to calculate "—week in office."

"He can call in absent to city hall," Will said in a hard voice. "Or you guys can hang up a closed sign for a week. This has to be a deadly slow time of year anyway."

"Not so much. A lot of people are planning for spring." Moira hesitated. "I guess I'm pretty much done, though."

Will looked closely at her, but didn't gloat at her capitulation. He only nodded and got out to come around and help her. Once they were inside, he said, "Nap?"

"I might as well lie down." Her back was killing her.

"I'll give you a massage."

"I'd love that," she admitted.

He followed her into the bedroom and sat on the bed once she'd settled herself on her side, facing away from him. Then he lifted her shirt and went to work, those big strong hands unerringly finding every ache and kneading as if she were stiff bread dough. Pure bliss.

Eventually his touch became more gentle. He was soothing her to sleep, and it worked.

The backache returned more fiercely that night. By the following day an occasional contraction rippled across her stomach, turning it rigid beneath her touch. Moira didn't tell Will. He'd fuss worse than he already was.

One week exactly before her due date, Moira couldn't sleep at all. The contractions become more painful, more frequent. Will had sprawled onto his back beside her. If he'd had his arm around her, his hand settled in its usual place, he would have felt the waves of tension seizing her. But she waited and let him sleep, her gaze on the clock.

Finally, she groaned and had to pant when the sharpest one yet gripped her in bands of steel.

"Huh? What?" Will rolled toward her.

She could only keep panting.

"Oh, God," he said. "That's it, sweetheart. One, two, three, four. You can do this."

He got her dressed, got her to the hospital. He had to go park and she could tell he'd been running when he re-joined her. Moira fumbled for his hand and held on tight. She needed him. She did. His voice, his touch, his eyes, became the center of her world.

Eight hours and forty-five minutes later, Caleb Graham Becker was born.

CHAPTER TWELVE

IT WAS ALL WILL COULD DO to tear himself away from Moira's side. The sight of his wife nursing his son was so stunning, he had a giant lump in his throat and wasn't sure he could have said a word. Caleb hadn't taken much urging to latch on to his mommy's breast. He was so small, so precious. And for all that Moira looked exhausted, her hair sweat-dampened and matted, she was also lit up from inside with a glow that made her beautiful. Will hadn't known he could feel so much.

But she finally said, "You'll call Mom?" and he reluctantly nodded.

"Yeah. Sure." He started toward the door. "I'll be right back."

For a moment he wasn't sure she'd even noticed he was leaving. He felt a sharp slice of pain. For all that he'd held Caleb first, had been the one to lay their baby in Moira's arms, Will had this momentary fear that she had what she needed now, and it wasn't him, that he was on the outside looking in.

Then she looked up and gave him a smile that started soft and grew radiant. "Oh, Will," she murmured, and he found himself grinning idiotically at her. How foolish to get his feelings hurt for nothing.

"I'll hurry," he repeated, and left.

He went downstairs and stepped outside, startled to realize it was daytime. A part of him felt it should still be the middle of the night. He glanced at his watch. 11:20 a.m. Almost lunchtime. He had the same sense of disorientation he did after an international flight. The last hours had seemed entirely apart from the normal flow of time.

Shaking his head, he stepped aside from the double doors as a family pushed an old woman in a wheelchair in. He took out his cell phone and called Moira's mom first.

"You have a grandson," he told her, smiling as she exclaimed and wept and begged for details.

"Quite a bit of hair, I think you'd call it auburn. Not as bright as Moira's, but there's some red in it. I couldn't tell with his eyes, they were kind of muddy. Maybe they're going to turn brown. Uh…he's eight pounds, nine ounces. Thank God he was a week early," he said fervently.

Her mother laughed. "Has he said his first word yet?"

Discovering his legs were a little shaky, Will leaned against the stucco wall and laughed, too. "No, and I don't think he's quite ready to crawl, either. Now, if he'd had another week…"

"Think what a grump his mother would have been by then."

He was still laughing when he called Becker Construction and told Clay the news. Clay didn't weep, but he sounded staggered.

"Man. Are you going to call Sophie?"

"Yeah. You'll tell Jack?"

"Hell, yes! Can we come up and see the kid in a couple of days?"

"Any time after we're home and Moira's rested."

He then called his sister, who predictably enough did cry. She also, if he was hearing right, was jumping up and down while screaming, "So cool!" But then she went quiet, and finally said softly, "And you named him after Dad. That was, um…"

Will had to clear his throat. "I'm glad Moira liked the name."

"Oh, Will."

She, too, promised a visit, although thought she'd probably wait a couple of weeks.

Then Will made one more call, to Gray. "Moira and I have a son," he said.

"A son. Well. Damn." The pause made Will wonder if Moira's best friend wasn't fighting some tears of his own. "Have you named him yet?"

"Caleb." Will smiled even though he was only looking at the parking lot. "Caleb Graham."

"For me." He made a choking sound. "Damn."

"We should be home by tonight if you'd like to run over."

"You're okay with that?"

"Why wouldn't I be? You know Moira will want to see you."

"Yeah. Damn." Gray's vocabulary seemed to have deserted him. Will hoped he didn't have any important meetings scheduled in the next few hours.

Him, all he wanted to do was get upstairs.

Once there, he found that Caleb had been taken away for further assessment and to give Moira a chance to rest. She was sound asleep. Knowing she'd expect it, he backtracked briefly to the nursery and stared through the glass at his son, bundled like a burrito in a thin, pale green blanket, his spiky dark red hair covered by a tiny blue knit cap. As Will watched, Caleb's mouth moved and his face momentarily scrunched up in a frown, then smoothed out as he relaxed into sleep. Will stood there for ten minutes or more, unable to tear his eyes from this small person he'd barely met and yet loved so much. Nature in all her mystery, he thought ruefully.

Realizing suddenly that he needed to be with Moira, he returned to her room. She lay on her back clutching the white cotton blankets to her neck, as if she'd been cold when she fell asleep. He pulled up a chair beside the bed and sat looking at her with much the same wonder he'd felt watching his newborn son. Between the books he'd read and the class, Will had thought he'd had a pretty good idea what childbirth involved, but he'd discovered that he hadn't known at all. Now, he was in awe of what Moira had endured. He flexed his hands—they still ached from the strength of her grip as she struggled to ride the ebb and flow of contractions too powerful to be mastered.

Her eyelids were near translucent and her copper lashes lay against purplish bruising beneath her eyes. He doubted she'd had a good night's sleep in weeks. But…they had their son. Will felt exultation so fierce, he couldn't remember why he'd even hesitated about changing his life so that he could be here with her and Caleb.

Her breasts rose and fell; her lips were softly parted. A great bubble of emotion swelled in him as he fought the hunger to touch her: to smooth back the damp strands of copper hair plastered to her high, curved forehead, or to caress her cheek. He could hardly wait until tonight, when he could hold her.

I love her, he thought, waiting for that painful, glorious pressure in his chest to ease, although he wondered if it ever would entirely. And if what he felt was really love, or only the by-product of what they'd gone through together. It was logical that nature would want to ensure that he stay to protect and raise his child. What he felt, maybe this was the male version of the hormones that had a pregnant woman at their mercy.

But he didn't think so. He was pretty sure he'd started falling in love with Moira Cullen one week shy of nine months ago, and had kept tumbling ever since.

And now that love was all tied up with what he'd felt the moment the nurse laid baby Caleb in his arms and he gazed into those unfocused, bewildered eyes and known that nothing would ever be the same.

This, he thought with bemusement, is what his father had felt when he was born. He wished like hell Dad could be here. Wanted to think Dad *was* here, in some sense.

Right this minute, it was almost impossible to imagine how Moira's father could have failed to feel this savage certainty that he would do anything for her, give anything at all to make her happy, to keep her safe. Did the son of a bitch ever give his daughter a passing thought? Would he give a damn if he knew how his absence had damaged her?

Maybe, Will thought, he was wrong in suspecting that half the turmoil he sensed in Moira had to do with a childhood devoid of a father. She wanted her own child to have one, but maybe on another level she didn't. Maybe she didn't believe in fathers at all, or at least not their staying power.

The hospital sounds outside this room hardly made an impression on him. Will only smiled an absent thanks when a nurse brought a freshly warmed blanket to cover Moira, who gave an unconscious sigh of pleasure when it settled over her. He just kept looking at her and wishing their marriage was different, that she felt any faith at all in him.

MOIRA WAS SITTING ON THE SOFA nursing Caleb when Will walked into the living room. Surreptitiously, she adjusted her blouse, knowing it was silly when he'd seen all of her at one time or another, but feeling shy anyway. His gaze flicked to Caleb, greedily suckling, lingering either on his son or the swell of her now overabundant breast, she wasn't sure which, before settling on her face.

"He's hungry again already?"

"I'm hoping to get him down for the night," she said.

"Greedy little bugger," Will said fondly, then sat in the easy chair facing her. He stretched his legs out, crossed them at the ankles and relaxed, but didn't pick up his book. Apparently he was simply going to watch her.

After a minute of pretending he wasn't, she said, "I should have driven Mom to the airport today."

"She understood why you didn't."

Her mother had come only for a few days instead of the couple weeks she'd offered when Moira thought she'd be on her own with a newborn. Mom and Will had gotten along splendidly, as far as Moira could tell; they'd taken turns cooking and cleaning the kitchen, and had had several long, quiet conversations Moira wished she'd overheard.

As dearly as she loved her mother, though, it was almost a relief to have her gone now. With Will still not working, they hadn't needed the help, which had made Mom really a guest who had to be entertained. Will had made an effort to leave them alone sometimes, but Moira was too confused about how she felt about him and their marriage to have any desire to confide even in her mother.

They'd decided last night that Will would take her to the airport, because it was up to a two-hour drive each way, depending on traffic. Too long for Moira to leave Caleb, since she was nursing, and Will had quietly said, "I'd rather we not take him, with it so cold out there and the roads icy."

Still, Moira felt a little bit guilty now. She frowned, thinking about it. No, that wasn't really what was bothering her. Mom *hadn't* minded. It was more complicated, she thought. Things had changed without her realizing how much it would affect her relationship with her mother. Some of it was little stuff. Already she and Will had developed a kind of verbal shorthand, an ability to read each other's minds, that sometimes had left Mom excluded; a couple of times Moira had caught a fleeting expression on her mother's face that in retrospect Moira realized was sadness. This visit was the first time Moira had ever kissed her mother good-night then gone off to bed with a man, and *that* was different. It just…had felt as if they'd lost some closeness that they'd both always taken for granted.

It was the first time she'd found herself speculating about her mother's choices, too. Moira didn't remember her dating very often, and never seriously. Had Mom not *wanted* to remarry? It had always been her and Moira against the world, although—to her credit—she hadn't tried to cling when the time came for Moira to leave for college.

Moira frowned, forgetting that Will was watching her. Was it an accident that her own life was ending up an echo of her mother's? Or would have, if not for Will's stubborn refusal to take no for an answer?

"What are you thinking?" he asked now.

It took her a second to recall what they'd been talking about. Her not accompanying Mom to the airport. That was it. "Just Mom. About today…I know she understood. It's not that."

When she hesitated, Will said, "You miss her?" His gaze was keen on her face. She wondered what he was thinking.

"I guess I mostly feel bad that we didn't need her more. You know?"

He nodded. "If it had been a busier time of year, I might have picked up some work for Clay while your mom was here to take care of you. To give you two time alone. But he's got crews idled as it is, so I didn't want to ask."

Moira looked at him in surprise. "Are you thinking about going to work for him?"

After a minute Will shrugged. "Maybe later. Not long-term, and not for now. First I want to do the bedroom."

The guest room was to become Caleb's, but they'd agreed to wait to redecorate until Moira's mother came and went. Although they had bought a crib, Caleb was currently sleeping in a bassinet beside their bed. Now that Mom was gone, though, Will was going to paint and put up a wallpaper border. Moira didn't sew very often, but she'd bought fabric to make a valance for the window, too. Will would be taking down the bed and storing it in the basement.

"You know," he said, "we might want to think about putting on an addition."

Moira had been switching Caleb from one breast to the other, something that was easier to do when she wasn't trying simultaneously to whisk the cup of the bra up with lightning speed to cover her breast even as she freed the other one. But that brought her head up. "An addition?"

"To the house?" He looked amused but also…wary, she thought. "Another bedroom or two maybe. Do you really want to be without a guest room?"

"Well, maybe not forever, but…"

"Your office is too tiny to make a decent bedroom. I might want my own office down the line, too. And then if we have more kids…"

They hadn't even decided whether they were going to stay married, and he was talking about them having another baby? Something that might have been jubilation tangled with apprehension.

"Wow." She cleared her throat. "You're, um, thinking way ahead."

"Why not? I'm free right now, I could do most of the work." He shrugged again. "Think about it."

Moira made herself speak calmly. "I think I'd like to wait until we know better where we stand."

"What the hell does that mean?"

"We agreed we'd talk when Caleb was a little older." Her stomach squeezed into a ball at the thought, and she silently pleaded, *Argue. Tell me we don't have to, that you never plan to leave.*

But…he didn't. His eyes narrowed and she had the sense that he was mad, but he only said tightly, "If that's what you want."

No. No, it wasn't.

Caleb's mouth slipped off her breast. Moira eased him against her shoulder and patted his back until he gave a sleepy burp and nestled into her.

"I'm going to put him down," she murmured.

Will didn't move as she stood and went down the hall. Moira hesitated once she'd settled Caleb into his bassinet. The coward in her wanted to hide out in the bedroom and *not* return to the living room. Will was in a strange mood tonight. She couldn't imagine what had set him off, unless… Had *he* felt excluded while Mom was here?

Heavens. Maybe, Moira thought unhappily, she'd made both of them feel unappreciated.

And maybe that wasn't it at all. Maybe she was seeing Will's naturally pushy personality in action.

But when she entered the living room, he only said, "Like some ice cream? I was thinking a bowl would be good."

She moaned. "You can't keep tempting me like this."

"Nursing takes a lot of calories."

"Yes, but look at me." Moira laid her hands on her still too-soft stomach. "I have so much to lose."

He pushed himself to his feet. "There's no hurry, you know."

"Easy for you to say," Moira muttered.

"So no ice cream?"

She sighed. "Mocha almond fudge?"

"Yep."

"Oh, God. Just a scoop. Okay?"

Will grinned and disappeared into the kitchen.

He brought two bowls back, hers containing one perfect round scoop, his mounded high. After a resentful glance at his bowl, she concentrated on eating her own ice cream in tiny increments, stretching it out, letting the richness melt on her tongue.

"Why do you worry so much about your weight?" Will asked after a time.

Moira looked up sharply. He sounded too casual.

"What did Mom tell you?"

He lifted those dark eyebrows. "About?"

Okay, maybe not.

After some internal debate, Moira said, "Even before prepregnancy, I wasn't exactly a sylph."

"No, you had a luscious, curvy body that made me want to—" He broke off, color slashing his cheekbones.

Moira's eyes widened.

"You know what I wanted to do," he muttered. "I did it."

"You mean, I begged you to do it."

Abruptly, Will frowned at her. "Begged? I don't remember any begging."

"You were reluctant."

He snorted. "Yeah, that's why I insisted on walking you to your hotel-room door. Because I wasn't dying to take you inside and peel that dress off you."

"But you were such a gentleman. I thought—"

"Whatever you thought, it was obviously wrong. Any hesitation was only because of me planning to leave the country so soon." He hunched his shoulders.

"And I suppose I didn't like the idea of being a stand-in for the creep."

"The creep." She made an awful face. "Do you know, if I'd slept with him, and used that condom…"

Will didn't say anything. His expression was so unchanging, she could tell the thought had already occurred to him. And if it had…he must have wondered how she would have felt about Bruce Girard being the father of her baby instead of Will Becker.

"For your sake, I wish it hadn't happened," she said, meeting his eyes. "But for mine, I'm really glad. Glad you're Caleb's father."

His face relaxed, and she hadn't even been aware how rigid it had been. Voice scratchy, he said, "Don't be sorry. You think after holding Caleb I can regret anything?"

"No." Moira felt inexplicably mushy inside. "That would be awful, not having him, wouldn't it?"

They were both quiet for a moment, and she could see that he was as incredulous as she was at the very idea: no Caleb.

"You've managed to evade my question," Will pointed out.

She pretended not to know what he was talking about, even though she did.

"Do you really not know how sexy you are?" he asked.

With a shrug, she said, "Men tend to see me as best-friend material. I always figured it was the freckles. They positively shout girl next door. You know?"

"I've never lived next door to anyone who looked like you."

With no idea why she was arguing, Moira still shot back, "I'm just saying…"

"I watched you at the gala." Will sounded thoughtful. "For quite a while. I told you that."

She nodded.

"You danced. Men kept coming on to you, and I didn't need to hear you to be able to tell you were saying, 'Thanks but no thanks.'"

"That's ridiculous. I don't remember anyone special."

Will looked at her.

Well, there was Stan Wells, when she'd first arrived at the gala, but then she'd decided she must have imagined the way he had reacted. So maybe…

"I used to be fat," she blurted.

"Were you," Will murmured. It wasn't a question. She had the awful sense that she'd answered all his questions instead.

He might as well know. "When I was a kid," she said. "I don't know why. I was okay until…oh, third grade or so. The fatter I got, the more I wanted to eat. I'd sneak food. Mom would bake cookies and think they'd last for a week, only I'd have eaten the whole batch in two days. That's why I never learned to swim, you know. I didn't want anyone to see me in a bathing suit. I ended up getting dropped by the girls I thought were friends. And boys are such jerks in fourth or fifth grade."

"I don't think they can help themselves."

"They should," she muttered. "I pretended I didn't care, but I did."

"When did you lose the weight?"

"Oh, it was gradual. Being fat in middle school

was really horrible. I had crushes on boys, but I knew they'd never in a million years look twice at me." She shrugged. "They probably wouldn't have anyway, but..." Moira heard herself and cringed. "That's what I always think, you know. That no guy could be interested in me."

She hadn't known he could move so fast. One minute Will was lounging in the chair, the next he was on the sofa beside her, his hand grasping her chin.

"You're wrong. Guys can be. I am."

She gulped. "I think maybe my self-esteem issues are left from those days. After a while, you sort of... give up."

His thumb stroked her lower lip. His voice was a low rumble. "You shouldn't."

Wow. Moira gazed into his dark eyes and felt this swell of complicated emotions. "Thank you," she whispered.

He swore and took back his hand. "Damn it, there you go again."

"Again?"

"Why would you thank me for wanting you?"

"I was thanking you for being nice!"

After a moment he sighed. "Okay. I can accept that." He leaned back but kept watching her. "So, go on. How long did it take to *gradually* get slim?"

"I never got slim. It would have helped if I had. But...I'm not built to have skinny hips."

"A woman is supposed to *have* hips."

"Well, I do." She didn't know why he was being so insistent about this, but she was, after all, the one who'd decided to tell him why she maybe lacked confidence.

"By the time I was a senior in high school, I'd mostly lost the pudge. Too late to be a social success."

"You mean, the idiots you'd gone to school with didn't notice what was in front of their eyes."

She smiled at him. "You're good for my ego."

His mouth quirked in return. "I'd like to be."

"I finally dated and then had a serious boyfriend in college. End of tale."

"Okay, next question. Why do you hate the freckles so much?"

"Because hardly anyone else has them."

He waited, something he was good at. Moira couldn't help squirming under Will's patient regard. "Maybe because they came from my father." It had taken her a while to figure that out. "He was the redhead."

"Ah."

"What does *that* mean?"

Will took her hand and laced his fingers through hers. "Just that now it makes sense. You don't want to owe anything to him, but ignoring heredity is hard when it's right there every time you look at yourself in the mirror."

Moira made a face at him. "Plus, kids teased me about my freckles, too."

"*I* got teased for being big."

"Really?"

"Oh, yeah." He sounded wry. "I was always the tallest, from kindergarten on up. And talk about middle school. I had all the grace of a Saint Bernard puppy. My feet were huge." He lifted one and they both looked at it. "I wore a size twelve by the time I was in seventh grade. I tripped over my own feet. I was too clumsy to be any good at sports until later. Way later. I was probably eighteen, nineteen, before everything really started working together."

Why was she so dumbfounded? Did she really think she was the only person in the world who'd grown up knowing she was different, that she didn't *fit?*

"I like your size," Moira told him. "You're strong and gentle both. You make me feel…safe. Which I guess is a silly thing to say, since I'm not in any danger, but it's true anyway."

"I like your freckles." He lifted her hand to his mouth and kissed it. "And your hair, and your curves. Skinny, stringy women don't do it for me."

"A match made in heaven." She tried to sound sarcastic.

He grinned. "I keep trying to tell you."

They sat in silence. Will didn't let go of her hand. Moira had butterflies in her stomach that reminded her of Caleb's tumbles in midpregnancy. Her skin tingled. She wanted…

Will released her hand and, before she could feel disappointed, cupped her face and turned it toward him. Then he bent his head and kissed her. His mouth moved softly over hers, not demanding anything, only…asking. Her lips parted, but his kept dancing over them, nibbling, licking, almost kneading them the way his big, strong hands did on her back, seeming to *know* her body better than she did. Moira quit breathing. Eyes closed, she only experienced, wonder filling her.

Finally, Will eased back and waited until she lifted heavy lids and looked at him. "Someday," he whispered, "I want to kiss you all over. Just like that."

She swallowed.

"But not yet. I don't have enough self-control to stop. For now, we'll pretend we're shy thirteen-year-olds who know Mom or Dad is only a room away."

"Oh."

He stroked one fingertip from her chin down her throat. It was all she could do not to moan. In a low, husky voice, he said, "Okay?"

Moira bit her lip. "Okay."

"I think," he said, "it will be fun to flirt with you, Moira Cullen Becker."

Dizzy with unexpected pleasure, Moira tried for a saucy smile. "I might enjoy flirting with you, too, Mr. Becker."

"Good." He kissed her cheek, his breath warm, the small caress raising goose bumps on her nape. "And now, sweetheart, you'd better go to bed if you're going to get any sleep at all before our tyrant of a son starts screaming."

"Yes." She stood. "I take it you're going to stay up?"

"Yeah." His gaze was heated. "Cuddling you sounds a little too dangerous right now. I'll, uh, be along in a little bit."

Moira nodded, said, "Good night," and fled. To-night, she loved knowing that he'd risen to his feet and was watching her go.

CHAPTER THIRTEEN

CLAY CALLED AND ASKED if Will was interested in working, if only temporarily, as foreman on a job in Everett.

"Doug Redmond quit on me today," he explained. "No notice. Not really his fault. His parents have been going downhill, and now his dad has had a minor stroke. Doug and his wife decided to move to Texas and take care of them."

Doug was a nice guy who'd worked for Becker Construction as long as Will could remember. He was unimaginative but steady and reliable.

"You'll have to replace him," Will said.

Clay grunted unhappily. "I'm thinking maybe Ward Stevens, but I don't want to pull him from that drugstore we're building in Lake Stevens."

Will opened his mouth to comment, then closed it. The decisions weren't his anymore.

Instead, he said, "I wouldn't mind being busy for a little while. Moira doesn't plan to go back to work for another six weeks or so. It doesn't really make sense for us both to sit around staring at Caleb."

His brother laughed. "Is that what you do?"

"Just wait," Will said good-naturedly. "Man, there's nothing like seeing your own kid be born."

"Does he do anything besides sleep, nurse and piss?"

"He craps his diapers, too. And sucks his thumb. That's riveting."

Clay laughed. "Brother, you need to get out more."

Amused, Will said, "And you're giving me the chance."

Moira seemed fine with the idea when Will told her. Probably more than fine, he thought ruefully; having him hover 24/7 had to be getting on her nerves.

She was the one to catch his mood, though. They were loading the dishwasher and putting away leftovers when she said, "We haven't really talked about money."

"No." He guessed they should have. Knowing she was still paying utilities and a mortgage, if she had one, had been bugging him, but when he'd said something about splitting expenses she'd been evasive. He'd settled so far for buying most of the groceries and gas.

"Well…do you *need* to go to work for your brother?"

Will set down the saucepan he'd dried. "Do you mean, financially?"

"Yes."

He shook his head. "No. I have savings and investments. I put away most of my salary all those years. Living in the house we inherited from Mom and Dad, I didn't need much money."

"Then…why did you say yes?"

"I feel pretty useless sitting around."

"Now that you figure I don't need you anymore?"

That sent a cold chill through him. He hoped like hell she did still need him, if not in the same way. But he nodded.

"The thing is…" Moira hesitated again. "I could be wrong, but I just got an undertone there that you weren't very happy about working for Clay."

He went still, thinking about it. "I didn't realize," he said after a moment. "Hell. Are you reading my mind?"

Her face went blank. "If you don't want to talk about it…"

Damn it, he'd given the impression that he disliked her being so perceptive. He was shocked by a lightning quick thought: Did he? Will didn't let himself stop to examine the idea.

"No, you caught me by surprise. And you're right," he admitted. "It's not that I mind working for Clay. It's that…" He hesitated.

"You're used to him working for you?"

"That's part of it." Will fumbled his way, trying to figure out his own reluctance. Good God, was he oblivious to his own motivations? Did Moira understand him better than he understood himself? Unsettling thought. "Maybe more of it than I want to admit," he said finally, with a shrug. "It's not Clay, it's that I haven't taken orders from anyone in a lot of years. He started talking about promoting this guy and I almost said, 'I think you could do better.' But the truth is, he has to make his own decisions and his own mistakes. It was easier to keep my mouth shut when I wasn't around."

She closed the refrigerator. "I can see that."

"I don't want to work for anyone else." He frowned. "I don't think I want to run a business as big as Becker Construction again, either. I spent too much of my time shuffling papers, overseeing the books, hiring and firing. I guess I really do like building."

Moira smiled at him. "I understand. I didn't like working in a big architectural firm, either."

Will was swept by the odd realization that, in all

his adult life, he'd never had anyone he could talk to like this. He'd been the boss at work, the grown-up, the parent, at home. He'd become stuck in his roles. He had never felt able to confide, to talk problems out like this. Even though parts of this conversation had been oddly unsettling, Will thought he could easily learn to depend on having a real partner.

But all he said was, "Thanks," and that came out roughly. "I've committed to this job, but I think I'll say no next time."

"You do take commitments seriously, don't you."

Will tensed. "Shouldn't I?"

She seemed to shake herself. "Yes, of course. Don't listen to me." And she changed the subject, leaving him frustrated by his inability to figure out what she was really thinking half the time.

HE GUESSED HE *had* been getting restless, because something settled in him once he started leaving for work every morning and coming home tired but satisfied. A brief stretch of good weather allowed them to get the roof on and walls framed in on a strip mall that would house three businesses. Tenants were already lined up for all three, so they were building to spec instead of planning open spaces. Will made any decisions and Clay didn't attempt to assert authority. During their brief business conversations, they were both tiptoeing around, Will realized, which reinforced his feeling that he shouldn't take on another job for his brother.

Damn, he looked forward every day to getting home to Moira and Caleb. Caleb changed so fast, and that was part of it. Will hated to miss anything. But mostly, he found himself thinking about Moira. He'd want to share something he'd heard, or a joke, or a random thought. He'd remember the plush feel of her lips beneath his, the delicate indentations of her spine when he slipped his hand under her shirt and tugged her close to him. He thought about the nightly pleasure-torture of sleeping with her, of waking up to find her head on his shoulder and her breasts pillowed against his side. He'd remember the luscious white swell of her breast revealed when she was nursing their son, and the occasional glimpse he caught of her nipple, damp and swollen, when Caleb's mouth slipped from it.

He kissed her every day at least twice. The brief goodbye kiss in the morning was becoming a satisfying routine. She'd blush, but lift her face to his so naturally he rejoiced. Come evening, he would touch her whenever he could, and sooner or later he'd bend his head and explore her mouth. Most nights, he read for a while or went online after Moira disappeared to bed. He had to cool off before he could get under the sheets with her so temptingly close. He might have been able to maintain his sanity better if he wasn't sleeping with her, but he loved holding her at night. He was living for her six-week checkup and the all clear from the doctor. Will hoped and prayed she felt the same. Or—hell— that she was at least *willing*.

Weekdays, she'd taken over doing most of the cooking. When he walked in the door, Moira would greet him, hand over Caleb and disappear to the kitchen, giving him some time alone with his son. By three weeks old, Caleb was staying awake more and holding his head up pretty well. He started cooing, a soft sound that always made Will smile. Usually Moira would nurse him again and put him down for a short nap while they ate dinner. Some nights he'd refuse to fall asleep, and they'd take turns bouncing him against a shoulder while they ate.

Painting the bedroom only took a couple of days. Moira commented on how much more quickly he worked than she could have.

"Dad made me learn the business from the ground up," Will explained. "I painted the entire first summer I worked for him. Over the next few summers, I learned to wire and plumb a house along with framing a window, hanging a door, reading blueprints." He shrugged. "I took the same tack with Clay and Jack."

Her brows rose. "But not with Sophie?"

Will laughed at her tone. "Are you accusing me of sexism?"

"Should I be?"

"No. Sophie worked one summer in the office, but letting her even set foot on a construction site was out." He chuckled, thinking about his sister's quirks. "She's really smart. You know that."

Moira nodded.

"She couldn't build a decent tower with wooden blocks when she was a toddler. I doubt that, to this day, she could assemble a Barbie house. She's got a great memory, so she gets herself most places with no trouble, but she can't read a map. We finally figured out it's some kind of spatial thing. She worked in a vet clinic a couple of summers, she's a whiz on a computer, but she'd be a menace with a tool in her hand."

"I've heard about people like that. I'd never have guessed."

"Sophie does plenty of things well. When she has kids, her husband can assemble the toys."

"Are there many that *need* assembling?"

"Are you kidding?" He looked at her. "There was this pink plastic dollhouse that must have taken me four hours to put together one Christmas Eve. I was up half the night, determined to have it under the tree. I did a lot of swearing." He grinned, remembering. "I kept worrying she'd hear me and sneak down the stairs. Maybe she secretly still believed in Santa Claus and found out he had a foul mouth."

He loved Moira's laugh.

Caleb was a month old when she took him for his first doctor visit.

"He's—what a surprise—in the ninety-ninth percentile in height," she reported that evening. "Ninety-seventh in weight. He's going to be big like his daddy."

"You mean, he'll start tripping over his own feet before we know it," Will said, pleased despite himself. He was amused to discover how much he liked the idea of his son taking after him.

"Well…he has to learn to walk first."

Caleb was five weeks old when Moira called Will one day when he was at work. In the middle of talking to the plumber, he was going to ignore the call until he saw Moira's number on the screen.

He felt a jolt. Not Moira's number. *Their* number.

"Excuse me for a minute," he told the plumber, and turned away. God, what if Caleb was sick? he thought with quick panic.

"Moira," he said, walking outside. "Is something wrong?"

"No, I didn't mean to scare you. I had to tell you." Excitement rang in her voice. "Will, Caleb smiled! I was nursing him, and he let my breast go and just beamed. Now, every time I smile at him, he smiles back and flaps his arms. Oh, I can hardly wait for you to get home and see."

"Damn." He closed his eyes, overwhelmed by a flood of emotion. "I wish I'd been there. Oh, hell. You make me want to come home right now."

"He's about to go down for a nap, anyway. I— Well, I probably shouldn't have called, but I had to tell you."

Voice low and husky, Will said, "I'm glad you did. I'll never mind you calling me, Moira."

"Oh." Abruptly shy, she said, "Okay. I'll, um, see you when you get home. I'm making a stir-fry tonight."

Thoughts of stir-fry and smiles got him through the rest of the afternoon. He walked in the front door wondering if Caleb would smile for him, too, or only for his mommy, and not liking the twinge of jealousy.

But Moira, her own smile glowing, was waiting for him with Caleb in her arms, and when Will reached for him and said, "Hey, big guy," his son lit up. He focused hard on his daddy's face and grinned a huge, toothless grin. Eyes that had turned brown sparkled. If Will hadn't already been in love, he'd have gone down for the count.

Moira had trouble pulling herself away to fix dinner, and he didn't blame her. Who needed any other entertainment?

After Caleb fell asleep Moira told Will about her day. She'd grocery shopped with Caleb in the stomach sling he seemed to enjoy. "Mom called," she reported. "I think she'll visit again pretty soon. It's killing her not being able to see Caleb."

"Has she ever considered moving over here?" Will asked.

"I don't know." Moira's forehead crinkled reflectively. "She seems to like her job, and she has friends. On the other hand, she's been grumbling more and more about the cold. She's getting arthritis in her hands, you know, and it's worse during the winter." She was quiet for a minute. "I think I'll ask her."

Will nodded. He thought Moira would like having her mother nearby. He wished the idea didn't feel like a threat to him. Would she turn to her mother instead of him?

Feeling petty and uncomfortable with it, he listened as Moira continued to chatter. She'd talked to Gray today and to a new client.

"I'm meeting with her and her husband next week. They've bought some property at Port Susan and want me to design a house for them. I thought I could start working here at home."

They'd talked about her doing some of her work from home, and perhaps hiring a part-time nanny instead of putting Caleb in day care.

"You must be going stir-crazy," he realized. "Unless you're getting addicted to soap operas."

Moira scrunched up her nose. "I've taken to watching a couple of talk shows, but no soap operas. And no, I'm not going nuts yet, but…it has been a big change. It's weird, having this completely different rhythm to my days. And no one to talk to. I can't tell you how much I look forward to you walking in the door."

His voice roughened. "No more than I look forward to getting home."

"Oh," she said softly. "I didn't realize."

It was way too soon—too risky—to tell her how much he thought about her, how much she meant to him. She and Caleb gave him a sense of purpose. They *were* his purpose. That made him feel a little uneasy sometimes. He'd wanted to do something meaningful with his life, something bigger than being the devoted husband and father he'd fallen into being. He'd had no choice but to make the decision he had, and he wouldn't change it if he could. He wanted to be here with his wife and son, not in Zimbabwe building medical clinics. He just wished…hell, he didn't know what. That he could have his cake and eat it, too, he guessed.

She was a little shy with him for the rest of the evening, and Will wondered what she'd seen on his face. When she finally said, "I'm going to bed," he stood with her.

"Let me kiss you good-night."

Her face warmed, but she came to him and wrapped her arms around his neck. Will bent his head and nuzzled her ear, her cheek, her throat, inhaling the scent that was Moira's alone. The rush of desire was almost painful. He'd made love to her once, and that was ten months ago. He'd been sleeping with her now for over two months, and it was killing him.

He brushed her lips with his. "When's your doctor appointment?" he murmured.

"Next week," she whispered. "Wednesday."

He groaned and kissed her with more hunger than he'd meant to unleash. Damn, he wanted her. He ended up with his tongue driving into her mouth and his hands wrapping her hips and lifting her against him, so that she couldn't help feeling how aroused he was. What gave him hope was that she held on tight and danced her tongue around his. They were both breathing hard when he let her go with another groan.

"Go to bed."

Wide-eyed, she took in his expression, then backed away. "Um…good night, Will."

"Good night."

He paced the living room until the quiet sounds of her getting ready for bed had ceased. Then he grabbed his parka and went for a walk. He'd been taking a lot of late-night walks recently. Only heavy rain stopped him. The frigid night air worked as well as a cold shower. He could go back with some hope of actually sleeping.

Will still didn't feel ready for bed after his walk. Instead, he turned on his laptop and browsed the internet. He did that some nights, too, when he wasn't in the mood to read. A foundation employee he'd known in Zimbabwe was regularly blogging and posting pictures. Will always started by checking if Gary had added anything new. Then he browsed for similar projects in Africa, or sometimes went to tourist sites. He wasn't much of a photographer himself, but he liked looking at pictures of Victoria Falls or the fascinating wildlife. He hadn't been in Africa long enough for glimpses of elephants or impala or even a lion lounging not far from the road to become routine.

Tonight Will found photos posted by someone who'd recently gotten home from visiting grandparents still farming near Chinhoyi, and was admiring a spectacular one of cormorants roosting in the branches of a long-dead tree poking from the waters of Lake Kariba right at sunset when he heard a sound and turned his head to see Moira. She wore flannel pajamas with cartoon characters on them. Her hair was loose and tousled, her eyes fixed on the computer monitor.

In an odd voice, she asked, "Where's that?"

"Lake Kariba, along the Zambia-Zimbabwe border. It flows into the Zambezi River then on to Victoria Falls."

"Oh." She was already backing away. "I didn't mean to interrupt you. I just got up to… It doesn't matter."

He had a really bad feeling that it did matter. "Did you want to talk to me?" he asked.

"No, I— It's nothing." She smiled, although it wasn't much of one, said, "Good night again," and disappeared down the hall.

His body tensed with the desire to go after her, but he made himself stay where he was. He'd wake Caleb if he chased her to the bedroom. Something told him she wouldn't want to talk right now, anyway.

Somewhat grimly, he decided that Caleb needed to start sleeping in his crib, in his own bedroom. Sure as hell before next Wednesday night.

Will had lost interest in browsing scenic pictures of Africa and closed out the internet, then turned off his computer. He rubbed his forehead and felt as guilty as if Moira had caught him viewing pornography. Damn it.

The next moment, anger rose. He'd been doing something completely innocent. He was entitled to his interests. Why should he feel guilty? He'd quit the job for her, he'd married her. He was here, wasn't he, giving her his all? She had no business looking wounded because he was browsing the internet.

A rough sound escaped his throat. He hated his memory of the expression on Moira's face. It made it hard to hold on to the anger.

But maybe he'd been imagining things. Moira probably hadn't read as much into what she'd seen as he feared she had. It was that damn, irrational guilt making him see what wasn't there.

Still, he had no desire to go back online or read. Instead, he followed her down the hall and went to bed. But when he quietly got in on his side, he stayed there, hoping Moira was sleeping and not lying very still, wanting him to keep his distance.

SPYING WAS REALLY LOW and Moira hated herself for it, but the next morning after Will left for work, she turned on his laptop, went online and called up the list of websites he'd recently visited. What she saw made her feel as if she'd been kicked in the chest.

Scrolling down, she realized he was obsessed. She'd let herself believe he wasn't going to bed at the same time as she did because he was having trouble resisting the desire to make love to her. Now she knew. He could probably hardly wait for her to go to bed so he could go online and vicariously live his dream.

The one she'd stolen from him when she told him she was pregnant with his child.

Hastily, half wishing she *hadn't* looked, Moira closed down the computer and went to her office. While Caleb was sleeping, she'd do rough sketches of some ideas for the Russells, the new clients she'd told Will about. Molly Russell had said enough on the phone about what they wanted to get Moira thinking, and she did that best on paper.

But she felt too agitated to accomplish a thing. She wasn't used to not knowing how to handle a problem. It wasn't like her to be so completely clueless.

Of course, there was a reason she was. She had

next to no experience in relationships. Worse yet, she'd never been in love before.

But now she was. So desperately in love, and with a man whose life she'd seriously mucked up. A man who probably wished he'd never met her.

She closed her eyes and remembered him gently rubbing her belly and saying, *I wouldn't want to be anywhere but here.* And *You think after holding Caleb I can regret anything?*

Yes! Yes, she thought he did. Oh, she did believe he loved Caleb. The tenderness on his face when he held his son was unmistakable. And she believed that he did want her. A man couldn't fake an erection, which he seemed to have pretty frequently these days.

But then…men liked sex. Getting a hard-on didn't mean much.

What should she *do?* Offering to let him go would be useless; he was fixated on a goal, the same way he'd been after his father died. He might be miserable, but that wouldn't count. Marrying her, being a husband and father, was now his main goal in life, and she was pretty sure it would take dynamite to shake him from it.

And—oh, God—she didn't *want* to let him go. She could have survived without Will, if she'd never let him know she was pregnant. She knew she could have. But now that she'd had him, she couldn't bear the idea of life without him.

If only Gray hadn't bullied her into telling Will.

Moira made a face. She'd have contacted him sooner or later anyway. Later, maybe, without Gray's push, but she knew she'd have done it. Will had deserved to know.

She spent a really unhappy day, but pulled herself

together enough to greet him when he got home as though nothing was wrong. She thought his gaze was rather searching as he took Caleb from her, but she had the excuse of needing to stir the spaghetti sauce simmering on the stove. And she got lucky in that Caleb chose tonight not to want to sleep, so he was a distraction during dinner.

Afterward, he would have liked to fall asleep, but she refused to let him.

"He only woke up once last night," she told Will. "And that wasn't until nearly three. Maybe if we keep him awake now he'll sleep through the night. I talked to Charlotte yesterday, and she says Emily did before she was six weeks old."

Caleb let out a frustrated cry.

"Mommy doesn't really mean that," Will told him, holding his son up to look into his eyes. "She'd miss that middle-of-the-night feeding. She told me how much she loves getting up with you. Snuggling you when the house is all quiet and dark. She's grumpy tonight, that's all." He blew a raspberry on Caleb's plump cheek. "Don't listen to her."

"You know," Moira said, "I've been thinking about pumping some breast milk so he could start getting used to taking a bottle. If I did that, *you* could get up and snuggle him in the middle of the night. Just think. It could become your special time."

He laughed and bounced an increasingly disgruntled Caleb against his shoulder. "Now Mommy is getting nasty."

"Goo ga."

"Hey!" Face alight with pleasure, Will looked at her. "Did you hear that? He's talking."

"That was a new sound." Wow. The dumbest things could make her teary-eyed. It wouldn't be that long before Caleb was saying *Mama* or *Dada.*

"What a smart boy," his father crooned, sounding as besotted as she was.

Oh, she had a million doubts, but never that he loved Caleb. Watching Will Becker, big and kind and sexy, walk in circles around the living room with their baby cradled in his arms, all she could think was, *But what about* me? *Can't he love me, too?*

After she put Caleb to bed, Moira returned to the living room. She was in such turmoil, her chest felt crowded inside, as if she was stuffing too many emotions, too many doubts, into it. *Say something,* she ordered herself. *Don't be a coward.*

Will was texting someone on his phone when she came back to the living room. "Jack," he murmured, finishing and setting the phone aside.

"Last night," Moira said. Too abruptly, probably too loudly. "I know you're spending a lot of time online. Do you…do you look at stuff about Africa a lot?"

His jaw tightened. "I'm still interested. I do a little browsing."

A little? she thought incredulously, remembering the list of sites he'd visited.

Feeling incoherent, she began, "It's just…" Swallowed. "Maybe we should talk about it."

"Moira, the fact that I read someone's blog or look at pretty pictures of Africa has nothing to do with you and me." His voice was tighter than usual. Was it temper ruffling his usual calm? "For God's sake, don't read something into nothing."

What could she do but nod? She wasn't sure the

lump in her throat would have let her speak anyway. *Nothing?* The very fact that he was defensive told her *nothing* was definitely something.

But she was a coward after all. Enough of one that she wouldn't light that stick of dynamite, that she would keep taking whatever he would give and pretend she didn't guess how deep his regret ran. And she would hope that he meant it when he said he liked her freckles and her hair and her curves; that he did, at least, want her.

CHAPTER FOURTEEN

Tuesday evening, Will said, "Why don't we try Caleb in his crib tonight. Since he's made it through the night a couple of times now."

Call him prudish, but he didn't think he'd be able to enjoy making love with Moira when Caleb was right there, only a few feet away. Will knew it was dumb; it's not as though Caleb would know what his parents were doing, and that was assuming he even woke up. And it took a heck of a lot to wake him up. Will had seen Moira vacuum right around his bassinet while he snoozed on without a twitch. Whatever Caleb did, he *concentrated*.

Not surprising, since Will knew he was known and occasionally reviled for the force of his determination and single-mindedness. And he'd seen Moira lost in her work, oblivious to ringing telephones or conversations around her.

Moira's gaze found and shied from his. "Um…that's probably a good idea. Let's see if we can keep him up another half an hour."

"Good idea." He sat on the far end of the couch from her, stockinged feet on the coffee table. He'd spent a lot of time looking at her tonight. Tormenting himself. "Your doctor appointment still on for tomorrow?"

She murmured agreement and played "This little

piggy went to market" with Caleb's toes. He might be getting sleepy, but he smiled with delight nonetheless. She moved on to his other foot. Will might have believed she wasn't thinking about anything else, but her pink cheeks betrayed her self-consciousness.

This last week had been a strain. For both of them, he suspected. It was partly that near-argument about his continuing interest in Africa. The tension between them had never dissipated. His fault, maybe—he'd continued to stay up long after she went to bed, feeling bloody-minded but doing it anyway. Making a point. Marriage didn't mean giving up all privacy, all outside interests. It was unreasonable of her to imply—even if only by one stricken look—that he should. The fact that he'd had no interest since in reading about Africa was irrelevant; if he wanted to, he could.

Guilt still ate at him, and that still pissed him off. But he had also been forced to do some thinking, which was probably a good thing. Truth was, he'd been drifting. Taking this job for Clay just to have something to do. He had a new life now, and he had to make it matter or he was going to end up unhappy.

So he'd actually spent some pretty productive time on the internet, leading to a meeting today that had him excited. He'd been looking forward all afternoon to telling Moira about it.

Truth was, he wouldn't have had the self-discipline to go to bed at the same time as she did, anyway. Sharing a bed as if they were nothing but friends had become an impossibility. If he cuddled with her, she'd notice he had a raging hard-on. It was bad enough climbing into bed beside her once she was asleep. He still stayed on his side, careful not to touch her. Every muscle in his body would be rigid with restraint, when all he wanted to do was reach out for her. He'd relived their one and only lovemaking a thousand times. The feel of her under him, the sounds she made, the tightness of her body when he pushed inside her. Sleep did not come easily. It was worse when she had to get up to nurse Caleb and would slip back into bed beside Will. Knowing she was awake, wondering if she was thinking about him, remembering his touch, too, was enough to make him feel like fire ants were crawling over his skin.

Torture.

They'd never actually talked about whether they'd make love, but the knowledge that soon they *could* had become part of the very air they both breathed. Every time Will looked at her, it was on his mind. The fact that Moira had gotten shyer made him pretty sure she was thinking the same. Wanting the same. Please, God, she wanted the same.

Will had hardly took his eyes off her all evening. Usually, when she nursed Caleb, he made no pretence that he wasn't watching. He was fascinated by the voluptuous swell of her breasts, the moist dark peak of her nipple when Caleb let go of it. In a different way, Will loved the sight of their baby nursing. That small, perfect hand often seemed to pat his mommy's breast, as if in appreciation. The two of them together, mother and child, made his heart swell until it filled his chest.

He changed Caleb's diaper and brought him to her to nurse, as usual. Sat down, watched as she lifted her shirt and reached for the catch that would free one breast, then shot to his feet. He couldn't take it tonight.

Voice hoarse, he said, "I'm going for a walk."

"Oh." Her color heightened. "Okay."

She was tiptoeing down the hall when Will came in, shaking the water from his hair like a wet dog. He took his coat off and said unnecessarily, "It's raining." Then he recognized her unusual caution. "You put him in his crib?"

Moira nodded. "He was already asleep."

"Will he notice when he wakes up?"

"What do you think?" she scoffed.

He grinned. "Of course he will," he said. "Caleb's a smart boy."

"And he's going to be a mad boy."

"Can I go look?"

She narrowed her eyes. "If you wake him up, on your head be it."

Another grin, and he slipped silently down the hall. The ceramic nightlight shaped like a mouse cast a faint, golden glow that allowed him to make out Caleb, a tiny lump under his comforter, his face slack and peaceful. When Will just as quietly stepped back out of the room, Moira was hovering at the other end of the hall.

Will waited until he'd reached her. "He's cute."

"Yes, he is. And I'm going to bed, too."

"I wanted to talk to you about something first," he said.

Moira studied him. She must have heard that he was serious, because she looked apprehensive when she said, "Sure."

She sat on her usual end of the couch, bare feet tucked beneath her, Will in the big easy chair across from her.

"I've been thinking about the future," he said.

Her face stayed unnaturally still, but he saw the way she squeezed her hands together, the fear in her eyes.

"Work," he clarified, before she could do more than stare at him.

Air escaped her with a force that was audible.

Will raised his eyebrows, but when she didn't say anything, he went on, "I'm bored with what I'm doing. No, more than that—dissatisfied. We build solid, Becker Construction doesn't cut corners, but… this kind of job I'm doing, the best you can say is it's workmanlike." He shrugged. "Nothing wrong with that, but I think I'd like to build something that might endure. Even be admired fifty years from now, a hundred years from now."

"Which means building for clients with money. Lots of money."

He grimaced. "Yeah. The opposite of what I was striving for in Africa. I do realize that."

"So what have you decided?"

"I guess I have two sets of ideals. One pushes me to do something for people who genuinely need help. The other is to build real quality." He leaned forward, letting her see passion he most often kept disguised. It was one of those pieces of himself that he had to share if they were to have any hope. "I think I can do both," he said. "I might start a small construction firm. Build one house at a time. Focus on the details, connect with the real craftsmen in our area who do fine stonework or cabinetry or wrought-iron railings. Do work I can be proud of."

Moira nodded. "That's part of the reason Gray and I struck out on our own."

Will nodded in acknowledgment, unsurprised by

her understanding. "The other part of what I'm thinking is that I'll provide my services free or at minimal cost for projects I believe in." He paused. "I've already found the first one."

"Really?" She was leaning forward slightly, too, as though he'd captured her by his intensity.

"I found an organization looking to build an apartment house for women with children who are trying to make a new start. Most of the women served were in abusive relationships. Bright Futures works to provide counseling, help find jobs, whatever the clientele needs. They'd like to be able to offer housing, too, for up to a year while the women get their feet under them. The idea is that the women can turn to each other, that the apartment building will give the residents a community, too."

"Is the funding in place?"

"They've got property in Stanwood, but they thought they were a year or more away from starting. No plans yet, for one thing. If I don't charge for my work as contractor, and I get deals where I can find them for materials, we might be able to break ground this spring."

Moira didn't even hesitate. "I can draw the plans free."

He smiled. "I thought you might say that."

"I've been suckered?"

"Yeah, you have."

He could all but see her brain racing. "There should be a community room. Not only the separate apartments, but a space for the women to get together. Maybe even for some communal child care. How many apartments?"

"Six or eight."

"I'm ashamed that it never occurred to me to volunteer my skill for something like this."

"Don't be." He made his voice low, husky, intimate. "I thought maybe it was something we could do together."

That was one of the things he'd realized this past week, when he'd sat here long after she'd gone to bed. He'd hated the gulf that had opened between them. He wouldn't let himself be disappointed if she didn't want to be involved in whatever project he took on, but…he'd liked the idea of sharing it with her. He'd liked that a lot.

"Yes." Her face was alive with the same excitement he felt. "This is great timing, Will. I could get started any time. As soon as you can set it up for me to meet with whoever will be overseeing us."

"I'll talk to them tomorrow," he promised. He sat back in his chair, looking at her with pleasure. This had gone even better than he'd hoped. "Now you'd better get to bed. Thank you for listening to me."

Moira stood then, in a flurry, came to him and kissed his cheek. He felt his evening beard rasp under her soft lips. "I like your ideas," she said, her voice a little husky. "Both of them."

"Good." He made no move to touch her or pull her down for a deeper kiss although, damn, he wanted to. He had no doubt his expression was rueful. "I think I'd better read for a while. My self-restraint is flagging."

"Oh." Heat bloomed in her cheeks again. "Okay."

All he could do was sit there trying not to hear the muted sounds of her getting ready for bed—water running, the toilet flushing, the glide of the closet door—

and try to figure out how he could kill an hour or two, when all he wanted to do was make love to his wife.

WEDNESDAY HAD TO BE THE LONGEST damn day of his entire life. Will considered himself a patient man, but he'd used up all his patience these past few months.

Why hadn't he tried to seduce Moira before she had the baby? She'd probably convinced herself that, as big as she'd gotten, he didn't want her. Truth was, he'd been half-aroused most of the time since their wedding. She'd been carrying his baby and was round and ripe and bursting with fertility. What was sexier than that?

But he'd told himself it was too soon, that she needed to get to know him, decide she could trust him. Will had given serious thought to trying to coax her after he'd made the move into her bed, but her bleeding episode had scared him. He wouldn't do anything that might threaten their child. And…she had gradually relaxed with him, so his original plan had been working.

What he *hadn't* thought about was how torturously long the six weeks until Moira got the all-clear from her doctor would turn out to be. Ten months, one week exactly since he'd made love to her. Hell, since he'd had sex. He didn't know how he'd survived.

He got home at five-thirty to a flustered wife and a cranky baby. Caleb had not enjoyed his first night in his own bedroom. He'd woken up every couple of hours all night long and sobbed. Moira and Will took turns going in and rocking him back to sleep. They were all three heavy-eyed this morning. Under other circumstances, Will might have been thinking about nothing but hitting the sack.

Taking Caleb into his arms and enjoying Moira's

pink cheeks and green eyes that wouldn't quite meet his, Will hid his grin. He was thinking about nothing but bed, all right, although sleep didn't have anything to do with it. And it was pretty clear that Moira had her mind on the same thing.

He kissed Caleb's chubby cheek and strolled as far as the kitchen doorway in pursuit of his wife, who'd skittered away the instant she handed off their kid. "Smells good," he said amiably. "What are you cooking?"

"Meat loaf and baked potatoes."

He spotted a pie cooling on the counter. "And you baked."

"Cherry," she said tersely, keeping her back to him as she fussed unnecessarily over whatever vegetable she had steaming in a saucepan on the stove.

"À la mode?" he said hopefully.

Mouth prim, she shot him a look. "For those who can afford the calories."

"You're determined to stick to your diet, aren't you?"

"I will never be fat again," she said in a steely voice.

"Can't you splurge sometimes?"

She rolled her eyes, looking for a moment like a disgusted teenager. "Why do you think I put on almost forty pounds while I was pregnant? Remember the French fries? The milk shakes?"

"I suppose it's natural I eat more than you do," he realized.

"Ya think?"

Amused, he let it go. "Did Caleb sleep all day?"

There was more steel in her voice. "I didn't let him. My sympathy was at a low ebb today, I can tell you."

"Yeah, I almost crawled into my pickup for a nap." Will surprised himself with a jaw-popping yawn. "Damn. Well, let's hope he's resigned himself tonight to his crib."

Moira yawned, too. "Oh, don't get me started."

Very casually, he asked, "How'd the doctor visit go?"

"Fine." She kept her back to him. "Great. She said I'm fine. Everything's…"

Fine.

Under other circumstances, he'd have grinned. As it was, his blood pooled in his groin. "Good," he said after a moment, his voice rusty. "I'm glad you're—" not *fine.* Anything but fine "—recovered," he finished firmly.

She nodded, still without looking at him. Will retreated to the living room.

While he entertained Caleb, Moira dished up dinner. They settled him in a reclining baby seat while they ate. Moira cheered up when Will told her that someone from Bright Futures, the nonprofit organization that wanted to build the apartment house, would be calling her the next day.

"I can't tell you how excited they are. An architect and a contractor. And I talked a buddy of mine who owns an electrical contracting firm into offering his work cut-rate. You remember Dennis Mattson—he was at our wedding."

"Dennis was nice." Sounding thoughtful, she said, "I know a plumber who might be interested, too. Let me give him a call tomorrow."

"Maybe we can build up a network of, er…"

Moira arched her eyebrows. "Persuadable people?"

He chuckled. "Yeah, something like that. Good meat loaf," he told her.

Seeing Caleb's eyelids sinking, she said, "Oh, no you don't," and tickled his stomach. He started and began to cry.

Will saw her frustration and guessed that she was exhausted. The thought made his heart sink. Was she too tired? Damn it, damn it.

He stood immediately and picked Caleb up, holding him tight to his chest, one large hand engulfing the baby's entire back. He silently begged, *Please cooperate. Please.*

CALEB WAS SO TINY AGAINST the breadth of his daddy's powerful body. The sight of Will with their baby always moved Moira, but tonight she felt especially emotional. Somehow, it was more amazing to see a man as big and strong as Will being so extraordinarily gentle.

His eyes met hers and seemed to darken. "Are you all right?"

She nodded and gave a sniff. "I just…sometimes…" She flapped a hand.

His mouth curved. "Yeah. I know what you mean."

She saw that he did. He so often seemed to. How did he understand her so well? Was figuring her out part of what he'd taken on when he decided she and Caleb were going to be his priority?

"Poor boy," he was murmuring. "I know you're sleepy. But, see, there's a big picture you're missing. Mommy and I are sleepy, too. And if you nap now, we're in trouble."

Caleb didn't care. In the next hour, Moira began to feel that they were tormenting him, keeping him awake. She might have buckled, but Will displayed a more ruthless streak than she'd seen yet. He shook rattles, bicycled Caleb's chubby legs, made obnoxious noises, played bounce the baby. Caleb alternated between grumpy and delighted.

Maybe it was her own tiredness, but a giggle kept bubbling in Moira's throat.

"Mean Daddy," she said.

Amusement and something else in his eyes, Will retorted, "Desperate Daddy."

That didn't strike her as nearly so funny. In fact, she had to clench her thighs together to contain a wickedly physical response to his expression and the low, rough sound of his voice.

They were both watching the clock. At eight on the nose, Will stripped off Caleb's sleeper and quickly and efficiently changed his wet diaper. Then he thrust their baby at her.

She already had her blouse unfastened and her bra unhooked. Caleb latched on with his customary eagerness. She gave him a couple of minutes, then switched him to the other breast. The entire time, Will sat staring. Tingling all over, Moira felt as if her skin was flushed from her toes to the crown of her head.

The suckling slowed. Caleb's small body went slack and his mouth slipped from her breast. Not looking at Will, she eased the baby to her shoulder, patted him until a burp escaped him, then stood. Will rose, too, and by the time she reached the bedroom, the lights in the kitchen and living room had already gone out.

She turned on the nightlight, laid Caleb in the crib and tucked his flannel quilt up to his chin. He never stirred.

Will was already waiting in their bedroom, where the lamp cast the only light. Her pulse skipped.

He watched her walk toward him. "Moira." He spoke barely above a whisper. "Sweetheart."

She swallowed.

"You know I want to make love with you."

She nodded. "I want that, too." In her attempt to keep her voice low, too, she sounded almost sultry. She hadn't known she could. "We shouldn't until…until things are more settled. But I don't care."

After nursing, she hadn't bothered buttoning up her blouse. Will caressed her cheek, then stroked his fingertips down her throat until he reached the front clasp of her bra.

"You have the most beautiful breasts. Watching you nurse has been killing me."

"They're…awfully big these days," she said awkwardly. "I'm always leaking."

"Beautiful," he repeated huskily. He flicked open the clasp and her breasts spilled out. His big hands enveloped them the way she'd remembered. Her nipples peaked against his palms, and he rubbed gently, squeezed, whispered about how much he wanted her. She stood for the longest time doing nothing but soaking in his touch, as if every cell in her body was starved for it. Finally, she had to touch him, too, and she tugged his sweatshirt upward.

As though they'd both lost all patience in that moment, they fought to remove each other's clothes. She was hardly aware of losing her shirt or bra; her hands were already on the metal buttons at the fly of his jeans. So quickly, they were both naked, and only then did she remember to be self-conscious.

She crossed her arms protectively. "Don't look at my stomach."

Will groaned and thrust his fingers into her hair. "How many times do I have to tell you how sexy you are? I like you soft. You just had a baby. You *should* be soft." His voice was ragged, the gaze that swept her so darkly appreciative Moira couldn't help but believe him.

"Where have you been all my life?" she asked, and quit trying to hide herself.

He laughed, scooped her up and laid her across their bed. Coming down beside her, he kissed her, a deep, drugging kiss that tumbled her back in time, to that first night. All the lonely months that had followed, all her fears, slipped away, forgotten if only for this moment.

His mouth finally left hers to nibble and lick and kiss her neck and her shoulders, her breasts and belly, her thighs and calves and the sensitive arches of her feet.

"Such pretty freckles." He was nuzzling his way up her legs. "You make me want to connect the dots. All the dots."

She half sobbed at the pleasure his mouth brought her. She wanted to explore his body, too, but that seemed too leisurely for this first time. "Please." Moira gripped his shoulders, felt the muscles bunch beneath her fingers. "Will. Now."

He surged up the length of her body, found his place between her legs and thrust into her. Then they were both groaning, their bodies rising and falling in a rhythm that came so naturally, they might have done this a hundred times instead of only once. And yet there was nothing smooth about it. She strained upward, fighting him each time he pulled back, moaning at the depth of his plunges. The end came too quickly. She cried out and faltered; he had to grip her hips and lift her so that he could drive deep inside her again. Once, twice, three times, his body bucking and shuddering above and inside her. And then he sank onto her, and she pressed her lips to his damp skin and couldn't tell whether the vibration and thunder of the heartbeat she felt was his or hers.

THAT WEEK WAS THE SINGLE happiest of Moira's life. When Caleb napped, she eagerly started work on plans for both the Russells' Warm Beach house and the Bright Futures apartment building. She hadn't felt so creative or excited in ages, she realized. Of course, the pregnancy had tired her, but it was more than that— maybe she'd needed the break. She loved talking to Will about her ideas, too. She and Gray used to talk about their work that way, but had done so less and less in recent years. Perhaps they'd both gotten stale, or simply too busy.

She adored being a mother, watching her gorgeous baby boy thrive and change day by day. His eyes had turned a warm, chocolate brown, lighter than his daddy's, but so pretty. She kept wondering whether he'd have freckles. A few would be okay, a dusting across his nose, maybe. A little wryly, she thought, *a sprinkle of cloves, instead of a warehouse club-size canister dumped.* Already she could see him as a tough little boy, missing a front tooth or two and grinning, both mischievous and deceptively innocent. She began to wonder if she really had to go back to work full-time.

Maybe she and Gray should start thinking about bringing in an associate. They hadn't so far, but they both had families now.

Then there was nighttime, after Caleb was asleep. From the minute Will walked in the door at the end of the day, Moira could hardly think about anything *but* going to bed. With him. Making love. Falling asleep with her head on his shoulder, her legs tangled with his. Waking to find his hand on her breast, his morning erection pressed against her belly or hip. If they were lucky and Caleb gave them time, they made love then, too.

Life was so perfect, it shimmered like the highway ahead did sometimes in the desert. She had this funny, uncomfortable feeling, as if she were a little girl who'd been trusted to carry a precious family heirloom and was proud and thrilled even as fear curdled in her stomach that she'd trip or do something foolish and drop it. The vision of it shattering was almost more real than the loveliness in her hands.

That was silly, of course, but being scared that this was only an idyll wasn't. Will wasn't in love with her, he hadn't married her because he couldn't imagine living without her. He'd made the best of it, and he did want her, but…for how long? They'd never had that talk, and she wasn't brave enough to suggest that they do. She didn't want to hear any harsh truths, however gently phrased. She didn't want to think about how only days ago Will was waiting for her to go to bed so he could go online and…and visit his former lover. That's what it felt like. As if she knew a big part of his heart was taken, and that it was only because he was a good, kind man that he hid his hurt and disappointment.

For which *she* was responsible.

Moira felt adolescent, the way her worry continued to niggle at her. The fact that Will had loved his project in Africa—had loved Zimbabwe—didn't take away from anything he felt for her and Caleb. She was adult enough to know that. They weren't teenagers, to demand complete and utter devotion of each other. They'd both had lives, had work that was important to them, family and friends, opinions and values and goals that weren't necessarily shared.

This common sense had zilch effect. She kept wondering how the Bright Futures project could possibly compare to what he'd been accomplishing in Africa—an apartment house for a few mothers and their children, a temporary refuge against a dozen medical clinics and community hospitals that would have improved thousands and thousands of lives. Saved many of those lives. Was this another way he was...settling?

She wanted to clap her hands over her ears and shut out the doubts, but how could she? She wanted so much to believe she was lovable, but that didn't mean Will did—or could—love her.

And yet...he seemed happy. And he *was* in love with Caleb. She kept reminding herself of that.

On Wednesday the week after they had begun to make love again, Moira became so engrossed in drawing that she didn't notice when the mail was dropped through the slot in the door. Will picked it up off the floor when he got home, glanced through it and handed most of it to her before taking Caleb with an exuberant grin and a kiss for her.

But he kept one envelope aside.

She wasn't sure what he did with it. She didn't see him open it at all. Maybe it was junk mail. He didn't seem to get much personal mail; Sophie and he emailed and even, occasionally, used Instant Messenger rather than exchanging letters. She knew he talked to her and both his brothers regularly.

Moira didn't really think about that piece of mail until the next day, when she passed the end of the breakfast bar where Will kept his computer, a battered address book and a heap of work-related notes to himself. She loved his handwriting, an emphatic scrawl that was a complete contrast to her own exceedingly tidy, careful script.

A long white envelope, torn open, lay there on top of his notes. The typed letter was beside it. One fold concealed the bottom, but she could see the letterhead—the foundation he'd worked for. It was probably nothing. He hadn't tried to hide the letter. He might have automatically gone on their list of potential donors, for example. But her heart had began to pound hard, and she couldn't stop herself from reaching out and unfolding the piece of paper. Reading. And feeling sick, when words leaped out at her.

We regret losing you… Projects have bogged down… Your skill at dealing with local authority… And finally, their hope that he'd fulfilled the *obligation* that had interrupted his planned commitment to them. Might he be able to return to Zimbabwe?

They wanted him back. And he *had* fulfilled his commitment to her.

An obligation. She felt sick. *I'm nothing but an obligation.*

The last months of her pregnancy had been hard.
The first weeks with a newborn, too. But she and Caleb
would be fine without Will now.

Except that her knees almost gave away at the
thought of him leaving. The pain that filled her was
nearly unbearable because she knew she couldn't keep
him here. Not if he truly wanted to go.

But how did she find out?

CHAPTER FIFTEEN

WILL KNEW THE MINUTE he walked in the door that something was wrong. Moira was quiet, closed off. Preoccupied rather than upset, he wanted to think. Or maybe Caleb had been cranky today and she was tired.

During dinner he asked a few questions about her work, talked about an aggravating delay brought about because he'd rejected the shoddy cabinetry that had been delivered today.

"Damn, I'm going to be glad to be done with this job," he said with feeling.

She appeared to be concentrating on her salad, although he couldn't see that she'd eaten much. "I can imagine."

"Is something wrong?" he finally asked bluntly.

Her eyes, a darker green than usual, briefly met his. "No. I just thought we should talk tonight. Once Caleb's gone to bed."

A sense of foreboding tightened his stomach. What the hell?

The evening seemed interminable. Moira insisted on cleaning the kitchen while he played with Caleb, who then resisted going down for the night. When he finally did and Moira returned to the living room, Will said, "All right. What is it?"

She sat on what he thought of as her end of the

couch, well out of his reach. "I saw the letter from the foundation."

Well, shit. He hadn't meant to leave it out.

"It's flattering they thought I did such a good job. But I'm not going back."

Finally, she looked fully at him. Her voice was completely steady. Even cool. "Maybe you should, Will."

"What?"

"I thought about it all day. I've appreciated more than I can say what you've done for me. I hope you know that. But I don't need you the way I did. Not the same way. We'd agreed in the first place this would be temporary. You gave up so much. And now...now it looks like you don't have to."

He let loose with an obscenity. Fear clawed at him. "We're married, Moira. I gave up one commitment for another—to *you*—and I'm sure as hell not going back on it."

"Will, this is your chance." She sounded almost as if she was pleading with him. "We didn't marry for love. Neither of us was thinking about a lifetime when we did it. You've been wonderful, but you can still follow your dream. I'll welcome you to stay whenever you can get back to the States to see Caleb. And...he'll be here when your two years is up. I promise I won't ever try to keep him from you. I swear."

"Moira, what I want has changed."

Her gaze pierced him. "Tell me that you didn't feel longing when you read that letter. Be honest, Will. Please. Please." For the first time her voice faltered. "You read that and thought, I could go back. Didn't you?"

"I won't lie to you," he said hoarsely. "I felt a pang. But that's all."

"You hate the work you're doing right now, and starting your own contracting business isn't what you ever intended to do with your life." She was relentless. "It's second best. All of this is." Her vague gesture encompassed him, her. Them. "I don't want a marriage with a man who came to it reluctantly and stayed out of a sense of obligation. That's...not fair to either of us."

She did deserve better, and he could give it to her. He loved her. But he had the breath-stealing fear that she wasn't asking for his love. Was she telling him that he wasn't what she wanted and needed?

"When we made love, did it feel like obligation?" Now his voice was harsh. Only anger could combat pain. "Is that what you were offering? Did you think I expected payback because I'd taken care of you when you needed me?"

Finally, color rushed over cheeks that had been too pale. "Of course not. We enjoyed sex. We enjoyed sex a year ago, too, Will. That didn't keep you from going to Africa. Why should it now?"

Now the shock, anger and hurt were so damned knotted together, he couldn't separate them. "Are you asking me to leave, Moira? Is that what this is about?"

"No, I..."

He swore. "I'd have sworn last night—this morning—that you were happy. Is it just the letter?"

The flush had left her cheeks. She was marble-white now, her freckles standing out starkly. He wondered if she was even breathing. "You know I'm...not very confident about some things. And you know how much I hated the fact that you gave up something you'd been dreaming about for years. It broke my heart, when I saw your face that night when you were looking at pictures of Zimbabwe online. I suppose I thought you couldn't have it back, once you made the decision. But it turns out you can, Will. It's not like you can't still be a father to Caleb. He'll need you more later, anyway, when he's older."

Granite hard, he said, "I'm not going, Moira."

Eyes huge and beseeching, she said, "Will you think about this? Please? Don't…don't just be stubbornly set on sticking it out because you think you promised. That's not enough. We'll both be miserable later. I need you to be honest. Please," she repeated. "Please don't lie to me."

"Moira…"

She shook her head and stood suddenly. "I can't talk about it anymore. I've said what I had to say. Just… think. Now I'm going to bed. No," she said, when he started to rise. "I'd rather go alone tonight. I'm not in the mood—" Moira stopped as if her throat had clogged, then rushed away.

Frozen halfway between standing and sitting, he heard the quiet snick of the bedroom door shutting. His knees gave out, and he sank into the chair. That damn door hadn't been shut in a long time. Should he be grateful that she trusted him to hear Caleb?

At the thought of their baby, Will felt a huge crack in his almost-numbness, one that let him glimpse such agony he couldn't bear it. How could she know him so little that she'd think for an instant he'd want to spend two years half a world away from his son?

From her?

He sat there for hours, the house quiet and almost

unbearably lonely around him. Once Caleb did awaken and cry. Knowing he couldn't be hungry yet, Will rocked him back to sleep. The small weight nestled against his chest felt so sweet, Will only reluctantly laid him back in the crib and retreated from the softly lit room. The door across the hall stayed closed. Either Moira hadn't heard Caleb's cries, or was lying there tensely hoping she wasn't needed.

What if she did kick him out? Will tried to imagine going home to his brothers' house—and he thought of it that way. It wasn't home anymore. *This* was home now, with Moira and Caleb. And he sure as hell couldn't talk to anybody about what had gone wrong, not even his brothers. Clay was becoming a friend, but still, Will had never in his life talked about his feelings with any of his siblings. With anyone, really, before Moira.

And this… No, he needed to wrap his mind around everything she'd said first. She'd asked him to think, and he would.

He eventually laid down on the couch, not even bothering to convert it into a bed. It was too short, but he wouldn't have slept well, anyway. He waited in the morning until he heard Moira go in to Caleb, then he showered and dressed for work. Thank God for work, he thought, with an edge of desperation. When he came out, Moira had already fried bacon and was scrambling eggs. He ate, they were civil, but he didn't kiss her goodbye. It was the first time they'd parted in a long time when he hadn't kissed her.

The morning was too busy for much brooding. One of the tenants came by to inspect the work and discuss some minor changes. Will's crew was doing finish work, and on impulse at noon he said, "You're on your own this afternoon. Call my cell if you need me," and left.

He drove over to Forest Park and found a bench with a view of the playground. The day was chilly but clear and several well-bundled mothers pushed their kids on swings or watched them scramble on climbers. As he'd be doing someday with Caleb.

Had he been lying to Moira? To himself? If he weren't bullheadedly determined to make their marriage work because he viewed this commitment to the mother of his child as the right thing to do, would he want to take up where he'd left off in Zimbabwe?

He sat for a long time, imagining himself getting back on the airplane, ending up in Harare. Walking into his house there to the smell of cooking, sitting down in solitude to his *sadza,* served by Jendaya. He remembered his last trips in the country, the lengthy negotiations with regional officials, the open-air meetings with villagers, the glimpses of wildlife and ancient rock art. And gradually he relaxed, because what he remembered best was how colored his every day had become by his worries about Moira, his memories of their one night together.

It would be a thousand times worse now. There wouldn't be a minute when he wasn't haunted by thoughts of her and Caleb. He'd enjoyed what he was doing there, he'd found it satisfying, but it didn't compare to being a husband and father.

How could she think...?

He groaned, remembering the night she'd walked in unexpectedly when he was online looking at photos of Zimbabwe. He sat without moving, aching when he pictured the stricken expression on Moira's face as she'd hastily retreated. She'd tried to talk to him, and he'd shut her down. But she'd been right, and he was wrong.

There was a reason he had only gone online after she'd gone to bed, or when she wasn't home. Face it: he'd been trying to deceive her, to convince her that he wasn't thinking anymore about the job and dreams he'd given up. He'd deceived even himself, because what he'd done was leave that door cracked open.

With what she saw, with his refusal to talk about it, he'd confirmed Moira's belief that he'd chosen duty over heart. That wasn't true, but it also hadn't been quite honest of him to pretend he had no regrets.

Had a part of him, hidden inside, still thought maybe he'd help Moira out for a while, then go back to what he'd been doing? He couldn't be sure, but he was ashamed of himself that his commitment hadn't been as absolute as he'd believed it was. He felt sleazy, as if he *had* been looking at big-breasted naked women online.

The door was shut now, but maybe too late. He'd hurt her, and he had refused to see that that's what he was doing. *Please God,* he thought bleakly, *don't let me be too late.*

No matter what, he was done. She and Caleb mattered more than anything else in the world to him. That *was* the truth. He'd finally been finding his way to a life that would satisfy him in other ways, too, he realized. He wouldn't like to disappoint the people at Bright Futures. He'd committed to them, too. Nor would it be hard to keep finding projects like that, ways he could do good here.

But…what if he couldn't convince Moira? The fear devastated him. Just thinking about losing her, he knew how much he loved her. Her, and Caleb. How could he go on without them? He couldn't conceive of being an every-other-weekend father to his son. Seeing Moira only to hand off their child would be hideous.

If she didn't believe in his commitment, would she believe he loved her? Will didn't know.

He kept searching through her words for clues, and not finding them.

I don't want a marriage with a man who came to it reluctantly and stayed out of a sense of obligation. The question was, did she want marriage with *him?*

Leaving that aside, he began to think about why she'd had such a hard time from the beginning believing he would want her enough to give up anything for her. He'd always known that she was strong, but even that first night Will had seen the vulnerability beneath. He'd peeled back layers since, and could see the scars she tried to hide even from herself. The father who hadn't given a damn. The years she'd seen herself as fat and been rejected socially. The sense she'd always had of being likable, but not…desirable.

Hands shoved in the pockets of his parka, legs stretched out in front of him, Will stared at the playground without seeing a soul. It might as well have been deserted. All he saw was Moira, only Moira. Her face that time he'd told her how much sadness he saw in her. He remembered her telling him once that he was a good man, so good she was afraid he'd lie to her to keep her from thinking she was taking advantage of him.

She had never believed he would want to stay with her. He'd *known* that, without letting himself understand how deep her fears ran. In her memory, she'd had to beg him to make love to her in the first place. The pregnancy was all her fault because all he'd done was be kind to her. His enthusiasm in bed was…hell, who knew? A man getting laid?

That's what I always think, you know. That no guy could be interested in me.

Making love at least once a day this past week, waking up next to her, eating breakfast with her, coming home to her, had been so good, like an idiot he'd believed that her fears about him had been laid to rest. Of course it wasn't that easy. Moira's deep-seated belief that he had made a huge and terrible sacrifice for her and for his baby had only dozed, waiting to be reawakened by that letter he'd so carelessly left out.

Carelessly, because it hadn't meant that much to him. A sound escaped him as he exhaled. Had he really even felt a pang? Reading the letter, he *was* flattered. Sorry the clinics weren't being built as quickly as they had all hoped. He'd had a moment of renewed guilt at having failed to keep a promise. But he hadn't been tempted at all. He'd tossed the damn thing aside without a second thought because he'd found something a hell of a lot more important. Love.

Had Moira really not seen how happy he was? How much he needed her? How many times had he told her he lived to get home to her and Caleb? Will was still baffled that she could really think it was all a lie, him making the best of an obligation he'd reluctantly shouldered…but she did.

What an idiot he'd been, not telling her he loved her. He had known for a long time what he felt. But… that door had still been cracked open behind him, too, and he guessed that's what had kept the words unsaid. Yeah, Moira had plenty of self-doubts. What had she said? *After a while, you sort of give up*. But she'd been married to a man dumb enough not to say, loud and clear, "I love you," and keep saying it. And she wasn't a woman able to hold on to faith in the face of his silence.

He surged to his feet, wanting nothing more than to get in his truck and head home to West Fork to confront her. To tell her he was crazily, permanently in love with her, and she could by God *learn* to believe it.

As the engine roared to life, he felt a hard kick in his chest. Was he kidding himself, thinking she wanted him to love her? Moira had never said anything to indicate she was in love with him. He was judging solely on the way she responded to his kisses, to him in bed, the expression in her eyes sometimes, the trusting way she slept in his arms. The fact that she had agreed to marry him in the first place. He'd presented marriage to her as a sensible solution to their dilemma, but Will knew he wouldn't have gone that far if he hadn't already felt too much for her. And he couldn't imagine that she'd have accepted him if *she* hadn't felt enough to know she could live intimately with him. They'd both gambled on something they hadn't been willing to name, not at that point. And he'd believed—still believed—they had won.

But he had to hear her say those three words, too. *I love you*. Until he did, until he had her in his arms again, he was going to stay scared.

"There," Moira said, lifting Caleb from the small plastic bathtub she'd set on the kitchen counter. "That wasn't so bad, was it?"

The first few weeks of his life, he'd wailed every time he was put in water. He'd progressed to looking worried, and tonight he'd become briefly entranced with a floating soap bubble. He'd grinned once, too, kicking his legs and splashing the counter and her.

Bundled in a towel, he wriggled happily.

"Now I'm wetter than you are," she told him, kissing him on the nose. She carried him to her room and laid him on the bed while she peeled off her shirt and grabbed a dry one from the drawer. But, unable to resist, she picked him up before she put the T on, loving the feel of his plump, naked body against her own bare skin.

She'd read in books about how important touch was to babies. Dry diapers and enough formula weren't enough. Something inside shriveled and died if babies weren't cuddled often enough. They lost the potential to feel emotions and trust for the rest of their lives.

Holding Caleb, Moira wondered if that's what had happened to her. Not when she was a baby, of course; she knew her mother had loved her. But later. After college, she'd had no one to hold her. An occasional hug from a friend or her mom wasn't the same as this, loving and warm, or the thigh to chest, skin-to-skin contact she'd had with Will. His kisses and his arms around her, the way he had of constantly touching her, that big hand making her feel secure in a way she didn't ever remember feeling. Sitting on the edge of the bed, tears welling in her eyes even as her body soaked up the contact with her baby, Moira ached for Will's touch. For Will.

No, she hadn't lost the potential to feel these emotions, but hope had certainly shriveled in her. The belief in forever.

Cheek pressed to her baby's head, she gasped with

the pain, and tried to believe she'd done the right thing in giving Will an out. The only thing possible, for the man she loved.

Caleb began rooting for her breast and, no matter her inner turmoil, she opened the cup of her bra. He happily latched on.

Even as she bent and kissed the silky, damp hair on top of his head, she let herself consider an idea that would once have been unthinkable.

What if Will had meant what he said? What if he really *had* felt only a pang? What if he truly *wanted* to stay with her and Caleb?

What if she hadn't been acting out of love for him at all, but out of her own fears? Her own belief that he couldn't possibly choose her over his dreams?

He'd been angry, she knew he was. If he didn't think she wanted him to stay, might he be mad and hurt enough to call the foundation today and say, sure, what the hell, I'll go?

An awful sound escaped her. Caleb let loose of her breast and lifted his head to stare at her with perplexed brown eyes.

Moira made reassuring sounds despite the anguish that tore through her. She kept looking at her baby— at *their* baby—and thought as she often did how well he blended parts of her with parts of Will. The eyes were Will's, if a lighter shade than his. The square, determined chin was his, too. The red in Caleb's hair was from her, the nose, she thought, hers. He proba- bly *would* have freckles, but also his daddy's size and, someday, powerful shoulders and big feet.

She wished desperately that she'd been brave enough

to tell Will she loved him. He'd have been kind no matter what. Why had she been so afraid of baring herself?

Now, all she could think was that, while Will had been angry, mostly what she remembered was the pain in his eyes, the hoarse disbelief in his voice. And she hadn't listened to what he tried to tell her, had refused to hear.

Caleb had fallen asleep. Moira slipped away, fastening her bra and pulling on her T-shirt. He only scrunched his eyes tighter closed when she put on his diaper and carried him to his crib.

She stood for a moment, looking down at him, her chest hurting. Will would be home after work. They could talk then. It wasn't as if he'd left her because of the things she'd said. All she had done was ask him to think, to be honest with himself. That wasn't so bad, was it? She *wanted* him to be honest.

And maybe it was better that she'd never told him she loved him, even if that was cowardly. Because he might tell her tonight that what he really wanted was to go back to Africa. If so, it was better that he never knew. She wouldn't bind him further with more guilt, barbed to draw blood.

WILL STOOD ON THE PORCH and actually thought about ringing the doorbell. The way he and Moira had left it last night and this morning, he didn't know how welcome he was.

But, damn it, he lived here, and after a minute he shoved the key in the lock and opened the door. The foyer was empty. There was a moment of silence and he had the sudden, irrational fear that the house was empty.

But the next instant, she stepped from the living room with Caleb in her arms, as if he was coming home from work any other day.

"Will," she whispered, her face pinched and eyes huge.

Caleb beamed at the sight of his daddy. Without saying a word, Will held out his arms, and she put his son in them. Damn. His eyes burned.

Moira backed up, as if to give him space. For a moment he laid his cheek against Caleb's head and inhaled the clean, milky scent of baby.

"How could you think even for a minute that I'd walk away from you?" he whispered. He had to blink away the blur in his eyes to focus on her face. "I miss you every day, just going to work."

"Oh, Will." She flung herself at him. He barely got his free arm out in time to catch her. He lurched back and pushed the door closed.

Their baby was squished between them. Moira wrapped both arms around Will's torso as if she were drowning and he was the life preserver. She burrowed her face against his chest. She was trying to talk, but the words were muffled in his shirt.

Caleb struggled in protest. Heart pounding, Will said, "Let me put Caleb down. Sweetheart, let me set him down."

It seemed to take her a minute to hear. Then she slowly let her arms fall and backed away. Her face was wet. Will looked around and saw a crib-size comforter on the arm of the sofa. He grabbed it and spread it on the floor with one flick, then laid their son down on his tummy. Caleb pushed up right away, stronger than he'd been a few days ago.

Will turned and hauled Moira into his arms. Once again, she pressed herself to him as if she wanted to crawl inside him. He wanted that, too. Holding her as close as was humanly possible meant more to him right now than anything else on earth.

He heard himself saying things, but he didn't know if they were any more coherent than whatever she'd mumbled into his chest. He was crooning to her more than making any sense.

It had to be a couple of minutes before she began to relax. Just a little, then a little more, until her body didn't feel as frantic to him and he could loosen his own grip some. Finally she stepped back, her wet, puffy face wrenching his heart, and cried, "Oh, I've got to blow my nose." She fled for the bathroom.

While she was gone, Will swiped his eyes with his forearm. He crouched beside Caleb and patted his diaper-padded butt. "Look at you," he murmured. "Man, you're going to be crawling before we know it."

When he heard the bathroom door, he stood and watched Moira come down the hall then, more hesitantly, across the living room to him. Her face was still puffy and the red splotches didn't go well with the golden dust of freckles, but she wasn't crying anymore and, damn, she looked beautiful to his eyes.

After a hesitant moment, she said, "I kept being afraid you wouldn't come home. That you were mad, and I'd hurt your feelings, and you wouldn't want to see me."

"You did hurt my feelings," he said gruffly, but he was reaching for her to draw her close.

"I just…needed to know…"

"I understand," he heard himself say gently. He

rubbed his cheek against the top of her hair. "I gave you every reason to wonder."

"I…" Moira went very still in his grip. "Did you get in touch with the foundation?"

"Yeah. The day the letter came. I sent them an email saying thanks, but I'm not available."

She pulled back enough to look up at him, searching his face with grave eyes. "You truly didn't want to go?"

"And leave you and Caleb?" His voice sounded rusty now, the hurt thickening it. "No. I didn't want to go."

Moira retreated farther. The hands that had been pressed to his chest writhed as she wound her fingers together. "I thought I was doing the right thing for you. But today I realized I was listening to my fears more than anything." She swallowed. "Did you think, Will? The way I asked?"

"Yeah. I thought. And I realized that I'm not very good at communicating with people. Not about what I feel. I've never had to try before. I also realized that I wasn't completely honest with you. I was trying to hide the regrets I did feel. And that was stupid. I can talk to you. I just thought—" He stopped, lost for words.

"That I'd assume exactly what I did last night."

He frowned. "But maybe you wouldn't have, if I'd been open all along. If I'd said, 'I loved it in Africa, but I love it here, too. With you, Moira.'"

"Is that what you'd have said?" she whispered.

He nodded.

"Will." The strain on her face was heartbreaking, but no more so than the hope. "Do you really want to stay married to me?"

His throat closed, his chest spasmed. In a harsh

whisper, he said, "More than I've ever wanted any-thing in my life."

"Oh, Will." She rushed into his arms again, and they were ready for her. She pressed her face to his shoulder, and he buried his in her cloud of copper curls. They rocked in place, a subtle, reassuring motion that came instinctively, comfort at its most primal. He knew he was probably holding her too tightly, but she didn't seem to mind, and he couldn't make himself unlock his arms from around her.

"I love you," he said to the top of her head. "Maybe you can't feel the same way about me, but don't ever doubt me. I love you so damn much, it about ripped me apart when I was afraid you didn't want me."

Without loosening her arms at all, Moira tilted her head back to look at him. "You love me?" she asked, her voice cracking at the end, the vulnerability and un-certainty in it as excruciating as a blade between the ribs. "You really love me?"

He tried to smile. "I think I must have fallen in love with you that first night. I knew I shouldn't do something as dumb as go in that hotel room with you, but…I couldn't not. From the minute I saw you in the ballroom, I couldn't look away. I never got your face out of my mind. You'd have heard from me as soon as I got back from Africa. I think I'd have spent two years praying you didn't meet someone and get mar-ried while my back was turned."

Her eyes filled again with a rush. "I fell in love with you, too. And, oh, so much more when you came to see me. And listened to Caleb's heartbeat, and laid your hand on my stomach to feel him move. The expression on your face—" She choked to a stop.

"I should have told you," Will said. "I thought you weren't ready to hear those words. But I should have said them anyway. Maybe you'd have known that I wouldn't leave you. *Couldn't* leave you."

She was the one smiling now, although her lips trembled. "I don't know if I'd have believed you."

His fingers tightened. "Do you now?"

There was something dazed in her eyes. After a moment she gave the smallest of nods. "Yes. I do. Part of me thinks I'm dreaming, but...I do believe you. Oh, Will. I love you so much!"

He kissed her then, using mouth and teeth and tongue to show her how hungry he was for her. The kiss wasn't just about wanting her body. Although he did. God, he did. She kissed him back so fervently, he knew she felt the same. She still wanted to get inside him, and she wanted him inside her just as much.

Caleb let out a cry. When his parents ignored it, he got serious with a frustrated wail.

Will and Moira separated, only a few inches. He felt a grin stretching his mouth and loved the answering smile on hers.

"Oh, dear," she said. "He thinks this is his time of day with Daddy. He's not used to us ignoring him."

Will stooped and picked up Caleb, murmuring, "You felt left out, didn't you? I'm so sorry, buddy. So sorry."

Moira kissed Caleb's cheek, then briefly rested her cheek against Will's arm. "This is my second favorite time of day. When you come home."

"What's your favorite?" he asked in a low rumble.

She gave a little laugh. "You know."

Cradling Caleb in both arms, Will bent his head

and nuzzled his wife's ear. "Mine, too," he said huskily. "And I'm already thinking about it."

A little shyly, she said, "Good."

Gently bouncing Caleb, Will said, "So, what's for dinner?"

Moira laughed. "A pot roast."

"Even though you were afraid I wasn't coming home?"

Her smile, glorious and uncomplicated by any doubt whatsoever, stole his breath. "But you see," she said, "I was being optimistic."

He lifted his eyebrows. "I've cured you of pessimism?"

As if startled, she was quiet for a minute, her lips parted. When she answered, she sounded bemused. "I think maybe you have. Or at least, that I'm learning. What a funny feeling."

On a surge of emotion that filled him to aching, Will said, "You'll get used to it. I'll help. I promise."

"You're a good and kind man, Will Becker," she told him.

"And an honest one."

"Yes, I believe you are." Her mouth curved once again. "There I go again. Optimistic." The smile turned into a laugh. "I'll get dinner on. That will bring bedtime closer."

"Our favorite time of day." Will took a deep breath. "Damn, it's good to be home," he said, and headed for the bathroom. Their son needed a clean diaper.

Bedtime would come soon enough.

* * * * *

HOLLY JACOBS

In 2000, Holly Jacobs sold her first book to Harlequin. She's since sold more than twenty-five novels to the publisher. Her romances have won numerous awards and made the Waldenbooks bestseller list. In 2005, Holly won a prestigious Career Achievement Award from *RT Book Reviews*. In her nonwriting life, Holly is married to a police captain, and together they have four children. Visit Holly at hollyjacobs.com. You can snail-mail her at P.O. Box 11102, Erie, PA 16514-1102.

Be sure to look for other books by Holly Jacobs in Harlequin Superromance—the ultimate destination for more story, more romance! There are new Harlequin Superromance titles available every month. Check one out today!

UNEXPECTED GIFTS
Holly Jacobs

For all the amazing teachers who work in the Erie School District's Teen Parenting Program, especially Jeanne Bender, Mary Fuhrmann, Connie Sementilli and Bonnie Sobeck. Thanks for letting me be a part of the amazing work you do. You have touched so many students' lives, and the ripple effects from your work will be felt for years to come. And for Sharon Lorei, who was an "Eli Cartwright" sort of teacher in my life.

PROLOGUE

"There's no way to cheat nature."
—*Pregnancy, Childbirth and Parenting for Teens,*
by Mary Jeanne Lorei

ARIEL MAYORS KNEW that, until recently, she'd been teacher's pet. A favorite. The student who could do no wrong.

She'd cultivated that status with the same care that a gardener used looking after prized orchids. By the time Ariel had reached her senior year of high school she'd practically perfected the art of perfect. She was always the first one to raise her hand, the first one to volunteer and almost always the best student in class.

Popularity was a game that she didn't just play with the teachers, she played it with fellow students as well.

To garner the girls' admiration she made sure she never poached boyfriends, that she always offered a shoulder in any cry-worthy moment and that she was never without an extra Tampax in her purse for those time-of-the-month emergencies.

She'd discovered the basic truth that once you'd borrowed a tampon from someone, it was hard to hate them.

Ariel was a cheerleader, which provided her a ready-made social group, and also meant she was one of the girls all the boys wanted to date. She knew this part of her popularity didn't stem from any planning of hers. Biology had blessed her with blond hair and a long, lithe body. But she'd worked at the rest—worked on knowing what clothes to wear, how to apply makeup flawlessly. She worked at knowing when to laugh, when to draw closer, when to pull back.

Well, she thought, she'd known when to pull back until that one night in Charlie Markowski's Lumina van.

She stood in front of Ms. Cartwright's desk. Her teacher wasn't beautiful, but there was something appealing about her averageness. Brown shoulder-length hair, blue eyes. A little shorter than Ariel's five feet, six inches. Ms. Cartwright was the kind of person who was so normal-looking she could easily get lost in a crowd in a way Ariel never could. That was, until she smiled. Then Ms. Cartwright was beautiful. Ariel wasn't sure how that worked, she just knew it did. She wanted to be like Ms. Cartwright someday. Calm, collected—a woman in charge of her own destiny. Someone who got more beautiful when they smiled.

Only Ms. Cartwright wasn't smiling today.

"Ariel," Ms. Cartwright said, disappointment right there in that one word and echoing so fiercely in her favorite teacher's expression.

Ariel had disappointed so many people in the last few weeks. She'd worked so hard to please this one woman, and now, she'd disappointed her, too.

"Ariel, Mrs. Brown came to see me. She says she found this in your book." Ms. Cartwright slid the small piece of paper across the desk. "Is this crib note yours?"

"Yes," Ariel whispered.

"Pardon?"

"Yes."

"Do you have an explanation?"

"I worked at the restaurant last night and planned on studying during my break but Dale, the dork manager at Barney's, wouldn't give me one. We had a bus come in and…" She simply shrugged. What more was there to say? She'd done it—she'd cheated. She could add that to her growing list of descriptions.

Cheerleader.

Student council rep.

Straight A student.

Pregnant teen.

Cheater.

Ms. Cartwright didn't yell, didn't scream. She just shook her head sadly and asked, "Do you really think this is the way to handle things? By taking the easy way out?"

"I just didn't know what else to do."

"Did it occur to you that you could go to Mrs. Brown and explain the situation to her. Or, you could have come to me. It's part of my job description…helping you find options. There are always some. I know you're new to the program, but it's pretty much our mantra—finding options." She sighed. "Listen, Ariel, this stopped being about you when you became pregnant. You will be this baby's role model. He or she will look to you to see how to live. Is this what you'd want *your* child to do? Do you want them to take the easy way out?"

"No. I didn't think of it like that."

"You have to learn to think about everything you do in that way—how it will affect your baby. You need to do what's best for them, always. Even when it's difficult for you. Now, how do you think we should handle this?"

"You know, those are the kinds of questions all us kids hate. You make us decide on a fair punishment."

"I make you take responsibility for your actions. Most teens have a few more years to learn about actions and consequences—the girls in this program don't have the luxury of time. *You* don't have that luxury."

She looked pointedly at Ariel's stomach and the barely there baby bump.

"Ariel, I see so much potential in you. Don't blow it. If you have a problem, come see me, see Mrs. Brown. There are people here for you. Don't forget that."

"Maybe I should start by writing an apology to Mrs. Brown?"

"I think that's an excellent place to begin. Come see me tomorrow and we'll talk about what else you think is required in order to make this right."

Darn. Ariel had hoped that a letter of apology would be all that she had to do to smooth this over. Obviously, it wasn't.

"Okay, I'll think about it and see you tomorrow." She practically sprang for the door, anxious to escape Ms. Cartwright's sympathetic gaze. It would be easier if the teacher would get pissed off and yell. But no, not her, she only looked as if her girls screwing up hurt her.

Ariel turned the doorknob, and pushed at the door, ready to make her escape when Ms. Cartwright's voice stopped her. "And Ariel?"

She turned back and saw pain in Ms. Cartwright's smile. She'd do almost anything to replace that look of disappointment with one of pride.

"You can't cheat nature. You are going to be a mother in a few months and there are no crib notes that will let you fake your way through being a good parent. And that's what you owe this baby. Being the best parent, the best example you can be."

"Yes, ma'am."

"And for that matter, Ariel, life happens. You can't cheat your way through it, either. There are no crib notes. You have to live each day as well as you can. I'll see you tomorrow."

Finally, dismissed, Ariel hurried away before Ms. Cartwright could say anything else profoundly painful.

There were no crib notes for being a parent. For being an adult.

Ariel desperately wished there were.

CHAPTER ONE

"There are four stages of mourning. Denial. Sadness. Anger. Acceptance. Becoming pregnant in your teens means that some dreams have to be put away, others altered. It's a death of one future. You have to mourn that loss before you can move ahead and plan a new future...one that includes the baby you're carrying."

—*Pregnancy, Childbirth and Parenting for Teens,*
by Mary Jeanne Lorei

THERE WAS SOMETHING completely undignified about peeing in a cup. It took a certain knack that Elinore Cartwright didn't feel she had acquired and, to be honest, she didn't know that she wanted to be presented too many more opportunities to develop it.

Despite the fact she was nowhere near a master, she managed the fill the little paper cup. She washed her hands and then, clutching the paper gown at the back, hurried across the hall to her assigned examination room. She hoisted herself back onto the table.

Sitting on paper, wearing paper, covering herself with a square piece of quilted paper. Every movement was a festival noise.

The only nonpaper item she was wearing for her less-than-happily anticipated annual checkup was her wildly striped toe socks. She'd left them on partly because now that it was the end of October, her feet wouldn't be warm again for at least eight months, and partly because she felt they dressed up her paper ensemble.

She sank back onto her paper-shrouded shrine and waited. Right on cue, as her body relaxed, her thoughts picked up steam, tumbling over themselves. There was no flitting involved, just a terrible tangled twist of to-do items and worries.

To-do: Call Zac Keller and set up a meeting for the end of the week.

Ariel Mayor. She replayed their talk from earlier this afternoon. It had seemed to go well. She saw a lot of potential in the girl. As a matter of fact…

To-do: Pull together Ariel's information and see if Zac would agree that she'd make an excellent test-run for the new Community Action, Teen-Parent Apprentice Project.

It had been almost fifteen years since Eli had started the George County School District's teen parenting program. George County was a large, primarily rural county just south of Erie, Pennsylvania. Her job was to find ways to cut the county's number of teen parents, and help those who were pregnant or already parents graduate and go on to be worthwhile members of the community.

The statistics said her program was working. She experienced that warm glow of pride she always felt when she thought about the inroads she'd made.

The number of teen mothers in the county was falling, the number of teen moms who graduated was climbing. And there had been a nice bump in the number of her mothers who went on to college or some type of vocational training after graduation.

This new project was just another way of helping her girls. Partnering local businesses with the students in the program. Giving the teens jobs with flexibility, jobs that would provide crucial work experience.

It sounded as if Ariel was already working hard, too hard, at that restaurant. This program might be just the ticket for her.

And despite Ariel Mayor's slight bump in the road, Eli was determined that this girl would be one of her successes.

Her to-do list was replaced as a niggle of worry crept into the forefront of her thoughts. She'd figured passing so easily from fertility to menopause was a good thing. After half a year of erratic cycles, her periods had just stopped a few months ago with no other problems arising. No hot flashes, mood swings, trouble sleeping.

Eli took this as another sign that her life was pretty much perfect. She had Arthur, who, although he was a little less than exciting, was good company and a dependable boyfriend. She had a job she loved, a great family and good friends. And now, she'd had a pain-free transition into menopause at the ripe old age of forty-four.

At least, that's what she thought until Dr. Benton had asked to run a few tests. One of which involved peeing in that stupid cup.

How long did it take to do whatever voodoo test he was doing? And what did he think was wrong?

Cancer?

That horrible C word.

Cancer of what? Cervix, uterus, ovaries? Maybe that was it, cancer had eaten all her eggs, so her periods had stopped.

She tried to force her thoughts back to her long to-do list. It was much more pleasant.

Okay. To-do…

Her mind was blank. She was saved from trying to fill it though when Dr. Benton opened the door.

"Go ahead and just tell me. Cancer has eaten all my eggs, right?"

He laughed.

Hmm, doctors didn't normally laugh when telling someone they had a cancer, right?

She took a deep breath and let it out slowly, feeling better. She sat up and all the paper crinkled merrily. "I have an active imagination. So what's the news?"

"You're not in menopause—"

"Then it is cancer. Cancer of the uterus? That's why my period stopped."

"You're pregnant."

"Cancer of the cervix?"

"Pregnant. As in going to have a baby."

She laughed. "Funny. Ha ha. You can tell me. Just say the words, I can take it."

"Eli, you're not sick, there's nothing wrong with you that I've found. Although you are pregnant."

"But…I can't be. I mean, Arthur always uses condoms, and…" She paused, trying to process what Dr. Benton was saying. "You can't get pregnant if you're in menopause, so I'm not pregnant."

"You're not in menopause. You're pregnant. Some of those missed periods were because you're going to have a baby, not because of menopause. You're going to have a baby in around six or seven months. Somewhere around May or June would be my guess. We'll have to do some tests to be sure."

"But—"

"Listen, Eli, I've been your doctor for a long time, and I know this comes as a shock. Why don't you go home, take some time and process it all, then come see me again next week and we'll talk? We'll do a few more tests. I want to do a sonogram so we'll have a more accurate idea of your due date since you have been experiencing erratic cycles."

"But—"

"And here." He reached into his pocket and handed her a prescription. "Prenatal, prescription vitamins. Get it filled and start taking one a day."

"But—"

He patted her hand. "It's going to be all right."

Eli went into a type of brain-fogged automatic pilot. That was the only way to explain how she managed to dress and check in with the receptionist. She agreed to the first appointment that was offered without consulting her calendar, bundled into her jacket, and made her way to her car—her brand-new MINI Cooper. A more nonbaby car couldn't be found. She drove a MINI, so there was no way she was pregnant.

The fog started to clear.

Dr. Benton, bless his heart, was wrong. That was the only explanation. She'd seen one of those news shows about doctors and their inaccurate tests. That's what this was. The test was faulty.

Or, since Dr. Benton was getting on in age and probably needed reading glasses, he'd misread the results.

Either way, he was wrong. She was not pregnant.

With a newly found, albeit fuzzy, plan, Eli put her foot to the floor and hurried to her neighborhood pharmacy. While she waited for them to fill the prescription that she probably wouldn't need, she grabbed a basket, then walked up and down the aisles until she found the pregnancy test section.

Six.

There were six different brands of pregnancy tests.

She read the boxes. Digital tests. Plus or minus tests. One box had three individual tests in it…for people who thought they were pregnant frequently? There was no way she would want to go through this sinking feeling more than once.

She studied the boxes. All claimed to be ninety-nine percent accurate.

She took the first box and threw it in her basket.

Just to be on the safe side, she grabbed a second brand and added it.

She started down the aisle. Surely, the tests would prove Dr. Benton was wrong.

But what if they were faulty as well?

She turned back and hurried to the display. She put one of each brand of test in her basket.

There. She'd take all of these and when all six told her she wasn't pregnant, she'd call Dr. Benton and insist he either check the expiration dates on his tests at the office, or that he make an appointment for an eye exam.

Maybe both.

He was going to be embarrassed, she was sure. But she'd laugh it off, and make certain he understood she didn't blame him.

Yes, tell him no harm, no foul.

By the time she got home she was feeling a surreal

sense of calm. Everything would be fine once she peed on the six small wands. All of them promised results in three to five minutes.

She glanced at the clock. Dr. Benton would probably still be at his office. She'd call him right away so he could figure out what the problem was...faulty test or aging eyes.

She hurried into the bathroom and discovered peeing on sticks was infinitely easier than peeing in a cup.

She lined them all up on the counter and left, determined not to watch them. She didn't need to. She knew what they were going to show—she wasn't pregnant.

She stood outside the bathroom door, trying to decide what to do while she waited. Aimlessly, she went down the hall and thumbed through her mail that she'd set on the antique washstand she'd found last summer on her New England vacation with Arthur. They'd meandered with no real destination in mind, stopping in small towns and villages along the way.

She ran a finger over the stand, and couldn't help it if her sleeve slipped up, exposing her watch. She didn't mean to check the time and was disappointed to discover that only one minute had passed.

She walked through the house, feeling slightly removed—as if she were a visitor seeing it for the first time. She remembered every item, its history and any sentiment it carried.

Everything was orderly in her tiny, perfect-for-one-person, but not-for-a-baby house. There was her bedroom, with the froufrou pillows on the bed. Arthur hated them and felt that the few seconds she spent putting them in place every day were wasted time. It probably added up to an hour or more a year, he'd told her. Arthur was a big fan of time management, and try as she might, she couldn't seem to convince him that time spent on aesthetics wasn't wasted at all. She liked how the pillows looked on the bed, how the entire room's decor came together. That was worth an hour of her year.

She peeked in her equally neat and appealing office. She'd spent three weekends stripping, then refinishing the oak floor. She'd used a high gloss on them and they truly shone. The deep red walls, the pulled back curtains…her office was an oasis.

This time she didn't try to convince herself that glancing at her watch was an accident.

Two minutes to go.

She went to the kitchen, hoping she'd left a glass or plate in the sink, something she could rinse, but there was nothing.

Her house was too small, too settled for a baby.

She couldn't be pregnant because she'd built a single person's home.

She glanced at her watch again.

Finally knowing beyond any doubt just how Marie Antoinette had felt as she marched toward the chopping block, Eli opened the bathroom door, then one by one picked up the wands.

Pregnant.

Pregnant.

Pregnant.

Pregnant.

Pregnant.

Her hands trembled as she picked up the last one. One little stick of hope, which was the only branch she had left to hang on to.

Pregnant.

Shit.

Eli wasn't sure how long she sat on the bathroom floor staring at that last stick. It was long enough for the realization to begin to penetrate, long enough that the ramifications of that stick, along with the other five, hit home.

She was pregnant.

Her feet were numb and tingling. One of the changes she'd noticed since hitting her forties was that she could only kneel for so long before all the blood stopped pumping into her legs.

She was well beyond her blood pumping limit.

And she was pregnant.

She wasn't sure what to do. Who to turn to.

She wanted to cry, but had preached to her girls that news of a baby should never be greeted with tears. She'd had so many young moms in her office, crying their eyes out. She understood their feelings, but it struck her as a very sad way to welcome a child into existence, so she wasn't going to cry.

But if she wasn't going to cry, that left her nothing to do with the huge lump that was sitting squarely in the center of her throat.

What to do?

Call Tucker.

She made her wobbly feet walk into the living room and dialed her friend's number. "Could you come over? I need you." She'd known that would be all it took.

Tucker didn't ask any questions, didn't hesitate. "On my way," she replied. That was like her friend. Tucker never expected anything from anyone, but gave unhesitantly to everyone.

Angelina Tucker was Eli's inspiration for starting the teen parenting program. Sixteen years ago, Tucker had been a senior and Eli had been a teacher in the home-ec department for five years. That's what they'd called it then. Now, it was family and consumer sciences.

When Tucker had found out she was pregnant, she'd come to Eli for help, and Eli had discovered how very few options and avenues there were for the young girl. She'd fought for Tucker and had become her advocate. The following year she began to put together a program for the entire district.

Tucker had come into her first classes and talked about her experiences as a teen mother. Eli had used her as a peer role model for her girls.

As they worked together, something shifted, and Tucker had become a friend. A good friend. Eventually, a best friend.

Eli was even little Bart's godmother.

Okay, Bart wasn't all that little anymore. But Tucker was just the same, hard on the outside, a pushover on the inside.

Tucker would know what to do.

Eli went to the living room and just sat on the couch and waited. When Tucker came, everything would be fine. She clung to that thought.

Tucker didn't knock, but burst into the house fifteen minutes later. There was no prelude, no opening line. She just asked, "What happened?" Concerned lines were etched on her face and she ran her fingers through her short, curly brown hair, which made it look more wild than it usually did.

"I'm pregnant."

Eli had never seen anything stop Tucker in her tracks, but this did.

Tucker plopped down next to Eli on the couch and was quiet a moment.

Then, as if some reserve energy source engaged, she turned to Eli and smiled. "Okay. If anyone can deal with this, it's you. You know all your options. You've got your education, a good job, a nice house…good friends." There was a firm certainty in Tucker's voice that worked as a balm on some of the raging emotions that roiled through Eli.

"Oh, and you've got Arthur," Tucker added as an afterthought.

"Yeah." Eli realized that when the news had finally sank in her first thought was to call her friend, not Arthur. She didn't want to analyze what that meant. There were too many other things she needed to concentrate on. "I'm a few months along. I thought it was menopause."

Tucker smiled. "Surprise."

Despite her worries, Eli managed a weak smile of her own. "Yeah."

"I remember when I found out about Bart, I was sort of stunned. I went and talked to this very wise teacher and she asked, 'What are you feeling'? She made me dig through all that junk and really pick the emotions apart. So, I'll ask you, what are you feeling?"

Eli tried to sort through the swirling vortex of feelings that were overwhelming her. She grabbed at one. "Terrified. I mean, I'm forty-four. Once upon a time I wanted kids, but I never met the right man, it was never the right time. Years ago I decided that it wasn't meant to be. I have hundreds of kids as in my students. That's enough. I've organized my life in a childless sort of way. I can't have a baby."

"Well, then…" Tucker let the words hang there.

Eli shook her head, surprised at the fierceness of her reaction to Tucker's unspoken suggestion. "No. That's not an option for me. I mean, I just can't."

"Fine, then that's progress. You've made a major decision…you're having this baby. And you're terrified, you didn't expect to have a child. What else are you feeling?"

Eli waded through the mishmash of her emotions. "Foolish. I mean, I work with pregnant mothers for a living, and I didn't realize I was pregnant? That's sad. But in my defense, we used protection every time, and I'm old. Practically ready for menopause."

"Terrified. Foolish. Old. What else?" Tuck pressed.

"Apprehensive. I have to tell my parents before they leave for their winter in Florida…and Arthur, of course."

"I remember how much fun telling my dad was. But lucky for me, I had this great teacher go with me. Lucky for you, you have a friend who's here if you need backup with your parents."

Eli noticed that Tucker didn't offer to come tell Arthur with her. She laughed. "What about when I tell Arthur?"

"I'd just antagonize him by—oh, I don't know—breathing or something."

"And he'd reciprocate. It's fine. I'll take that one on my own." The fact that her boyfriend and her best friend didn't get along made things difficult. Eli had learned to compartmentalize her life. Tucker and the rest of her friends, her school life, on one side, and Arthur on the other.

"What else?" Tucker asked.

Eli pulled her thoughts from Arthur and went back to the question at hand. What else was she feeling? She searched, and finally caught on a weak, almost whisper of a feeling. "Under all of that, there's a bit of excitement. I mean, I never thought it would happen, that I'd have a baby. Truth of the matter is, I'm going to be a mother. Sure there's a lot to figure out, and it's not convenient, but then it was that way with Bart and look at how tight the two of you are."

She stopped a second and added, "I've never asked before, but do you regret it? I mean, I know you love him, but do you ever regret everything you had to go through?"

"There are parts that I wouldn't want to relive, but he's such an amazing kid, I can't imagine what my life would be without him. I don't regret a minute of it. Having him led me to where I am. I have a kid I adore, a job I love and a friend I might never have found if I hadn't shown up in her classroom that day asking for help."

Eli couldn't think of anything to say to that.

Tucker didn't seem to mind. After another silent moment passed, she asked, "You want me to call Bart and tell him that he's on his own for dinner? We'll order a pizza and pig out. You can do that guilt-free now that you're eating for two."

Eli laughed, which she knew had been Tucker's intent. "No. I'm fine now. Well, not quite fine, but on my way to it. I need some time alone to sort it all out.

Though it's so good to know that you're just a phone call away. You really helped settle me down."

"I'm no expert. I mean, I just paint stuff for a living—"

Tucker always underplayed her talent, and Eli felt obliged to interrupt and correct her description of her job. "A graphic artist. What you do is art, Tuck."

Tucker shrugged and stood. "Doesn't matter what you call it, I'm a simple woman who has to say something before I leave. It's something no one but you ever said to me. Congratulations, Eli. This baby will change your life. And though you don't see it now, it will change your life for the better. I just know it."

Tucker leaned down and, in an uncharacteristic display of affection, hugged Eli. "No matter what, you just remember that you're not alone."

She waved and hurried out.

Eli knew that Tucker was embarrassed at her actions. She wasn't a hugger, wasn't prone to inspirational speeches. However, this one hit the mark.

This baby was going to change Eli's life.

She could only hope Tucker was right and that it was for the better.

Eli spent the rest of the evening wandering from one room of the house to another, thinking. What was Arthur going to say? Would he be excited? And her parents? Were they going to be disappointed in her?

She knew she was well past the age where she needed her parents' approval, but that didn't stop her from enjoying it. It didn't stop the sting of imagining she'd let them down.

She went into the bathroom and cleared away the remnants of her momentary insanity. She was going to have a baby, and no amount of testing was going to change that.

Bathroom cleaned, she stood in the hall not sure what to do or where to go.

Finally, she went to her room, threw the decorative pillows onto the floor, rather than stacking them neatly on the chest, and climbed into bed fully clothed. She burrowed under the covers and willed sleep to come and take her away from all her worries.

When it didn't, she tugged up on her shirt and exposed her stomach. Gently she ran her hands over it. Not *it,* her baby.

Her baby was there.

She was going to be a mother.

She just let the enormity of that thought sit there, blocking all her other considerations.

She had six sticks and a doctor's test to prove that in a very short time she was going to be someone's mom.

She was going to change diapers and breast-feed. She was going to get up in the middle of the night and deal with teething.

Somewhere down the line she'd have to cope with a first day of school, book reports and science fairs. Even first loves.

She was going to be a mother.

And someday in about eighteen years, this baby would graduate from school and go away to college. Maybe stay away, too, if the right job came along.

Her baby would someday leave her.

A new emotion swamped her. Loneliness. She'd miss this baby she'd only just found out about. Her child would eventually find their own way, build their own life, one that didn't center around her. She'd be peripheral at best.

She rested her hand on her stomach and promised herself that when that day came she'd let go. Until then, she'd hold on tight and try to enjoy every minute.

Enjoy.

Yes, under the myriad emotions that had assaulted her since she got the news was excitement. Now joined by the promise of enjoyment. She was going to enjoy being a mother.

At least she thought she would.

Oh, there was still panic, terror, but she clung to the more positive emotions.

She was going to be a mother.

CHAPTER TWO

"Discovering you're pregnant means things will
change, but different isn't always worse…"
—*Pregnancy, Childbirth and Parenting for Teens,*
by Mary Jeanne Lorei

"MS. CARTWRIGHT, ARE YOU OKAY?" Ariel asked the next
day after class.

Eli had thought she was doing an admirable job
hiding her sleepless night and inner turmoil, but obviously, she was wrong.

She redoubled her efforts and pasted her best I'm-
okay smile on and nodded. "I'm fine, thanks."

"I promised we'd finish our discussion. I wrote the
note and will give it to Mrs. Brown this afternoon."

"Good. That's a great start." At the word *start,* the
girl's smile faded.

"You said we'd talk about what else I need to do?
I've been trying to think of what else could fix this,
but other than taking an F on that test, I can't think
of anything."

"Actually, Mrs. Brown and I talked about that.
Rather than fail you, we've agreed that you'll retake
the test. And then she'll deduct ten percent from whatever you get as a penalty."

"Thank you. I assumed I'd get an F and that would drop my GPA."

Eli smiled. Despite her own mind, she'd given Ariel's situation some thought. To be honest, thinking about Ariel was so much easier than thinking about herself.

"I have an idea," she told the girl. "After my meeting this afternoon, I'll fill you in."

Ariel looked nervous.

"It's not bad," Eli assured her. "As a matter of fact, I think this might work out to be a very, very good thing for you."

Suddenly Ariel's expression changed to a look children had worn on Christmas Eve for centuries. "Ms. Cartwright, do you want to give me a hint?"

Eli chuckled. "No. But come see me after school."

"You're sure?"

"Go. I don't want you being late for your next class."

When Ariel left, Eli went back to crunching figures and making sure her facts were in order. She wished she could find the enthusiasm for this meeting she once had. Today everything felt muted. Dampened. As if she were viewing the world through cotton gauze.

She kept eying the clock.

Finally.

Lunchtime.

She stood and smoothed her skirt, then without realizing it, her hand brushed her stomach, as if to make sure her baby was all right.

Baby.

Her baby.

It still felt so unreal. Part of her would have liked

to deny the reality, but those six little sticks wouldn't allow her to.

She had a standing dinner date with Arthur on Friday nights. So tomorrow, she'd tell him. She could almost imagine stoic, dependable Arthur's reaction. He would probably be as shocked as she was, but he'd be supportive. He'd understand her mixed emotions over this unplanned, life-altering event.

Together, they'd work it out.

Right now, she needed to put all that aside and get going or she'd be late for this meeting.

She stopped at the main office and checked out with the school secretary. "Doris, I'm not sure when I'll be back. If anyone needs me, I'll have my cell. Marion's covering my one o'clock class."

"Good luck. I know how important this meeting is to you, to the new program."

"Thanks. I'm pretty sure he's on board. Today we're supposed to finalize everything and decide on our test-student."

"You'll do fine. Just give me a holler when you get back in." Doris had been with the school longer than Eli. Longer than most of the staff. She was an icon. She ran the main office with a fluid efficiency and had an aura of everyone's favorite grandmother about her.

Her confidence in Eli's ability to make this work helped bolster her own flagging belief in herself.

She drove across Whedon, wishing that this meeting was in an office. She felt at home in that setting or in a classroom. But a local restaurant had sounded convenient when she'd agreed to it. Instead she now worried the location would detract from the business Zac needed to accomplish.

"Eli," he called, waving.

Despite the craziness since her doctor's appointment, seeing him made her smile. There was something engaging about Zac Keller. He was a nice-looking man who was defined by what he wasn't. He wasn't tall, wasn't short—maybe about five-ten. He wasn't fat, wasn't skinny, wasn't a bodybuilder, wasn't scrawny. He had average brown hair and a medium complexion.

But once someone met Zac, he stood out. Maybe it was the devilish look in his brown eyes—a look that said life was a joy and there was always mischief to be made.

"Hi," she said as she took the seat across from him.

His smile faded as he studied her a moment. "What's wrong?"

"Wrong?" she repeated dumbly.

"Wrong. Something's wrong."

First Ariel, now Zac.

Eli tried to school her expression and concentrate on the task at hand.

She passed a file to him. "Not wrong, exactly. Although…"

She jerked her head toward the file. He took the hint and opened it. "Ariel Mayor?"

She nodded. "I'd like her to be the first student we enroll in the program."

"And this troubles you because…?"

"She's having a hard time of it. To be honest, she's the type of student the Community Action Teen-Parent Apprentice Project was designed for. She's a senior who's always been a straight A student, popular with her peers and teachers. If you'd asked me, asked any of her teachers, we'd have told you that she was one of those kids who are blessed. Yet when her parents found out she was pregnant, at the beginning of the school year, they kicked her out. I got involved and learned that Ariel's home life was less than blessed. She's staying at an aunt's, working at a nearby restaurant, going to school, and other than one small incident, she's done a good job balancing everything. She's college material."

Eli paused, needing to make this absolutely pitch perfect. Working for Zac instead, in the CATA Project, could make such a difference for this girl. "Zac, I think it would be a shame if she didn't go to college because of the baby. She deserves to have the life she planned."

"With a baby in the picture, even if she goes to college, it won't be exactly as she planned," he pointed out.

"No, not exactly. But what in life ever goes exactly how we plan?" Eli might have said those same words a few days ago. And she'd have believed them. But now, they rang truer.

As if he'd read her mind, Zac asked, "You didn't plan to be here?"

Here? Pregnant? She almost snorted, but then Zac added, "Helping teen parents?"

Oh. Yes, of course, that's what he meant. "No. Truth is, I never planned this to be my life's work. I stumbled into it when a girl in my class became pregnant and asked for my help. When I looked for services in the district, I realized there was nothing."

"So you helped her yourself?"

She laughed. "Don't make it sound all noble. I liked her. Still do. Over the years, she's become my best friend. I'm surrogate aunt to her son."

"When the school district didn't help, you stepped

up and did it yourself. That's not a question. I know you, Eli. You couldn't stand by and not try to do something positive."

He'd said things like that before and as always it made her uncomfortable. Not in a stalker sort of way, but this man saw her in a way no one else did, not even herself.

"Don't glamorize it. I was in the right place at the right time and simply did what needed to be done. Anyone could have done it."

He snorted. "I don't want to argue with you, but you're wrong." As if sensing she was about to dispute it more, he picked the file back up. "So, Ariel's going to be our guinea pig?"

"If you agree. I noted in the file that she's never been in trouble, except for the recent incident. And I don't believe that would have happened if she hadn't been stretched so thin. That's where you come in. No more late hours, time for homework…support."

"Fine." He tapped the file on the table. "Ariel Mayor is our inaugural student in the CATA Project." He raised his water glass. "To many years of a successful partnership between us."

She clinked her glass against his.

"Now, let's order lunch and get down to the nitty-gritty of how we're going to make this work."

Eli had so much to do. So many things to think about. She knew she should excuse herself, instead, she found herself saying, "So, did you find out what the special is today?"

After they ordered, Zac asked, "So what else is new with you?"

If only she could tell him, but she wasn't about to

when her parents and Arthur still didn't know, so she simply said, "Not much. You?"

"Well, I was in some little Podunk town and I…"

Eli listened to Zac's story and soon forgot all her worries. Like Tucker had said, they'd be there tomorrow. Or rather tomorrow night when she went to see Arthur.

THE HOUR FLEW BY TOO FAST in Zac Keller's opinion.

He always enjoyed Eli Cartwright's company. There was something about her that touched him. Her enthusiasm for her work. The girls she taught were more than a job. He could see it in her expression as she talked about them. And this Ariel Mayor he'd just hired was obviously a favorite.

Eli'd talked of her boyfriend in the past, which was the only reason Zac hadn't long since asked her out. Even if he couldn't date her though, he could enjoy her company.

"Why don't we meet on Saturday morning? I'll treat you to coffee at Tim Horton's—the one next to Keller's Market. Then we can both go over and meet your Ariel?"

"You want me there?"

"Not for future student hires, but for this first one, I thought it might be a good idea if we both followed Ariel's progress closely. We can see what works, and where there's room for improvement. I'd like CATA to become one of Keller's pet projects, so I think it's best to really concentrate on this first student and make sure everything runs smoothly."

"I appreciate it, Zac. I don't know if you understand what this program could offer to our girls."

"I think I understand, at least as much as I can."

Eli glanced at her watch. "I better get going."

"See you Saturday, around nine, then? Tell Ariel to meet us at the market at nine-thirty?"

"Sounds good."

She stood, and he immediately followed suit. She thrust out her hand and they shook. "Thanks again, Zac."

"No problem. And Eli, I know we're just business associates, but if you want to talk about whatever's wrong, I'm here." Before she could deny there was anything wrong, or laugh at the idea of her needing his help, he took the bill and headed for the register.

She followed him, and handed him a ten, then, before he could protest, dashed out. "See you Saturday," she called over her shoulder.

Zac knew he should return to his office at the market, but he felt an uncharacteristic urge not to. So instead, he drove in the opposite direction toward his parents' house, under the guise of talking to his father about the business.

The house on East Street was a rambling building. The original one-story heart of the house was built in 1898, and generations of owners had added a room here and a room there, leaving a building with unusual lines. His parents had purchased it forty years ago, a month before they married, determined to fill the seven bedrooms with children.

They'd waited.

And waited.

After waiting ten years, with only their master bedroom in use, they'd decided on adoption.

Zac was their first child.

He was only five but he could still remember his social worker, Mrs. Bowler, pulling up in front of the house, with its flower beds and porch swing. He'd been sure that there was a mistake, that the man and woman waiting on the steps had wanted one of the other boys in the group home. But then the woman had knelt down, held her arms wide and said, "Welcome home, Zac." A feeling of disbelief and hope had filled him.

It was the same feeling he got whenever he pulled in to the driveway.

He hurried into the house. "Mom? Dad?"

He was already almost in the kitchen when his mother called, "In here, Zac."

Deborah Keller was a petite, well-rounded woman, with salt-and-pepper hair she'd pulled loosely into some kind of bun thing, and a smile that lit up the room. She swept Zac into a hug.

He sniffed the sweet scented air. "Cookies? Cake?"

"Gingerbread, *tateleh*." She glanced at the clock. "If you wait about ten minutes, you should be able to sample a piece and let me know if the new recipe is as good as the old one."

"You could probably twist my arm into staying." He pulled a stool up to the counter. "Cessy home yet?"

"Not for a while. If you have time to wait, I know she'd be thrilled to see you. The house is just too quiet since Layla went to college." His mom grinned at him. "Of course, if our older children started marrying and gave me grandchildren…" She let the sentence hang there, since he'd heard the entire spiel more than once.

"Just so happens I had lunch with a lovely woman."

"You did?"

His mom seemed so happy, he felt guilty about misleading her, and added, "Of course, she's got a boy-friend."

"A serious boyfriend, or just some man she's see-ing?"

He laughed. "I was only kidding, Mom. It's serious between them, I guess. They've been together now for five years." He'd collected a lot of Eli Cartwright trivia since he met her a few months back.

"Five years, and they're still dating?" She shook her head. "That's not serious, that's going with the status quo. Why, your father saw me at the fair—"

"And knew I'd met the woman I was going to marry right then and there," Abe Keller finished the sentence as he walked into the kitchen. He was a big man. He had a Grizzly Adams look about him. A bit wild. His hair was always unkempt and he went days on end without shaving now that he'd retired from Keller's and left the business to Zac.

Zac watched his father walk over and simply place his hand on his mother's shoulder—he'd noticed years ago that whenever they saw each other it was as if they needed to touch, to reconnect.

His hand still in place, his father continued the story. "And three months later, I married her. So, why are we trotting out that old story? Did your mom want to set you up?"

"No. I don't set my children up. I trust them to find their own dates. Zac was just telling me he had lunch with a woman who's been dating a man for five years. That's not a relationship."

"Now, Deborah, we can't measure other's rela-tionships by ours. If it works for them." His father shrugged.

But Zac could, and always would, measure every relationship against his parents'. This is what he wanted. Someone who needed to touch him, even if they'd only been a room away for a few minutes.

"She's not the one for me, Mom," Zac admitted with regret. "But when I find a woman as good as you are, one who's not dating someone else, you can be sure I'll whisk her off her feet as quickly as I can."

The timer buzzed. His mom busied herself with the gingerbread and his father took the stool opposite him. "So, if you didn't come to get set up…?"

"Thought I'd fill you in on the store."

The next forty-five minutes passed quickly as he and his dad talked business and his mother bustled around the kitchen starting dinner.

Then he heard someone enter before any of them saw her. "Zac." Cessy ran into the room at full speed, still wearing her coat and book bag, and threw herself full force at him, trusting he'd catch her.

He stood and did. He hugged his fifteen-year-old sister, Cessy, with her mass of curly brown hair, and her honey-toned skin. She backed up. He was five-ten, and she was almost as tall as he was now. "Stop growing, already, would you?"

"Poor little Zac, intimidated by a tall, strong woman?" she teased.

"If I see one of those, I'll let you know if I'm intimidated."

"Hey, you coming to my game on Sunday afternoon?"

"Wouldn't miss it."

"Good, 'cause May, Dom and Layla aren't coming in from Pittsburgh. And Seth—" Cessy stopped short and looked at him. No one talked about Seth, who couldn't forgive their parents for not being enthusiastic about him marrying Allie right out of high school. They'd loved her. The whole family loved her. Still, their parents had wanted them to wait, but Seth and Allie wouldn't. When she got pregnant, they'd started to mend the rift, but when Allie died… Zac wasn't sure what it would take for his parents and Seth to fix their relationship. Seth hadn't cut them off completely, but he'd erected a wall that their parents couldn't breach.

He knew Cessy was thinking the same thing as she glanced at their mother, and added, "So, it'll be you, Mom and Dad cheering me on."

"I'm pretty sure your brother can make enough noise that you'll never notice the rest are missing," his mom said.

Zac looked at Cessy's face and knew she'd notice. Cessy, more than the rest of them, needed her family around. Zac would rearrange his Sunday. He'd call Dom and May. Granted, they were in their mid-twenties, and busy with their own lives, but if he told them Cessy wanted them at the game, they'd find a way to be there. Layla would fuss about schoolwork, but if Dom or May did the driving, she'd have a little less than two hours in the car each way to study.

And Seth? Well, he'd try. That's all he could do.

Seth had never gotten over his parents not supporting his marriage to Allie, and since her death, he'd been ever more distant. But for Cessy, he might show up.

Zac would do all he could to get his whole family to the game because it was obviously important to Cessy.

That's what family did—supported each other when it was important.

And the Kellers knew that better than most.

FRIDAY PASSED QUICKLY.

Eli set things up with Ariel for Saturday morning. She smiled as she remembered the girl's excitement about the job. But that smile quickly faded as the reality of talking to Arthur that night hit her for the umpteenth time.

Eli had never thought of herself as a coward, but right now, she wanted nothing more than to call and cancel her date with Arthur.

Instead, she called Tucker, hoping her friend would tell her to suck it up and just get on with it. That was Tucker's normal attitude. Face whatever scared you. And yet ever since she'd told Tucker she was pregnant, her friend had continually surprised her. Instead of giving her a kick in the butt, she assured Eli that avoiding Arthur wasn't cowardly at all, that it would give Eli time to get her feet back on solid ground.

Eli had used similar phrases to girls entering the program. She'd meant them to be as comforting as she was sure Tucker intended hers to be, but until now Eli'd never realized how hollow they sounded.

She knew her feet weren't going to be on solid ground or anywhere other than limbo until she talked to Arthur and her parents. She wasn't sure how long it was going to take her to adjust to the turn her life had taken, and she couldn't wait any longer. She was pregnant and Arthur deserved to know he was going to be a father.

She clutched the bags with the Chinese takeout as

she got out of the car. She'd decided a private dinner was better than a public one for this news.

She stood outside his Brent Hollow condo. The development was for people over fifty. No one younger than that could buy a home here. And no children were permitted.

She was going to have to give up her MINI Cooper and buy a more sensible car and she hated the thought, but she was pretty sure Arthur was going to hate giving up his condo more.

She rang the doorbell and part of her wanted to bolt before he came to the door, but she held her ground.

Arthur opened the door. "Hi, honey." He kissed her cheek lightly.

He'd given her a key two years into the relationship. She'd felt it necessary to reciprocate. Neither of them used the keys often, though. They were still on doorbell-ringing status.

"Come in." He took one of the bags. "How's the pilot program going?"

He led her into the living room and set the bag on the table. They'd shared many meals here, sitting on the floor, in front of a fire during the colder months. He already had the wine open, two glasses waiting.

She sat down across from him, the familiar scene feeling comfortable. "Eli?"

She realized he'd asked about CATA.

"It's going well. Zac's agreed to my suggestion for our first student."

Arthur nodded absently. He didn't ask anything else about the program.

"So how was your week?" she asked, stalling, needing to catch her breath and find a way to gently break the news to him.

Arthur poured their wine, and Eli took up the glass and raised it to her lips, before it occurred to her that she couldn't drink it. She set the glass down and tried to gather her wits as she listened to Arthur go on about the students in his class as he dished up his dinner.

He didn't seem to notice she didn't follow suit.

"Arthur—" She got as far as his name and couldn't think of a way to finish the sentence.

I'm knocked up.

Knock, knock, guess who's knocked up?

What are your plans six or seven months from now?

You know the tour of Europe we've been talking about? What about a tour of local hospital maternity wards instead?

Arthur, I love you and we're going to have a baby.

Hey, Arthur, I'm pregnant. And do you know what irony is? I teach girls who experience unplanned pregnancies, and here I am. I wonder if I can write it off as educational expenses?

"Elinore, are you listening to me?"

She gritted her teeth at the use of her given name. Elinore was a name for someone older, more mature than she was. She was going to have a baby, for goodness' sakes, she couldn't be an Elinore yet.

She'd always hated it when he called her that, but today it grated more than it usually did.

"Eli," she snapped.

His fork full of General Tso's chicken froze midway between the plate and his mouth. "What is wrong?"

"I could give you a list, a long, long list of things, but topping it would be the fact I'm pregnant."

Arthur dropped the fork, and the bright red sauce splashed onto his shirt, but he didn't make a move to clean it off. He didn't say a word, but the wave of paleness that moved from the top of his head downward said it all.

Great. Just great. That was slick. What a gentle breaking of unexpected news.

Eli didn't say anything for a few minutes, letting him adjust to the shock.

When a bit of color seemed to seep back into his face, she said, "I know we didn't plan this. It's unexpected. When the doctor told me I didn't believe him. I thought I was entering menopause. I went to the pharmacy and bought one of each brand of pregnancy test there was and the results were all the same. I'm pregnant."

She waited for him to smile at her reaction.

Still nothing.

"I go for a second visit on Monday to have a sonogram, but the doctor thinks I'm either entering, or barely into my second trimester."

"Is it mine?"

Of all the responses she'd imagined, this hadn't even made the list of possibilities. "Is it yours?"

He nodded.

"Of course it's yours. I didn't cheat on you."

"I wish you would have." Arthur gave his head a small shake. "I can't have a baby. *We* can't have a… We talked about this up front. I'm almost ready to retire, and you have a busy and satisfying career. We have plans. I want to write my book, we're going to travel. We can't have this…"

"Baby, Arthur. It's a baby. Our baby. I know we

didn't plan it, but it's here, a reality we're going to have to cope with. It means adjusting some of our plans, but we can make it work."

He frowned. "Don't you see? I don't want to make it work. And there's nothing to say we have to. That you have to go through with the pregnancy."

Her hand immediately moved to her stomach, as if to protect their baby from the harshness of his suggestion. "Arthur, that's not an option."

"It is. I'd go with you, support you through the whole thing."

"I know it's a surprise, and I wouldn't condemn someone for making that kind of decision, but it's not for me. I couldn't terminate this pregnancy."

"And I can't be a father."

"Oh." Eli didn't know what to say to that. She'd expected him to be as taken aback at the news as she was, but she'd also expected him to hug her, to say he'd be there for her, that everything would be all right.

She hadn't realized how much she'd been counting on that.

"Arthur, we'll talk to someone and find a way to work this out."

He shook his head and his shaggy brown hair tumbled over his eyes. Normally, she'd reach over and push it back into place, but tonight she simply gripped her hands on her lap. "What do you suggest then?"

"If you go through with this, I can't be a part of it. I want nothing to do with the baby. Nothing."

There was a finality in his tone that cut straight through her. It was almost a physical pain. But Eli wouldn't give in to it. She sat up straighter. "Fine. You'll have to see a lawyer, have him draw up papers terminating your parental rights because I won't have you playing on-again, off-again father."

"That's not a worry because I have no wish to be anyone's father. I'll see my lawyer, have the papers drawn up. I'll open a college fund for the baby, in lieu of paying child support, if that works for you."

She wanted to tell him to keep his money, that they wouldn't need it, but a practical side of her knew that someday the baby would need substantial financial help with college.

"Fine." Somehow she found the strength to stand. "Goodbye, Arthur."

He stood as well, and moved next to her. "I didn't want things to end like this."

"I didn't, either." She'd barely begun to adjust to the idea of a baby, but when she'd pictured what it would be like to be a mother, she'd imagined Arthur by her side, learning to be a father. It was another future she'd have to let go of.

"Keep in touch." He moved toward her, as if to hug her.

Eli took a quick step backward. She didn't want to touch Arthur Stone. Didn't want the pity she saw in his eyes. She shook her head. "I don't think so. If we're going to make a break, let's make it clean. Call me when you've got the papers, and that will be the last you'll hear from me."

"Elinore—"

"Eli." And with all the dignity she could muster, she held her head high and walked out of Arthur's condo.

She got into her MINI and sat a moment, her hand pressed to her stomach. "Looks like it's just you and me, kid," she whispered.

Despite what she'd said to Arthur, she wasn't sure she could handle this. Wasn't sure at all. Unlike Arthur, though, she didn't have a choice. She couldn't walk away.

She snapped her seat belt into place, put her key in the ignition, then the car in Drive and left.

Left Arthur, and left the life she'd thought she'd have.

For the first time in years, Eli Cartwright was driving without a map. It was disconcerting. It was terrifying.

Underneath all that, there was also just the tiniest bit of exhilaration. There was suddenly a potential that hadn't been there before.

Rather than driving home, Eli headed toward Tucker's, knowing her friend would be a hundred percent on her side.

But half an hour later, when Eli finished telling Tucker about her meeting with Arthur, her friend's reaction was far more vehement than Eli had imagined.

Tucker paced back and forth in her living room. "Penis. Goat-boffing, self-important eunuch of a man."

"Tucker, sit down next to me." Eli patted the empty couch cushion. "I feel I have to point out Arthur couldn't boff goats if he was a eunuch."

Tucker didn't stop pacing. Instead, she kicked the ottoman. "He could try. I hope—"

"Stop right there," Eli warned. "You're not going to tempt the fates by wishing any plagues—"

"I was going for some penis-eating venereal disease, but a plague would work."

Eli laughed. Tucker's reaction was almost a balm

to her wounded pride. "How could I have wasted five years of my life on someone who could desert a child?"

Tucker finally sat, but remained resolutely silent.

"You tried to tell me, and I appreciate your not saying 'I told you so,' but I'll say it for you—you told me so."

"I never in a million years would have expected him to just walk away from this. Oh, I thought he was a boring, pontificating prig—"

"Prig?"

"I've been reading historical romances again, and it's a good descriptive word. And though I thought it would describe Arthur, I still would never have guessed he'd abandon you. To be honest, I can't imagine him not having opinions—many, many opinions—on how a child of his should be raised."

"Actually, he doesn't want it to be raised. He wanted me to go for an abortion."

"Rat bastard."

Bart stuck his head in the doorway. "Mom, phone. It's a guy, some Tyler Martinez." He spotted Eli and waved. "Hey, Aunt Eli." He ducked back out again.

"Speaking of rat bastards," Tucker murmured more to herself than to Eli. She got up and took the phone. "Yes?"

She listened and was soon scowling. "Are you crazy? No." And without saying anything further, she hung up.

"Problems with a customer?" Eli asked.

Tucker shook her head and plopped back onto the couch. "Nothing you need to worry about. The way I see it, you've got more than enough on your plate."

"Maybe whatever's going on with you would distract me? And I so need to be distracted."

"Nothing's going on, really. Just a man asking for a date."

Tucker hadn't dated often over the years. Not that she wasn't asked out, but more often than not, she declined. Eli worried about her. Tucker was still young. She should go out and have a good time on occasion. "Is this guy a troll?"

"No. He's gorgeous, actually, in a sleek, magazine-ad way." Tucker's scowl made the idea of a gorgeous man seem less appealing than dental surgery.

"So he's boorish?"

"Not exactly. Despite his prissy way, he gets along great with Dad and the other guys in the garage."

"A prig like Arthur then?" She smiled as she used the word.

Tucker shook her head.

"Married? Twelve kids?"

Another no.

"Okay, so a gorgeous, interesting, unattached man who gets along with your father called to ask you out and you say no why?"

"I say no every time he asks."

"He's asked more than once?" This was the first Eli had heard about this Tyler Martinez, and she couldn't help but wonder if there were other men who'd asked Tucker out that she hadn't mentioned.

"He's asked me out a few times," Tucker admitted.

"What am I missing?"

"Some brain cells if you can't figure it out. I mean, I'm pretty sure his suits are designer—not that I know designer clothes. I mean, there's Jacqueline Smith stuff at Kmart, but otherwise?" She shrugged. "Anyway, I'm pretty sure that's what his stuff is, and he's certainly got money to burn."

Eli shook her head, genuinely confused. "Still not getting it."

"Look at me, do I look like the type of woman a man like that would be interested in?"

Eli did look. Tucker was wearing a holey pair of jeans, some steel-toed work boots and a T-shirt that proudly proclaimed It's NASCAR or Nothin'. The T-shirt was worn thin from too many washings, and hugged Tucker's body in such a way that no man could miss that despite the work clothes, Tucker was all woman. "I don't see why he wouldn't be interested, Tuck. I mean, if I were a man, I'd try to date you."

Her outrageous comment had the desired effect. Tucker laughed. "If you were a man I'd probably say yes. But he's different. Too different."

"Tucker, this Tyler, or any man, would be all kind of lucky to have a woman like you."

Tucker pulled back, not physically, but emotionally. Eli could talk herself blue in the face, but Tucker would never believe that she was beautiful. It had nothing to do with designer clothes, and everything to do with the kind of woman Tucker was.

And part of what made Tucker Tucker was her complete and annoying stubbornness, which reared its head now. "Let's change the subject back to you. What are you going to do now?"

"I made plans for dinner with my parents tomorrow night. I expect it's going to go about as well, or even worse, than how it went telling Arthur." She loved her parents, saw them at least once a week when they were in town, and talked to them frequently when they wintered in Florida each year. The fact that she would be an unwed mother was not going to impress them. She was forty-four, but obviously the desire to please a parent didn't go away with age. It might even have gotten stronger.

"I think you're wrong. They might not be happy, but they'll stand by you. I have no doubt of that."

"You're right. It still won't be pretty."

"Maybe you're wrong."

"Yeah, maybe. And maybe the earth is going to start rotating backward, and all the bad guys will suddenly become good guys forever and ever."

She snorted. "And maybe prigs will fly."

Maybe.

But Eli wasn't betting on any of it.

CHAPTER THREE

"Time. It can feel as if you don't have nearly enough time to get everything done. Remember, despite all you need to do, take time to have some fun."
—*Pregnancy, Childbirth and Parenting for Teens,*
by Mary Jeanne Lorei

ELI NORMALLY LOVED SATURDAYS. She loved knowing she didn't have to get up and do anything. She loved the idea of leisurely walks, and reading the paper—front to back—over a second cup of coffee. Then possibly doing the crossword puzzle in ink over a third cup.

Today, there was no sense of happiness at the thought as she glanced at the clock. 8:00 a.m.

She didn't have time for the paper before her meeting with Zac, and even if she did, there'd be no coffee. No caffeine for her for the rest of the pregnancy. And probably not while she was breast-feeding, either. If she breast-fed. Would she breast-feed?

Another decision.

One she simply couldn't face.

She had to get together with Zac Keller and Ariel Mayor, then she had to hurry home and clean the house before her parents' visit.

Not that her house was a mess. And she didn't generally clean before her parents came over. But since she was about to break the fact she was pregnant with no father in the picture, she figured the least she could do was tell them in a spotless house.

After all, that wasn't too much to ask, was it?

And why on earth did she let Zac talk her into meeting at Tim Horton's? To smell that wonderful coffee and not be able to have a cup was going to be sheer torture. Okay, she could probably order a decaf, but seriously, if she couldn't drink the real thing, why bother?

She hurried out to the car, pulling her winter coat tighter.

Winter hadn't even officially arrived—heck, autumn was only halfway gone—but she was ready for spring.

The thought stopped her in her tracks. By late spring, she'd have her baby. Right at the end of the school year. She'd be a mother. Her whole life would change.

Sometimes, she'd forget she was pregnant. Then, she'd have one of those moments of awareness.

She *was* pregnant.

She *was* going to be a mother.

She kept repeating the words as she drove to the coffee shop.

There was no denying it. The life she'd planned was gone thanks to this baby. A small spurt of anger surprised her. She didn't blame the baby, but she was mad at the circumstances. Arthur could throw up his hands and walk away. She was stuck. Her body wasn't ever going to be the same. Her life was never going to be the same. It wasn't fair.

It wasn't fair. She couldn't count the number of

times girls said those words to her. Her response? Life's not fair. Deal with it.

She realized she'd been parked in front of the coffee shop for…she wasn't sure how long.

Yeah, life's not fair. Deal with it.

Right now she had to deal with Zac Keller.

She hurried inside and scanned the place. She spotted Zac in line and approached him.

A slow smile spread on his face. "You made it."

"We'd agreed, so of course I made it."

"What would you like?" He nodded at the menu.

"A house decaf." She wanted her caffeine. Wanted it desperately. Already, the baby was impacting her life. Her decisions.

"After all our meetings, you switching to decaf just seems wrong."

He was teasing, and Eli knew it, so she smiled. "I'm turning over a new leaf. Actually, a few new leaves." Whether she wanted to or not.

"How does Arthur feel about these changes?"

"Arthur's out of the picture." It was the first time she'd said the words out loud in conversation. It made the fact he was gone seem more real. More permanent.

"We broke up," she added, more for herself than for Zac.

"Oh." Zac paused. "Sorry."

"Our relationship had progressed as far as it could. It was time to make a clean break."

Zac seemed puzzled, and Eli waited for him to ask her more questions, but after a moment, he nodded. They waited in silence for their coffees.

She wondered what he was thinking.

But he didn't give her a clue. After their drinks

were in hand, he simply said, "Why don't we take the coffees next door to my office and I can show you the schedule we've put together for Ariel."

"Great."

ZAC AND ELI CONTINUED in silence as they walked to Keller's Market. Other than the first day, they'd never met in his office. He always insisted they meet over a lunch or coffees. It seemed more relaxed, more personal. And that was just what he'd wanted to be with Eli Cartwright.

The news that she'd broken up with her boyfriend meant he was free to get even more up close and personal.

He'd love to ask her out right away, but he knew he should wait and give her some time to recover from the breakup.

How much time did it require?

Hours?

Days?

Not weeks. No, weeks was too long. Some other guy was bound to ask Eli on a date as soon as the news got out that she was available. Zac wasn't going to lose out to some quick-on-the-draw stranger.

Since he knew he had to wait, this once, keeping things all business was probably for the best. That was why he suggested taking their coffees to his office.

"Zac?" Eli said.

He noticed they were standing in his office doorway. "Sorry. Thinking about things I have to do." Mainly asking out Eli. "Have a seat."

He had a copy of Ariel's schedule in his briefcase,

but handed her the one on his desk instead. "Here you go."

She reached for it, and for the briefest second, their fingers touched. Zac didn't think of himself as a sentimental sort of man, which is why his awareness of that smallest of touches surprised him. Of course, it shouldn't have. Yet, everything about Eli Cartwright touched him.

"It looks—"

Eli was cut off as Cessy burst into his office. "Z-man, help. I need a ride to—" Cessy stopped short as she caught sight of Eli. "Sorry, Ms. Cartwright. I'm not used to Zac having people in his office this early on a Saturday morning. I'm much better behaved on weekdays. Uh, the principal didn't send you in to talk to Zac about my inability to be quiet in class, did he?"

Eli laughed. "No. I'm not here about you."

Zac knew he should reprimand his irrepressible sister, but she stood there grinning and practically radiating happiness. He couldn't muster up even a small tsk of disapproval.

She ran a hand over her brow. "Phew. I'd rather the principal talk to Mom and Dad any day of the week. They're pushovers. Zac, he's tough."

He laughed. "Yeah, that's why you're coming to me for a ride somewhere, because of my world-renowned toughness?"

"Zac, I say you're tough in front of people so they won't catch on to what a marshmallow you are." She fished in her pocket and pulled out a small thing to twist her wildly curly hair into a ponytail.

"So, where are we riding to?" he asked.

"I was sort of hoping you'd drive me over to Grove

City's outlets after I finish my morning shift. They're having a preholiday sale, and I'd really like to go do some early Christmas shopping."

"Mom and Dad said you could go?"

She shook her head. "I'm going to ask after I have everything set up. It makes it harder for them to say no if I have all my bases covered."

He chuckled. "Sure."

"Thanks. See you later, Ms. Cartwright." His sister gave a small wave, then proceeded toward the door.

"Hey, Cessy," Zac called, halting her progress, "don't forget I'm sending down a new employee for you to show the ropes to."

"I won't forget. And I'll have her swinging from the ropes before the morning's over," she promised. "And Zac, don't forget your promise…I'm Cecily out in public." And with that reminder, she ran out of the office.

"So Cecily's your sister? You don't look anything alike."

Zac knew that was an understatement. "We're both adopted. Actually, I'm the oldest of five. We were all adopted, so there's no family resemblance, but maybe that's why we're so tight. Cessy—" remembering his promise, he corrected himself "—pardon me, *Cecily* is fifteen, she's the youngest."

"I should have put the last names together. She's a whirlwind. I don't have her in any classes, but I see her around school and hear her name on the announcements a lot because of sports. It's hard not to know who Cecily Keller is."

"That was a very polite way of saying Cessy is loud. When she asked if you were here on a mission from the school, it was only because it wouldn't be the first time we'd had reports of Cecily's—" he searched for the appropriate word to describe his sister "—exuberance."

"That's an apt description."

"I was going to use boisterous, but exuberant sounded—"

Cessy interrupted as she burst back through the door, a tall blonde behind her. "Hey, Ariel's here. Ariel, my brother Zac Keller. Zac, this is Ariel." Introductions made, she turned to Ariel. "Go pretend to listen to him—he likes it when employees act as if they hold him in high esteem and appear to hang on his every word."

"Something my little sister doesn't even bother to pretend to do."

Cessy cackled. "Like I'd feed your overinflated ego, Mr. Keller, sir." She dropped her voice to a stage whisper. "You're making Ariel nervous, Z-man."

"I'm not nervous," Ariel protested, standing straight and squaring her shoulders as if to prove the point.

"Good, 'cause I can assure you, my brother's a pushover. Go listen to his spiel, then I'll show you around." Cessy flew back through the door, shutting it loudly behind her.

Zac turned to Eli. "You're sure you're not here on behalf of the school to talk to me about my sister?"

She grinned. "She's just exuberant. Remember?"

He grinned. "Hi, Ariel. Have a seat."

Eli patted the chair next to her. "Come sit down."

When Ariel was settled, both women looked at him. He didn't want to dive right into business. He wanted to put the girl at ease. "You and Cecily are friends?"

"We know each other, Mr. Keller. The school's small enough that it's hard not to know everyone. But she hangs out with the jocks—" she stopped abruptly and amended "—basketball team, and until recently, I hung out with the cheerleaders."

"Two different circles in high school terms," Eli explained.

"But we get along, Mr. Keller," Ariel added hastily.

"Call me Zac. We're not very formal at Keller's."

He could see the girl was nervous. Eli must have sensed it, too. She slid the paper she'd been looking at before Cessy's entrance toward Ariel. "Zac was showing me the schedule he drew up for you."

"It's only preliminary. We can fine-tune it as you get comfortable and see what works. And later, when the baby comes, we'll adjust it even more."

Ariel studied the schedule for a minute. "Thanks. This is so much better than the hours at the restaurant."

"Well, if it gets to be too much, say something. I thought we'd start you out on the register. And Ariel, Keller's offers partial scholarships to any of our employees who are going to college. You need a good work record, and at least a B average at school, and we can help defray some of your education costs. Ms. Cartwright has glowing things to say about you, including the fact that you are definitely on the college track."

"Really?" Ariel looked surprised.

He wasn't sure if she was asking *really* about the partial scholarship, or *really* about whether Eli really had glowing things to say about her. He simply answered, "Really."

"I appreciate the opportunity, Mr. Keller. I'll do my best to make you and Ms. Cartwright proud. I've made so many mistakes lately, but I will try to do better."

"Ariel, everyone makes mistakes," Eli assured her.

"Life happens. What truly defines us as people is how we handle what life throws at us."

Zac nodded. "Do your best. That's all we ask for here at Keller's. And remember, I'm here if you need anything." He figured that about covered what he needed to say today, so he added, "Why don't you go find Cecily and let her show you around? Tell her to put you on the clock for the tour. And make sure she takes you to Millie, to fill out all the paperwork."

Ariel stood. "Really, Mr. Keller, Ms. Cartwright. Thank you."

Eli reached up, took Ariel's hand and gave it a squeeze. "You're going to do great, Ariel. I'll look for you when I'm getting ready to go."

Just as Ariel left the room, Eli's cell phone rang. She pulled it from her bag, glanced at the number and asked, "Do you mind?"

"No problem."

She got up and stepped outside the office. Moments later she was back.

"Problems?"

"No. My parents called to cancel our dinner plans. Seems some old neighbors are in town only for the weekend, and they're seeing them." She sat back down with a sigh. "It's a relief, actually."

"You don't get along with your parents?" He knew better than most that not all parents were created equal. He hated the thought of Eli growing up in a bad situation.

"No, I didn't mean it to sound that way," she assured him. "It's nothing like that. I have some news for them, and I don't think they're going to like it, so the reprieve is not a bad thing."

"Do you want to talk about it?" As he said the words, Zac admitted that he wished she would confide in him. She looked so stressed at the thought of whatever she needed to tell her parents. He wanted nothing more than to ease some of that burden.

"Thanks. But I'm not really ready to talk to anyone about it. At least, not yet."

She probably needed to tell them she'd broken up with the boyfriend. Maybe they'd liked him and that's why she was reluctant to tell them. "Hey, if you were going to be with your parents, that means you don't have plans anymore, right?"

She nodded slowly. "Right."

"Why don't you come with us to Grove City? We could ask Ariel to come as well. From what little you've said, it sounds as if she'd appreciate having some fun. We could all make a day of it."

"I don't know. There are a million and one things I should be doing."

"I'm all for doing what should be done, but sometimes, there's merit in taking a break. And to sweeten the offer, there's a great restaurant right outside the outlet mall. We could grab something to eat and take your mind off your parents."

"Are you sure? I don't want to intrude on your time with your sister."

Zac didn't want to tell her just how sure he was and scare her off. So he settled for, "Of course, I am. I mean, I'm smart enough to want an ally while shopping at an outlet mall with a teen."

She chuckled. "Ah, so asking me was selfish on your part."

Eli's laughter. It was one of the things about her

that got to him. She worked with kids who were in such tough straits. He'd seen how she went to the wall for each and every one. And still, despite the fact she dealt with such trying experiences, she still managed to find the joy in things.

"Eli, I can assure you that my asking you was definitely in my own self-interest. Absolutely selfish."

"Glad to know you have a flaw or two, Zac Keller. Anyone who's too perfect makes me nervous."

"You think I'm perfect?" he teased.

"I did, but now I know that you have an occasional selfish moment. It makes you seem more human."

"Well, don't talk to Cessy too much about me, she'll tell you so many flaws that I'll go from human to subhuman in record time."

"I doubt that, Zac. You are truly one of the nice guys."

The phrase *nice guy* set his teeth on edge. His ex had used the phrase when she'd broken up with him. *You're such a nice guy. I'm sure you'll find someone else, someone better.*

He couldn't help but remember the phrase, "nice guys finish last."

He pushed away the thought and tried to remain upbeat. Eli was available. He was available. They were going to spend the day together.

Nice guys sometimes finish first.

And if he had anything to say about it, this would be one of those times.

BEING WITH ZAC WAS EASY. Cecily and Ariel ran from store to store, while Eli and Zac trailed behind at a more sedate pace. They'd gone into one store that sold Waterford crystal and Zac had bought a beautiful frame. "My mom will love it," he said with a hint of embarrassment.

"Real men buy crystal frames," she'd assured him as they strolled together.

They went by a maternity shop, and part of Eli wanted to go in and look. She'd never been in one before. She'd never had the need, and never thought she would. She knew Zac would have obliged her, but she wasn't ready to confess.

She wasn't ready for anyone else to know.

She'd received a parental reprieve, and so for one more week, she'd hold on to her news and hopefully adjust even more to the idea of being a mother.

So she just walked past the maternity store. There would be plenty of time to shop at one later.

"So, fill me in about your siblings. Cecily is the youngest. You're the oldest."

"Then there's Seth. He's a cop in Erie—we don't see him much anymore." There was a sadness in his voice, telling her there was some kind of trouble with Seth. He didn't share, and she didn't ask.

"Next there's May," he continued. "She's in Pittsburgh trying to find herself. This week she's a waitress, I think. I've offered her a job at Keller's, but she wants to make it on her own. Then there's Dom. He's graduating from Pitt in the spring, then Layla, who's at Carlow University in Pittsburgh."

"Wow. How on earth did your mom manage all of you? Six kids. I can't imagine." Trying to wrap her brain around raising just one child was taxing at best.

"Mom's…" He paused. "She's all heart. We were

the kids no one wanted to adopt. Older. Damaged. But Mom put us all together and made us a family."

"She sounds wonderful. And you are lucky."

Zac nodded. "I am. We all are, and we know it. And Mom is fantastic." He paused. "Are you going to the girls' basketball game tomorrow at the school?"

Eli planned on staying at home tomorrow to figure out how to turn her guest room into a nursery. It was just an idea. One she wasn't sure she was ready for. Having a baby's room in the house would make everything seem so much more real.

A girls' basketball game would be easier. "I might go."

"Great. So you can probably meet the whole Keller clan. It's sort of like taking medicine. Best to get it all over with at once."

"What a way to talk about your family," she mock-scolded. "I'm sure they're all lovely."

"If by lovely you mean loud, then yes. All of us. Maybe especially my dad, who likes listening to his music as loud as possible. Mom banned his CD player to the garage, but even then we'd hear the music inside the house. Mom would holler at him because it was so loud, and after he turned it down, he'd say, 'Loud? Why it was quieter than inside the house,' in a puzzled way. It was a standing joke. He was the only one who laughed, but it made him laugh every time. He was the king of one-liners. You'd say something like, 'My head hurts.' His favorite response? 'Does your face hurt?' When you said no, he'd add, ''Cause it's killing me.' He cracked himself up with that one as well."

Eli laughed. "He sounds like a riot."

"Now, he does. When you're fifteen and on the

phone with a girl, not so much. What about you? Your family?"

"Just me. An only child of two only children. Quiet. That's the best way to describe our house. Mom and Dad are great, though. I see them most every weekend when they're in town. This weekend's pass is a fluke." Unexpected, and just this once, welcomed.

"When they're in town?"

"They've become snow bunnies. Heading for Florida before the snow, and not coming back until it's long since melted. But even when they're down south, we're close."

"That's nice. One of Mom's cross-stitched sayings goes, 'It's not the size of the family, it's the size of its heart.' In our case, sounds like we both have big ones." He groaned. "Okay, I feel emasculated by saying that out loud."

Eli laughed. "No, you sounded sweet. And I find it hard to believe your mom had all those kids and still found time to cross-stitch?"

"Actually, there's something my mother made in every room at my place. One Christmas she made all us kids a cross-stitch that said, 'I didn't carry you for nine months, but once I met you, I knew you were mine. So, now I'll carry you in my heart for the rest of my life.'" His voice gave a little hitch.

"Oh, Zac, that's lovely."

He looked embarrassed. "I don't know why I told you that. That one's not in the public portion of the house."

They were standing in the middle of the mall. And without thinking about it, Eli took Zac's hand and gave it a light squeeze. "I'm glad you shared it."

"Hey, Zac."

Eli realized she was still holding Zac's hand and dropped it.

Cecily didn't seem to notice as she opened a bag and pulled out a top. "Look what I've got to wear after the game tomorrow."

Ariel stood behind her, bagless. Eli wished she could offer the girl money to buy a new top. But she was Ariel's teacher, and had already edged too close to the boundary that should exist between a student and teacher. Plus, she suspected Ariel was too proud to accept it.

Zac was scowling in the general direction of Cecily's shirt. "Where's the rest of it?"

"Funny. Ha. Ha. It's all there." She turned to Ariel. "My brother thinks he's Mr. Funny. He's so not."

"And you know Dad's worse than I am," Zac continued. "And you know what else? It's practically winter. Turtlenecks are in season."

"Funny. You're almost as funny as Dad now, Zac, and that means not at all." She turned back to Ariel. "Tell, him Ariel. Tell him this isn't bad."

"It's a very popular style, Mr. Keller."

"Seriously, Ariel, don't go calling him 'Mister.' I told you, it gives him a swollen head. Soon he'll expect all of us to be Mistering him all over the place. And Z-man, that's so not going to happen."

"Don't listen to Miss Incorrigible, Ariel." Zac tried to sound stern, but knew he didn't manage it well. "Before she can start a fight with me, why don't we all head over to Elephant and Castle for dinner."

"You're not saying much, Ms. Cartwright," Ariel said as they walked toward the car.

"I'm an only child, but even I know better than to get in middle of a brother-and-sister sniping war."

Cecily and Zac continued their banter as they traveled the short distance to the restaurant. And they kept it up even after they were seated in a booth, only letting up when the waitress came over. "Can I start you all out with something to drink?"

When it was Ariel's turn, she said, "Water."

"Oh, come on," Zac prompted. "We're celebrating your new job and Cecily's first game tomorrow. This one's on me. You can do better than water. How about a milk shake? It's got milk in it, so it's good for you."

"Strawberry, then," Ariel said.

Eli realized that Ariel had been worried about paying for the dinner. She could have kicked herself for not making sure Ariel knew the meal was on her. While the girls were busy talking, she nodded at Ariel and mouthed the word *thanks* in Zac's direction.

IT WAS SEVEN O'CLOCK when Zac drove to Keller's Market parking lot. They'd already dropped Ariel off at her aunt's and Cecily was in the backseat.

Zac got out and walked Eli to her car.

"Thanks for a wonderful day." Eli had so enjoyed not having to worry. She'd enjoyed listening to Zac and Cecily's playful arguing. She'd enjoyed the meal. It had been especially sweet to hear Ariel and Cecily yakking—just two teenagers talking about school. Her conversations with Ariel had centered around her pregnancy, her schoolwork and her job. The dinner reminded her that Ariel was still a girl. A girl in the process of growing up too fast. "Really, I had a great time."

"You didn't buy anything. I don't think I've ever been shopping with a woman who didn't buy anything."

Eli shook her head. "Maybe you've been shopping with the wrong women."

Zac laughed. "Maybe."

She unlocked the door and opened it. Zac still stood there. "Did I forget something?"

"You were considering coming to the game tomorrow. I could pick you up. You're on my way and carpooling...we'd be saving the planet and all that." He hesitated. "That is, if you want to."

Wanting to drive with Zac had nothing to do with saving the planet, although Eli had tried to live green before green was the fashionable color. "That would be great."

"You'll have to give me your address."

She gave him her best teacher's look. "I thought you said I was on your way?"

"Eli, Whedon is at best a fifteen-minute drive from border to border. Okay, that's an exaggeration. You could probably drive the circumference of the town in fifteen minutes, with time to spare. Everything is on my way."

Eli laughed even harder as she dug in her bag and pulled out a card. "Here you go."

"Always prepared. I like that in a woman." He pocketed the card. "I'll be there at one."

"I'll be ready."

Zac stood there as she started the car and pulled away. She glanced in her rearview mirror and saw him finally moving toward his own car.

She went directly home and had barely taken off her coat when the phone rang.

She kicked off her boots, exposing her favorite striped socks, and ran for the living room. "Hello?" she answered breathlessly.

"Are you okay? Nothing wrong with the baby?" Tucker asked, anxiousness in her voice.

"I'm fine. I just walked in the house and ran for the phone." She flipped on the lamp and sank down onto the couch.

"I wanted to see how it went with your parents."

"They canceled. So I went to Grove City and did some shopping at the outlet mall." There was silence on the other end of the line. "What's up, Tuck?"

"I've been calling you all day. At home. On your cell."

She dug through her purse and found her cell phone at the bottom. "The battery's dead. Sorry."

"No problem." Tucker paused. "Want to do something tomorrow?"

"I could in the morning, or late afternoon. I have something at one."

"Something?"

Eli pulled her feet onto the couch and covered them with the throw. "A girl's basketball game at the high school."

"Oh, I like basketball." Tucker muffled the phone, as if she were putting her hand over the receiver. "Hey, Bart, want to go to the girls' basketball game tomorrow?"

Eli could hear Bart's voice, although she couldn't make out what he was saying.

Tucker came back on the line. "He says it's only a scrimmage, but sure. We'll meet you there, unless you want me to pick you up?"

Eli wasn't sure why she felt embarrassed, but she did as she replied, "I sort of have a ride already."

"Oh? With who?"

"Zac Keller. You remember, he's helping me out with the new CATA Project."

"Hot, single Zac Keller, whose family owns Keller's Market…the chain. That Zac Keller? You're *going with* Zac Keller?"

"Yes. It's only carpooling. You know, to save the environment."

Tucker snorted. "Eli, you're a catch…pregnant or not."

"Shh! I don't want Bart to overhear you. I need to tell my parents before I tell anyone else."

"So what happened with telling them today?"

"They had unexpected plans and canceled. I'll tell them next week."

"You sure you don't want me to come with you when you do? Your parents always liked me, and maybe I'd serve as a reminder that unexpected pregnancies sometimes turn out to be a blessing in disguise. I could bring Bart's last report card. All A's…not that I'm bragging."

Eli laughed. "You're bragging. But mom-brags look very good on you, Tuck. And thanks again for the offer, but I can handle this. More than anyone, I know how these things go."

"But it's not the same when it's you. When you're worried about your parents being disappointed in you."

"I'll handle it. I'll handle it all, Tuck."

"Just remember, you're not alone."

"I won't forget." Eli's hand rested on her stomach, and she thought it felt a little rounder.

She wasn't alone. Not ever. Friends. Family. And soon, a baby.

CHAPTER FOUR

"First things first. You need to tell those you love that you're pregnant. You're going to need their support."

—*Pregnancy, Childbirth and Parenting for Teens,*
by Mary Jeanne Lorei

ZAC ARRIVED ON TIME to pick up Eli and held open her jacket. She looked startled. "Sorry. I know some women take offense, but my mom's lessons on how a gentleman should behave stuck."

"I don't ever take offense when none is meant." She stuck the hat on herself. "Okay, I'm good to go."

"Just like that? A jacket and hat—no primping? My sisters always take forever to get ready to go anywhere. Even just a basketball game."

"I might have when I was younger, but such is the way of age. You've figured some things out." Eli smiled as she opened the door, letting him go through first, then followed him and used the key to turn the dead bolt.

"Only some things? You always seem to have everything sorted and in order." He opened her car door.

Eli climbed in, saying, "If only you knew."

Zac walked around the car and got in the driver's side. "Ah, is that a cryptic reference to whatever was bothering you the other day? That offer to listen is still there."

She paused and looked him directly in the eye, as if seeing him for the first time. "I may take you up on that someday. But not today. Today is for basketball and Niagara pride."

The school parking lot was overflowing with cars. And as they made their way into the gym, the home side was awash with blue and white.

"There they are," Zac said, pointing to his family sitting in the bleachers. He did a quick head count. Everyone had made it, including Seth, although he sat apart from his parents. Cessy would be surprised and pleased.

"Hi, this is Eli. Eli, my mom and dad, Abe and Deborah Keller. And…" He listed each name, trying to see his family through Eli's eyes. Was she taking in the different colored skin, the lack of any similar features? Was she seeing the braces on Dom's legs?

"Eli, come sit by me," his mom invited, patting the spot next to her.

Eli went over and took the seat between his mom and May. There was no way Zac could squeeze in, too, so he sat behind them between Dom and Seth.

"Thanks for coming," he said to his brothers. "Cessy seemed to really need us all here."

"No problem." Dom nodded at Eli. "By the way, nice-looking lady."

Zac didn't say anything. He turned to the still silent Seth. "Thanks."

"I'm here for Cessy" was Seth's flat response.

Zac had tried in the past to mend the rift between his parents and Seth, but his brother would have none of it, and not wanting to start a fight today, he didn't say anything.

"You two serious?" Seth jerked his head in Eli's direction.

"She recently ended another relationship, but…"

Any further conversation was put on hold as the home team entered the gym. Cessy was easy to spot. She towered over her teammates.

A woman and boy arrived and sat down by May, Eli and his mom. Zac realized he hadn't planned this very well. What he'd hoped would be a continuation of yesterday's good time wasn't working out that way.

"Hey, it's fine. You can go be with her at halftime. I won't be insulted," Dom assured him.

"That obvious?"

Dom laughed. "Maybe not to everyone, but I'm not everyone. I'm your brother. And I am good at reading people. Even if I wasn't, you've always been pretty much an open book."

Zac laughed. It wasn't only Cessy who'd needed to connect with the family. He did, too.

He glanced over at Eli and she seemed totally relaxed with his mom. Good. He wanted her to fit in. He hoped she'd be spending a lot more time with them in the future.

THE GAME WENT FASTER than Eli thought it would. The home team won by three points.

Cecily Keller was an amazing player, especially for a freshman on the varsity team.

Eli had planned to ask Zac to drop her at home as soon as the game ended, but Mrs. Keller had proclaimed a family dinner was in order to celebrate the first scrimmage, and while Eli thought her I'm-not-family excuse should get her out of going, it didn't.

Tucker and Bart were dragged along, too.

"I could have told you arguing with my mother was useless," Zac explained as he escorted her into the rambling Keller home. They waited on the porch for Tucker and Bart to get out of their car and follow them.

"I don't think you two formally met. Angelina Tucker, this is Zac Keller. And this is Tucker's son, Bart."

Zac led them back to a huge kitchen and started introducing Tucker and Bart to his family. Even as he picked on his siblings the genuine affection was apparent.

Mrs. Keller pulled bowl after bowl out of the refrigerator, and took the lids off of two Crock-Pots. "Dig in, everyone."

It was chaos.

Pandemonium.

It was wonderful.

"Are you as freaked out by all these people as I am?" Tucker asked as they sat together in a relatively quiet corner of the living room. Bart had disappeared with Cecily, leaving the adults on their own.

"You two hiding, too?" Zac's brother, Seth asked.

He was teasing. Until now, he'd been monosyllabic at best. Eli could sense there was some rift in the family, and Seth's avoidance of his parents confirmed that. It was like a dance. Every time his mother headed in his direction, he countered and moved in the opposite one.

"Do you need anything?" Seth continued, without waiting for either of them to respond to his first question.

"In your dreams," Tucker said with a scoff. "My son's got socks in his drawer that are older than you."

Seth looked flustered for a moment. "I didn't mean it that way—" he began, then saw Tucker was teasing and smiled. The expression looked a bit rusty, but he managed to tease back, "Hey, I'm a cop. I spend my life protecting and serving the community. That ages a man rapidly. Heck, I might be chronologically seven years younger than my big brother, but my soul is so much older than his paltry thirty-four years."

"Listen, Seth, you seem like a nice guy, but I'm not interested. And Eli's—"

For a second, a horrifying second, Eli thought Tucker was going to say she was pregnant. *And Eli is pregnant.* But when Tuck said, "And Eli isn't interested, either," Eli breathed a sigh of relief. She should have known better.

Eli laughed. "Sorry, Seth."

"Hey, you can't blame a guy for trying." He sat down on the couch next to Tucker. "But since I know you're not interested, you're safe. I'm hiding out with you two."

"I thought you were a big, brave cop. I didn't know that involved hiding."

"Sure it does. Don't you watch cop shows? They're always staking out someone…."

The two of them continued their banter, while Eli digested Seth's words. Zac was only thirty-four. Ten years younger than she was.

Not that it mattered. It wasn't as if there was anything more than a friendly business association between them. But still, she'd thought Zac was older. Around her age, at least.

"…Zac," Tucker said.

Eli had been too preoccupied to catch the first part of Tucker's sentence, but Zac's name was enough to draw her back.

"That's how it goes. Zac always got all the girls because he was older."

Zac had somehow edged close to their conversation when she was lost in thought.

"Wrong, little brother," he corrected. "I got the girls because I was oh, so much prettier."

Eli studied him, and still didn't see a younger man. She just saw Zac. Someone who was a friend. A nice guy.

"I'm sure that's what they said, but they only said that to make you feel better about your rather large nose," Seth countered.

"You know what they say about men with big noses…?" Tuck started, then stopped. "Or maybe it was big hands."

"I think this conversation has gone about as far as I'm comfortable with," Eli said as primly as possible.

"Come on with me," Zac said. "These two can duke out the whole age issue without our help."

Eli couldn't see any way not to go with him and not seem rude, so she got up and followed him.

He led her to the back porch, which looked out over a beautifully landscaped yard. "Does your mom do the gardening or your dad?"

"Both. After all these years, they still enjoy bumming around together. They consider working in the garden a date. Groceries, too. Us kids always called them geek dates, but it's actually sort of comforting knowing they still get along. Does that make sense?"

She nodded. "My parents are like that. A unit. I can't imagine one without the other. They're heading down to Florida in a few weeks. They love to call me with news of their adventures. Mom got Dad to try ballroom dancing lessons a few years ago, and now they like to hit the clubs. Picturing my mom and dad club-hopping is a bit bizarre."

"It's nice knowing people who can raise kids, and still maintain a sense of self. That's what I want someday."

Eli didn't nod, didn't say anything. Once upon a time, she'd have said the same thing. And not too long ago, she'd have said she'd found that with Arthur. But their relationship had been a sham.

And now with the baby coming?

She couldn't imagine she was going to be able to balance her job and raising a child with finding a new boyfriend. So odds were, she was out of the running for that kind of relationship. The kind her parents and Zac's had.

The thought saddened her.

"I never called my parents' outings geek dates, but now that I know the term, I could. Antiques. Mom's crazy about antiques and Dad tends to indulge her. Those would probably qualify."

Zac grinned. "Do you like antiques?"

"Sure. I grew up with them. I don't know as much as my parents, but I have a fondness for old stoneware."

"I know a place in Mill Village, Abercrombie's. They've always got interesting things. Maybe we could drive out sometime."

Was he asking her for a date? She liked Zac. He made her laugh. But she wasn't ready to tell people she was pregnant, and once she did, she figured he wouldn't be interested in dates, if that's what this was.

"As just friends, right?"

"I'd like to think we're friends," he answered.

"Good. I can use all the friends I can get. But I'm not in the market for anything more than that. It's only been a few days since Arthur and I broke up." She felt a bit presumptuous saying it, but still she respected Zac and wanted to be honest. She didn't want to muddy the water of their friendship with unrealistic expectations.

He'd find out soon enough she was pregnant, and that would remove all her worries, but until she was ready to share the news, she wanted to be clear.

"Just friends." There was a hint of something in his voice as he said the words—something Eli couldn't quite identify.

Whatever it was, it made her heart do a weird little double beat. As if she could possibly be attracted to Zac Keller. But she wasn't. For a myriad of reasons she knew she wasn't attracted and never could be. They worked together on the CATA Project, he was younger, she was barely out of a long-term relationship…and she was pregnant. All good reasons to make sure their relationship stayed platonic.

She should say no to his invitation to Abercrombie's, but instead, she reiterated, "Friends," then found herself saying, "That sounds great."

"How about tomorrow, after you're done at school?"

"I have an appointment tomorrow after school." He gave her a look that said he thought she was trying to blow him off. She wasn't. So she quickly added, "But Tuesday would work."

"Tuesday it is."

TUESDAY AFTER SCHOOL, Eli waited for Zac in a chair by the window in her living room.

Her appointment yesterday had been a snap. They'd done a sonogram to get a measurement, and determine when the baby would be born. But Dr. Benton was pretty sure she'd have her baby toward the end of May. Eli would be able to work the school year, and spend the whole summer with the baby.

Her baby.

The idea still felt surreal, but she thought she was getting used to it.

Her hand drifted toward her stomach. The baby resembled a blob on the sonogram, and though the technician tried to point out things, no matter how much Eli tried, it was still a blob.

She heard Zac pull up out front.

He laughed as she hurried down the drive. "Wow, that was fast."

"I was watching for you. It's a beautiful day for a drive."

"So, how did your appointment go yesterday?" he asked as they started towards I-79.

She tried to remember what she'd told him, but couldn't, so she simply said, "Fine."

"And how are you doing…I mean with the breakup and all."

The breakup.

Arthur.

She hadn't heard from him and—she hated to admit it, even to herself—barely thought of him since she'd told him about the baby and he'd bailed.

What kind of person did that make her?

She dated Arthur Stone for five long years, and she hadn't felt the loss of the relationship.

Hadn't missed him.

"Hey, you got really quiet. Are you sure everything's okay?"

"Just thinking. It's a teacher's curse. You can leave the school building, but you never quit working."

"So, how goes CATA?"

"I have two other businesses interested and…" She babbled about her job, because in truth, it was easier to think about that than think about everything else.

Maybe that's why she'd agreed to go out with Zac today. He didn't know about the baby, so there were no sympathetic looks like she got from Tucker, there was no shock like there had been with Arthur, and there was no nervousness that she hadn't told him yet like there would have been with her parents.

He was just Zac. A nice guy who was a friend.

And she was just Eli. Someone who liked antiques. Someone who enjoyed a drive on a fall afternoon.

The rest of it…she'd worry about that later.

Specifically this weekend, when she saw her parents.

FOR THE FIRST TIME IN her adult life, the weekend came too soon, in Eli's estimation.

"Mom, Dad…" Eli started as she sat across from them in her very neat living room.

She'd practiced her speech over and over again. She knew what she had to say, but she wasn't sure she was ready for what would follow.

She stared at them. Gail and John Cartwright. Childhood sweethearts who still held hands, as they did now, sitting on her sofa. Both wore expressions of trepidation. She worried that she'd scared them with her opening: I've got big news.

"Listen, you know I love you. You've tried to raise me right and I appreciate that. I've tried to live up to the ideals you set for me. What I'm going to tell you might upset you. And though it's certainly not what I planned…"

She paused.

She'd been here before so many times. Only *she'd* been the moral support for a girl who was telling her parents she was going to be a teen mother. She tried to remember her advice.

Tell your parents you love them, and that though this wasn't what any of you had planned, this baby is a gift and you're going to do everything you can to be worthy of the life that's been entrusted to you.

"And though I know this isn't what I had planned, I have to tell you that I'm…"

The word *pregnant* hung for a second on the tip of her tongue. Once she said it, once it was out in the open, everything would change.

"I'm pregnant."

Her mother clapped her hands to her mouth and her father sat stone-faced and unreadable.

"Mom. Dad. Say something. Say anything." She waited for them to tell her how disappointed they were. That this wasn't how they'd raised her.

"Oh, Eli…"

Wait for it. Wait for it, she commanded herself, steeling herself for her mother's words.

"I'm going to be a grandmother." Her mother hugged herself with apparent glee. "Oh, my. I'd given up hope.

Will I be Grandma? Grammy? Granny—no. I hate that one. Mammy? Nana? Bubbi?" The words rushed over one another, tripping to get out.

Her mother sprang from the couch as if she were too excited to stay still any longer. She hugged Eli tight.

"Mom—" *You're happy* was what she was going to say, but her mother interrupted.

"Oh, Eli, I'm going to be a grandmother."

She took a deep breath that Eli could feel, as she was still caught in her mother's death-grip of a hug.

"Gail, I don't think Eli can breathe," her father said. "And that can't be good for the baby."

Her mother let go immediately.

"Come and take a seat, honey, before you keel over." Her father made room for her on the sofa next to him. "Congratulations, Eli." He smiled, but his brows puckered in such a way that she could tell he was worried.

There was no puckering, no worry in her mom's expression, as she asked, "Now, when's your due date? Do you know?"

"May."

"Why isn't Arthur here with you, telling us?" her father asked.

There it was again, the pucker.

Well, they'd taken the news about the baby better than she'd imagined, so maybe they'd take the news about Arthur better as well.

"You see, Arthur's not going to be a part of this. We broke up and—" *I'm doing this on my own* was going to be the rest of the sentence, but her doorbell rang and interrupted her. "Hang on a minute."

Eli hurried to the door. Zac was there, with pizza boxes and a DVD. "Hey, I brought food, hoping it would keep you from being annoyed that I've just dropped by uninvited and unannounced."

She heard her parents' footsteps and knew they'd followed her. She turned and they were standing in the doorway studying Zac.

"Mom, Dad, this is my friend, Zac Keller. Zac, my parents, John and Gail Cartwright."

Zac handed Eli the pizzas and walked up to her parents. "Mr. and Mrs. Cartwright, it's so nice to meet you. Eli's said such lovely things about you. My mother totally fell for Eli when she was over, and said her parents must be wonderful to have raised such a great daughter."

Her mother looked hurt. "You told his family first?"

"Told my family what?" Zac looked confused.

Eli realized that her mother had misunderstood. "Mom, it's not what you think. I—"

Her father cleared his throat and interrupted. "Elinore, you know we've always supported you and your decisions. And though we haven't seen Arthur in a few months, it didn't sound as if you'd been separated very long. After all, today is the first you've mentioned it. So how long could you have known this man? This is a monumental undertaking for two practical strangers."

She was in trouble when she was Elinore.

"Dad, I—"

This time Zac interrupted. "Mr. Cartwright, Eli and I have worked together for quite a while on her new CATA Project. Now that it's time to implement it, well, so far so good. We've become quite close. She's an amazing woman."

"The CATA Project is a huge undertaking," her mother said. "But John's talking about the baby."

"What baby?" Zac asked, clearly baffled.

"Yours and Eli's," her father responded, looking stern. "And I need to ask you, sir, what are your intentions with my daughter?"

"Baby?" Zac asked Eli.

She nodded. "We'll talk later. But Mom, Dad, this is ridiculous. Zac's not—"

"Afraid to answer your question, Mr. Cartwright," Zac finished. "My intentions, in regard to your daughter, are to do whatever she wants to make this easier on her. I've liked her longer than she knows."

"Liked her?"

"More than like, if I were honest, but I'm taking it slow, so as not to frighten Eli off."

"You two obviously didn't take it slow enough," her father groused.

"Enough," Eli said loudly. "Everyone keeps interrupting me. I am not some child who needs to be defended, or explained."

"Yes, exactly." Her mother came over and put an arm gently around Eli. "Enough, you men. My daughter's pregnant and I'm thrilled. I have so much to do. So much to think about. I have to learn to knit, and we'll have to go shopping for the baby. Oh, Eli, I've wanted to be a grandmother for so long."

Eli was on the verge of telling all of them that the baby was Arthur's, but her mother's last statement stopped her. "Really?"

"Oh, yes."

"But you never said anything."

"I wouldn't want you to feel as if I were disappointed that I wasn't. I didn't want to pressure you. But no matter how this baby came about, know it's going

to be loved and spoiled beyond all sense and reason."
She glanced at Zac. "And no matter how long you've
known the father, we'll accept him, too."

Her mother walked over to Zac and hugged him.
"Welcome to the family, son."

"Stop. Please. Zac. Is. Not. The. Baby's. Daddy."
She enunciated each word as clearly and succinctly
as she could.

"Eli and I are friends who are working our way up
to dating," Zac added helpfully. "But I'm thrilled about
the baby. I have five siblings, and am pretty handy with
babies, if I do say so myself."

"You dumped Arthur, got pregnant by someone else
and now are dating this man?" Her father's voice held
a sad disbelief.

"No. I didn't dump Arthur. He dumped me and the
baby—his baby. And I'm not dating Zac."

"Not yet, but hey, a guy can hope." Zac grinned.

What on earth was with him? Eli gave him a sharp
jab with her elbow.

Her parents both looked as confused as she felt.
"Gail, I think we'd better go and let these two work
out what's going on with them."

"You're right, John." She hurried to Eli and swept
her into her arms. "No matter who the baby's father
is or isn't, or how long you've known him, don't you
worry. Your father and I are here for you every step of
the way. And…" She squeezed Eli tighter. "Eli, a baby.
I'm beside myself with happiness."

Suddenly her mother's face clouded over. "John, we
were leaving in a week for Florida. I don't know if I
can go now. Eli might need me. I—"

"Mom, Florida's a couple hours' flight. I don't want

this to undo any of your plans. You'll be home long before the baby comes."

"But I—"

"Gail, we'll talk about Florida and what Eli does and doesn't need from us later."

For a moment, Eli wasn't sure her mother was going to agree, but then she slowly nodded. "Okay. Tomorrow, Eli. I'll talk to you tomorrow after you and Zac here sort things out." She turned to Zac. "It was very nice to meet you, young man. We never really liked Arthur, you know."

And with that surprising last sentence, her mother took her father by the hand and said, "Come on, John. Let's take a drive into Erie and do some shopping on Peach Street. We can stop at Babies 'R' Us and then…"

The rest of her mother's plans were muted as they closed the door.

Zac took back his pizzas from Eli and started walking toward her kitchen. There was nothing left for her to do but follow and ask, "What on earth was that all about?"

He set the boxes on the counter. "What?"

"Don't *what* me. You didn't come right out and deny the baby was yours. And then you claimed we were dating. We are not dating."

He opened up one of the lids. "Do you want to get us plates?"

On autopilot, she opened the cupboard, grabbed two plates, then took a handful of napkins back to the island's counter.

"So what gives?"

"A," he began, as he put a piece of pizza on a plate and slid it in front of Eli, "I didn't know you were pregnant, and didn't know the circumstances with your parents. So I just tried to go along with it."

"I didn't ask you—"

"And B," he said, taking the other plate and another piece of pizza and sliding it in front of himself, "we haven't been dating only because I wanted to give you time to get over your breakup with Arthur. I have no interest in becoming your rebound guy, but I'm every bit interested in dating you for a long time to come. I was trying to be considerate and ease you into the notion."

"Well, you can obviously see that's out of the question now. I thought it was just friendship, Zac. If I'd known you were hoping it was anything else, I would have said something and put a stop to it. Truth is, I was selfish. I had fun hanging out with you. It was easy to forget…well, everything. All the changes I'll be going through—my life will be going through. The time we were together I wasn't worrying about the future, about how I'm going to handle becoming a mother. I'm sorry. You deserve so much more than that."

"And you deserve all the friends and support you can get. If you don't mind me asking, if you're having his baby, why did you break up with Arthur?" Zac took a bite of his pizza.

"I had a choice. Arthur or the baby. I chose the baby."

He dropped the pizza back onto the plate, swallowed and asked, "He didn't want it?"

"He's got his life mapped out and this wasn't on the map."

"So, did you…you didn't plan on a baby?"

"Once upon a time, I thought I'd have a houseful of kids. I never found the right guy, and it was never the right time. So somewhere along the line, I decided it wasn't going to happen and I've set up a quiet life for myself."

"That's going to change real fast." Zac chuckled. "I've got younger siblings and I can assure you, babies aren't quiet."

"No, they're not—I do know that much. But it's a drop in the bucket compared to what I don't know. You'd think the fact I've done this, dealt with situations like this, for years, that I'd have it all together. I don't, I've got a lot to figure out. And I will. I've watched too many girls cry because they're pregnant. I won't do that. This baby might be unexpected, but it's being greeted with…" She searched for the right word. *Joy* wasn't quite it. "It's being welcomed."

Zac nodded, as if he'd never doubted it for a moment. "Eli, I want to keep seeing you."

"As friends," she clarified.

"I want to see you in whatever capacity you'll allow me to," he said.

"I don't want to lead you on, Zac. I've got a lot on my plate. We can be friends, but there's too much stacked against us being anything more. If that can be enough, then yes."

"Fine. If that's what you want."

"That's what I want," she assured him.

"Then friends it is."

A COUPLE OF HOURS LATER, Zac turned off the television. It was ironic that he'd thought to woo Eli by bringing a chick-flick movie disguised as an action-adventure, called *Adventures in Friendship.* Two best friends cavorting through Europe, running from the big bad mafia and discovering they have deep romantic feelings for each other.

He wondered if there were any mafia guys interested in chasing after a grocery store manager and a teacher. Maybe that would convince Eli they could still be a couple.

But she was pregnant.

A baby.

The news was a shock, and he wasn't quite sure what to do about it.

"Zac, I don't want to be rude, but I really have some things to get done around the house, and I expect my mother and father to stop by once she's done buying out every baby store on Peach Street."

He took the hint. "Yeah, I'd better go."

She stood at her door, watching him walk to his car. He wanted nothing more than to go back, hold her and tell her everything would be all right.

But he'd wait.

Zac had gotten very good at waiting.

Rather than drive home though, he went to his parents'. It was never quiet there, and he wanted something to distract him.

He found his mom in the kitchen, which was no surprise. The fact that he didn't see his dad or sister, was.

"Where's the gang?"

"Cessy had basketball practice, and your father's picking her up."

His mother was stirring a pot of something as he sat down at the island counter. "You'll stay for dinner?"

He meant to say "Yeah, of course." Instead, he blurted out, "Eli's pregnant."

His mother stopped stirring and took the stool opposite him. "And what are you two going to do."

"No, it's not mine. It's her ex's. He found out and dumped her."

"I'm sorry. That has to be hard on her."

"Mom, does it make me lower than low to be glad he's gone? Even knowing about the baby? I know I should hope they get back together, but I can't."

She studied him for a long moment. "You care about her." It was a statement, not a question.

"I have for a long time. While he was in the picture, I let it go. But now? I know that her being pregnant with another man's baby should change things, but it doesn't. I still want her. I still want to date her, to get closer to her. But a baby. Someone else's baby? She says she can't do that to me."

"Zac, the heart doesn't care about such things. If you like Eli, her being pregnant doesn't change that. Maybe it adds complication, but life's complicated, and so are relationships.

"Your father and I wanted many children, and when that didn't happen we decided that maybe our children weren't going to grow in my womb. Maybe they were out there waiting for us. So we contacted social services. They told us you weren't clear to be adopted, but we could foster you, that they expected your biological parents' rights to be terminated. And I said yes.

"There you were, Zachary Manhiem, a tiny little boy with dark brown hair that sorely needed a trim. Your clothes were too small, and your expression was too guarded. But I knew—I knew as soon as I saw you that you were ours."

"I remember that day." He couldn't remember the

last time he'd eaten, and he'd never been to school. Someone in the neighborhood had called and reported his mother to social services. He'd never known who, but he owed whoever it was a debt of gratitude.

When he'd gone to the group home, the only thing he'd brought from his past was a piggy bank.

"You were so small, yet so old. You kept your distance. You were polite. Quiet. You always did what you were asked. You had a way of looking at me and your dad, as if you were assessing us. You were careful.

"A few months after you arrived, you started school. That first day, when I came to get you, you said—"

"I didn't think you'd come."

"And I told you that I'd always come get you, that you were my son and I loved you." There were tears in her eyes, even after all these years.

"That Christmas I told you the stories of Christmas and Chanukah, trying to blend your traditions with ours. You asked what you were. And I told you—"

"That I could be whatever I wanted to be. And I said, I want to be a Keller. I want to be your son."

"You chose to be Zachary Keller. A man of honor, of heart. A man I'm so proud to call my son. About Eli and her baby, give it time. You've always made good decisions and pursued them with no doubts, no hesitation. Some people take longer. Eli's experiencing so much change right now. Patience. If it's love, you'll both figure it out."

"We haven't known each other long enough to use the L word."

"So, you'll see each other more and figure out if you should use the L word. Because if you love Eli, I'm sure you'll fall in love with this baby. Our family knows, so much more than most, that a family isn't tied by genetics, it's tied by love. If you're meant to be a family, you'll find a way."

"So, I should date her regardless?"

"Be her friend. It sounds like she could use them right now. Then see what happens." His mother echoed Eli's words.

"So, I'll be her friend."

His mom was right, Eli could use all the friends she could get. For now, that's what he'd be. And later? Well, they'd see.

CHAPTER FIVE

"The second trimester is a time of change. Most mothers feel wonderful during these months. The morning sickness and excessive tiredness of the first trimester has diminished. Women feel good. They're starting to become used to the idea of the baby."
—*Pregnancy, Childbirth and Parenting for Teens,*
by Mary Jeanne Lorei

ELI STRAIGHTENED THE CORNUCOPIA in the center of her table. Last month she'd sworn that Halloween was her favorite holiday, but looking at her house all decorated for Thanksgiving, she had to confess, Thanksgiving might be, after all.

Her hand drifted to her stomach.

Her baby.

Next year at this time, she'd be putting the cornucopia on the table while holding the baby on her hip.

She could see it in her mind's eye. How often she'd realized that this time next year, she'd have a baby. It was easy to imagine.

She was getting used to the idea of the baby.

And she was getting used to having Zac around.

He was coming to pick her up soon.

She'd talked to her mom this morning. Her parents had settled back into their Florida home, but unlike most years, her mother kept hemming and hawing about coming back to Pennsylvania because she was worried about Eli. Eli spent most conversations assuring her mother she was fine, and today's call was no exception. Her mom worried about her being alone on Thanksgiving, but Eli assured her that she would be with the Kellers, and with so many Kellers, there was no way she'd be alone.

The doorbell rang as if on cue, and she said goodbye to her mother and hurried to the door. She glanced at her watch. He was early, but she was happy. That pretty much summed up her relationship with Zac. When he was around, she was simply happy.

She threw the door open...and froze. "Arthur?"

Her bubble of happiness popped.

"Is this a bad time?" He looked as if he were hoping she'd say yes it was a bad time. Worse than that, he looked downright queasy.

Good mothers think about what's best for their baby, not what's best for themselves. Knowing the father was what was best for her baby, she'd need to make an effort when it came to Arthur. "It's fine. Come in."

She opened the door wider for him.

It had been a little more than a month since she'd seen him. She waited for the pang of longing, for some feeling of regret that things turned out the way they had. When those emotions didn't surface, she waited to feel fury—he'd treated her badly, and treated their unborn baby worse.

Still, she felt nothing, except maybe a sense of wonder about what she'd ever seen in him.

Should she offer him a drink? She didn't know what

the protocol was when dealing with an ex-lover who'd abandoned you and your unborn child.

"Did you want something, Arthur? Did you bring the papers from the lawyer, perhaps?" she finally asked. She didn't see any papers, but maybe they were tucked inside his coat.

"No. I haven't been to the lawyer yet." He sounded almost angry at her.

Maybe that's why her hackles were up as she countered, "Then why are you here?"

"I missed you. I worried about you. I came to see how you were doing." There was still no tenderness in his admission.

He'd only mentioned her, which annoyed her even more. Arthur could ignore the baby, but she couldn't—wouldn't. "I'm doing fine. And the baby's doing fine, not that you asked."

"This was a mistake. I just wanted to see how you were doing," he repeated. He turned as if to leave.

"Arthur."

He stopped, hand on the doorknob, and faced her.

"Arthur, what do you really want?"

He ran his fingers through his always well-styled hair, leaving it mussed. "I don't know, Eli. I know what I don't want more than what I do want."

"What don't you want?"

Slowly, quietly, he said, "I don't want a baby. I don't want our lives to change. I don't want to lose you, but if you're keeping the baby, I don't know how to keep you."

"I'm sorry, Arthur." And as she said the words, her annoyance with him faded. She *was* sorry. Sorry that she'd wasted five years of her life on this man. Sorry that he couldn't see what a blessing this baby could be.

"Arthur, keeping me is out of the question, no matter what you do from here on out. We're over. There will be no reconciliation. However, if you decide you want to be part of the baby's life…" She let the offer hang there.

He ignored her mention of the baby, and honed in on her comment about their relationship. "You can't just write off a five-year relationship."

"I didn't, you did."

"Eli—" He stopped, as if he didn't know what to say.

So Eli said the words that had to be said. "Arthur, you and I? It's done. There's no going back." And to herself, she admitted that she didn't want to go back. She didn't miss Arthur the way she should if she truly loved him. "But whether you're a dad who takes an active role in the baby's day-to-day life, or a father who spends a few days here and there with the baby, I'll work with you. Children should know their fathers."

The books said so. Studies said so. And Eli had seen enough teen relationships to know that most of the time it was better if a child's father was present.

"I want *you*," he blustered with a petulant whine in his voice.

She gritted her teeth at the sound, but didn't address his childishness. "Arthur, I don't mean to be cruel, but I don't want you carrying around false hope—I don't want you."

His face blanched at the baldness of her words. "I—"

"Go figure out what you want as far as the baby is concerned. That's the only decision you have in front of you. Either you want to play a role in his or her life, or you're going to the lawyer and terminate your parental rights."

"Eli…" He just stood there, undecided.

"It's all right, Arthur," she said with gentleness. "You take some time and figure it out. Right now, you have to go. I'm waiting for someone."

"A date?"

"A friend," she corrected.

"A male friend?"

She nodded, unsure where this jealousy was coming from. Arthur had been many things during their relationship, but jealous was never one of them. "A colleague," she clarified. "And a friend."

"A friend who's coming over on Thanksgiving? Friendly colleagues don't tend to share holidays with each other."

"Arthur, I don't have to explain myself to you. You lost the right—if you ever had it—to approve my itinerary when we broke up. Now, if you'll excuse me." She opened the door as a not-so-subtle hint. Cold November air rushed into the hallway.

It would snow soon.

She was sending her boyfriend of five years packing, and rather than crying, she was thinking about the weather.

"Eli—"

"Goodbye, Arthur. Figure out what you want to do and get back to me."

"Can I call and check on you?"

"No, but you can call and check on the baby."

As she held the door open, she saw Zac pull up on

the street in front of her house since Arthur's car was parked in the driveway.

Arthur saw her looking past him and turned to look as well. "That him?"

"Go home, Arthur."

Arthur didn't move. He waited until Zac got up to the door. "Arthur Stone," he said, extending his hand.

Zac didn't take it. "Zac Keller."

"Him?" Arthur asked again.

"Go home, Arthur" was her flat response.

Arthur finally took his cue and started toward his car.

"Sorry," Eli said to Zac.

"You don't have anything to apologize for."

"Maybe not, but I feel as if I should. Come on in, while I get bundled up."

"How was your day?" he asked.

"Nice. Well, until about ten minutes ago."

He jerked his head in the general direction of her driveway. "Did he give you trouble?"

"No. Not trouble, really. He's just confused. He doesn't want the baby, but he still wants me."

"And you, what do you want?"

ZAC HELD HIS BREATH AFTER he'd asked the question and forced himself to exhale. He knew that he wasn't officially dating Eli, but this last month they'd spent a lot of time together. Basketball games. Sunday dinners with his family. He'd even had dinner at her parents' before they left for Florida.

No, they weren't dating, but they were creeping ever closer. He'd felt a sense of certainty that it was only a matter of time until they were officially a couple.

And now Arthur was back.

What did this mean?

"I told Arthur that *us* wasn't an option. In fact, *us* wasn't ever a viable long-term option."

"You were together for five years," he declared, not so much because he wanted to remind her, but because he wanted to understand.

"Yes. Being with Arthur was easy. It didn't require any work. Any commitment. We had regular nights we were together, and we both did our own things as well. And I'll confess, on the nights I didn't see him, I didn't pine over him. There should be some pining in a good relationship, don't you think?"

Zac wasn't sure *pining* was the word he'd use for the days he didn't see Eli, but he did miss her when they weren't together. He wasn't sure that she'd recently analyzed their growing friendship, and he didn't push her to.

Rather than answer her pining question, he said, "So, are you ready to head to Mom and Dad's? The whole crew is going to be there."

The trip to his parents' was a quick one. They stopped to pick up Ariel from her aunt's, since the teen wasn't invited to her family's celebration. Zac couldn't understand how any parent could cut a child off so completely. He could imagine being disappointed, or even angry, but he'd still want to be there for his child. When Marge at the store mentioned that Ariel's aunt, an airline attendant, would be out of town, and her parents hadn't invited her home, Zac had issued the invitation.

Despite their age differences, Ariel had grown close to Cessy, and he was pretty sure it was Cessy who'd

convinced Ariel to accept their invitation to Thanksgiving dinner.

"Thanks, Mr. Keller. Hi, Miss Cartwright," she'd
said as she climbed into the backseat.

Ariel and Eli chatted the rest of the trip.

His parents' house was awash in light as they pulled
up in front. A huge autumn leaf wreath hung heavily
on the front door and thwapped against it as Zac threw
the door open. He didn't need to call out or check what
room they were in, they merely followed the dull roar.

"Z-man," Cessy cried as she ran across the kitchen
floor. "You brought her. Hey, Ariel, Ms. Cartwright."

"Hi, Cecily." Eli smiled as Cessy engulfed Ariel in
a huge hug.

"Thanks for not calling me Cessy, Ms, Cartwright.
Some people—" her voice rose in volume as she said
the words, leaving no doubt that her family was some
people "—can't seem to remember I'm not four."

"Sorry, squirt, you'll always be four to us," Zac said
and tweaked a hair that had strayed from her ponytail.

"Squirt?" Cessy stood up straight.

The whole family started discussing Cessy's squirt-
ness and Zac saw his mother come up to Eli and talk
to her quietly.

Cessy dragged poor Ariel down the hall, presum-
ably to her room.

Zac found a quiet corner and just observed. He loved
that his family had embraced Eli as one of their own.
She tried to help with the dinner preparations, but they
all kept telling her to sit down and put her feet up.

Zac followed her when she finally gave up and
pulled up a chair in the family room. "They like you."

She snorted. "Maybe, but they won't believe I'm not an invalid."

"None of us have ever really been around a pregnant woman. I mean, we've done babies. I can remember when Cessy came home. She was so tiny and, Eli, she had so much hair, we all swore it weighed more than she did. They're just worried about you."

"When you put it that way, I suppose I'll have to content myself with being waited on."

As if on cue, Seth came in and handed Eli a glass of something red. "Cranberry juice. Mom said to tell you it's all juice and organic and that you should drink it."

"If you don't like cranberry juice, we'll cover for you," Zac said.

Eli laughed. "No, the baby and I like it just fine."

At the mention of the baby, Seth visibly winced and hurried back to the general pandemonium.

"Did I say something?"

"No, it wasn't you." Zac toyed with how much to say, and opted to leave it at that. Today wasn't a day for sad stories, it was a day for family and giving thanks.

Zac didn't get to keep Eli to himself for long. His sisters arrived en masse and swooped Eli away. "Mom might not let you lift a finger, but come into the kitchen and visit with us."

Zac got up and found his brothers and Dad in the garage. "It's safe," Dom called. "Come on in, quick before they follow you."

They were all gathered around his father's ancient black-and-white television, that had a screen comparable to the size of an iPod's screen.

"Seriously, guys, why watch the game on this, instead of on the flat-screen in the family room?" Zac asked.

"Now, Zac, you know your mother never ventures out here if she can help it. We're hiding until the meal's served."

"She'd find us too quickly in the family room," Dom added, then laughed. "She's scary when it comes to the holidays. Do you remember that holiday she wanted to take a picture of all of us in front of the Christmas tree, with a menorah in the shot?"

"I have that picture as my screen saver," his dad admitted. "And it wasn't so bad. I had the fire extinguisher in hand before the fire spread from that one branch."

They all laughed. Well, everyone except Seth, who might have had a small smile. It was hard to tell.

They crowded around the small TV, watching the college football game and sharing family stories until his mom came to the door and called. "I knew you were all hiding. But that's okay. The girls and I decided since we got dinner on the table, you all get to do dishes."

They laughed and followed their dad into the house. That's what Zac associated the most with being home—laughter. And as they all gathered around the table and gorged themselves on turkey and all the trimmings, there was a lot of laughter. A lot of noise. Eli and Ariel seemed to fit right in, both joining in the conversations. His parents had an awful habit of sharing embarrassing childhood stories, not just of him, but of all his siblings.

"You just wait, you two," his mom said to both Ariel and Eli. "One minute you're holding the most precious baby in the world in your arms, and the next, they're twelve and you're getting a call from the neighbors because they've climbed out their bedroom window... again."

"Ah, come on, Mom," Cessy cried right on cue. "Are you ever going to let me live it down?"

"Darling, I told you somewhere around the second time I caught you at it that I wouldn't."

Cessy turned to Ariel and Eli, who were sitting next to each other on the opposite side of the table. "I thought my biological mother might have been an alien and that's why she left me. I was hoping my alien superpower was flying."

Their whole family knew why Cessy's alien fantasies didn't include her father. Zac felt the familiar sense of pain as he remembered.

"Turns out her only alien superpower was annoying her older brothers," Dom, ever the peacemaker, teased in hopes of making everyone let go of the sad memory and laugh.

It worked.

Zac glanced at Eli. She gave him a look that said she'd caught the awkward moment, and that she was sorry, but she didn't ask any questions. And Zac knew she wouldn't. She would let him tell her when and if he was ready.

He smiled and gave a small nod, letting her know it was okay. Then he glanced at her plate, specifically at the place where his mother's dressing had been, but was now conspicuously empty. He glanced at her with a question in his eyes. She nodded.

He reached for the bowl that was in front of him. "Hey, Mom, can you pass this to Eli?"

"Your dressing's delicious, Mrs. Keller."

"It's the chestnuts. They give it just the right crunch."

"Hey, Zac, how did you know Eli wanted the dressing?" Cessy asked. "Maybe I wasn't the only alien Mom and Dad adopted. Me and my flying abilities, and you and your ESP."

"Nah, they've got that same thing Mom and Dad have. That conversations-with-their-eyes thing," Layla assured her. "I've always thought I don't want a guy who can't talk to me without saying a word."

"And I assure you, Lay, that most men I know would soooooo—" Dom drew the word out to annoy her especially "—appreciate having their only speech with you confined to ones without words."

Layla tossed a dinner roll at him.

He picked it up, poised to toss it back, when their mom said, "Children, we have guests."

And there it was, that look Layla had been talking about. His mom looked at his dad, and though both of them maintained a stern expression, they were laughing with each other.

They were talking without saying a word.

In that one quick glance between his parents, he'd seen not only their amusement, but also the love they had for each and for the family they'd built.

In Eli, he could see she'd seen his parents, and that she was as touched as he was.

Zac had dated women before, but he'd never met anyone he felt he could build a relationship with like his parents'.

Until now.

And as they resumed their regular holiday chatter,

Zac acknowledged that he was most thankful for that sense of potential he had with Eli.

LATER THAT NIGHT, AFTER they'd dropped Ariel off at her aunt's, Zac pulled up in front of Eli's house.

She was exhausted, but she lingered in the car, not wanting the day to officially end. "I'm supposed to tell you thank you from my mom for rescuing me from a solo Thanksgiving."

"Did you tell her that Tucker invited you, too?"

"Oh, she knew. But if you've ever eaten Tucker's cooking, you'd know you did indeed rescue me." Tucker was great with a paintbrush in hand, but give her a pair of oven mitts and watch out.

"So, I have a long weekend for the holiday," Zac said. "I've got to check in at the store tomorrow morning, but the rest of the day is mine. What if I come pick you up and take you to lunch?"

"Zac, you must have better things to do."

"You say that every time I ask to spend time with you. Since my sister is convinced we can talk without talking, just like my parents, want to guess what I'm saying without saying?"

Eli tried to look serious, but all she could do was laugh. That seemed to be a common theme with Zac. They talked, they enjoyed each other's company and they both laughed a lot.

"Okay, tomorrow for lunch." She opened the door. "I'd better get in."

Before she got out, Zac leaned over and kissed her cheek. It was light, platonic even, and yet, she felt a bit breathless in a way that had nothing to do with the blast of cold air that flooded the car.

"Uh, well, thanks for a lovely day, Zac. I'd really best get in."

And in his eyes, without him saying a word, she could see that he knew his light buss on the cheek had flustered her, and that he was pleased.

She brushed a fingertip over the spot as she opened the door.

What was she going to do about Zac Keller?

CHAPTER SIX

"Holidays and family gatherings can be a very busy time, and an especially trying time for a pregnant mother. You can do as much as you're comfortable doing, but remember to pace yourself."

—*Pregnancy, Childbirth and Parenting for Teens,*
by Mary Jeanne Lorei

THE TIME BETWEEN THANKSGIVING and the Christmas break always flew by, in Eli's opinion.

Fall leaves and turkeys were replaced by Christmas lights and evergreens. Eli left for school in the dark, and it was dusk by the time she got home most evenings.

She sat at her desk before first period looking out at the grayish sky and admitted to herself that she was nervous.

Today was the day she was going to break the news to her students that she was expecting a baby. She'd made an appointment with Barry Werner, the principal, and told him this morning. Afterward, she'd told a few teachers, and knew that with the way the school grapevine worked, the entire faculty would know by now.

That left her students. And really, her stomach was

in knots at the thought of telling them. It was ridiculous and she realized it. She was an adult. She didn't have to make excuses to anyone. And yet…

Knot upon knot.

The bell for first period rang, and slowly, the girls filed in the room, one by one or in small clusters.

She had fifteen girls this year in her teen parenting class. Eli had other more traditional family and consumer science classes, but this one was nearest and dearest to her heart. Some of the girls, like Ariel, were pregnant, some already had babies. There were freshmen through seniors.

The room's volume had risen with their murmured conversations.

"Okay, everyone, find your seats."

Rather than abating, the noise grew even louder. Eli waited and everyone eventually sat down and looked at her expectantly. "Thanks. Now, before we get started on today's lesson, I have some news I'd like to share with you all."

The girls were staring at her, and Eli realized her hand was placed protectively over her stomach. "For so many years I've worked in the teen pregnancy program, teaching parenting and life skills. It was rather ironic, since I'm single and childless. Well, I'm still single, but I'm very happy to announce—" and as she said the words, it occurred to her that despite her nervousness, she really *was* happy to announce "—I'll be remedying the childless part in May."

The noise level rose again as the girls babbled their congratulations. Eli glanced at Ariel, who was resolutely staring at her desk and not meeting Eli's eyes.

A couple of hands flew up, and Eli didn't have time to ponder Ariel's reaction. She called on Felicity.

"Ms. Cartwright, are you going to get married to the baby's father?"

Eli had anticipated this question and had given her response plenty of thought beforehand. "In an ideal world, a child's parents are married. But you all know from personal experience that this is not an ideal world. So, to answer your question, no. I'm not planning to marry the baby's father. We'd been in a long-term relationship, but marriage is not in our future."

"He dumped you?" Kelissa asked.

"I wouldn't say that," Eli hedged.

Kelissa looked furious on Eli's behalf. "He didn't want nothing to do with a baby and he dumped you. Just like me. My baby's no-good daddy doesn't want nothing to do with me or the baby. That's fine. You've taught me to be independent, and I'm going to look after this baby on my own. You'll do fine, too, Ms. Cartwright, you know more than all of us put together. It's his loss."

"Yeah," Bobbi agreed.

Soon all the girls were offering her words of comfort, although she hadn't confirmed she'd been dumped.

Well, all the girls except Ariel, who was still staring at some imaginary spot on her desk.

Eli got the class back under control and started her day's lesson plan. The class flew by. When the bell rang again, the girls immediately started gathering their belongings. Ariel practically sprang from her desk and sprinted toward the door.

"Ariel, could I see you for a minute?" Eli called.

Ariel froze, and with apparent reluctance, turned around and walked back to Eli's desk, her head down.

"Mel, would you close the door after you?" she called to the straggler.

Eli waited until the door was shut. "Ariel, what's wrong?"

"Nothing."

She'd been a teacher too long not to know there was something very wrong here. "Is there something wrong with your baby?"

Ariel shook her head, and since she'd chosen another indistinct point to stare at, her blond hair flopped forward, hiding even her brow.

"Your aunt? Work? School?" Eli asked.

More head shaking.

"Ariel? Talk to me. I thought we were friends."

Ariel's head jerked up and she faced Eli, anger flashing in her eyes. "We weren't friends. We're not friends. You're just another stupid teacher, telling me what to do, and I'm just some dumb teenager who's screwed up her whole life by getting pregnant. You can't fix my life. Hell, you can't even fix your own life." And with that, Ariel stormed out of the classroom.

Eli sat at her desk, not sure what to do. Should she run after Ariel and apologize? For what? For getting pregnant and being dumped? For being human?

Somehow Eli made it until the end of the day. All she wanted to do was go home and hide. Hide from her life.

She opened the door to the silent house. The afternoons got dark early, so it felt gloomy, but she didn't turn on any lights. Instead, she went to her room, put on her oldest, most comfortable pair of sweats and her Mercyhurst College sweatshirt, made some herbal tea and sat at her desk, going over her plans for next week's mentor panel.

She made absolutely no headway. She aimlessly turned the pages of her notebook, and occasionally doodled in the margins, but her thoughts kept drifting back to Ariel.

She could rationalize Ariel's reaction. Ariel had lost everything she knew when she'd become pregnant. Her parents had kicked her out, her boyfriend had left her and she couldn't be on the cheerleading squad in her condition. She was mad. And in her mind, Eli had now let her down, as well, and in so doing had become a perfect target for some of that anger.

Eli had spent her entire teaching career trying to be a good example to her students, but while *she* knew good example didn't equal perfect, maybe Ariel had missed that bulletin.

Well, that was fine, because Eli wasn't exactly thrilled about her circumstances, either. She'd never planned on being in her forties, pregnant and alone. Yet, here she was. She looked down and what had started out to be a doodle had become an angry knot of scribbles.

She balled up the piece of paper and threw it at the garbage can…and missed.

Perfect. Just perfect. She'd made a mess of her life, her career and now she was making a mess in her house. She got up and picked the paper up and placed it in the can.

The doorbell rang. She couldn't imagine who it was, but truth be told she hoped it was someone trying to sell something—someone she'd be able to dismiss quickly. She opened the door to find Zac on the porch. "Oh, it's you."

"Wow." He was seemingly unphased by her lack of enthusiasm, as he walked past her into the house.

She shut the door, resigned to the fact she had a guest, like it or not.

"I thought we'd moved beyond such effusive displays of delight." He smiled, as if he could jolly her out of her funk. She noticed that his grins were so broad that they made the skin around his eyes crinkle. It was as if Zac's entire face took the business of smiling seriously.

He removed his coat and boots, and headed straight for her living room. Over the last month, he'd become quite at home at her house. "Uh, a bit dark, isn't it?" The only light in the room was coming through the window.

"Maybe I'm in a dark mood."

He clicked on the floor lamp next to the couch, sat down and indicated she should sit beside him. "Okay, so, what happened today to put you in a dark mood? Because Eli, you're the least dark person I know."

She sat, not because she was obeying him, but because she was pregnant and she should probably sit. "Nothing happened."

"Liar." When she didn't respond, he asked, "Want me to call Tuck for you? I mean, I know you two have been friends longer than we have. It won't hurt my feelings. If you can't talk to me, talk to her."

There was a tightness at the back of her throat that made it impossible to say anything. She literally couldn't seem to push the words past that point.

"Here, let me call her."

"No" was all she managed to get out before the tightness became a rush of tears. Not some little moisture leaking from her eyes, but a full gush.

"Hey, hey," Zac said and without asking, without waiting, he simply pulled her into his arms.

She started to pull away, but he held tight. Not in an uncomfortable way, but rather he held on in the way that only a good friend would know how to do.

She leaned on his shoulder and continued crying as he patted her back and murmured a string of there-theres, I'm-heres and it's-all-going-to-be-okays.

"But it's not," she finally managed to reply, her head still buried in his now soggy shoulder.

"Can you explain?"

She nodded and lifted her chin from his shoulder. She felt slightly deflated after her hysterics. Deflated and embarrassed. "I'm so sorry. That's so not like me."

"Eli, a few tears can't scare me off. And I know it's not like you, so I know something's happened. I meant what I said, if you can't tell me, I'll call Tucker, or your mom, even if she's in Florida, she's just a phone call away. Hell, even my mom. You have to talk to someone. I hate seeing you like this."

ZAC WANTED TO PUNCH someone. He just needed Eli to tell him who.

He liked to think of himself as a peaceful, easygoing guy, but right now, he had to crush whoever had upset her. He'd never felt such an overwhelming need to protect someone since the day the social worker came for Cessy.

He shut out the memory and concentrated on the here and now—on Eli's needs.

"It was just a very bad day," she said, softly.

"Is something wrong with the baby?"

"No. No, nothing like that. I mean, other than the fact I can't button my pants anymore. Since last week."

"And that's set you off? It's okay. You'll get back into them after the baby."

"No, no, I know I'll get back into them. And I'm not so vain that it freaked me out, but it did make me realize I couldn't put off telling people at school any longer. I mean, once you're wearing maternity clothes, the news is sort of out there."

"And it didn't go well?"

"The teachers, my colleagues, were supportive. Well, I really just told the ones I'm close with, and figure that the news would make it to the rest of them in record time. The principal was supportive as well. Of course, he asked if I'd be needing time off for the wedding."

"Subtle as a brick."

"No, it wasn't mean. He's met Arthur and assumed that we'd—" She cut herself off. "Anyway, I told him no, there was no wedding in the works. That Arthur was out of the picture. The principal's a nice guy, but he's a guy, and he got this look on his face that said he was afraid I'd start crying, but I didn't. He seemed relieved and told me congratulations and to let him know if I needed anything. I spent the day telling more people."

"And that's why you're crying? Someone else said something?" Again, the need to find whoever had made Eli cry was as overwhelming as it was a surprise. Chest thumping he-man was not Zac's normal M.O. but it was out in full force.

"No. All the teachers were great. And Doris, the secretary, jumped up and hugged me and swore she was going to get her knitting supplies out the minute she got home. Between her and my mom, this baby will have booties well into his or her forties. No, that all went well. It was later, when I told my students." She gave a little post-cry hiccup.

"They didn't take it well."

"Most of them did. It's just, Ariel didn't. I know that teachers aren't supposed to have favorites, and yet we're human and we do. I try to make sure I don't show her favoritism, but she reminds me so much of Tucker. You wouldn't think she would. I don't know if I ever mentioned that Tucker's real name is Angelina, but no one ever calls her that. It's too girly, she'd tell you off if you tried. And Ariel has always struck me as the personification of all things girly. So, on the surface, they're nothing alike, but inside, where it counts, they're very much the same."

"And you care."

"Probably more than I should. Tucker's dad was supportive after he adjusted, but she didn't have a mom to go to, and Ariel...well, I get the feeling her aunt is more about materially looking after her than emotionally. Her aunt's sort of young, she's gone a lot and I don't think she knows what to do for Ariel. Tucker and Ariel...they both needed that maternal gap filled. And I tried."

"And when you told her, there was no support from her? She hurt you."

Eli shook her head. "I shouldn't let it get to me. I mean, I understand her reaction. She's a scared, angry teen, and I was a place for her to vent."

"After all you've done for her—"

"I did my job." Even though Eli'd stopped crying and was barely hiccuping any longer, he still pulled her back into his arms. He thought she'd protest, but she simply returned his embrace.

"Eli, what you do for Ariel—for all the girls—is so much more than your job."

She mumbled something against his chest, then simply went still, allowing him to comfort her. That was what all he wanted to do, and more.

She was obviously done talking. He could feel her relax in his arms, and for the longest time he just held her as he desperately tried to think of something, anything, to cheer her up.

"Hey, wanna go shopping this weekend?" He could have shot himself for breaking the comfortable silence because Eli's head popped up off his shoulder.

"Is this a pity shop? See the pregnant woman cry and toss her a shopping bone?"

"No, this was a totally selfish request. I desperately need help buying Christmas presents for the ladies in the family. Dad and the boys are easy. I just buy them a subscription to *Sports Illustrated,* or something, and they're happy. But you can't just buy women magazine subscriptions. They get testy."

Sitting there wearing an old college sweatshirt, her face streaked from her tears, she smiled and looked utterly beautiful to him. "How can I say no? I mean, saving your mom and sisters from a magazine subscription is a worthy cause."

"Then it's a date."

"Zac, we've had this discussion." She scooted toward the end of the couch, putting as much distance as possible between them. "I just want to be clear."

"Eli, answer me this—do you like spending time with me?" He wasn't sure she was going to answer, but slowly she nodded her head. "And I like spending time with you. So, what's the difference if we call it two friends going shopping together, or dating?"

"A world of difference, and you know it. Maybe we shouldn't go."

"Or maybe we should—" Zac was done. He'd been playing the nice guy since September. He'd been her buddy, her pal, and while he loved that, he wanted them to be a proper couple. So in a decisive, non-buddy, non-pal way he moved closer to her and kissed her. He didn't hold her, although he wanted to. He wouldn't force the kiss, but she didn't back up. If anything she deepened it. She made a small sound of pleasure in the back of her throat that was almost his undoing.

After months, Zac Keller was kissing Eli Cartwright the way he'd longed to since the day they'd met.

He could have gone on doing so for much longer, but slowly, he withdrew. "I think we could safely go shopping and call it a date."

"Zac, you're younger than me and I'm pregnant with another man's baby."

"I think there's a chance you're saying those things to remind yourself, more than remind me, why you're scared. I'm not scared by our age difference. I mean, you wouldn't think anything of it if I were the older one, would you?" She didn't answer. She didn't have to.

"So, that's a double standard, isn't it?" He added, "As for the baby, well, I'll admit, the timing's odd and we're not talking about forever, only a date, but Eli, the idea of a baby that's not mine isn't a deterrent, either. You know that my siblings and I are adopted, just looking at us, it's obvious. I learned a long time ago that being a family has everything to do with love."

At the word she frowned and sniffled some more.

"But we're not talking about love," he hastily assured her. "We're talking about a Christmas shopping date. I'll come pick you up, we'll head to Erie and the Millcreek Mall, and since it's a date, you'll let me take you to dinner afterward. I'll open doors for you, and hold your chair."

"What if we're sitting at a booth?" she asked softly.

Zac hadn't realized how tense he was, but as she teased him, he felt his neck and shoulder muscles release. She was going to say yes. "I'll take you someplace that has tables."

"This is probably not a good idea. We haven't even talked about the fact I'm on the rebound."

There were many things in life that Zac didn't know, and he was the first to admit them. But this one he knew with utter certainty—Eli wasn't on the rebound with Arthur. Whatever they had was over. "No, I think there's a month or so that's the rebound zone. And we were friends hanging out then. You're past that, so we can date without worrying."

She patted her small baby bump. "Not worrying?"

He leaned forward and gave her a small tender kiss on the cheek. "I'm not worried in the least."

"Zac, you're crazy."

About you was the response he'd have liked to give, but he'd taken this as far as he dared tonight. They were going on a date. That was enough progress for an evening. "Hey, have you met my family? I'm the sane one."

She gave him a more convincing smile. "Yes, I have met them and they're quite sane."

"Oh, come on, you're just being nice. They're nuts."

"You're nuts about them."

"Guilty." And because she seemed to be feeling better and he was feeling daring, he went ahead and added, "And I'm nuts about you."

She gave him a tsk-tsk. "What am I going to do about you?"

"Right now, you're going to follow me into the kitchen, where I'm going to check your refrigerator and find something to feed you. Then, I'm challenging you to a brisk game of Scrabble. I saw the box in the closet."

"Feed me first?"

"Hey, when I totally trounce you, I don't want you crying because you were at a disadvantage because you were hungry."

"As if you'll beat me. My mom and Tucker refuse to play with me because I win a lot. And by a lot I mean, most of the time."

"How about your dad?" he asked, as he walked toward the kitchen with her trailing after him.

"Who do you think taught me how to play? Our games were cutthroat."

"Well, we'll have to see how we match up." He was pretty sure they'd be a good match, win, lose or draw.

THE NEXT DAY, ZAC CHECKED Ariel's schedule and was waiting in the employee's room when she clocked in. "How's it going, Ariel?"

Ariel looked nervous. "Fine, Mr. Keller."

She hurried to her locker and stowed her coat and

purse, and pulled out her cashier's smock. Carefully buttoning it over her swollen stomach, she turned and saw him waiting. "Really, everything's fine. I love working here."

But it wasn't fine. He could tell. "And you? Are you okay?"

"Sure. How about you? I hear congratulations are in order." There was a hardness in her tone.

He didn't confirm or deny he was Eli's baby's father. He just said quietly, "Whatever there is between Ms. Cartwright and me is our business, Ariel."

"Sure, yours and the baby's. That's what Ms. Cartwright always says, that it takes two people to make a baby and both are responsible for it." She snorted. "Sometimes the guys don't get her classroom notes on the subject though."

"There are similarities between your situation and Ms. Cartwright's, but there's one major difference. She's an adult. A self-supporting adult who knows what she wants." He paused and asked gently, "Why does this bother you so much?"

"Why?" Ariel kicked her locker door shut. "'Cause there she is, Ms. Cartwright, a teacher who knows about this stuff. And still, she makes a mistake—"

"Did she say the baby was a mistake?" he asked pointedly.

Ariel shook her head.

"Well, why would you assume it is?"

"I—"

"Listen, I'm not sure why you're so mad at her. And I don't want to get in the middle of it. I will say, however, that you hurt her. And though I know Ms. Cartwright doesn't play favorites, you're special to her. I don't know how you couldn't know that."

He walked out of the room without looking back.

He knew that Eli wouldn't appreciate his interfering, but he couldn't stand to see her cry as she had last night. And if he were honest, he had to admit, it wasn't only Eli, it was Ariel. He'd grown close to the girl, and knew that she needed Eli.

Maybe his words would make a difference.

THAT FRIDAY, ELI BUSTLED around the classroom, setting up for the day's panel discussion. Three of her former teen-parenting students were coming in to talk to the current students and serve as role models. Mentors.

Tucker had agreed to participate, although it took a lot of arm-twisting and laying on the guilt.

She was the first one to show up. "I'm here. I even put on semi-grown-up clothes, and you know how I hate that."

Rather than her normal paint-splattered jeans and T-shirt, she had on a pair of dark brown slacks and a navy sweater. She'd taken her hair out of its quintessential ponytail and soft curls framed her face.

Sometimes Eli forgot how beautiful Tucker was.

"Tucker, it's time like these that I know you care."

Tucker missed the teasing in Eli's voice and simply nodded. "And I even put on makeup. Not a lot, but some. I hate that, too."

Eli laughed. "You're a good friend."

Tucker laughed as well. "Yes, I am. Still, you're going to have to make it up to me. Maybe we should go out to dinner and a show on Saturday."

Eli was about to say yes, when she remembered

she'd agreed to go out with Zac. "Maybe Sunday?" she countered.

Tucker plopped into one of the chairs Eli had set up at the front of the room. "Come here and sit. What's up on Saturday? You have a look, Eli."

Eli ignored Tucker's invitation to sit and went to her desk instead. She knew why she was reluctant to tell Tucker. If she said the words, it would make the date real. Instead, she simply replied, "Nothing's up. I just have plans."

"What kind of plans? Plans that center around a certain grocery store owner?"

Eli busied herself with a stack of papers, trying to ignore Tucker's question.

Tucker, however, was a force of nature—impossible to ignore. She sprang out of the chair and hurried next to Eli at the desk, putting herself directly in Eli's line of sight. "A date? You finally broke down and are going on a date with him?"

"It's Christmas shopping." She took the pile of papers and moved it to her file cabinet. "And maybe dinner."

Tucker followed her. "That sounds like a date."

"Don't get too excited." She dumped the papers into an empty file at the front of the drawer because she had no idea what they were and where they actually belonged, and this way, later, she could find them easily.

She practically tripped over Tucker, who was directly behind her. "Seriously, Tuck, it's nothing major."

"I like him a lot more than I liked Arthur. Of course, you know that's not saying much, so let's say that I really like Zac, and I like who you are when you're with him."

Eli wanted to ask what Tucker meant by that last line, but didn't because she also wasn't sure she wanted to hear what Tucker had to say. "Arthur and I were compatible, though. Zac and I? There are a lot of strikes against us."

"Like what?" Tucker took her by the hand, led her to the chairs, sat in one and gently pulled Eli into the other. "Tell me."

It took Eli a moment to remember her own arguments. "His age…my age."

"Huh?"

"He's younger. And I'm pregnant…let's not forget that. Pregnant with another man's child. Those are two big hurdles."

Tucker shrugged. "I still think he's better than Arthur. And if Arthur's an example of compatible, then maybe it's time to think about something different."

They didn't get any further with the discussion since Greg and Deborah, her former students, came in. Hugs were exchanged and they all caught up for a few moments.

Eli didn't miss the fact that Tucker was giving her a look. And she knew what it was saying. Coward. Tucker thought Eli was simply avoiding getting hurt with all her excuses about Zac.

And maybe she was, but that wasn't necessarily cowardly, it was being careful.

The students arrived on the heels of her guests, and after the obligatory minutes of shuffling and settling in, Eli started.

"As I told you yesterday, we're going to hear from guest speakers today. They'll each take turns telling you a bit about their experience as teen parents, and what they're doing now. When they're done, they'll take questions from you. We'll start with Angelina Tucker." Tucker grimaced as Eli used her first name. "She's the reason this program exists today. It was almost sixteen years ago that Tucker came to me for help when she found out that she was pregnant. There were no programs in the district to assist girls in her situation and—"

Tucker interrupted Eli's introduction. "And you all know Ms. Cartwright. When she found out there was nothing out there to help me, she just helped me herself."

The girls all laughed.

Eli continued. "Today, Ms. Tucker's a successful graphic artist. She specializes in motorcycles, and there are people all over the country who want a bike that Tucker's worked on. Tucker, why don't you take it from here?"

"Hi, everyone. Let's just forget that Ms. Cartwright mentioned my first name. I'm Tucker. Not Ms. Tucker, Miss Tucker, or Mrs. Tucker. Just Tucker. And before someone raises their hand to tell me you have to call me something formal, I'll save you the effort, I'm not a teacher, so you don't."

The girls all laughed, and Eli smiled. She'd had Tucker come in for years, and it always went this way. Tucker had an instant connection with the girls that stemmed from the fact she was genuine. There was no artifice in her, and the girls responded to that.

"And it doesn't seem like that long ago I was a student here. A pregnant student. My boyfriend wanted nothing to do with a baby, and he'd made that perfectly clear. My mother was dead, I didn't have any aunts or sister, so I came to Ms. Cartwright. She came with me when I told me father. I figured he'd do me in, but my dad, well, he was great. He's been my son's father figure. But he didn't know much about pregnancy or babies. It was Ms. Cartwright who got me prepared, who came with me to childbirth classes...."

Eli could feel her cheeks warming as Tucker continued on her Eli-fest. She didn't know how to stop it. Tucker made it all sound so much more than it was. She hadn't done anything special. She'd just helped a student. That was her job.

She glanced at Ariel in the back row. She'd purposely avoided Eli ever since Eli had announced her pregnancy. She didn't know what to do about Ariel. Maybe there was nothing she could do. Maybe she shouldn't even try.

She was Ariel's teacher. She'd done her job—was doing her job. That she'd somehow failed to live up to Ariel's expectations wasn't her fault.

Tucker finished and Eli got up and introduced Greg Warton, a local disc jockey who'd been her first teen dad through the program. "Okay, I know you all know this, but teen parents aren't just teen moms. My girlfriend and I..."

There were currently no boys in the program, despite the fact Eli actively recruited. Maybe if she found a male teacher...

She introduced their third panelist, Julie, and when she finished, Eli said, "I'm sure you all have questions. Please raise your hands and remember to be polite."

Forty-five minutes later, the class ended. She ushered the kids out and thanked all her panelists.

Tucker was the last to leave. "You okay?"

"Sure."

"So, you'll call after your date with Zac and we'll go out on Sunday?"

"I wish you wouldn't call it that." Date. She knew she'd agreed, but the word weighed heavily on her.

"Is that what he's calling it?" Tucker persisted.

She remembered his kiss and nodded.

"Then maybe you should get used to calling it that, too." Tucker paused and said, "Date. Date. Date. Come on, Eli. You can do it."

"Date." She tried to sound put out, but with Tucker standing there grinning at her, it was impossible. She suspected she even had a hint of a smile on her face. "Date. I've said it. Are you happy?"

"Getting happier," Tucker admitted. "So, what are you going to wear?"

"Oh, man, you know things are bad when Angelina Tucker starts asking me about my wardrobe. To answer your question, I'm going to wear whatever fits."

"That bad?"

Eli lifted her top and revealed the rubber band that connected her pants button to the button hole. It was a stopgap measure at best. "I think it's time to admit that I need maternity clothes."

"Well, we could go shopping." Tucker's offer was made with obvious reluctance. "I remember I had this great teacher who took me out and helped me buy a few necessities when I no longer fit in my clothes."

"And I remember I had this student who decided maternity clothes were horrible and spent the last five months of her pregnancy wearing sweatpants and her father's flannel shirts and T-shirts."

"I bet I could borrow some of his stuff for you, too.

Although, they might not be the most professional out-fits for a teacher."

"Thanks. And thank your dad, even though he didn't make the offer. But I'll probably have to break down and buy some maternity clothes soon."

"Okay, so call me and we'll skip the movie and just do the maternity store and lunch."

"Shopping for clothes is your idea of torture."

"Yeah, but I like you enough to suffer for our friend-ship."

"It's a date."

"See, you can use the word without grimacing." Tucker started for the door. "Call me after that other big date."

"I'll call you, all right...." Eli was talking to the door.

What was she doing? Single, pregnant and dating a younger man?

CHAPTER SEVEN

"Maternity clothes. Some women love them. Some hate them. But as your waistline expands, they become a necessity. Today's trends are much more fashion friendly."
—*Pregnancy, Childbirth and Parenting for Teens,*
by Mary Jeanne Lorei

THE NEXT DAY, ZAC found a parking space…way at the back end of the lot. He was glad he'd dropped Eli off at the door to the mall. She'd protested that she was perfectly capable of walking, but he'd simply pulled over next to the entrance and waited until she got out. She'd grumbled as she did.

He smiled as he waded through the three or so inches of snow that had fallen since the plows had been through.

It might not be officially winter until the end of December, but in Western Pennsylvania, winter could arrive anytime after Halloween—sometimes before. It was still early enough in December that this current batch of snow would probably melt, but it would be sticking around soon enough.

Thinking about snow was easier than worrying about what was his first official date with Eli. It wasn't what he'd have chosen, but Eli was still tepid, to say the least, about dating him. Although she didn't seem all that tepid about him personally. As a matter of fact, their kiss was pretty hot.

That thought warmed him as he hurried toward the mall.

Eli was stubbornly standing outside the Sears door waiting for him. "Why didn't you go inside where it's warm?"

"You know, Zac, scolding a woman isn't the best way to start a date."

Before he could respond, she continued, "And I was outside because I like the snow. I like watching the hustle and bustle here, especially this time of year." She dug in her pocket and stuffed a bill into the Salvation Army kettle as they walked by it. "I just love the season."

That didn't surprise him in the least. "So, where do we start?" he asked as they stood in the concourse. Zac knew it fed into stereotypes, but he couldn't help it. He hated shopping.

"You need to get things for your sisters and mom?"

He nodded.

"Do you have a guideline money-wise?"

He gave her his figure.

She smiled. "Oh, this is almost too easy. Let's go."

Eli was an organized, no-nonsense shopper. That didn't surprise him. They had a very pretty locket for his mom within the first half hour and then headed toward one of the trendy teen stores to find something for Cessy.

"So, how did your panel go yesterday?" he asked as they strolled down the concourse.

"Fine. I started the role-model panel my second

year with the program. We didn't have any real graduates, so I found former teen parents throughout the
community. They were wonderful and the kids enjoyed them, but it's so much more rewarding to see the
kids you worked so hard with come back as success
stories. Tucker came in. She's always a great role model
for the kids. She has an ability to really reach them."

He heard the word she wasn't saying, so he sup-
plied it. "But?"

She stopped in front of a candy cane pole at the
Santa Claus station. Her frown contrasted with the
smiles on everyone else's faces. "But what?"

"There was a 'but' in there," he insisted. "Remember what Cessy pointed out. I can hear you even when
you're not talking." He looked up and saw a sprig of
mistletoe hanging off the pole. He didn't mention how
much he'd like to indulge in the age-old custom. No, he
simply waited for her to tell him just what the *but* was.

Eli's silence was broken when she sighed. "*But* even
Tucker couldn't reach Ariel…at least not on my behalf."

"She's still upset?"

Eli shrugged and looked disheartened. "I can only
assume, since she's not talking to me. Oh, she'll answer
if called on in class, but otherwise, nothing."

Eli started walking down the concourse again. Santa
had a line of kids waiting to see him, and there was a
holiday train running around in circles behind him. Its
merry whistle seemed to punctuate Eli's words.

Wanting to comfort her, and knowing it was risky,
Zac took her hand in his. "Want me to talk to her?"
He hadn't really talked to her before, he'd simply men-
tioned that Eli was upset. This time he'd be more firm.

Eli didn't withdraw her hand from his. As a matter of fact, she gave his hand a firm squeeze. "No. But thanks. Like I said, she needs a target and I'm convenient."

"How is everyone else reacting?"

"Fine. Better than fine. The other teachers are great, and Lainey came up to me the other day and said that she always liked my class, but now she really knows I get it because Arthur dumped me like her boyfriend dumped her." She paused. "You know, I've always done everything I can to reach the girls. I don't know why I never gave this approach a try before now."

She was trying to make a joke, but it fell flat.

"Eli, it'll all be okay." He paused and asked, "So have you heard from Arthur lately?"

"Not since that last time. I want him to give me the parental termination papers and just step away. I don't like ambiguity."

"It will work out." It made him feel like a schmuck, but truth be told he was relieved she hadn't heard from Arthur. If he really thought Arthur was the man to make Eli happy, he'd have tracked the guy down himself. But he didn't think Arthur was the man for Eli. Zac very much believed he was. "Really, it will all end up the way it was meant to be."

"Most days I believe that. Sometimes, though, it's harder." She hesitated and then added in a blatant attempt to change the conversation, "But Zac Keller, I didn't think you were the kind of guy who believed in destiny."

"We all grew up listening to Mom talk about how we were all meant to be a family. That it was destiny. So I've always believed in it." He squeezed her hand. "And sometimes I believe in it a lot."

She looked away, and he knew he'd come on too strong, too fast.

When she continued looking at the other side of the mall, he knew it wasn't just that he'd made her uncomfortable. Zac turned and saw she was checking out a maternity store. "Want to go in?"

"No, that's fine. Tucker offered to come with me to shop for clothes."

"I take it from your expression that she doesn't enjoy shopping."

"You hardly know her, and yet you know her so well. I'll confess, I'm no window-shopper. I tend to come into a store or mall, get what I need, then get out. But Tuck's barely stepped foot in any store other than a grocery store, and most of the time, her dad does their grocery shopping. No, her offer was a firm sign of how deep her friendship goes. Besides, I can't imagine going into a maternity store is any more your cup of tea than hers."

"Well, the good news is, Tucker will owe me one. And I'm guessing she's a very good person to have in your corner. Come on. If you can help me shop for my mom and sisters, the least I can do is go with you to look around a maternity store since we're here."

"I do need some pants. Desperately."

"Then, let's go." Zac liked to think of himself as a brave man, but walking into the maternity store with Eli was one of the bravest things he'd done in a while.

One of the saleswomen approached them before they'd taken more than two steps inside. Soon thereafter she led Eli off. There was a seating area in the back, so Zac sat, content to wait. He noticed a book on a nearby table. *What Every Father Should Know.* He picked it up and thumbed through it. Chapters titled "What To Do When She's Breast-feeding" and "Emotional Roller Coasters." *"Remember, that while your role might not be as obvious as the mother's, babies need a father's care. Boy or girl, they need a male role model...."*

Eli's baby would need a male role model. Would Zac be around long enough to be it?

He glanced at Eli as Eli had worn a bulky sweater under her coat, but when she moved the right way, her stomach's small bulge was evident. He noticed her hand rested lightly on it, as if the baby inside were her touchstone, something she needed to reassure herself was still there.

It was too soon to talk about being there for this baby, in his heart he already was. He'd have no trouble being a father. He couldn't help but think of his parents and siblings. No, he didn't need to be related to this baby genetically in order to parent it. He wasn't sure Eli got that yet.

"Being Daddy is More Than Just Tossing Around a Football," a chapter in the book proclaimed.

He thought of his father. Abe Keller hadn't been much on tossing footballs, but he'd been there in so many ways. School plays, PTA meetings. His dad had even been one of the chaperones on an overnight trip to Cleveland when Zac was in eighth grade. He hadn't thought anything of it at the time, but later he realized that being trapped in a hotel room with four boys might not have been his father's idea of a good time.

No, there might not be any shared DNA between them, but Abe Keller was a great father and a real role model for what a dad should be.

Zac wanted nothing less for Eli's baby. And he didn't think Arthur came close to stacking up. The man was...

He forced himself not to think about Arthur.

That's not what Eli needed. She needed a friend. She needed support.

And he hoped she was beginning to need him.

She appeared with a stack of clothing in her arms. "I'm going to try a few things on, if you're sure you don't mind."

He held the book up. "I'm reading. Take your time."

He watched her walk toward the changing room. She had a bit of a waddle because of the large stack of clothing. Soon she'd be waddling because of the ever expanding girth of her stomach. She'd be cute.

He turned back to the book and flipped to another chapter. "Adoptive Fathers."

"Being a father is more than biology. Parents aren't tied to their children by blood, but rather by love. Remember that. Your baby needs you. Your wife needs you...."

The chapter echoed so many things his parents had taught him.

"Good book?"

Zac looked up and saw Eli standing in front of him, two big bags in hand.

"Wow, that was fast." He set down the book, got up and took the bags before she could protest. "You obviously got some shopping done."

"Yes." She turned shy. "And I know this wasn't exactly the best first date ever, I mean, it's different all right. Sitting around a maternity store while your date shops."

"Eli, you don't get it yet, do you?" he asked as they left the maternity store.

She stopped to the side of the entryway and studied him. "Get what, Zac?"

He set down the bags containing her maternity clothes and his Christmas presents. "I don't care what we do, I just like being with you. Whether we're talking about the CATA Project, watching a basketball game or shopping—I like it because you're there, too."

"You're right, I don't get it. I'm pregnant. I'm getting fatter by the minute and…" She looked truly confused. "I just don't get it. I'm nothing special."

"Now, there's a subject for a great debate because I disagree."

He'd given Eli's hang-ups about dating him some serious thought. It was time to lay it all on the line.

He didn't need any special insight to see that she was going to be a tough sell.

"Let me ask you something."

"Okay."

"Don't look so worried. It's not about you and me, it's about Tucker. I take it she dates on occasion?"

Eli appeared confused. "Very rarely, but yes, she dates."

"And she has a kid?" he asked.

Eli nodded.

"And it doesn't bother you that she dates?"

He saw the lightbulb moment, when she understood where his questions were going. "Zac—"

"Come on, Eli, just so we're clear. You don't have any fundamental problem with the idea of single moms dating, right?"

"You're right, I don't have problems with single

moms dating. But I'm not quite a mom yet, I'm a mom-to-be. And may I point out, I agreed to a date."

"You reluctantly agreed to a date. If I were a less confident man, I'd have been wounded by the extreme coercion I've had to exert to get you to agree. Now, what you're saying is that if I'd been willing to wait until after you had the baby, you'd have been more comfortable with the idea of dating me?"

"When you put it that way, my reluctance sounds stupid. It's not the pregnancy alone. It's the fact you're younger." She stared at him stubbornly.

He wasn't buying it. "I'm not younger by that much."

She snorted. "I could have practically babysat you."

"No, you couldn't have. I'm pretty sure I read an article about the fact Pennsylvania doesn't have a law on the books about what is old enough to babysit, but it said eleven was considered old enough by the courts. And I know my mom never let us babysit until we were twelve. So, no, you couldn't have babysat me."

"Almost," she insisted.

"It's sort of a double standard, isn't it? I mean, if a girl was dating a guy who was older, you wouldn't think anything about it."

"I don't know—"

"And given that women statistically live longer than men, it really makes more sense for women to date younger guys."

She smiled.

It was the smallest upturn of her lips, but it was indeed the beginning of a smile.

"Zac—"

"Lastly, let me simply point out that when you're

past your twenties, a few years doesn't really represent any huge life-experience gap. For instance, what do you listen to in the car?"

There was no hinting now, Eli wore a full-out smile. He could sense she was weakening.

"Country," she admitted.

"There you go. I love country. Rascal Flatts, Taylor Swift, Carrie Underwood. I'll confess, I watch *American Idol* and liked her even then."

"Me, too. I love it."

"Well, there you go. We watch the same shows, and can talk the same music language. So, what it comes down to is—do you like me? I feel like I'm back in school, but still I'll ask, if you weren't pregnant, and if my age wasn't a factor, would you like me enough to date me?"

"And if I hadn't just gotten out of a long-term relationship."

He'd won. He knew it. He wasn't going to gloat, but if that was the last of her arguments, then Zac knew he'd won. "No, that one doesn't count. Whatever we have growing between us is absolutely not a rebound relationship. We waited quite a while before today's first date, so no. You don't get to use that argument, either." He grinned to let her know he was teasing.

"It seems I'm not winning any argument today." Eli went from smiling to out and out laughing.

"So, we're an item? Dating?"

She shook her head. "You're crazy and beyond persistent."

"Your answer?"

"Fine, so we're dating."

"That wasn't so hard, was it?" It was a huge hurdle. Zac felt like celebrating.

The holiday crowd was bustling around them, and he purposefully turned the conversation to something lighter. "So, how long are you off for the holidays?"

SOMEWHERE DURING HIS reflections on dating, Eli had admitted to herself her real reason for not wanting to date Zac—she was afraid. Arthur had been comfortable. Easy, even. They both maintained their own homes, their own spaces. They didn't mingle at each other's jobs. They were together regularly, but neither had ever done much calling on days they didn't see each other.

Now, here was Zac, and nothing about him was easy. He'd found a way into her life and sort of filled in all the cracks and rounded off the edges. He called every day until one day she realized she was waiting for his call. Looking forward to it, even. And she saw him all the time. There was no regularity about it. He was simply with her whenever possible.

She'd met his family and had a standing invitation to weekend dinners. They'd even included Tucker. It took two years before she'd met Arthur's sister, and even after that, when Ashley came to town Arthur was apt to see her on his own.

"There's a Christmas party coming up for the Keller's Markets' employees. Want to go?"

"You're sure you want to introduce me to the people you work with? I mean, I'm more and more pregnant with each passing day and they're bound to specu-late.…"

"I don't care what people think. I've liked you for a very long time. There was an instant attraction when I met you, but as I got to know you it went beyond that. The only thing that kept me from actively pursuing you was that you were in a relationship and seemed happy. And I grew to care about you too much to do anything that would dim that happiness." He paused and added, "And I don't poach. I've never poached. You were the one case where I was tempted. But now you're not in a relationship, and I'm not in a relationship. So, we'll go out."

"And if people talk?" she asked.

"People always talk, Eli. When Mom and Dad adopted us, they talked."

His response confused her. "About?"

"About the fact they had kids of mixed races. Or when they adopted someone like me, who was older, people worried that I'd be a bad seed. When Mom and Dad adopted more than three kids, they talked about the fact they were crazy…they were getting older and would never be able to handle a big family. People talked then, Eli. Odds are they'll talk now. That kind of talk seems to be a part of the human condition. But I don't care. Do you?"

She knew that if she and Zac got any more deeply involved there were bound to be hurdles.

As much as she knew that maybe she should care, the truth was, she didn't care at all.

She took his hand in hers. It felt solid. It felt right. "No, I don't care what anyone says."

Eli had spent months feeling a bit crazed by all the unexpected changes in her life. She was someone who liked to have things planned out. And yet, here she was inviting another change...and rather than finding that daunting, she couldn't seem to stop smiling.

For the first time in months, she felt like she was getting something right.

CHAPTER EIGHT

"A new baby is a gift. Sometimes, when circumstances aren't ideal, it's hard to remember that, but in every baby there's a sense of potential, a dream for the future...and that is a gift, regardless of the circumstances."

—*Pregnancy, Childbirth and Parenting for Teens,*
by Mary Jeanne Lorei

"JINGLE BELLS, JINGLE BELLS..." Eli sang giddily.

Zac laughed. "Someone's got the Christmas spirit."

"Everyone was so nice at your work party. I'd been worried."

"I told you not to be."

"You might not have noticed, but I don't *always* listen," she said cheekily. She hung up their coats and walked toward the kitchen, but stopped in the doorway and turned to face him.

Zac was forced to stop, too. "Problem?"

Eli pointed at the ceiling. "The only problem is a boyfriend who neglects to follow tradition."

Zac looked up and a slow grin spread across his wind-chapped cheeks. "Why, Ms. Cartwright, what could that greenery be?"

"I suspect it's mistletoe, Mr. Keller. What do you suppose we should do about it?"

Zac didn't need a second invitation. He pulled her into his arms and kissed her which was just what she wanted.

Eli had discovered that kissing Zac was addictive.

It hadn't gone any further than kissing, and while part of her wanted it to, the other part—the part that needed to take this slow—was relieved that it hadn't. She moved her hands along the contour of Zac's back, loving the feel of him. Wanting to be closer…

The doorbell rang, interrupting both her thoughts and the kiss.

"Argh" was her not quite verbal response to the interruption.

"Argh?" Zac teased, though he sounded equally breathless. "I think I'm flattered."

"You should be." The doorbell rang again. "Who do you suppose that could be?"

"Tucker and Bart? Or maybe your parents?"

"They're on a cruise, so I doubt it." Eli hoped beyond hope that it was Tucker, who was a good enough friend not to take offense if Eli asked her to make the visit a short one.

"Merry Christmas," Eli cried as she opened the door. "Oh."

Arthur. To say he was the last person she expected to see would be a lie, but to say he was one of the last people she wanted to see was pretty much a given.

"Merry Christmas, Eli."

She stood there, not saying anything, not opening the door any farther.

Arthur.

Her silence and immobility must have gone on too long, because he finally asked, "May I come in?"

She let him into the entryway, glancing at Zac. "Sorry. This shouldn't take long."

"Don't worry. I'll go start the water for tea." He went into the kitchen.

"He's here?" Arthur asked.

She looked at her ex, who seemed none too pleased to find Zac at her house. "He's a friend. Now, what did you want, Arthur? Did you bring me the papers?"

"No. Could we go into the living room and sit down?"

"No, I don't think there's a need. Just tell me what you came here to say. I have company to get back to."

"I saw the lawyer and he's drawn up the papers to terminate my parental rights, as well as set up a trust fund for the—" he stumbled on the word "—baby."

"Great. Get back to me when they're signed." Eli felt a twinge of regret that it had come to this.

"That's just it." He stood ramrod-straight, his shoulders squared as he added, "I went down to sign them yesterday, and I couldn't do it." He looked as if he expected a fight.

Fighting wasn't what Eli had in mind, it never had been. "Are you saying you're planning to take a role in the baby's life?"

She was torn between believing that her baby had a right to know its father, and the knowledge that her life without Arthur in it was easier. What kind of mother would that make her? Putting her comfort over what was good for the baby?

"Is that what you're saying?" she repeated.

The unflappable college professor slumped a little and leaned against the wall, as if in need of support. "No. Yes. Maybe. I don't know. I just don't know, Eli.

I'm so confused. I never wanted a…baby. And yet…"
He shrugged.

She was tired of his waffling.

"I don't know how to help you with that, Arthur.
To be honest, I've been confused. Having a baby
in my forties wasn't what I expected, either. I had
a life planned. Everything laid out. This wasn't a
part of it."

"I know. I'm making a mess of all of this. I want
to be a good guy, the kind who would stand by you in
something like this, but every time I resolve to do just
that, I see a kid or a baby and they're messy, demanding and…"

"And messy and demanding has never been something you've dealt with well. That's why I was a perfect
girlfriend. I never asked for more than you could give.
Our relationship was orderly. Dinners Friday nights.
Something Saturday or Sunday afternoon. A standing date for the phil. I don't want to make it sound
like this was all your fault. Let's face it, I was content
with the status quo. It was easy for us, Arthur. But
this isn't easy."

"No. No, it's not. And I miss you, Eli."

She realized he wasn't calling her Elinore anymore.
Was he trying to please her?

"I loved knowing on Fridays we'd go out to dinner,
or planning something for the weekend. I loved knowing that I had someone to go to the philharmonic with
me. We were good together."

Eli realized that when he rattled off the things he
loved, he never mentioned loving her—and she hadn't
mentioned it, either. She didn't love him. And at this
moment she knew with utter certainty that he had never

loved her. "I can't help you decide what to do. Being part of the baby's life because you feel you have to, because you'd be able to think of yourself as a good guy, isn't enough." She heard herself start to lecture him and stopped. It wouldn't do anyone any good. "Listen, figure out what you want to do about the baby, then let me know."

She started to open the door, but Arthur put his hand on top of hers. "I truly miss you, Eli."

She wasn't sure what to say, so she simply slipped her hand out from under his.

"Please…"

"Arthur, you and I, we're over. I've told you. It's not a question you need to consider. That one's been answered. All that's left is for you to decide what you're going to do about the baby."

Arthur hit her doorjamb with his fist. "I don't know, damn it. I didn't ask for this."

"No, you didn't, neither did I. And yet, here we are."

As if that outburst had used up his energy, his shoulders slumped again. "I didn't come here to fight. I just missed you and wanted to wish you a merry Christmas."

"You, too, Arthur."

As he stepped away, he suddenly looked older than someone in his mid-fifties.

Eli watched until he got into his car before slowly closing her front door. Then she leaned into it, her face pressed to the winter-cold glass.

A sense of emptiness swept over her. She couldn't have really said why. She'd spent five years of her life with Arthur. And realized anew why it had been so easy to let him go: she had never loved him.

Zac held Eli for a while, enjoying the feeling of having his arm around her shoulder. Her arms were wrapped around her stomach, as if trying to protect the baby from a world where its own father didn't want it. Zac took his free hand and rested it on top of hers. Instantly, her being pregnant became real to him for the first time. He felt a sense of protectiveness—he'd do anything to save this child even one tear, one hurt feeling.

This wasn't his baby, but as his hand stayed on Eli's hands and stomach, that didn't matter. He loved this child sight unseen.

A baby who would need to be cherished...to be loved.

Arthur might not be sure if he could do it, but Zac knew in his heart that he already did. Completely.

And thoughts of losing the baby hurt as much as the thought of losing Eli.

The man had deserted both Eli and the baby. In Zac's book, that meant Arthur had forfeited his rights. Zac didn't see a way to make her understand that.

"Thanks for holding me," Eli said as she stirred. "You're a good man, Zac."

Her compliment embarrassed him, given that a more noble man, a better man, would be more understanding of her conflicted feelings about Arthur.

Zac thought a distraction might help. "We were going to deliver the baskets to Keller's employees tonight. Are you still feeling up to it?"

"I wouldn't miss it for the world."

"Well, bundle up and let's go."

Zac always volunteered to take holiday baskets to the employees, even when his dad still ran the markets.

Zac enjoyed trying to sneak up to the employee's home and leave the basket without getting caught.

This year, he'd borrowed one of the store's trucks and had it loaded with the baskets. For three hours he and Eli made their way through Whedon, making deliveries to Zac's staff. Eli wanted to be the one to do the running, but he worried that she'd slip and fall on the snow-covered sidewalks, so he convinced her to be the driver.

She took the role to heart and sped away from each scene like a bank robber making her getaway, laughing with delight each time.

Zac could have stayed like this forever—just driving around town with Eli and listening to the sound of her delight.

But all too soon, there was only one basket remaining. "It's Ariel's," he told Eli. It was bigger than anyone else's because so many of the employees had come to him and asked him to include something they'd bought Ariel or the baby.

"That's not a basket, that's a crate," Eli said, smiling.

"Are things any better between the two of you?"

"No, not really. But I understand her, Zac. It's not my situation that's truly upset her. Ariel feels powerless, deserted even. And she's not just mad, she's pissed. Yes, her aunt's taking care of her, but her parents and boyfriend are gone. She's pissed at me, because deep down she trusts me. She trusts that I'll still care. I'm it, and though it stings a bit, I get it."

While Zac knew she meant every word she said, he also knew she was still hurt, and he wished he could do more to spare her that.

They pulled up in front of Ariel's aunt's place. He

started to open the door, but Eli said, "Hang on a minute."

She dug through her purse that sat on the floor of the truck, and pulled out a beautifully wrapped gift. "Would you include this, please?"

He didn't ask what was inside, but simply took the small box and said, "Sure."

He went to the back of the truck, took out Ariel's "basket" and tucked Eli's gift in, then dashed to the porch, rang the bell and sprinted away. As soon as he was next to Eli, she gunned the engine and took off with all the speed of their other getaways, but this time there was no laughter.

He saw her glance in the rearview mirror, and turned to see for himself that Ariel was at the front door.

"Merry Christmas," Eli whispered.

Zac kept glancing at her as she drove them along Whedon's main street and he saw in Eli what he'd always seen...a beautiful heart. He knew she'd try to downplay it, but Eli Cartwright gave herself unstintingly to her students. She was generous with her ex. And Zac knew if she ever loved him, he'd be the luckiest man in the world.

And he also had no doubt there was no *if* left for him. He loved her.

Zac Keller loved Elinore Cartwright. And nothing would ever change that.

DEBORAH KELLER HAD A penchant for gathering people to her—especially, it appeared, during the holidays. Eli was just like the rest, happy to oblige her.

It was Christmas evening, and the Keller's family

room was filled with family and friends…and people they barely knew.

Ariel and her aunt were sitting as close to the fringe as the ample room would allow. Deirdre Mayor wasn't what Eli had imagined. She didn't look as if she could be more than a few years older than Ariel, her niece.

Deirdre hadn't said much to anyone, and when Eli tried to engage her, asking about her job as a flight attendant, Deirdre had seemed so uncomfortable that Eli had finally abandoned the effort.

Eli had talked to her mom and dad that morning. Her mother spent most of the conversation apologizing for not being there for Christmas. "If we'd known you were pregnant we'd never have booked the cruise…." she said over and over.

Eli reassured them both that she'd be spending the day with the Kellers, and they'd all celebrate together next year with the baby, which was always a topic that was sure to brighten her mother's mood.

"Any idea what this is all about?" she whispered to Zac, who shook his head. After they'd had their dinner and cleaned up, they'd all been summoned to the family room.

Mrs. Keller stood up. "First, I want to say I'm so glad to have all my children with me, and our new friends as well. I'm hoping those new friends will indulge me as I read a letter I received several days ago."

From her pocket Mrs. Keller produced a couple sheets of paper. "'Dear Mrs. Keller,'" she read, "'Enclosed please find a copy of an essay Cecily wrote for my English class. The topic was, what does family mean to you.'

"'My students frequently inspire me, but I don't

think I've ever been brought to tears by an essay before. I believe this is something you and your entire
family will treasure. Sincerely, Helen Asti.'"

Mrs. Keller shuffled her papers and took a deep
breath, as if she were going to start reading some more,
but Cessy interrupted. "Mom, please don't." Cessy
hid her face in the arm of the couch. "I'm so embarrassed," she moaned with the drama that only a teen
could muster.

"Cecily Keller, this is beautiful, and not only am I
going to read it, I'm thinking about having it framed."

Cessy groaned even louder, and her sister Layla patted her shoulder.

"There's no stopping Mom when she gets like this,"
Dom said from his seat across the room.

"You're right, Dom, there's not." Mrs. Keller cleared
her throat. "'My family, by Cecily Keller.'

"'When I was in fourth grade, our class made cards
for our families for Thanksgiving. We traced our hands
and turned them into construction paper turkeys. After
school, I ran out and gave mine to my mom when Les-
lie, a girl in my class, came up and said, "You're supposed to give it to your mom." I was confused and told
her this was my mom, and she said it couldn't be 'cause
we didn't match. Until that moment, I don't think I ever
thought that way about my family.'

"'Oh, I knew my brother Zac always called me
cocoa because my skin is the color of chocolate, and
there was no way to miss that Mom is as pale as a white
person can get. But I never saw those differences.'

"'After that, I did. I noticed the looks my family
got when we went out together. None of us are alike.
We have brown hair, black, reddish-brown and blond.

Some of us are very tall, a few are vertically challenged.'

"'When I was ten, we all went to Disney World and Mom made us wear matching T-shirts that proudly proclaimed The Kellers. We got looks there, too.'

"'The fact that we all were so very different made us stand out, and any school kid will tell you that standing out can be a problem. So I hoped no one would notice.'

"'The Kellers took me home weeks after I was born. I have biological parents, but I never knew them. Then when I was five, my biological father took me back. I still remember that day. My whole family stood on the porch as the social worker led me away to her car. I didn't understand what was going on. My mom had told me that I was going to live with my real dad, but I felt that my *real* father was the man on the porch physically holding my brother Zac, who was struggling to get to me. I was only five and I knew who my family was. The stranger the state decided should have custody was nothing to me. The six months he kept me were bad. I don't talk about them. But they taught me something.'

"'Before, I wanted to hide how different my family was, but then I figured out that biology might determine your skin and hair color, it might determine if you're tall or short, but it's your family that makes up your heart. It's your family that makes you whole, the person you really are.'

"'I took my family to school later that year for show-and-tell. Though in fourth grade we'd really outgrown the tradition, Mom stood by me and my entire family showed up and let me introduce them to my class. And I told all those kids that my family didn't match on the outside, that we never would, but we matched on the inside and that's all that counts.'

"'And that's what family means to me.'"

Eli was crying like everyone else was. The men were more circumspect about it, blinking rapidly, discreetly wiping their eyes, but they were crying, too.

"Mom," Cessy whined, "I can't believe you did that."

"And I can't believe my daughter wrote such a beautiful essay. I remember the day you took us to school, but you never said why you did it." Mrs. Keller brushed away her own tears. "Well, I'm going to frame this essay, Cessy, and some day when you're grown and have a family of your own, I'll show it to them, and let them know that matching on the outside doesn't matter to me…"

Zac leaned closer to Eli, whispering, "And it doesn't matter to me."

Gently, he put his hand on her stomach, and Eli knew Zac Keller had accepted her baby, even if it wasn't his.

She took Zac's hand and squeezed it, letting him know she understood.

When their eyes met, she truly got what Cessy had teased them about—talking without saying a word. And she'd been right because Eli could see not only his feelings for her, but also for the baby.

Ariel and her aunt made their excuses a few minutes later. Ariel hadn't said more than an obligatory greeting to Eli, but she'd noticed the girl was wearing the necklace she'd had Zac tuck in the Christmas box. *Believe,* it proclaimed. And Eli silently wished that Ariel would learn to believe in herself, and to believe that things would work out. Until Ariel could do that, Eli would just believe for her.

She and Zac spent another couple hours at his parents'. It was loud, and a bit crazy, but Eli had to admit, she loved Zac's entire family.

He drove her home, and as they pulled into her drive, she asked, "Can you come in for a few minutes? I have something for you."

"That's funny because I have something for you." Zac reached in the back and pulled out a bag, then followed Eli to the porch, where she dug through her purse for her keys.

"I don't always have this much trouble finding my keys. Maybe it happens when you're around because you make me nervous."

"Do I?" He'd moved closer and she could feel his warm breath on her very cold neck. But her shivers had nothing to do with the warmth, and everything to do with the proximity of him.

He affected her like no one ever had.

Finally, she snagged her keys and opened the door.

He made himself at home, taking off his coat and boots before she'd managed, and by the time she walked into the living room, he'd snapped on the lights and even plugged in her tree.

"While you're over there, grab the present wrapped in red."

He came back carrying it, with his shopping bag as well.

"You first, please," she said. "I've wanted to give it to you for more than a week."

He tore into the paper with childlike abandon. "Wow."

That was exactly the reaction she'd hoped for. "I'll confess, I asked your mom to find the pictures for me."

He held the painting gently studying it.

"I have a student who's so talented, and she really could use the extra money. It's not professional, but I think it's beautiful. Your mom said she's jealous because she said she's never managed to get everyone home at the same time for a family portrait and she's going to have Katie paint a second one for her."

The painting was of the Keller family. All six kids and Mr. and Mrs. Keller. After listening to Cessy's essay tonight, Eli was even more pleased with the picture.

"Eli, this is one of the best presents I've ever received." He leaned over and hugged her. "Seriously, the best." Zac reached down, grabbed his bag and thrust it at her. "Here. Open the smaller one first."

She was much neater at taking off the paper, mainly because she'd always loved dragging the suspense out. Right now, the box was potentially anything, but in a moment, she'd know what it was and the magic would be over.

So she slowly worked the bow off, then the tape, and finally found a small tan, cardboard box and slid the lid off…and started laughing. While the box was small, it was rather large for a key ring. And as she held the silver key ring that looked as if someone had bedazzled it with the most gaudy jewels they could find, she continued laughing.

"When I saw it, it practically glowed, and I thought you might have an easier time finding something that shiny in your purse."

"Oh, I guarantee I will."

"Now, open the flat one." She did, and found tickets. "I got us season's tickets to the Broadway series at the Warner Theater. I couldn't help but notice that most of your CDs are show tunes."

For five years, Eli had done the philharmonic with Arthur. And she loved the music, but he'd never once asked, or noticed, that she loved Broadway even more. And here was Zac, who'd not only noticed, but had also bought tickets for them both.

The fact that their tickets added another layer of permanence should have felt rushed, but instead felt comforting. She liked the idea of Zac being around for a long time.

"I don't know much about Broadway," he continued, "but you'll teach me."

She'd barely managed a thank-you when he said, "Okay, the last one's not technically for you."

Eli took the much larger box from the bag and opened it. There was a chipped and well-used piggy bank.

"I know it's not the prettiest thing in the world, but it's all I had when I came to the Kellers'. I'd been in foster care for two years, and they moved me from home to home, and I brought that bank with me. I squirreled away every penny I found, and in my mind, I was going to save enough to run away."

Eli had a mental image of Zac as a little boy, clutching his piggy bank and dreaming his dreams. She blinked hard, fighting back the tears. Trying to lighten the mood, she gave it a small shake. "It's empty, now. So what did you do with your riches?"

"Yes, it's empty. After I'd been with Mom and Dad for about a year, the adoption was official and I finally figured out they weren't going to send me anywhere else. Then the Kellers asked me if I would mind having a little brother or sister. I told them, wait a minute and went upstairs and I emptied the bank. I took my fortune—all eight dollars and sixty-two cents—down to Mom. I didn't know how it worked, and guessed they were going to buy a brother or sister for me, and I wanted to help. It's been empty ever since and collecting dust at my place. For years it was my security blanket of sorts… The only thing that stayed the same. It occurred to me that maybe the baby could use a little security."

Eli ran her fingers lightly along the beat-up pig, then gently set it on the coffee table, and turned to kiss the amazing man who'd come into her life at the most unexpected time, her baby sandwiched between them.

CHAPTER NINE

> "When the mother first feels the baby move, it's just the slightest flutter. First-time moms might not recognize it for what it is. Soon, the baby's movements will be unmistakable."
>
> —*Pregnancy, Childbirth and Parenting for Teens,*
> by Mary Jeanne Lorei

"HAPPY VALENTINE'S, MOM," Eli said as she answered the phone on Sunday morning.

"How did you know it was me?"

Her mom had asked this question before, but anything more complicated than an electric mixer was out of her mother's comfort zone. "Caller ID, remember?"

"I forgot you were my little techno-geek." Her mother paused and asked, "I got that right, right? Techno-geek?"

Eli laughed. "Yes, you did." She took the phone with her into the laundry room.

"See, I do pay attention sometimes. And happy Valentine's Day to you, too. Are you doing anything special tonight?"

"Zac's taking me to lunch, then he's coming with me to my first childbirth class."

"Are you sure that's a good idea? Maybe Tucker could be your partner, or I could come home—"

Eli stopped. "Mom, we've been through this. Don't cut short your winter in Florida. You'll be home long before the baby's born. And come on, you've met Tucker. I'm sure she would come to the classes with me if I asked, but Mom, it's Tucker."

Eli pulled a towel from the dryer.

"Tucker has had a baby, so I'm sure she could handle it," her mother insisted.

"Handle it? Yes. But be a comforting support system? She was an Amazon when she gave birth. I think she grunted a couple times, but she was so stoic, even the nurses commented. I'd feel as if I had to live up to that, and Mom, I'm no Amazon."

Eli was realistic. She was going to try to do a natural childbirth, but if the pain got too intense, she reserved her right to have drugs. To be honest, she would have felt she was letting her friend down.

Plus, she wouldn't admit it to her mom, but she wanted Zac with her. They'd grown so much closer since Christmas and—

"Fine. I just worry about you and Zac."

"You like him." Her inflection made it sound like a statement, but it was a question.

"We liked him when we met him, Eli, but…"

The word hung there ominously. "But?"

"But your father and I worry. Things are going very fast between the two of you, and with all the changes in your life…" Her mother paused. "I want you to be careful. You've never been a fan of change. Do you remember when you were four and I made you give up your crib finally? It was three weeks until I slept again."

"Mom, I've heard the story but I don't remember."

"Or, how about when we moved to Whedon. You swore you would ride your bike every day to our old place. When you realized it was too far, you spent a day sitting in the principal's office because I could make you go to school, but I couldn't make you pay attention in class."

"Seven, Mom. I was in second grade." Eli did remember the move. It was traumatic for her. She'd missed the security of her old school and her established friends. She missed knowing where everything was in her house and room. All these years later, she remembered the feeling of a hole in her life.

"And you carried your blanket to school every day that whole year, stuffed in your book bag so your new friends wouldn't know, but you just needed it near. I want to be sure that Zac isn't another blanket, something to keep near when you're going through a big change."

Eli felt a niggle of concern, but quickly pushed it aside. Zac wasn't merely convenient to have around. "He makes me happy, Mom. Happy in a way I can't remember being."

"I'm glad," her mom assured her.

"I know you worry, Mom. But this is one time you don't have to. Zac's good for me."

"I'll call tomorrow to see how your class goes tonight."

"Talk to you then."

Eli sat on the floor of her small laundry room, dirty clothes surrounding her. That worry niggled at her some more.

Was she just using Zac?

ZAC WASN'T SURE WHAT he'd expected at a childbirth class, but the instructor had started them off slowly. No birth video to feel squeamish about.

That was next week.

"Arthur came by yesterday." Eli collected her mat and coat, and was heading for the exit.

"Oh?"

"He's been talking to a psychologist who told him he should embrace and explore his feelings for the baby. So, he wants to try. I suggested that he could come with me to my next sonogram. Maybe seeing the baby live on the screen, moving and so very real would help him figure things out. He said he'd try to make it."

They stood in silence. While Zac understood her insistence that Arthur had a right to be involved with the baby, he was still hurt. He was supposed to go to that appointment with Eli and she'd just dumped him to make Arthur feel better.

Granted it was just one appointment, but what if somewhere down the line it was something else, something bigger?

"Zac, I'm sorry Arthur's changed our plans."

Zac wanted to tell her it was okay, that he understood. And he did understand, but he wasn't okay with it. And admitting that made him feel small.

He tried to think of some excuse, but his silence must have stretched too long because Eli spoke up.

"Is something wrong? Arthur's visit?" she asked.

"It's not really—" He stopped. "I could lie to you, but I won't. Yes, it's Arthur's visit. It's his ability to walk in and out of your life at will. The baby's his. He doesn't want it. He changes his mind by the minute. Well, I don't. I want you. I want you more than you can know. There's no waffling, no indecision."

"He's the baby's father." She waited for him to respond. When he didn't, she continued, "I told you this was a mistake, but you're the one who insisted that single moms date and that it shouldn't be any different for them." She turned as if to leave.

"Eli, I meant every word I said—"

She wheeled around and faced him, her cheeks flushed. "Then I don't understand. I'm not getting back with Arthur. I've made that clear. But he deserves to be a part of the baby's—his baby's—life if he wants to be."

"Eli, I care about you. Hell, that doesn't even come close to covering how I feel about you…." Wasn't this the time to tell her that he loved her?

"But?" she prompted.

"Not *but,* an *and.* And I care about this baby."

"I still don't understand." She leaned against the doorjamb, both hands resting on her rounded stomach.

"Every time Arthur shows up, this feeling—" Zac shook his head. "I don't know how to explain it. It's not jealousy…"

"I'm glad because I've told you, I don't have feelings for Arthur anymore. He was familiar. Like teacher's in-service days the first Wednesday of every month, or grocery shopping on Saturdays. I'm not proud of the fact that I was willing to settle, but I don't feel anything else for Arthur."

"And yet, he's here. Waffling about whether he wants to be a part of the baby's life."

"He's the biological father, he has rights and— Damn it, Zac, we're going in circles here."

"I know we are. And if you were the kind of person who could ignore his rights, you wouldn't be the woman I've fallen—" He quickly switched direction. "Did I ever tell you about Cessy?"

It was a rhetorical question because Zac never talked about that time.

Eli shook her head. "No."

"She mentioned it in that essay at Christmas. I was in my twenties when Mom and Dad brought the tiniest baby I'd ever seen home. Mom laughed and said she might already have five kids, but she was a novice at the baby stuff. Diapers. Bottles. She'd never dealt with any of that before. Neither had any of us, but we were all older and pitched in and learned. Cessy didn't just have two parents doting on her, she had five siblings as well. We spoiled her."

"I wouldn't say spoiled. She's a beautiful girl inside and out."

Zac nodded. "I'd graduated college and was working alongside Dad at the store when Cessy... She was five and we were the only family she'd ever known, Eli. I was her big brother. She ran to me with boo-boos and secrets. Everything."

"So what happened?" Eli asked.

"Mom and Dad had been through adoption with the rest of us, but it was different with Cessy. There were more legal steps, and they—we all—were waiting for everything to clear so her adoption could be finalized. Her mother's rights were terminated at birth but there were problems with finding her biological father. When they did, he claimed he didn't know about her and that he wanted her."

Zac remembered his mother calling him, so hysterical that he couldn't understand a word she was saying. He'd driven to the house and found everyone in tears. "I wanted to fight. I'd have spent every cent I had and bankrupted the store if I had to in order to keep her.

But Mom and Dad—Eli, they said Cessy's father had rights. I was furious that they didn't do something to stop it. They were her parents. We were her siblings. *We* were her family. No DNA test would change that."

"Oh, Zac—"

"The night before the social worker was to come for her, I gave her a necklace. A small gold circle. And I told her that it was a hug. That anytime she missed us she could press it close and it would be as if we were hugging her. She didn't understand then, but the next day…"

Ten years later, that morning was still vivid in his memory. "She cried and screamed, Eli. Over and over."

TEARS WERE STREAMING DOWN Eli's face as she listened to Zac. She didn't even bother trying to wipe them away. Her heart was breaking for him, for Cessy, for the entire Keller family.

"I couldn't stop them," he continued, his voice ragged. "I couldn't save Cecily. I didn't lie, Eli. I can love your baby, sight unseen. It's not a question of that, it's a question of how will I survive if Arthur at some point takes…"

"Zac, it's not like that…Arthur's not taking anyone," she assured him.

"Eli, it is *just* like that. I want to be this baby's father."

Eli knew it was too soon to be talking in those terms, although she did wish Zac were the baby's father, too. "Listen, we're just dating—"

"There's more to us than just dating and you know that." She thought he was done, and maybe he'd thought so as well because he looked startled as he blurted out,

"I love you. I love this baby. Maybe it's right to let Arthur in if he wants, but I don't give a damn, anymore than I cared when Cessy's father wanted her back."

"Zac, you're not being fair."

"I know that, damn it. I'm jealous of something that hasn't even happened. I'm scared of losing you and the baby."

"Zac…" She wanted to reach him, to tell him it would be all right, but she couldn't do that. Maybe it wouldn't.

She hugged the baby.

Zac took a step forward and held the door open for her. "It's my problem. I'll drop you off, then. I need to go and think."

"Zac, I never wanted to hurt you."

"I don't want to hurt you, either, and I know that I am, but I'm not sure what else to do."

"I should never have said yes to dating you. I knew it was—"

He silenced her with a kiss.

"I'm an ass. Confused about a lot of things, but I know one thing. The day you agreed to date me was one of the best days of my life. Please don't give up on me."

When they reached Eli's place, he gave her a peck on the cheek and said, "I'll call you tomorrow."

She headed toward her house, hoping he'd follow, hoping he'd come inside with her.

But Zac was gone.

So many things had changed in her life over the last six months. She'd handled all of them. Though, if she lost Zac…that might be the one thing she wouldn't recover from.

She thought about calling Tucker. Or her mom. But Tucker would just be furious with Zac for her sake, and she didn't want that. And her mom would be on the next plane home, and she didn't want that, either.

So, Eli didn't call anyone. She turned away from her front door and went for a stroll. The sidewalks were finally clear again, rather than snow-covered, although there was still plenty of snow in front yards and occasionally, where the day's melting snow had pooled, there was ice.

The moon was full and bright enough to create shadows on the snow of the bare trees.

She made it onto Main Street, where the stores were closed and dark. A few bars and a coffeehouse still had lights on, but it was a Thursday, so they weren't heavily populated, either.

She could already feel Zac's absence. How had he become such an important part of her life? They'd worked together for a while on the CATA Project, but over the last months they'd gotten so close.

He'd said he loved her.

The weight of those words hung heavily. He loved her, and she'd hurt him.

"Ms. Cartwright?"

She spotted Ariel waddling out of the coffeehouse toward her, slinging her coat on as she walked.

"Ms. Cartwright, are you okay?"

Ariel had been avoiding her ever since she told the class she was pregnant. Oh, she came to school and still went to her job at Keller's Market, but the connection Eli had felt with her was broken. "Sure, I'm fine. Why wouldn't I be fine?"

They stood under a streetlight, which illuminated

the fact that Ariel's stomach was swollen to the extent that she couldn't zip up her coat. Eli worried about her out in the cold. "You'd better get inside."

"Come with me. I'll treat you to a decaf coffee or tea."

"No, that's fine—"

"Ms. Cartwright, I know I've been a jerk. I've known all along I was being a jerk, but I didn't know how to stop. It seems once you start, it can grow exponentially, picking up steam on its own."

"You weren't a jerk. I let you down." And now, she'd let Zac down as well. If she could handle Arthur a different way she would, but she couldn't.

"No. I just finally figured out you were human." Ariel offered Eli a wry smile that was so much older than her seventeen years. "I'm sorry."

"It's okay, Ariel. I understand…understood."

"Well, show me that you really forgive me. Let me buy you an herbal tea."

Eli didn't know how to say no after that, so she followed Ariel to the coffeehouse. After the dark sky, the well-lit room seemed overly bright.

She and Ariel sat down at a table. "Ms. Cartwright, you're not okay."

Eli could see the concern on the girl's face. "Yes, yes, I'm fine. How about you? How are things at your aunt's?"

"The same. She said I could quit work if I wanted, but I like it at the grocery store. Everyone's been nice. They had a shower for me last week, did I tell you?"

Eli didn't point out that Ariel hadn't been saying much of anything to her outside of the classroom, but she didn't mention it. "No."

"It was great. I got all kinds of stuff for the baby. Mr. Keller even got me a crib."

Zac hadn't mentioned it, but then he wouldn't. He wasn't the type of man who did things in order to be praised. He did them because they needed to be done. "He's a very nice man."

"And a good boss."

Eli nodded. "I'm so glad the store's working out for you. I have two other businesses in town lined up for CATA." She needed to get that organized before she had the baby. There was so much to do before the baby came.

Where would Arthur or Zac be when that happened? When she first found out about the baby, she'd thought Arthur would stand by her, but it soon became apparent that wasn't going to happen. Then for months, she'd believed Zac would be there.

And now, maybe he wouldn't.

If he walked, she wouldn't blame him. When he'd told her about Cessy, she realized that it wasn't a story he shared with people, and she'd also realized how the idea of Arthur popping in and out of the baby's life must hurt and scare him.

And while she understood, she couldn't help but feel as if her heart was breaking.

Eli started to cry. Not a few dainty tears. But rather big wet drops that ran down her cheeks. Her nose immediately clogged and she took a napkin and wiped it.

"Ms. Cartwright, it's okay. Being pregnant makes you cry and stuff. But this isn't about being pregnant, is it?"

"I think I just lost…" She couldn't even say his name. "I mean, having the baby's father leave me hurt, but to lose…" It occurred to her that she was about to unburden herself to an already overburdened student. "Never mind. You're right. It's only hormones."

"I'll go get you that tea," Ariel offered.

While she was gone, Eli took a tissue from her pocket and tried to get herself under control as she sipped her tea and listened to Ariel's chatter. The girl was keeping up a running commentary for her sake, trying to distract her.

It was sweet.

It wasn't working, but it was really sweet.

"So, how are the childbirth classes coming?" Eli asked.

"My aunt went with me. Hee hee hoo. Hee hee hoo," she breathed. "I'm pretty good. She tries to help, but ends up out of breath in the end." Ariel paused and asked, "Are you taking classes?"

"Sure." She'd taken them with Zac. Maybe she should ask Tucker to take over for him.

"I wasn't sure." Ariel dumped another bag of sugar into her teacup. "I mean, you're a teacher and have taught this stuff for so many years."

"Ariel, I may have taught it, but I never lived it. I think you and I are both going to find out that the reality of it is so much different than just reading about it."

"Oh, I've already discovered that. I'd read about morning sickness, but you don't get how bad it can be until you spend every morning and most evenings kneeling in front of a toilet, hoping you can keep something down." She nodded. "So, who's your partner?" she asked.

"A friend."

"Someone I know?"

Eli didn't want to answer. Ariel was finally talking to her again, and she didn't want to blow that.

"I'm teasing, Ms. Cartwright. I know you and Mr. Keller are dating, that he's going with you."

"Ariel, Mr. Keller and I—"

"Ms. Cartwright, I meant it. I know I was a jerk. I know your baby's dad left, and that Mr. Keller likes you."

"How?" Eli asked.

"He came to see me right after you told us you were pregnant. He basically told me I was acting like a spoiled brat and to get over it."

"He shouldn't have spoken to you like that…at all."

"He didn't put it that way. He was a lot more polite about it, but I could see how much he cared about you. And even after I didn't follow his advice, he's still been really nice to me at work. He's the best boss I ever had. One of the nicest guys I've ever met. If I were a little older…" Her grin said quite clearly she was joking.

Eli laughed.

"Here's the thing, Ms. Cartwright. It's easy to get wrapped up in yourself when you're pregnant. They don't say it in the books, but it's probably part of the whole process. I mean, every day your body changes, the baby grows. You have to worry about what you eat and pretty much anything you do may be affecting the baby. So, it makes sense that everyone who's pregnant spends so much time thinking about themselves. It's not a bad thing. It just is. That's what happened with me. I forgot that you're human. And that's why I was mad. It was all about me. But maybe you've got some of that, too, and you don't see how lucky you are having Mr. Keller around. I know the baby's father was a skunk—"

"He's not. It's just that this baby wasn't what he had planned." Eli defended Arthur out of habit more than a firm belief that he wasn't a skunk.

"Yeah? Too freakin' bad for him. Charlie said the same thing when he walked—that he didn't sign up for a baby. Really? Well, I didn't either, and neither did you. And yet, here we are, two very knocked-up women handling it. They're both rat bastards, if you ask me. But Mr. Keller, he didn't walk away. He stayed. And it's not even his baby. That makes you lucky in my book."

Ariel got quiet and turned to look out the window, giving Eli a moment to process what her student had just said.

She was lucky.

Zac didn't like Arthur walking in and out? That was understandable.

He'd admitted it to her and shared a traumatic event from his past in order to make her understand. That was honest and brave.

He'd said he loved her and that he loved her baby sight unseen.

Coming from some men, that might be a line, but with Zac, she knew there was honesty in the statement.

She hadn't been nearly as honest with him. She owed him that.

"Ariel, I need to go, but I want to thank you. You've helped me work through some things. And I really... well, thank you."

"You know how you said that being pregnant is different than teaching it?"

Eli nodded.

"Well, looking at other people's lives and giving advice is easier than figuring your own out."

"You are a very wise girl…." She paused and corrected herself. "Woman. You're a very wise woman, Ariel Mayor. And I know you're going to make something out of yourself. That you've got a wonderful life in front of you…you and this baby."

Ariel reached out and took her hand. "You, too, Ms. Cartwright."

"Thank you. And right now, there's a person I really need to talk to because of you."

Eli hurried home, got her car and drove to Zac's. She didn't want to take time to think anything through. She just wanted to get to him and say the words that were suddenly burning to come out.

She knocked on his door and he answered, looking horrible.

"I know you want to be alone and think, but I wanted to tell you that I think I love you, too. I don't want to pressure you. I understand your feelings about Arthur. And if he wants to see this baby, to be a part of its life, I'll let him. But there's no chance of him being a part of mine again, at least not romantically. Days, weeks, months have gone by, and I don't miss him. But one evening of you leaving early and I feel bereft. I missed you."

"Say it again."

She stood on her tiptoes and kissed his cheek. "I love you. I just wanted you to know. I owed you the same honesty that you'd given me."

Eli turned and started to walk away, but Zac grabbed her hand and gently pulled her into his arms, and kissed her. His feelings right there on the surface. He loved her. He loved her baby. He wanted her.

He held her as if she were in fact the most beautiful woman in the world.

All her worries and doubts fell away.

He led her into the house and kicked the door shut. There was an urgency in his kiss, but despite that there was tenderness in it, too. She still had her coat on as she stood sandwiched between him and the wall, locked in a kiss that she hoped would never end.

And when it did, when he finally withdrew, there was an almost physical ache.

"Say it again." Zac looked at her, his need evident in his expression.

"I love you," she said for a third time, the words coming out so much easier this time. "I love you. It's a crazy time to fall in love, but I don't think love follows a schedule. I can't pinpoint the moment it happened. It sort of crept up on me so slowly I didn't even realize it. Somewhere between that lunch last fall, when I told you Arthur and I had broken up, and today, I fell in love with you. And I know you have concerns. So do I, but—"

"Not now. Not tonight. Any concerns or problems will be there tomorrow."

And he kissed her again.

Part of Eli knew she should protest. She wasn't the type to bury her head in the sand and ignore issues. She liked to face them head-on. But as Zac deepened the kiss, the only thing she could think of was getting even closer.

He held her with one arm, but his free hand moved down and rested lightly between them on her belly.

Eli didn't think she was self-conscious, but she felt shy about her ever-changing body.

"Zac, I—"

"Shh. You're beautiful, Eli. The most beautiful woman I've ever seen." He stroked her stomach. "And this baby. I meant it when I said, I've fallen in love with it, too." He gently caressed her stomach. "I want to be here for you now, and after it's born. I'm in this, Eli. No matter what, I'm in this."

He didn't mention Arthur, but she knew that her ex still troubled Zac.

"But—"

"No. Not tonight. We'll work it all out. Right now, I want you to stay with me. Spend the night."

It was what she wanted, too.

But she must have hesitated too long because Zac added, "I mean, I could just hold you, if doing more would hurt the baby."

He was giving her an out. She could spend the night in Zac's arms without making love to him. And yet, despite the fact she felt ungainly and shy, somehow, because it was Zac, it didn't matter. "There's no problem."

That was the only invitation he needed. He took her hand and led her to his room.

"I'm nervous," she confessed as she looked at his bed. It was a bachelor's room. Spartan in its furnishing. A bed, sheets and blankets, a nightstand with a stack of books and a chest of drawers.

"Eli, seriously, just spend the night with me. We'll sleep. I want to hold you. I could hold you forever and it wouldn't be enough."

And as she looked at him, Eli knew he meant it, which eased her shyness. She walked back into his arms and kissed him, then reached up to unbutton his dress shirt.

He pulled back. "Are you sure?"

She nodded.

Carefully, he tugged her shirt up over her head. Her breasts were huge. Well, not huge, but significantly larger than they'd ever been. Even in her no-nonsense maternity bra, she felt exposed.

And when she glanced down, she realized she'd worn her maternity pants that had the elastic panels in the sides. They looked like normal pants, although her stomach seemed huge to her as she peered down at it.

Zac's shirt was unbuttoned and he tore that off as well, and quickly slipped out of his white, cotton T-shirt.

She thought he'd remove more clothing, but as if sensing her feelings, he didn't. Instead, he took her hand and led her to the bed.

"You look beautiful."

He gently placed a hand on her stomach. At that moment, the baby kicked.

"That's amazing."

"It doesn't freak you out?"

"I love you," he said. "I love this baby. Nothing about being with you freaks me out."

And she saw in his eyes that he meant every word. He didn't see her ponderously large breasts or swollen abdomen. He saw her. Just her. And he thought she was beautiful.

And because he did, she felt truly beautiful. There was no more awkwardness, no more hesitancy. She gave him everything she had.

He was gentle and tender as they learned each other's bodies.

She forgot to be self-conscious. She forgot everything but this man...this moment.

In his arms she felt safe.

She felt treasured.

She felt loved.

And for tonight, that was enough.

CHAPTER TEN

"The third trimester is a time of change. Your pregnancy is even evident to strangers. You're gaining weight and your body is changing almost daily. Most women find this troubling, possibly scary. Just remind yourself that these are normal reactions for both teens, and for older moms. And that we must embrace our fear and not let it beat us down."

—*Pregnancy, Childbirth and Parenting for Teens,*
by Mary Jeanne Lorei

A MONTH AND A HALF.

Zac couldn't help but marvel at how happy he'd been the last six weeks. Cessy complained last week that if he didn't stop his incessant smiling his face was going to get stuck like that.

As he watched Eli, he knew he was grinning in a way Cessy would have commented on if she were here. Eli was slicing apples for a pie, one fell and landed on her protruding stomach.

He chuckled.

"Hey, men who laugh at pregnant ladies using their stomachs as a shelf don't get apple pie."

"Oh, I'll mind my manners, then."

"Good." She went back to slicing, looking as happy as he felt.

Tucker announced her presence by coughing loudly. "Okay, you two—" she paused. "Don't get all lovey-dovey."

Tucker was wearing paint-splattered clothes. She'd sided with him when he insisted that Eli not be in the baby's room while it was being painted, even though they'd used a low VOC paint.

Tucker had finished the edging so he could grab a bite to eat before he left for the office.

Zac listened to the two of them banter. They might not be related, but there was a sisterly connection. He had a vast degree of experience in how sisters sounded.

"Eli, I'm going to run home, shower and head to the market. But I'll be back before dinner."

"Don't be late, or I call the pie," Tucker said.

"A piece of the pie?" Eli asked.

Tucker shook her head. "Nope, I meant the whole pie."

"I'll definitely be back in time," Zac promised as he leaned over and kissed Eli goodbye.

"Okay, come on, you two. As Bart would say, no sucking face in front of me."

"You realize that if Bart was saying that to you, you must have been kissing someone," Zac teased.

"Not me. He said it about my pop. Turns out my father's got a new girlfriend and Bart walked in on them saying goodbye. I was sympathetic when he told me, but the two of you have made me even more so."

Zac laughed.

"Keep Eli out of that room," he said as he walked toward the front door.

"I've been watching out for Eli for years."

Eli waved a hand at both of them. "Hey, you two, I'm here and I'm quite capable of watching out for myself."

"Right," Tucker scoffed.

"I know you are," Zac said as they walked to the front door. "But I worry."

"You don't have to worry, Zac. I'm a big girl." She paused and added, "I'm older, remember? More years of experience."

That she was able to tease him about their age difference, which had once been a cause for concern with her, meant she was becoming more comfortable with the idea.

"I'll hurry," he promised as he kissed her again.

Kissing Eli.

Making love to Eli.

He put on his coat, leaned down for one more quick buss on the cheek, then opened the door to the raw wind.

A car pulled up in front of Eli's house and Arthur got out. It was as if the man had radar and could sense when Zac was happy.

"You're here again?" Arthur asked as he spotted him.

"I was just about to ask you the same question," Zac said.

At the last minute, Arthur had called off going with Eli to her sonogram appointment, and neither Zac, nor Eli had seen or heard from him since. Zac lived in hope that the man had finally given up.

Arthur didn't respond. He continued walking up to Eli's front door.

It took all of Zac's self-restraint not to follow him.

But Eli was right. She was a big girl and had been taking care of herself for years. She could handle Arthur.

Right?

"WELL, YOU TWO ARE GETTING all hot and heavy," Tucker said once Eli returned to the kitchen after seeing Zac off.

"Maybe." She could feel her cheeks burning as Tucker grinned in that knowing way of hers. "You know, your teasing us wasn't very helpful."

"Oh, come on. If you walked in on me sucking face, you'd be teasing me relentlessly."

Anxious to turn the conversation away from herself and Zac, Eli asked, "Speaking of which. Whatever happened to that guy who kept asking you out?"

"I kept saying no."

"And?"

Tucker shrugged. "I haven't seen him for a couple months. He told me he had business out of town and he'd call me when he came back. I told him not to bother."

Eli sat down on the stool next to her. "Oh, Tucker."

"You said 'oh, Tucker,' but I heard 'poor Tucker' in your voice." Tucker stirred her cup of tea, concentrating on it rather than looking at Eli.

"He sounded nice," Eli prompted.

She worried about Tucker. Worried that one day she'd chase away the right man for her.

"Sure, nice if you like designer suits."

"And if he wore jeans? Would that have helped?"

"Maybe. But he doesn't. Zac does. He looked fairly perfect in his painting jeans today." Tucker blatantly changed the topic back to Eli. "But."

"But he's not perfect, either. I mean, if he were a few years older he would be—"

"The age difference doesn't seem to be stopping you," Tucker interrupted.

"—and if I weren't pregnant, maybe we'd be perfect. Or maybe not. Maybe perfection doesn't enter into love."

"Oh, are we tossing the L word around already?"

Eli was saved from having to answer by a knock at the kitchen door. She glanced out the window and sighed, opening it. "Arthur?"

"Talk about a lack of perfection," Tucker muttered, then took a sip of her tea.

Eli wasn't sure if Arthur was glaring at Tucker because he'd heard her comment, or if he was just glaring at Eli because it was Saturday. The two of them had never needed much of a reason to do some glaring.

"Arthur, what did you need?"

"I need to talk to you."

So much for him just handing her the papers nullifying his parental rights. "Fine."

He obviously detected her lack of enthusiasm and frowned. He nodded in Tucker's direction. "Somewhere she isn't."

Tucker didn't even bother looking up from her tea. "I know that was a hint, pal, but I'm not leaving you alone with Eli. If you want privacy, try the living room, but I'll be in the house."

"You think I'd hurt her?" Arthur sounded affronted to his very core.

"You proved you would when she told you about the baby, didn't you?" Tucker asked. "Or how about last month, when you stood her up at the—"

"Okay, you two, enough." Eli thought about asking Tucker to leave, but that particular stubborn gleam in her friend's eye told her there wasn't much hope of that, so she said, "Come into the living room, Arthur, and say what you need to say."

Eli thought about sitting and offering him a seat, but she didn't want to drag this visit out longer than necessary, so she stood in the middle of the room.

"Now, what?" Her question came out sharper than she intended. "Sorry. What did you need, Arthur? Did you see the lawyer again?"

"Yes, I saw him."

"And the papers?"

"I have them, Eli, but I still haven't signed them yet."

"Arthur—"

"I can't, Eli. I've tried. I've tried over and over, but I can't. I miss you."

"Arthur…" She didn't know what else to say. She'd pretty much said it all again and again.

"How is the baby…?" He choked out the word *baby*.

"Everything's fine. The doctor's keeping a close eye on the two of us because of my age."

"If your age is an issue, then what about mine?" He tried to play it off as a joke, but it fell flat. "I mean, I'm a member of AARP. That's too old to be a first-time father."

Eli grabbed the notepad and pen out of the end table drawer and wrote. "Here's my doctor's name, the address and the appointment date and time. It's up to you." She didn't want to give him another chance. She remembered how Zac had reacted last time, and didn't want to start that up again.

She didn't have a choice, Arthur was the baby's father.

"I do miss you," Arthur said.

"Arthur, I'm sorry—"

"Yeah." He took the piece of paper from her outstretched hand. "I'll see you there."

He retraced his steps toward the kitchen.

Eli followed him. She felt bad for him, and yet, she could hardly remember the time when she thought she loved him.

He turned before he reached the kitchen. "Maybe just a dinner?"

She shook her head. "But I'll see you at the sonogram."

He nodded.

Tucker was washing dishes, and as soon as she spotted Arthur, she seemed ready to shoot out another zinger, but Eli shook her head, and Tucker's lips clamped shut. Arthur slipped his boots on and went out the door.

"So?" Tucker brought a mug of hot tea over and slid it in front of Eli.

"He's going to try another sonogram appointment. Maybe if he sees the baby, he'll feel more connected."

"Why? Why do you keep giving him chances? Just tell him to back off."

"He has rights, Tucker."

"You're a better woman than I am, Eli. If Bart's father came back today and wanted to explore his rights, I'd...well, let's just say, I wouldn't be inviting him to a sonogram appointment for a second time."

"I'm no better. And I'm ashamed to admit that there's a part of me that would like nothing more than to tell him to kiss off. But I've worked with girls in this situation for too many years. I've worked with some of the fathers, too. It's not an easy position for any of them. I always encourage my girls to give the baby's father a chance. How can *I* do any less? What kind of hypocrite would that make me?"

"I don't think I'd care. And that, my friend, is the difference between us and why you are indeed a better woman than I am. So, what do you want to do now? We could go see a movie or something. Bart's on a date—" Tucker stopped and looked as if she'd swallowed a bug. "I hate that my kid is old enough to date. Anyway, he's out. I'm footloose and fancy-free, so a movie, or—"

The phone rang and Eli held up a finger. "Hold on to that thought." She picked up the receiver in the living room. "Hello?"

"Eli, it's Zac. I was at the store and Ariel was working." He was all out of breath.

"Is something wrong?" A sense of panic filled Eli. Things between her and Ariel had finally become normal.

"I'm driving her to the hospital now. She's in labor. Her aunt's on a flight and is trying to get home, but she won't be back until later tonight, and her parents still aren't talking to her, so—"

"Which hospital?" Eli asked.

"St. Vincent's," Zac told her.

"Got it. I'm on my way."

"We're not that far ahead of you. I'd have just come to get you, but Ariel thought maybe her aunt would be home and able to come. So we stopped there, and I don't want to backtrack." He paused and added, "She shouldn't be alone."

"It's fine, Zac. I'll be there as soon as I can." She hung up and forced herself to take a deep breath. She talked about moments like this with her girls. It was easy to get frazzled and just run, but it was better to take a moment, a breath and just think.

What did she need? What might Ariel need?

"Eli?"

She'd forgotten all about Tucker.

"Sorry, the movie will have to wait. That was Zac. Ariel's in labor and her aunt's out of town, so he's driving her to the hospital in Erie."

"And you're going, too." There was no question, just a statement. "I'll drive you."

"I can drive myself," Eli insisted. "Besides, sitting around a waiting room would be less than exciting for you."

"I know, but hey, we'll have chick bonding all the way there and back again."

"Chick bonding?" Eli laughed because to the best of her knowledge, Tucker worked mainly with men, and seemed to prefer their company. "You hate chick bonding."

"Well, maybe most of the time, but not with you. There's a difference between spending time with women friends and spending it with guy friends. Women want to talk and be all feely about things. Guys just want you to pass the beer and pay attention to the game. They are simple creatures and easy to entertain."

Eli was grateful Tucker was giving her something to think about other than Ariel and she happily played along. "I thought this guy who wants to date you was giving you grief?"

"He's an anomaly. He's all touchy-feely. Mr. Designer Suit is part girl. Not in any physical way or in his mannerisms—no, he's all man there."

Tucker paused, and in any other woman, Eli would have been sure that the escaping hiss of air was a sigh of appreciation, but with Tucker she wasn't. It could just as easily have been exasperation.

"But emotionally? He's the girl." Tucker got a look in her eye that was definitely dreamy. And Eli was pretty sure the dreaminess had more to do with the all-man parts than the emotionally girly parts.

"Tuck, for someone who swears she's not interested, we do seem to talk about him a lot."

"Let's go," Tucker grumbled.

It wasn't a long ride from Whedon to Erie. It normally took Eli about twenty minutes on I-79. But with Tucker behind the wheel, they made it in fifteen. Still, it felt pretty close to forever to Eli. She was worried about Ariel.

Tucker parked her four-wheel-drive pickup in record time, too, and Eli hurried into the hospital. She checked in at the front desk, got Ariel's room number, then strode to the elevators. Tucker stuck close by until they passed by the waiting room. "This is where I stay."

"You don't have to. I—"

Tucker's stubborn expression, which Eli knew so well, was firmly set in place. "I'll wait, Eli. What else do I have to do other than sit around at home and wait for Bart? It annoys him when I wait up, so I'd rather wait here for you. And I'm going to confess, I really feel for the kid. I knew my dad would be pissed, but I never for a moment doubted he'd be there for me. Since her parents aren't here, I'll be."

Despite her cumbersome size, Eli hugged Tucker. As always, it seemed to catch her friend by surprise.

"Fine, Tuck. I'll come fill you in when I can."

She continued down the hall to find the birthing room, then softly knocked on the door. "Come in," Ariel called.

Ariel was in the bed with a very pale Zac standing by her side. "You're here." There was relief written all over his expression.

Eli went directly to Ariel's side. "I am," she said to Zac, then turned her attention to Ariel. "How are you doing, honey?"

"The doctor said I'm on the early side of things, but not to worry. Oh, and Mr. Keller is about to hyperventilate if he tries breathing with me one more time."

"Zac, Tucker's in the waiting room if you'd like to join her there."

Instead of the gratitude she expected, he put on a brave face. "I can stay if you want. Ariel was exaggerating. I'm a great breather."

Suddenly, Ariel started to take long, deep breaths.

"Oh, it's another one. I recognize the signs by now," Zac blurted. "I'll let you handle it and just wait with Tucker."

"SO MUCH FOR MALE BRAVADO," Zac heard Eli say as he beat a very hasty retreat.

Zac didn't care if running out of the birthing room was cowardly. He wasn't ready for this.

He all but sprinted the waiting room and found Tucker sitting there. She looked up and snorted. "Wimped out?"

"They didn't need me there. No teen mom wants

her boss around while she's in labor." The argument sounded plausible. Logical even.

"Wimped out, huh?" Tucker repeated.

Zac flopped onto the rather hard sofa and made an actual thwapping noise. "Yeah."

"Hey, you drove the kid to the hospital. I'd have called an ambulance for her." She gave a little shudder. "Laboring moms? Ick. The thought gives me the heebie-jeebies."

"You had a baby," Zac felt obliged to point out.

Tucker nodded her agreement. "Yeah, and since I've been there, done that, I can categorically say that I wouldn't recommend the experience to anyone. They talk about a rush of mother's love the second you hold your baby. My first thought was, 'ew, someone clean him off.'"

Zac laughed and felt more centered.

"But the love did kick in."

He'd seen Tucker with her son and he knew it hadn't just kicked in, it went into overdrive.

She quickly grew more serious. "Can I ask you something?"

"Sure," he said hesitantly. He was the first to admit as Eli's best friend, Tucker had the right to ask him questions, but that didn't mean he'd want to answer.

She didn't look any happier about asking them. "Since Eli's father is still in Florida, I'm going to fill in for him and ask, just what are your intentions toward Eli?"

"Pardon?" He wasn't sure what he thought she'd ask, but this wasn't it.

"I mean, you're there so often that you've become a fixture. You take her out on dates, but you also are just as comfortable hanging out with her. You're helping her get ready for a baby…for a baby that's not yours. I just want to know where you see this going."

"Where do I see it going? I see me and Eli, sitting in rockers on our front porch, grey-haired and wrinkled." As he said the words, he could indeed picture it. The two of them after a lifetime together. "Does that answer your question?"

Tucker shrugged. "Yes, I think it does. But does Eli know that's where you see this heading?" Before he could answer, she added, "When Arthur bailed, she recovered quickly. But since there's already more between the two of you than she ever had with him… I just don't want to see her hurt."

"I don't plan on hurting her."

"That I believe, but you have the power to. So be careful."

Zac didn't say anything after that, and neither did Tucker, for which he was grateful. He thought about her words. He had the power to hurt Eli.

What Tucker hadn't mentioned was that Eli had the power to hurt him.

Hours later, Eli wasn't sure just how many—the only time that mattered was the time between contractions, and that was growing shorter and shorter for Ariel—and there was still no baby.

"Come on, Ariel, you're doing great." Eli changed, "Hee hee hoo. Hee hee hoo. Long, slow breaths. You can do this."

The contraction ended and Ariel sank back against the pillow. "I don't want to do this, Ms. Cartwright. I want Charlie back. I want my mother here. I want my aunt. I don't want to do this."

Eli's heart broke for Ariel. She was a special girl who deserved to have her parents at her side. "Concentrate, sweetie."

"I called my mom. She just hung up on me."

Another contraction caught Ariel. Eli could recognize the signs now. "Breathe," she commanded again.

They fell into a rhythm.

Contraction. Rest a moment.

Contraction. Rest.

The doctor came in. "Let's see how we're doing." She positioned Ariel's feet in the stirrups and preformed a quick examination. "Ariel, you're one hundred percent effaced. You can push whenever you feel the urge."

Two contractions later, Ariel started pushing. The next forty minutes were a blur. Eli might not have been the one giving birth, but when the doctor held a baby aloft and cried, "It's a girl," she felt as exhausted and elated as Ariel.

"You have a daughter, Ariel," she whispered as she brushed the girl's sweat-sopped hair off her forehead.

"A girl," Ariel murmured as the nurse covered the baby up and handed her to Ariel. "Isn't she the most beautiful thing ever, Ms. Cartwright?"

"She is, Ariel. She is."

Ariel held the baby close and without looking up from her daughter asked, "Do you think you'd call Charlie and tell him. I mean, I'm not asking him to come over, or anything, but he should know he has a daughter."

"I'll go call him."

"And my mom? I mean, I know she hung up on me, but…"

But. Eli could read so much in that one word. But Ariel was hoping her mother would have a change of heart and come—that her mother loved her enough to be there now when she needed her.

"I'll call them both. I'll tell Tucker and Mr. Keller, too."

Ariel didn't look up from her daughter. "Do you think they want to meet her?"

"I think they'd love it, if you're up to it?"

"Just give us twenty minutes or so, okay?" the doctor asked. "We can have everyone cleaned up and comfortable by then."

"I'll be back in twenty," Eli promised, then she leaned down and did what Ariel's mom should have been there to do. She kissed Ariel's forehead. "Congratulations, hon. You did great."

She wanted to tell Ariel that as of this moment everything had changed. That being a mother was going to alter her views, but there was time enough for that later.

In the hallway, she telephoned Charlie Markowski. She'd gotten all Ariel's contact numbers weeks earlier and was glad of it.

Eli had to leave a message on Charlie's voice mail, and that was fine with her because all Eli could think of was Ariel crying for her mother, her aunt…and for Charlie. She was afraid her feelings would shine through if they had a conversation. Voice mail was easier.

Next, she called Ariel's aunt, and again got voice

mail. This time, she wished she'd actually spoken to Deirdre, who must still be in the air.

Finally, she called Ariel's mom.

"Mrs. Mayor, this is Ariel's teacher, Eli Cartwright. I'm at the hospital. She has a baby girl and—"

There was a click on the other end as Ariel's mother disconnected.

Eli had seen parents write off their daughters before, and she couldn't understand it. "No matter what happens to you, I'll always be here for you," she whispered to her baby, who was currently turning somersaults from the way it was kicking.

She hurried down the hall.

"It's a girl," she announced to Zac and Tucker in the waiting room.

"Come, sit down for a minute," Zac said. "This couch isn't exactly plush, but you look as if you need a break."

"That was the most amazing thing I've ever seen. Exhausting, but amazing. Let me tell you, I'm pretty sure that prepared me for childbirth better than any class film."

She sank back, closed her eyes and sighed.

ZAC SMILED AT TUCKER as they both realized that Eli wasn't merely resting her eyes, she was dozing.

He watched her as she slept. Her hands were folded on her stomach. He was startled when they moved, as if Eli had the hiccups. It took him a second to realize it was the baby.

The baby had hiccups.

It was a person in its own right. Soon, they'd be

back at the hospital and Eli would be the one cradling her new baby.

Hers and Arthur's.

He frowned.

"What's that for?" Tucker asked.

He'd forgotten she was still there.

"Just thinking."

"Thinking not exactly good thoughts."

He shrugged. "When Eli has the baby, where will I fit in?"

"I'm guessing this is about Arthur," Tucker said with a frown that Zac wasn't sure he could read. Either she was frowning at the mention of Arthur's name, or she was frowning about his concerns about Eli's ex.

"Listen, Zac—"

Whatever Tucker wanted him to listen to would have to wait as the nurse came in and said, "Ariel and the baby are waiting for you all. Don't stay too long, okay? They both need some rest."

Eli jumped awake and rubbed her eyes, looking slightly disoriented.

"Ariel's ready," Zac repeated.

"Let's go." She led them down the hall, then turned and asked, "How long was I asleep?"

"Not long," Zac assured her.

"You snored," Tucker teased. "Loud."

Eli didn't look as if she really believed Tucker, but Zac could see the small thread of doubt. "Did I?"

"No," he answered. She looked relieved. He added, "Well, not that loud, anyway."

She looked chagrined, then caught his smile. "Nice, you guys. Just pick on the tired pregnant woman."

She stopped in front of Ariel's door and knocked softly.

"Come in."

They walked in and Ariel looked content, as she sat cradling her baby.

She beckoned them closer. "Isn't she perfect?"

It was no hardship to admit she was. Ariel's daughter had a thatch of blond hair that was so pale it was almost white. She had a round face and brilliant blue eyes.

"She's beautiful, Ariel," Zac said as Eli cooed over the baby.

Tucker made a noise of affirmation, and though she didn't coo, she appeared decidedly mushy as she looked at the baby.

Ariel held her out to Eli. "Would you like to hold her?"

Eli took the baby as Ariel said, "I'm going to name her Elinore Charlotte Mayor and call her Nora."

"Oh," Eli said, and started to cry. With a loud sniff, she spluttered, "Ariel, thank you, that's such an honor." And she pulled the blanket back and gently touched the baby's cheek.

Something in Zac melted at the sight of her cradling the newborn. The baby rested on her own baby bump.

Little Nora yawned, and Eli laughed. "Look at her, Zac. Isn't she lovely? I can't believe that soon I'll be holding my baby."

Zac reached out and touched the baby's downy hair. "She's going to turn all the boys' heads in school, Ariel."

"And you know, as much as I chafed at my parents' restrictions, I can suddenly understand them better,"

Ariel admitted. There was a wistfulness in her voice, and Zac wished there was something he could do for her. He and Eli could support Ariel, but they weren't her parents. And he knew Ariel was hurt by their unwillingness to forgive her.

After cooing and cuddling the baby, Eli passed little Nora to Tucker, who despite her avowals in the waiting room, didn't show even the slightest baby bias.

"Zac?" Tucker held the baby toward him.

Not knowing what else to do, he took the baby. He'd never held one this small—Cessy had been a few weeks old when she'd come home, and a lot more filled out than Nora was. But as he peered down at her, he was amazed at how perfectly every feature was arranged. She yawned again, and opened her bright blue eyes and he would have testified in a court of law that she looked at him. Directly at him.

It was that easy—Zac felt connected to this littlest bit of humanity. "Ariel, you take as long as you need off from work, and you let me know—me, not the store—if you need anything, because our little Nora will never want for anything. I promise you that."

He couldn't make up for the people who'd deserted her, but he could help wherever she needed him to.

He was still holding Nora and planning a trip to the store tomorrow to buy out the baby supplies section, when the door opened and a gangly boy walked in. "Ariel, I..."

The kid stopped as if he didn't know what else to say and even without an introduction, Zac knew this was Nora's father.

"Can I hold her?" the boy asked Ariel.

Zac looked to Ariel, unsure what she wanted him to do. She didn't say anything, but nodded at him.

He walked over to Zac. "I'm Charlie. Charlie Markowski."

"Zac Keller. Ariel's boss and friend." Zac wanted to hold Nora close and protect her. And as he handed Nora over to Charlie, he felt what amounted to a knife in the heart knowing there was a very real possibility that one day he'd have to do it all over again. He'd have to hand Eli's baby over to Arthur.

And as he stood there, Zac watched as Charlie Markowski fell in love with his daughter.

It was that simple. He'd handed the baby to a boy who, as he held his daughter, turned into a man. The look on Charlie's face said he'd do anything for this baby. And when Charlie glanced up at Ariel, Zac could see that Charlie loved her as well.

Whether it was a love that could overcome all the obstacles they were facing, he wasn't sure. But it was real. And as Charlie walked over to Ariel, and together they gazed at their daughter, that love was a tangible presence in the room.

What if Arthur, who'd spent Eli's pregnancy bouncing back and forth, held his child, fell in love and finally decided he wanted to be a father? What if he convinced Eli to take him back, and to make them a family?

Zac had thought nothing would ever be harder than losing Cessy, but as he looked at the boy, so absolutely in love with a baby he'd spent nine months denying, Zac knew the truth of it. If Arthur came back and took Eli and the baby from him, there wouldn't just be a hole in his heart.

His heart would break.

Zac wasn't sure he'd survive it.

"Ariel, we're going to go and let you and Charlie bond with your baby," Eli said. "You call me if you need anything."

"I will. Thanks, Ms. Cartwright. Eli. Thanks for everything."

"You're welcome, honey." Eli leaned down and kissed Ariel's forehead again.

They all started to walk out of the room but stopped as Ariel called, "Ms. Cartwright. You talked to my parents, right?"

Eli took Zac's hand before she spoke. "I'm sorry, Ariel, but—"

"No, it's okay, Ms. Cartwright. I didn't expect it to make a difference."

"I'll call you tomorrow morning."

"She didn't expect it to make a difference, but she hoped," Tucker said when they'd safely shut the door. "I'd like to kick their asses."

"Got to admit, me, too," Eli said. "But Charlie came. Did you see his face as he looked at Nora? I hope he'll stay involved, even if Ariel and Charlie don't make it as a couple. Babies deserve to know their father."

Zac knew she didn't mean to, but Eli's words hurt. She looked so tired that he didn't have the heart to say anything.

"Eli, are you riding home with me, or…" Tucker paused.

Before Eli could ask to ride with him, Zac said, "I'm going straight into work today, then I'm heading home to sleep, so if you don't mind riding with Tucker?"

"Sure, that's fine." Eli looked confused. "Are you okay?"

"Yeah, I'm fine." But he wasn't. Wasn't at all. The image of Ariel, Charlie and Nora was giving way to one of Eli, Arthur and their baby. Zac tried to shut it out, tried to tell himself he was being foolish, and yet, he couldn't kill his doubts.

"I'll talk to you later," he promised and stalked away.

This was his problem. Not Eli's. His.

And one way or another, he'd fix it.

He just wasn't sure how.

CHAPTER ELEVEN

"The last weeks of a pregnancy are emotional for all moms-to-be, not just teens. There's no way to ignore the fact the baby you carry is a separate and individual person. It moves, it sleeps… it even gets hiccups. The baby is becoming more real by the day, and while that is exciting, you're about to leave behind the life you knew and step into an unknown future."

—*Pregnancy, Childbirth and Parenting for Teens,*
by Mary Jeanne Lorei

IT WAS MID-MAY and spring had finally arrived in Western Pennsylvania. After a long winter, it was good to see the sun, to see the landscape green, and it was especially lovely to be able to go out without a coat on every day.

The without-a-coat part was especially nice for Eli since she hadn't been able to button hers since sometime in April.

Tonight was the last childbirth class.

Somehow that made the fact the baby would arrive in mere weeks seem more real.

Eli said goodbye to their classmates and took a pillow. Zac took the other one and followed her out of the classroom. When they reached the hospital parking lot and got in the car, Zac turned on the radio. They listened to one country song after another on the drive back to Whedon.

The music was loud enough that conversation was all but impossible. And while Eli enjoyed country music, she enjoyed talking to Zac more. The fact that things had been off between them was becoming more and more apparent with each passing day.

They stopped at O'Brien's for their usual after-child-birth class dinner.

"You're very quiet," she said once they'd ordered. Even the thought of eating O'Brien's cheese soup, her current pregnancy craving, couldn't shake her sense of foreboding.

"Just one of those nights." With no subtlety whatsoever, he changed the subject. "How's Ariel?"

"She's doing great. And so's little Nora. Ariel's eligible to have a tutor until the end of the year. She's planning on attending her graduation ceremony. Every year moves quickly, but this year...?" Her hand rested on her giant stomach. "Maybe it's that I'm pregnant. It just feels surreal that the baby will be here soon. My mom's about ready to burst with excitement."

Her parents had arrived home the week after Ariel delivered, and her mother had tried to make up for lost time and lost shopping by personally buying out every baby store within a twenty-mile radius. "Did I tell you that Mom's already embroidered this gorgeous sampler for the baby's room? She's just waiting to fill in the name."

"That's great," Zac said.

Eli could pinpoint exactly when things had changed. The night Ariel gave birth. What she couldn't pinpoint was what had happened. All she knew was there was a distance between her and Zac.

"Hey, talk to me. Things aren't right, and I don't know why, but… I love you. You made me believe you loved me, too, but lately, I'm not so sure," she tried to explain.

That got his attention. He reached across the table and took her hand. "Eli, you can doubt many things. Frequently lately, I've doubted my own intelligence, but never doubt I love you. I couldn't stop loving you if I tried, and I love the baby. But I—"

"Elinore?" a voice interrupted.

She didn't need to turn to see who was there. To the best of her knowledge, Arthur Stone had never ventured into O'Brien's restaurant. But tonight, he was here.

Of course.

Arthur seemed to have developed a knack for interrupting her life at the most inopportune times.

She tried to think kind thoughts, to feel bad for Arthur and his upset plans, but all she could manage tonight was irritation. She was tired of making excuses for him. Ariel had been right when she said it was just too bad Arthur Stone's life was thrown into chaos with the news of this baby. Eli's had been, too, but she'd managed.

And here he was again, getting between her and Zac.

"Arthur." Her voice sounded colder than she'd meant it to.

He visibly flinched. And Eli couldn't help but notice he looked older. When they'd dated, she'd never really thought of the age difference between them. Now he seemed aged and tired.

She looked at Zac and realized she hadn't given a thought to their age difference in a long time. What had seemed like such a big obstacle didn't matter at all to her now.

"How are you?" Arthur asked.

"I'm fine." When he didn't ask, she added, "So is the baby." Two times Arthur had stood her up for appointments.

"Could we possibly meet sometime next week?" he asked.

"About?" she countered, although she didn't need to. She could almost write Arthur's script. He missed her, and maybe he'd try again to get involved with the baby.

As she stared at him, she knew she didn't want him to try again. She just wanted him gone. She felt guilty, but tried to remind herself what she always told her students: You can't help the way you feel, but you can help the way you act.

"I really need to talk to you. In private." He glanced at Zac, his meaning clear.

She sighed. Arthur's indecisiveness might be driving her crazy, but she saw Zac and knew it was hurting him. She remembered his pain-filled story about Cessy and no longer wondered why he was distant. Of course. He was worried about this…loving the baby and losing it to Arthur. She didn't know how to ease that worry.

She wanted to tell Arthur to get out and leave her and the baby alone. They had Zac. They didn't need Arthur.

But she didn't.

Couldn't.

As much as she'd love to.

"Fine. We can talk. But I'll tell you what I've been telling you all these months. You have two choices. Be a part of the baby's life, or not. There's no longer any choice when it comes to us. Ever."

Arthur didn't respond, but simply said, "I'll call you, then," and left.

Eli loved living in a small town, but at this moment, she'd give anything to be in a big city, where bumping into people just didn't happen like this.

She studied Zac, and knew he was thinking about the baby, about Cessy, about Arthur.

She knew he had to be because she was. "Zac, this is killing you, isn't it?"

"I won't lie. It is. But that night, after I'd told you about Cessy and we made love, I swore I'd be here for you and the baby. I'm in this. And I understand that you're connected to Arthur. I don't like it, but I understand it."

"But I'm not. *I'm* not connected to him. The baby is."

"I know. But Eli, biology might make someone a father, but never a dad. A dad is someone who cares. Someone who's going to be there day in and day out. I don't think that's ever going to be Arthur."

There was so much pain in Zac's voice, and it tore at her because she knew she'd put it there. She'd hurt him. "Zac, I love you."

"And I love you."

"If I could choose, if I had a choice, I'd pick you to be the baby's father. But I don't have a choice. I tell the girls all the time, that life just happens. There are no crib notes to cheat your way through it. You have to deal with it as it is. And as it stands, I love you. I don't love Arthur, but he's the baby's father and if he wants to be a part of this baby's life, I'll see to it that he is. Look at what happened with Charlie and Nora."

Zac visibly flinched as she said the words, and she felt cruel, but she needed to be clear. "Once he held his daughter, he fell in love with her. Maybe that will happen with Arthur. And he should be a part of this baby's life if it does."

She didn't enjoy it, but she knew she'd had to say what she had.

"He's had nothing to do with this baby, but he's the father? What about me? I've been here every step of the way. What am I to this baby? Let's say we get married. And little Junior does something wrong and I want to discipline him. Take away his bike for a week. Will you throw the fact that I'm not his father in my face? Tell me that I don't have the right to discipline him? Will we call Arthur to check that it's okay? I want to be there for all of it. For the big moments, for the small ones. I want to be the baby's dad, but I keep feeling as if you'll never let me."

"Zac, you're not being fair." The waitress came and they both were silent as she placed their orders in front of them.

"Can I get you anything else?" the waitress asked, her chipper voice sounding harsh because she was so obviously happy and they were so obviously unhappy.

"No, thank you," Eli managed to reply. When the waitress left, Eli repeated, "You're not being fair, Zac. If we stay together, certainly, you'd have a say in how the baby was raised, but it won't change the fact that Arthur's involved."

That *if* landed with almost an audible thud. She knew it.

"I know I'm not being fair, damn it. I want to be. I want to be that very cool guy who says, hey, whatever. I'd like to let it all roll off me, and take what I can get. But I'm worth more than just the table scraps in this situation. I want in, Eli. All the way in. No hesitation, no qualifications. I love you and I want to marry you."

Zac didn't give her time to respond, he just continued steamrolling along. "I want us to raise this baby as our own. I want to be the one who takes him out for ice cream to celebrate successes, and the one who sends him to time-out when he makes a mistake. I want to hear about his days at school, I want to worry about him, and I want to blame my grey hair on him. I want to be the one who loves his mother to distraction, and when we kiss, I want him to gag and beg us not to get all mushy in front of him like Tucker does."

"Zac, I want that, too. But no amount of wishing is going to make it so." She looked at him across the table. He was amazing and she'd brought him so much pain. "I think we need a break."

"What? I just told you, I'm in. This situation is no one's fault. It might hurt like hell, but we'll work it all out. I'll be fine."

But he wouldn't. She could see that even if he couldn't. The situation was too reminiscent of his sister's. It was killing him. And she loved him enough to do what he couldn't do. He was right, he was in this. And he'd never walk, no matter how much it tore at him. So, she'd walk for him. She'd walk away from him.

"I don't need a break from us, Eli," he repeated. "I love you."

"You don't understand, I need this," she lied. "The baby's here soon, and it's obvious, I'm not done dealing with Arthur. I know it's hurting you, and to be honest, Zac, I just can't deal with your problems on top of my own."

It was mean, but she also knew if she didn't sound convincing, he'd never let go.

"I need you to give me some space. Let me get my life in order and maybe then…" That was a lie, too. Arthur would always be a part of her life, and she couldn't deal with that fact hurting Zac day after day.

The soup that had sounded so good just a short while ago was left untouched and forgotten as she stood.

Zac stood as well and his voice was stiff as he said, "I'll take you home, then."

"It's not far, I'll walk. The baby and I need the exercise."

She grabbed her purse and coat and started for the door.

"Eli, please…"

She turned to see the man she loved. "I'm sorry, Zac. I'm sorry I ever said yes to anything more than our work sessions. I'm so sorry."

She quickly left the building before she burst into tears.

She'd hurry home and call Tucker, sure in the knowledge her friend would comfort her.

A WEEK LATER, ZAC WENT to the front door, hoping beyond hope it was Eli who was ringing the doorbell.

He tried to hide his disappointment when he found Cessy standing on the porch, glaring at him. "You're a jerk, Zac," she said by way of salutation as she pushed past him and entered his apartment.

She stood, ramrod-straight, still glaring at him.

"You want to sit down?" he offered, though he wasn't in the mood for listening to his sister's teenage angst.

Truth be told, he wasn't in the mood for much of anything other than being with Eli. He'd picked up the phone and dialed Eli about a hundred times in the last seven days. Every time, he'd hung up before he hit send.

"No, I don't want to come in. I don't want to chat and pretend to be all sympathetic with your plight because I'm not. Not at all."

"Hey, what did I do?"

"Mom was all worried when you didn't come to dinner on Sunday, but I said you were probably too busy with Eli, but you weren't, were you? I stopped at Ariel's and she told me that you broke up with Ms. Cartwright."

"How did Ariel know?"

"Bart heard his mom talking to Ms. Cartwright and got the gist of it. He said something to Ariel."

Zac had forgotten what high school was like. Rumors traveled quicker than the speed of light. "Cessy, I didn't really break up with her, she asked me to back off for a while, and I did."

"Jerk. Idiot. You've always been my hero, but Zac, right now, I'm…" Cessy paused and finally said, "Well, I'm disappointed in you." It was the killer phrase his mother always used to make any of her kids toe the line and do better.

I'm disappointed in you.

The phrase stung.

"She needs you," Cessy said. "That baby needs you."

"The baby has Arthur."

She snorted.

"He wanted another try," Zac stated. "And Eli gave it to him again because he's the baby's biological father."

"Hey, don't play that card with me, Zac. I met the man who biologically fathered me, and I lived with him for six months. I know better that's not what a parent makes. Dad is my father. Not that guy, who by some fluke or broken condom, knocked my mother up. Doesn't matter that this guy's the sperm donor. You can be the baby's father."

"That's not how Eli sees it and that's not how the legal system sees it. Cessy, don't you get it, when we lost you, the whole family had a big gaping hole in it. We missed you. I was your big brother, but I couldn't protect you. The law said that man had a legal right. And it would say the same thing about Arthur."

She shrugged. "So what?"

That wasn't the reaction he expected. "So, I don't think I can go through losing someone I love like that again."

"You've already lost. And the fact that you walked away—" he started to protest, and Cessy quickly amended "—even if she asked you to, means you've really lost. It doesn't matter that Arthur hasn't come to take the baby yet. You're done."

"But—"

"You're so afraid that you're letting the best thing that ever happened to you slip through your fingers." Cessy paused, then quietly, with less heat, said, "You know, all my life, I've looked up to you. I've wanted to be as good and brave a person as my big brother. But now I don't think I want to be. I don't want to be so afraid of losing someone that I wouldn't put up a fight."

"Cessy." She was getting it all wrong. He'd been willing to stay, to fight. He'd gone because Eli asked him. "Cessy," he repeated.

"Cecily, Zac. My big brother, the one I looked up to called me Cessy. You get to call me Cecily."

"Cecily, then. You don't understand."

"Stop. You don't understand, so I'm going to clue you in. Eli didn't ask you to leave because she needed space, she asked you to go because she knew this was hurting you and she loves you enough to want to make that pain stop. But she's as dumb as you are, even if she is a teacher. I'm going to explain this to you slowly, so it has a chance of getting through your extremely thick skull. You. And. Eli. Belong. Together. Everyone knows that, except the two of you. And even if Arthur decides to be a part of this baby's life, you'd still be there, too. You'd be a part of it. Love isn't something that gets smaller if it's divided. That baby will have enough to give some to you and Arthur."

"Cessy—"

"You're being stupid. I know that my leaving was hard on you, that it hurt you, but even if that man had kept me, even if I hadn't come home, I would always have known I was loved. That's a gift. I'd have remembered that. It would have been worth the pain of losing you to have had even one day of your love. How can you not feel that way about Eli and the baby? How can you turn your back on love?"

Zac didn't have an answer.

"These last few days, have you hurt any less?"

He shook his head.

"Well, there you go, Zac." She waved and flounced out.

Zac stood in his foyer mulling over her words.

Was that what he'd done? Had he actually turned his back on love?

CHAPTER TWELVE

"Every student lives for graduation day. A day
that marks the transition from childhood to adult-
hood. Teen mothers marked that transition when
they became parents. But that doesn't mean they
should stop thinking about graduation and their
future. Because, unlike their classmates, their decisions about their future will affect more than
themselves, they'll effect their child."
—*Pregnancy, Childbirth and Parenting for Teens,*
by Mary Jeanne Lorei

ELI HELD NORA as they sat in the row with the girls
from her program. Every time a teen parent graduated,
it was a triumph for the girl, for Eli, and it provided a
role model for the other students.

Parents and friends filed into the auditorium, and
the front dozen or so rows were empty, waiting for the
graduates to arrive.

"Your mama's graduating," she whispered in the
baby's ear.

Nora didn't pay any attention as she snuggled closer,
trying to find a comfortable position against Eli's giant
stomach. The baby kicked little Nora.

"Hey, behave," she scolded.

The baby had been much more quiet today than

usual, and she found the fact that it had stirred reassuring.

"You don't look very comfortable," came a voice that sent her heartbeat into overdrive. "Maybe I could sit here and help?"

"Zac." She turned and drank in the sight of him. It had been little more than a week. Most days she could believe that they'd figure things out after the baby came and Arthur decided what he was going to do. Somehow, they'd make it work for everyone. But then, the smallest hint of doubt would creep in and she'd worry that she'd lost him. But here he was and for now, that's all that mattered.

"Yeah."

She tried to tell herself that he was here for Ariel because she was part of the CATA Project. But as he sat in the vacant chair, she didn't believe it. He was here for her.

He didn't have to say a word. The way he reached out and touched her hand, she could tell that he'd needed to connect with her as much as she'd needed to connect with him. She took his hand in hers and held on.

She wasn't sure where her certainty had come from, but she reveled in it.

Zac was back for her.

He held out his free arm and took Nora. Despite the fact she enjoyed holding the baby, there was a sense of relief. Her stomach was so swollen it got in the way of pretty much everything these days. But despite her giant girth and her nagging backache, she felt marvelous. Zac was back.

"Eli, when this is over, could we talk?"

She nodded, not trusting herself to say something without bursting into tears. She'd missed him so much. Had so many things to share. About how the baby was kicking. About how it still seemed to like her right rib, pressing against it all day until by evening it just ached, and she'd sit with a hand on the foot moving it gently away and giving herself some relief.

She wanted to tell him so many things, to share so much of the minutia of her day.

But mainly she wanted to tell Zac that she loved him.

That she wanted to spend the rest of her life loving him.

That no matter what Arthur decided, she was sure Zac would never lose her or the baby. The emotion caught in her throat, preventing anything from coming out.

"Eli, are you okay?" he asked, as he put Nora on his shoulder and gently patted her back.

She nodded again.

"I missed you," he said. "I—"

The music started playing and the senior class began to file into the auditorium from the back. Eli had checked with the principal, and Barry had told her that Ariel would walk down this side of the gym.

She watched as gowned student after gowned student marched by. Soon, Ariel came into view wearing her blue cap and gown, along with her honor society cords.

And suddenly, all that emotion Eli had been trying to rein in, exploded. She could feel the tears streaming down her face, and tried to kneel down and get her purse and the giant stack of tissues she'd packed for just this occasion. The space between the seats didn't leave much room to maneuver herself, but she was managing until she felt a stitch in her back and she let out a sharp gasp.

"Here, let me." Holding Nora in one hand, Zac reached down with his other and retrieved her purse for her.

Eli tried to force herself to breathe normally as she dug for the tissues. In, out. Slow even breaths. It wouldn't do to hyperventilate. This was Ariel's night.

The graduating class had all reached their seats and sat down, then the audience did the same.

"Family and friends, on behalf of myself and the teaching staff, I want to welcome you to this celebration. We are here tonight…" Barry droned.

Eli had sat through years and years of graduations. She'd always felt a bit misty as she watched girls from her program graduate. But Ariel's graduation was special.

She reached over and touched Nora's peach-fuzzy hair, but stopped short because her back twinged again.

"Eli, are you sure you're all right?"

"I did something to my back. Probably just the stress of carrying all this extra weight."

He didn't look convinced.

"I'm fine, Zac. Really, I'm fine."

He gently held her hand as the baby slept and the various speakers came and went. Then one by one the graduates walked across the stage, received their diplomas, shook hands with Barry, then moved their tassels from the right side to the left.

"Laurel Lee."

"C. J. Manto."

"Charlie Markowski." Nora's father walked across the stage. He'd been true to his word in the hospital, helping with the baby and helping financially. Ariel had confessed they were dating again, though she'd qualified that most of their dates involved things for the baby. A trip to the zoo, a walk in the evening.

"Ariel Mayor." Ariel made her way across the stage, and like everyone before her, took her diploma and shook the principal's hand, then walked across the stage, turned to face the audience and moved her tassel from one side to the other.

Eli clapped until her hands hurt, but she didn't care. Ariel was her only graduating student this year, which just added to the specialness of the evening.

When the final diploma had been handed out and the ceremony ended, Ariel came to find them. "Thanks for being here, Ms. Cartwright and Mr. Keller. I saw Aunt Deirdre and I need to go find her, but I wanted to say thank you to you both."

Eli didn't ask about Ariel's parents, and neither did Zac. At least her aunt had made it.

"Congratulations, Ariel. We're both so proud of you."

"I brought something with me." Zac shifted Nora and took an envelope out of his pocket. "Keller's Market is proud to give you our first CATA scholarship to the college of your choice. If you pick one in town or nearby, you'll have a job with us throughout. If you choose a college farther afield, I have connections. I'll help you find another job with someone who will work with you."

Ariel opened the envelope and read the note then started to cry. "Mr. Keller, you don't know how much this means to me. To us. I—" She gave up trying to talk and hugged him, sandwiching Nora between them.

"Here, let me rescue the baby." Charlie took the baby from Zac and rather than ending her hug, it allowed Ariel to hold on longer.

When she finally broke free, she turned to Eli and hugged her as well. "Ms. Cartwright, I know that teachers are paid to be here and that it's not an easy job even if you stick to the job description and present lessons and grade papers. But you, you go even further. You cared about me. When I walked across that stage and took my diploma from Principal Werner's hands, it was because of you."

Eli felt the tears welling up in her eyes again and started digging through her purse for tissues. "Ariel, I just—"

"No. Don't. You're going to try and tell me it was nothing, that it was your job. But Ms. Cartwright, it was everything to me. And I know that I was more than a job to you. That all the girls in the program are more than a job. And I got accepted to Mercyhurst. They have a great education program. For a long time I didn't know what I wanted to do when I grew up. Having Nora forced me to grow up faster than most kids, and having you as a teacher made me know what I want to do. I'm going to be a teacher. Someday, I want to impact someone else's life the way you've impacted mine. You are what every teacher should be, Ms. Cartwright. Thank you."

Eli tried to say something, tried to make words form, but all she could do was moan as another spasm hit her back.

"Ms. Cartwright?" Ariel asked at the same time that Zac said, "Eli?" There was concern in both their voices.

"I think that maybe the back pain I've been having all day is more than a pulled muscle."

"Back labor. I remember you taught us about that," Ariel said. "I didn't have it."

"But I think I am. And I really think I need to go to the hospital. I'm sorry to cancel our dinner, Ariel."

"Come on, Ms. Cartwright, this is so much more important."

The pain subsided, and Eli gently touched Ariel's cheek with her finger. "Ariel, you are important to me, and we're going to take a rain check, okay? This day deserves to be celebrated."

"Yes, it does," Zac agreed.

"I'll be taking Ariel and her aunt out now, Ms. Cartwright," Charlie said, "and you guys can take her sometime after your baby's here, okay?" Still holding Nora, Charlie wrapped his free arm around Ariel.

"Thanks, Charlie." Looking at the three of them, Eli recognized a family in the making and though she knew odds were stacked against them, she hoped that Ariel and Charlie would make it.

"Come on Eli, let's go." Zac took her arm as if she couldn't manage by herself. She was about to tell him that she could, when another pain hit and she gratefully leaned on him.

"Hey, Mr. Keller, will you call me?" Ariel called.

"Sure." He dropped his voice and said, "Let's get you out of here before you have your baby on the floor."

"It would be a graduation first," Eli joked, smiling through the pain.

ZAC WASN'T SOME BIG-GAME hunter, and he'd never thought it overly prudent to bungee jump or skydive, but still he thought that when it came to bravery he had an ample amount. Instead, as he raced through the bustling downtown traffic to the hospital, he felt panic.

"Zac, how much longer?"

Eli had asked him that question countless times between Whedon and Erie. Finally, he was able to say, "Only a couple more minutes. I can see the hospital."

"Good. The E.R. entrance is in the back." Her voice was breathy.

"You okay?" He'd lost precious time because he'd been stupid enough to let Eli push him away. He should never have listened to her, or left. He should have stuck to her regardless.

"I'm fine," she managed to say.

Thankfully there were valets in the parking lot. Zac tossed them his keys, and took the slip, before helping Eli inside.

A nurse settled her into a wheelchair so she could escort them to the obstetrics floor.

"Well, Zac, thanks for everything."

Zac realized he'd never told her what he'd planned on telling her.

"Eli, I'd like to come…if you want me. I want to be here for you. I came tonight to talk, but I don't think right now is the best time. But please, let me stay. We'll talk later."

He was afraid she'd say no, but he could see the relief on her face. "Thank you."

While the nurses prepped Eli, he called her parents.

"We're on our way in," her mother told him. "It

would be nice if you'd at least stay with her until we get there."

There was a coldness in her mother's voice that had never been there before.

"I'm not going anywhere, Mrs. Cartwright. I planned on telling Eli after the graduation, but other things took precedence."

Just like that, her mother warmed. "I knew you'd work it out. I tried to understand why she did it, but still, I felt she'd been hasty and told her so."

"Maybe, but it was even worse that I listened and went anyway. I worked out a lot of things last week, ma'am."

"Things you probably should tell Eli before me." Eli's mother laughed. "We'll be there soon. I'm glad you'll be staying, Zac."

He'd be staying for a lot longer than the delivery if he had his way. He was just about bursting with the need to tell Eli his feelings, but he knew right now she had other things to concentrate on. "I'll look after her, Mrs. Cartwright."

"Let me be the first to welcome you to the family, Zac. I knew you'd be a part of it when I saw the way you looked at my daughter that first time I met you, right after she told us about the baby. That look…that's why I wasn't sure if the baby's was yours or Arthur's. You mean a lot to Eli, and I'm sure you'll mean a lot to this baby, too."

Eli's mother's words meant so much. "Thanks, Mrs. Cartwright. I—"

The nurse interrupted. "Mr. Keller, Eli's asking for you now."

"Mrs. Cartwright, I have to go." He snapped his

phone shut and hurried into the room. "I texted Tucker, and I called your mom."

"Great. She's so—"

Another pain hit and began a cycle of contractions and breathing, brief rests, then back at it again. He fed Eli an occasional ice chip, helped her concentrate on breathing, but basically felt useless. He hated to see her in pain.

The nurse told him that back labors tended to be more intense, and helped them position Eli more comfortably. But more comfortably wasn't nearly comfortable enough in Zac's opinion. When they offered her pain meds, Eli insisted that she didn't want to miss a moment.

Eventually, her doctor came in and after checking Eli assured them it was time.

Zac very thankfully remained by Eli's head, and well out of the viewing range as he continued to play cheerleader. "Breathe, Eli… Huff. Huff. Huff."

"I can see the baby's head. This one's got a full head of hair, Mom," the doctor said. "Don't push, Eli. Let me just ease the baby's shoulders through. Breathe. Breathe."

Zac breathed along with her, huffing in hopes of controlling the urge to push.

"There, you're good," Dr. Benton said. "Push the next time you have the urge."

There was no waiting. Eli pushed and cried out as she flopped back on the pillow.

A minute later, the doctor cried, "It's a boy!" And as if on cue, the baby wailed. The doctor held the baby aloft and placed him on Eli's chest. "Would you like to cut the umbilical cord, Dad?"

Zac didn't know how to respond, so he looked at Eli. "Zac? Only if you want."

"I want."

He followed the doctor's instructions, made the cut and realized that this baby, who'd been a part of Eli for nine long months was now a separate person in his own right. This tiny little boy would learn to walk and talk. He'd go to school. Maybe play sports. He'd learn to drive.

And Zac wanted to be there for every new skill, every milestone.

He wanted to tell Eli and her son all of that and more, but there were just too many words, too many emotions, so he simply settled for, "I love you. I love you both."

"We love you, Zac. I know there's still things to say and there's Arthur—"

"You should probably call him," he suggested, more because he needed her to see he was going to be able to handle Arthur.

"Sir, maybe you'd be more comfortable waiting outside for a minute while we freshen up Eli and the baby?" the nurse asked.

"I could call if you want," he offered. He'd accepted that he was going to have to deal with Arthur for the rest of his life, since he intended it to be that way with Eli. He might as well get started with doing it the right away.

"Really?" Eli studied him, then nodded. "His number's in my cell, which is in my purse."

"You do ask a lot from a man, Eli," he teased. "I mean, going in your purse is the job for only a very brave man."

She smiled. "I really do love you, Zac Keller."

ELI HAD NEVER BEEN so tired in her life, and conversely, she'd never felt more alive. Her parents had come and seen the baby. It was all her father could do to pull her mom back out the door, and the only way he managed that was with Eli's assurance she'd need her mother's help when she went home the following day.

Zac had sat on the couch in the birthing room and had dozed off within minutes of her parents leaving. That left Eli plenty of time to watch him sleep. They still hadn't talked about what his being here meant, but she hoped that he was back to stay because he'd come to terms with the situation.

There was a knock at the door, which startled Zac awake. The baby stirred as well. "Shh," she whispered, then called softly, "Come in."

Arthur stuck his head into the room and for a moment, she thought he was going to bolt.

Instead, he stepped all the way in. "He called me." He nodded toward Zac. "I thought I should come."

Eli studied the man she'd once thought she'd loved and realized he'd never shared himself with her the way Zac had.

Zac had told her about the day they'd taken Cessy away. He'd given her son his piggy bank, which represented so much more that a place to save money—it had been a place Zac had saved his dreams. She wanted nothing more than to tell Zac everything she was feeling, but first there was Arthur.

He stood at the very end of her bed, looking at the baby.

"Arthur, would you like to see my son?" she asked. She untucked the blanket and moved the baby so he was facing the ceiling rather than turned toward her.

She saw Zac get up off the couch. "I should go."

"No, please. I need you." She wasn't trying to be cruel. She needed him here. She needed him to hear.

She could see from his expression that he thought staying would be awkward, but she'd said she needed him and so he stayed. "Okay."

Eli had known that Zac loved her, but how had she not known the second she had met him that she loved him?

Arthur eyed Zac, then addressed Eli, and finally the baby. "I thought about buying him something. It seemed that a father should bring a son a gift."

She could see Zac wince, but because he was behind Arthur, her ex didn't notice, and even if he had, she doubted he'd have cared. "But then it occurred to me that I don't feel like his father. I thought maybe when I got here and saw him that there would be some magic link. But there's not. I don't feel anything for him. You were right when you called him your son. He's yours Eli. I wish I was a better man, one who could stand by you and at least pretend this was what I wanted, but I can't. I don't want to be anyone's father."

He reached into his suit jacket's inner pocket. "Here are the papers. They're signed. And there's my lawyer's number along with some basics on the trust I'm setting up for him. You're supposed to call my lawyer with his name when you know it."

"I already know it. I'm naming him after my father and his father." She looked pointedly at Zac. "Jonathan Zachary Cartwright."

She saw the words impact on Zac. She remembered what Cessy had said at dinner…that she could talk to Zac without words. And right now, she didn't need words to know he was touched, and that he had taken to Johnny as his son long before she gave him his name.

Zac loved them both.

He'd come today even though he knew that Arthur might decide to stay. He'd come because he cared about them more than he worried about his own pain. "Jonathan Zachary Cartwright Keller," Zac corrected. "That is if you both will have me."

It was a proposal. And maybe in any other circumstances, proposing while someone's ex was standing there would have been bad form, but given everything they'd been through, it was fine.

She nodded.

Arthur looked at the three of them. "Good luck, Eli. I wish you all the best."

He kissed her lightly on the cheek, then turned to Zac. "You'll take care of them?"

"They're my family," Zac said simply, moving to Eli's side. "I figured it out. We match."

Arthur seemed confused, but Eli got it. She understood. "We match perfectly," she assured him.

"I'll let the three of you bond then, as all the books mention."

Eli looked surprised.

"Elinore, I'm an academic, I read up on the process. And I get it now."

"Get what, Arthur?" she asked.

He stood still, studying the three of them. "Get why I never felt a connection to this child…because I was never really his father."

Arthur turned and when he opened the door, Zac called, "Arthur, if you want to know how he is, if you want to check…"

Arthur glanced over his shoulder and shook his head. "I won't, but thanks. Just take care of them."

He left, and Eli focused on the man she loved.

Zac had one hand on her, one on Johnny. "You do realize that when I said his name would be Jonathan Zachary Cartwright Keller, I was asking you to marry me?"

"Elinore Cartwright-Keller. It has a nice ring." She picked up the baby and held him out to Zac. "Johnny, meet your father. Zac, your son."

Zac took the baby in his arms. Johnny was a bit red-looking, but Zac had only ever seen one thing more beautiful. He looked at Eli—so beautiful.

"Eli, remember at Christmas when you gave me that painting and I said it was the best gift I'd ever received?"

How could she forget. "Yes."

"I lied." His voice was husky with emotion. "You are. Johnny is."

"That's two things," she joked.

"No, it's not," Zac argued. "You and Johnny are one—a family. My family. Our family. We all match."

EPILOGUE

"Delivering your baby might seem as if it should be the end of the book, but there are still more chapters left. Because carrying and having a baby is the easy part. Raising that child, creating your own family…those are lessons you never stop learning."

—*Pregnancy, Childbirth and Parenting for Teens,*
by Mary Jeanne Lorei

ARIEL JIGGLED NORA on her knee and saw that Mrs. Cartwright, Eli's mom, was doing the same thing with Johnny. Both babies had reached a crawling-all-over age that made them less than happy about sitting through a marriage ceremony.

But Ariel had seen Mrs. Cartwright dab at her eyes, just as she'd dabbed at her own as Eli and Zac said their vows in front of a church filled with friends and family. Even Tucker, who was wearing a dress and standing next to Eli as her maid of honor, was misty-eyed.

"And I promise to stand by you through it all. You and Johnny are my world, my heart, my life," Zac vowed.

Cecily and Mrs. Keller burst into noisy tears, the rest of the Keller family looked on the verge of crying as well.

"I, Elinore, take you, Zachary, for better and worse. You came to me at one of the most confusing times in my life, and you gave me the strength to find a new path. Once I found it, it made sense that you were there, walking alongside of me. Wherever we go, I know I'll be just fine as long as you're there. I'm a teacher, but it took me until recently to figure out that life just happens… I didn't plan any of this, but I'm so lucky to have found it. To have found you. I love you, Zac…."

Charlie took Ariel's hand and squeezed it.

He'd asked her to marry him, but Ariel had said no. For now, it was enough that he was in her life, that he wanted to be a father to Nora. They were both still young. Maybe someday, when they were older, when they were sure they were marrying for the right reasons, but she wouldn't marry because it seemed convenient. And not just for Nora's sake. She wanted a family who matched. So, maybe someday…

For now though, Ariel would revel in Zac and Eli's wedding and enjoy the day. Tomorrow she had to go back to juggling her daughter, her college classes and work.

But it was worth it because Ariel had direction.

In a few years she was going to be a teacher like Elinore Cartwright-Keller and be a positive influence in her students' lives like Eli had with her kids.

That thought, that goal, was enough to get Ariel through the hardest moments. She was going to take it one day at a time because like Ms. Cartwright had said, life just happens. There were no crib notes for it.

* * * * *

*Unexpected
Christmas plans...*

One Frosty Night
by **Janice Kay Johnson**

Olivia Bowen would rather avoid this holiday season.
Even her satisfaction at improving the family business
doesn't make up for the loss of her beloved father and the
sudden tension with her mother. Olivia questions how much
longer she can live in her hometown. And her decision is
further complicated by Ben Hovik.

She should keep her distance—he broke her heart years
ago. Yet his compassion and their still-sizzling attraction
are seductive. Could she be falling for him again? When
she spends Christmas with Ben and his teenage son, she
wonders if this might be the first of many more...

AVAILABLE NOVEMBER 2014 FROM HARLEQUIN SUPERROMANCE
WHEREVER BOOKS AND EBOOKS ARE SOLD.

⬦ HARLEQUIN®

super romance®

More Story...More Romance
www.Harlequin.com

HTHMS1014-4

This cowboy isn't so easy to catch!

Reclaiming the Cowboy
by Kathleen O'Brien

When Mitch Garwood ran away with Bonnie O'Mara, he thought he'd found forever. But all his dreams crashed the morning he woke alone. Months later, he's immune to her reappearance. Even if she's now using her real name— Annabelle Irving—and ready to tell him her secrets, he's done.

Too bad the situation is not that simple. Annabelle's willingness to leave her money and position behind so she can work at Bell River Ranch and be near him surprises Mitch. Despite his resolve, the spark of attraction flares again. The most compelling part? Her determination to win him back!

AVAILABLE OCTOBER 2014 FROM HARLEQUIN SUPERROMANCE WHEREVER BOOKS AND EBOOKS ARE SOLD.

H HARLEQUIN®

super romance®

More Story...More Romance
www.Harlequin.com

HTHMS1014-3

A *Romance* FOR EVERY MOOD™

JUST CAN'T GET ENOUGH?

Join our social communities
and talk to us online.

You will have access to the latest
news on upcoming titles and special
promotions, but most importantly,
you can talk to other fans about your
favorite Harlequin reads.

Harlequin.com/Community

Facebook.com/HarlequinBooks

Twitter.com/HarlequinBooks

Pinterest.com/HarlequinBooks

American Romance

Returning to Crooked Valley is to ex-soldier Duke Duggan more terrifying than the battlefield. Still, Duke has only one reason to be back—taking control of his late grandfather's ranch. But being thrown headfirst into ranch life sees Duke like a fish out of water.

That is until he sees Carrie Coulter again. He may be steadfastly proud, but Carrie has learned never to take no for an answer—especially from a cowboy crying out for her expertise.

As Christmas approaches they finally let the magic of the season sweep them away!

Look for

The Cowboy's Christmas Gift

by DONNA ALWARD

Part of the *Crooked Valley Ranch* miniseries from Harlequin® American Romance®.

Available November 2014 wherever books and ebooks are sold.

HAR75543

HARLEQUIN®

American Romance®

Her Christmas Wish

The last thing rodeo cowboy Daniel Baron needs is a commitment. After a lifetime of feeling like an outsider among his larger-than-life stepfamily at Roughneck Ranch, Daniel is ready to leave the ring—and Texas—behind forever. Except he can't stop thinking about the woman he just met—beautiful, bighearted…and pregnant.

Look for
The Texan's Christmas
by TANYA MICHAELS

Part of the *Texas Rodeo Barons* miniseries from Harlequin® American Romance®.

Available November 2014 wherever books and ebooks are sold.

HARLEQUIN®

A *Romance* FOR EVERY MOOD™

Save $1.00

on the purchase of any
Harlequin Series book.

Available wherever books are sold, including most bookstores,
supermarkets, drugstores and discount stores.

- ✄

Save
$1.00

on the purchase of any
Harlequin Series book.

Coupon valid until December 31, 2014. Redeemable at participating retail outlets
in the U.S. and Canada only. Limit one coupon per customer.

52612015

5 65373 00076 2   (8100)0 11987

Canadian Retailers: Harlequin Enterprises Limited will pay the face value of this coupon plus 10.25¢ if submitted by customer for this product only. Any other use constitutes fraud. Coupon is nonassignable. Void if taxed, prohibited or restricted by law. Consumer must pay any government taxes. Void if copied. Millennium1 Promotional Services ("M1P") customers submit coupons and proof of sales to Harlequin Enterprises Limited, P.O. Box 3000, Saint John, NB E2L 4L3, Canada. Non-M1P retailer—for reimbursement submit coupons and proof of sales directly to Harlequin Enterprises Limited, Retail Marketing Department, 225 Duncan Mill Rd., Don Mills, Ontario M3B 3K9, Canada.

U.S. Retailers: Harlequin Enterprises Limited will pay the face value of this coupon plus 8¢ if submitted by customer for this product only. Any other use constitutes fraud. Coupon is nonassignable. Void if taxed, prohibited or restricted by law. Consumer must pay any government taxes. Void if copied. For reimbursement submit coupons and proof of sales directly to Harlequin Enterprises Limited, P.O. Box 880478, El Paso, TX 88588-0478, U.S.A. Cash value 1/100 cents.

® and TM are trademarks owned and used by the trademark owner and/or its licensee.
© 2014 Harlequin Enterprises Limited

HIINC0413COUP

HARLEQUIN®

SPECIAL EDITION

Life, Love and Family

Coming in November 2014

THE SOLDIER'S HOLIDAY HOMECOMING

by *USA TODAY* bestselling author

Judy Duarte

Sergeant Joe Wilcox is back where he never expected to be—Brighton Valley, which he left long ago. He's in town because he promised to deliver a letter for a fellow marine to Chloe Dawson, who broke his late pal's heart. But before he can do so, Joe is struck by a car and gets temporary amnesia. Joe can't remember who he is, but he's intrigued by the lovely Chloe. Can the soldier and his sweetheart find happily-ever-after just in time for Christmas?

Don't miss the latest edition of the *Return to Brighton Valley* miniseries!

Available wherever books and ebooks are sold.

HSE65849